Anne Holt is one of Europe's most popular and respected authors. She has worked as a lawyer, a Minister of Justice, an assistant district attorney, a TV news anchor and a journalist. She lives in Norway.

Praise for *Punishment*:

'A thoughtful, tense novel . . . This is the first of a new series. I look forward to the subsequent ones'
Observer

'A genuinely puzzling and deeply unsettling thriller. Anne Holt is the latest crime writer to reveal how truly dark it gets in Scandinavia'
Val McDermid

Also by Anne Holt

Punishment

THE FINAL MURDER

Anne Holt

Translated by Kari Dickson

SPHERE

First published in Norway in 2004 by Pirat
First published in Great Britain in 2007 by Sphere
This paperback edition published in 2008 by Sphere

A CIP catalogue record for this book
is available from the British Library.

ISBN 978-0-7515-3715-4

Typeset in Calson by M Rules
Printed and bound in the UK by CPI Mackays, Chatham ME5 8TD

Papers used by Sphere Books are natural, renewable and recyclable products,
made from wood grown in sustainable forests and certified in accordance
with the rules of the Forest Stewardship Council

Mixed Sources
Product group from well-managed
forests and other controlled sources
www.fsc.org   Cert no. SGS-COC-004081
© 1996 Forest Stewardship Council
FSC

Sphere
An imprint of
Little, Brown Book Group
100 Victoria Embankment
London EC4Y 0DY

An Hachette Livre UK Company
www.hachettelivre.co.uk

www.littlebrown.co.uk

For people today, only one radical shock remains – and it is always the same: death.

Walter Benjamin, *Central Park*

She no longer knew how many people she had killed. It didn't really matter anyway. Quality was more important than quantity in most professions. And that was true of her business too, although the pleasure she once gained from an innovative twist had dwindled over the years. More than once, she'd considered what else she might do. Life was full of opportunities for people like her, she thought to herself every now and then. Rubbish. She was too old, she felt tired. This was the only thing she could really do. And it was a lucrative business. Her hourly rate was sky-high now, naturally, but so it should be. It took a while to recover afterwards.

The only thing she really enjoyed was doing nothing. And where she was now, there was nothing to do. But she still wasn't happy.

Perhaps it was a good thing that the others hadn't come, after all.

She wasn't sure.

The wine was certainly overrated. It was expensive and left a sour taste in her mouth.

One

To the east of Oslo, where the hills flatten out down towards Lørenskog, a station town by the Nita River, cars had frozen solid overnight. People on foot pulled their hats down over their ears and wrapped their scarves tighter round their necks as they trudged the few perishing kilometres to the bus stop on the main road. The houses in the small cul-de-sac fended off the frost with drawn curtains and snowdrifts that blocked the driveways. Huge icicles hung from the eaves of an old wooden villa at the end of the road down by the woods, disasters in waiting.

The house was white.

Inside the front door with its lead glass and moulded brass handle, at the end of the unusually spacious hall, to the left in a study, dominated by minimalist art and lavish furniture, sitting behind an imposing desk between boxes of unopened letters, was a dead woman. Her head had fallen back and her hands rested on the arms of her chair. A track of dried blood ran from her lower lip, down her bared neck, split round her breasts and then joined again on her impressively flat stomach. Her nose was also bloody. In the light from the ceiling lamp, it looked like an arrow pointing to the dark hole that had once been a mouth. Only a stump remained of her tongue, which had obviously been carefully removed. The cut was clean and sharp.

It was warm in the room, almost too hot.

Detective Inspector Sigmund Berli from the Norwegian National Criminal Investigation Service, the NCIS, finally closed his mobile phone and looked over at a digital thermometer just inside the southeast-facing panorama window. Outside, it was nearly 22 degrees below freezing.

'Amazing that the windows don't break,' he said, carefully tapping the windowpanes. 'Forty-seven degrees difference between inside and outside. Incredible.'

No one seemed to pay him any attention.

Under her silk dressing gown with its golden collar, the dead woman was naked. The belt lay on the floor. A youngish policeman from the Romerike Police took a step back when he saw the yellow coil.

'Shit,' he gasped, then ran his fingers through his hair in embarrassment. 'I thought it was a snake, like.'

The woman's missing body part lay beautifully wrapped in paper on the blotter on the desk in front of her, only the tip protruding from the middle of all the red. A plump, exotic plant; pale flesh with even paler taste buds and purple red wine stains in the folds and cracks. A half-empty glass was balanced on a pile of papers near the edge of the desk. The bottle was nowhere to be seen.

The detective sergeant cleared his throat. 'Can't we at least cover her tits? It just seems mean that she has to . . .'

'We'll have to wait,' Sigmund Berli replied as he put his mobile back into his breast pocket. 'I'm going to keep trying.'

He went down on one knee to get a closer look at the dead woman.

'Adam would be interested in this,' he muttered. 'So would his wife, for that matter.'

'What?'

'Nothing. Do we know anything about the timing yet?'

Berli stifled a sneeze. The silence in the room made his ears ring. He got up and needlessly brushed dust from his trousers with stiff movements. A uniformed policeman was standing by the door to the hall. He had his hands behind his back and was shifting his weight from one foot to the other as he stared out of the window, away from the body. Some Christmas lights still hung in one of the spruce trees. Here and there, you could see the bulbs glowing dimly under the branches and tightly packed snow, where it was dark.

'Does nobody know anything here?' Berli barked in irritation. 'Don't you even have a provisional time of death?'

'Yesterday evening,' the other man eventually replied. 'But it's too early . . .'

'To say,' Sigmund Berli finished his sentence. 'Yesterday evening. Pretty vague, in other words. Where's . . .?'

'They're away every Tuesday. The family, that is. Husband and daughter, who's six. If that's what you . . .'

The sergeant smiled uncertainly.

'Yes,' Berli said and walked halfway round the desk.

'The tongue,' he started and peered at the package on the desk. 'Was it cut off while she was still alive?'

'Don't know,' the sergeant answered. 'I've got all the papers for you here. As we've finished examining everything and everyone's back at the station, you might . . .'

'Yes,' Berli said, but the sergeant wasn't sure what he was agreeing with. 'Who discovered the body, if the family was away?'

'The cleaner. A Filipino who comes every Wednesday morning at six. He starts down here, he said, so he doesn't wake anyone too early, and then works his way up. The bedrooms are upstairs, on the first floor.'

'Yes,' Berli repeated with no interest. 'Away every Tuesday?'

'That's what she said,' the sergeant answered. 'In all the interviews and suchlike. She sends her husband and daughter away every Tuesday. Then she goes through all her letters herself. It's a matter of principle . . .'

'Right,' mumbled Berli cynically, and stuck a pen into one of the boxes of letters. 'I can believe that. It'd be impossible for one person to go through all of this.'

He pointed at the dead woman again.

'*Sic transit gloria mundi*,' he said and peered into her mouth. 'Her celebrity status isn't much good to her now.'

'We've already gathered lots of clips and cuttings and everything is ready . . .'

'Yeah, yeah.'

3

Berli waved him away. The silence was overwhelming. No people could be heard on the street, no clocks ticked, the computer was turned off. The red cyclops eye of a radio stared at him mutely from the glass cabinet by the door. There was a Canada goose on the mantelpiece, frozen in flight. Its feet were faded and it had hardly any feathers left in its tail. The ice-cold daylight painted a colourless rectangle on the carpet under the south-facing window. Sigmund Berli could hear his blood pounding in his ears. The uncomfortable feeling of being in a mausoleum made him run his finger down his nose. He couldn't decide whether he was irritated or at a loss. The woman still sat in the chair with her legs open, bare breasts and a tongueless gaping hole. It was as if the horrendous crime had robbed her not only of an important body part, but also of her humanity.

'You lot always get pissed off if you're called in too late,' the sergeant said eventually, 'so we just left everything as it was, even though we're done with most things . . .'

'We will never be done,' Berli said. 'But thank you. Smart thinking. Especially with this lady. Does the press . . .?'

'Not yet. We hauled in the Filipino and we'll hold him for questioning for as long as we can. We've been as careful as possible outside. Securing the evidence is important though, especially in snow like this and suchlike, so I'm sure the neighbours are wondering what's going on. But no one can have tipped off the press yet. And in any case, they're all too busy with the new princess right now.'

A fleeting smile became serious.

'But then again, obviously . . . Fiona from *On the Move with Fiona* murdered. In her own home and in this way, well . . .'

'In this way,' Berli nodded. 'Strangled?'

'The doctor thinks so. No stab wounds, no bullets. Marks on her throat, you can see . . .'

'Mmmm. But take a look at this!'

Berli studied the tongue on the desk. The paper was elaborately folded, like a low vase with an opening for the tip of the tongue and elegant, symmetrical wings.

4

'Almost looks like a petal,' the younger policeman said and wrinkled his nose. 'With something horrible in the middle. Quite . . .'

'Striking,' Berli muttered. 'Whoever did it must have made this beforehand. I can't imagine you'd kill someone like this and then take time out to do a bit of origami.'

'I don't think there's any suspicion of sexual abuse.'

'Origami,' Sigmund Berli repeated. 'The Japanese art of paper folding. But . . .'

'What?'

Berli bent down even closer to the severed organ. The sergeant did the same. The two policemen stood like this for a while, forehead to forehead, breathing in time with each other.

'It's not just been cut off,' Berli said finally and straightened his back. 'The tongue has been split. Someone has split the end in two.'

For the first time since Sigmund Berli arrived at the scene of the crime, the uniformed policeman at the door turned towards them. He looked like a teenager, with an open face and spots. He ran his tongue over his lips, again and again, while his Adam's apple jumped up and down above his tight collar.

'Can I go now?' he whimpered. 'Can I go?'

'Throneowning,' the young girl said and smiled.

The half-dressed man drew the razor slowly down his throat before rinsing it and turning round. The child was sitting on the floor, pulling her hair through the holes in an old swimming cap.

'You can't go like that, love,' he said. 'Come on, let's take it off. We can find the hat you got for Christmas, instead. You want to look beautiful when you meet your sister for the first time, don't you?'

'Throneowning,' Kristiane repeated and pulled the swimming cap on even further. 'Hairgrowing. Throne hair.'

'Do you mean heir to the throne?' asked Adam Stubo, rinsing off what was left of the shaving foam on his face. 'That's someone who's going to be a king or queen in the future.'

'My sister's going to be a queen,' Kristiane replied. 'You're the biggest man in the world, really.'

'You think so?'

He lifted the girl up and held her on his hip. Her eyes roamed uncertainly, as if eye contact and touch at the same time would be too much. She was nearly ten and small for her age.

'Heir to the throne,' Kristiane said to the ceiling.

'That's right. We're not the only ones who had a little girl today. So did . . .'

'Princess Mette-Marit is so pretty,' the child interrupted and clapped her hands. 'She is on TV. We had cheese on toast for breakfast. Leonard's mummy said a princess had been born. My sister!'

'Yes,' Adam said, and put her down again before carefully trying to remove the swimming cap without pulling her hair too much. 'Our baby is a beautiful princess. But she's not heir to the throne. What do you think she should be called?'

The cap came off eventually. Her long hair clung to the inside, but Kristiane didn't seem to feel any pain as he loosened the rubber from her head.

'Abendgebet,' she said.

'That means evening prayers,' he explained. 'That's not her name. The girl in the picture above your bed, I mean. It's German for what the girl is doing . . .'

'Abendgebet,' Kristiane said.

'Let's see what Mummy says,' Adam said, and pulled on his trousers and shirt. 'Go and find the rest of your clothes. We have to get a move on.'

'Move on,' Kristiane repeated, and went out into the hall. 'Hoof on. Cows and horses and small pussy cats. Jack! King of America! Do you want to visit the baby too?'

A big mongrel with yellowy-brown fur and a tongue hanging out of his smiling mouth came tearing out of the girl's bedroom. He whined eagerly and scampered in circles round the girl.

'Jack will have to stay at home,' Adam told her. 'Now, where's your hat?'

'Jack's coming with us,' Kristiane said cheerfully and tied a red scarf round the dog's neck. 'The heir to the throne is his sister too. Leonard's mummy says we've got equality in Norway, so girls can do what they want. And you're not my daddy. Isak's my daddy. So there.'

'All very true,' Adam laughed. 'But I love you lots. And now we have to go. Jack has to stay at home. Dogs aren't allowed in hospitals.'

'Hospitals are for sick people,' Kristiane said as he put on her coat. 'The baby's not sick. Mummy's not sick. But they're still in hospital. Spot the pill.'

'You're a little rationalist, you are.'

He kissed her and pulled her hat down over her ears. Suddenly she looked him straight in the eye. He stiffened, as he always did in these rare moments of openness, unexpected glimpses into a mind that no one could fully grasp.

'An heir to the throne has been born,' she quoted ceremoniously from the morning's announcements on TV, before taking a breath and continuing: 'A great event for the nation, but most of all, for the parents. And we are delighted that it is a bonny princess this time.'

A muffled ringing interrupted from the coat rack.

'Mobile telephone,' she said mechanically. 'Dam-di-rum-ram.'

Adam Stubo stood up and frantically felt all the pockets in the chaos of jackets and coats until he finally found what he was looking for.

'Hallo,' he said reluctantly. 'Stubo here.'

Kristiane calmly started to take off her outdoor clothes again. First the hat, then the coat.

'Hold on a moment,' Adam said into the phone. 'Kristiane! Don't . . . Wait a moment.'

The girl had already taken off most of her clothes and was standing in her pink pants and vest. She pulled her tights down over her head.

'No way,' Adam Stubo said. 'I've got fourteen days' paternity leave. I've been awake for over twenty-four hours, Sigmund. Jesus, my daughter was born less than five hours ago and now . . .'

Kristiane arranged the legs of her tights like two long plaits down her front.

'Pippi Longstocking,' she said, pleased with herself. 'Diddle, diddle, tra la la la la.'

'No,' Adam said so brusquely that Kristiane got a fright and started to cry. 'I've got time off. We've just had a child. I . . .'

Her crying morphed into a long howl. Adam never got used to this slight child's howling.

'Kristiane,' he said in desperation. 'I'm not angry with you. I was talking to . . . Hallo? I can't. No matter how spectacular the whole thing is, I can't leave my family right now. Goodbye. And good luck.'

He snapped the phone shut and sat down on the floor. They should have been at the hospital a long time ago.

'Kristiane,' he said again. 'My little Pippi. Can you show me Mr Nelson?'

He knew better than to hug her. Instead, he started whistling. Jack lay down on his lap and fell asleep. A damp patch grew on his trousers under the dog's open, snoring mouth. Adam whistled and hummed and sang all the children's songs he could think of. The girl stopped crying after forty minutes. Without looking at him, Kristiane pulled the tights off her head and slowly started to get dressed.

'Time to visit the heir to the throne,' she said flatly.

The mobile phone had rung seven times.

He hesitated before turning it off, without listening to the messages.

A week had passed and the police were obviously no further forwards. It didn't surprise her.

'Internet reports are useless,' the woman with the laptop said to herself.

As she hadn't bothered to subscribe to a local server, it was also extortionate to surf the net. She got stressed when she thought of all that money being eaten up while she waited for a connection on the slow, analogue line to Norway. She could, of course, go to *Chez Net*. They charged five euros for fifteen minutes and had broadband. But unfortunately the place was full of drunk Australians and braying Brits, even now in winter. So she didn't bother, not now anyway.

There was remarkably little fuss in the first days after the murder. The little princess had the full attention of the media circus. The world truly wanted to be deceived.

But then it started to get more coverage.

The woman with the laptop simply could not stand Fiona Helle. It was an unbearably politically correct response, but there wasn't much to be done about that. She read phrases like 'loved by the people' in the papers. Which was fair enough, given that the programme had been watched by well over a million viewers every Saturday, for five series in a row. She had only seen a couple of shows, just before she came away. But that was more than enough to realize that for once she agreed with the cultural snobs' usual, unbearably arrogant, condemnation of popular entertainment. In fact, it was just one such vitriolic criticism in *Aftenposten*, written by a professor of sociology, that made her sit down in front of the television one Saturday evening and waste one and a half hours watching *On the Move with Fiona*.

But it hadn't been a total waste of time. It was ages since she had felt so provoked. The participants were either idiots or deeply unhappy. But they could hardly be blamed for being either. Fiona Helle, on the other hand, was successful, calculating, and far from true to her love of the common people. She waltzed into the studio dressed in creations that had been bought worlds away from H&M. She smiled shamelessly at the camera, while the poor creatures revealed their pathetic dreams, false hopes and, not least, extremely limited intelligence. *Prime time*.

The woman, who now got up from the desk by the window and walked around the unfamiliar sitting room without knowing quite what she wanted, did not normally join in public debate. But after watching one episode of *On the Move with Fiona* she had been tempted. Halfway through writing a letter from an 'outraged reader', she'd stopped and laughed at herself before deleting it. She had been in a good mood for the rest of the evening. As she couldn't sleep, she allowed herself to indulge in a couple of TV3's terrible late-night films and had even learnt something from them, if she remembered rightly.

At least feeling angry was a form of emotion.

Readers' letters in newspapers were not her chosen form of expression.

Tomorrow she would go into Nice and see if she could find some Norwegian papers.

Two

It was night in the duplex villa in Tåsen. Three sad street lights stood on the small stretch of road behind the picket fence at the bottom of the garden, the bulbs long since broken by excited children with snowballs in their mitts. It seemed that the neighbourhood was taking the request to save electricity seriously. The sky was clear and dark. To the northeast, over Grefsenåsen, Johanne could make out a constellation she thought she recognized. It made her feel that she was totally alone in the world.

'You standing here again?' asked Adam with resignation.

He stood in the doorway, sleepily scratching his groin. His boxer shorts were stretched tight over his thighs. His naked shoulders were so broad that he almost touched both sides of the doorway.

'How much longer is this going to carry on, love?'

'Don't know. Go back to bed.'

Johanne turned back to the window. The transition from living in a block of flats to a house in this neighbourhood had been harder than she'd expected. She was used to complaining water pipes, babies' cries that travelled through the walls, quarrelling teenagers and the drone of late-night programmes from downstairs, where the woman on the ground floor who was nearly stone-deaf often fell asleep in front of the telly. In a flat you could make coffee at midnight. Listen to the radio. Have a conversation, for that matter. Here, she barely dared open the fridge. The smell of Adam's nocturnal leaks lingered in the bathroom in the morning, as she had forbidden him to disturb the neighbours below by flushing before seven.

'Why do you creep around so?' he said. 'Can't you at least sit down?'

11

'Don't talk so loud,' Johanne whispered.

'Give me a break. It's not that loud. And you're used to having neighbours, Johanne!'

'Yes, lots. But they're more anonymous. You're so close here. It's just them and us, so it's more . . . I don't know.'

'But we get on so well with Gitta and Samuel! Not to mention little Leonard! If it wasn't for him, Kristiane would hardly have any . . .'

'I mean, look at these!'

Johanne stuck out a foot and laughed quietly.

'I've never had slippers before in my life. Hardly dare to get out of bed without putting them on now!'

'They're sweet. Remind me of little toadstools.'

'They're supposed to look like toadstools, that's why! Couldn't you have got her to choose something else? Rabbits, bears? Or even better, completely normal brown slippers?'

The parquet creaked with every step he took towards her. She pulled a face before turning back to the window again.

'It's not exactly easy to get Kristiane to change her mind,' he said. 'Please stop being so anxious. Nothing is going to happen.'

'That's what Isak said when Kristiane was a baby too.'

'That was different. Kristiane . . .'

'No one knows what's wrong with her. So no one can know if there's anything wrong with Ragnhild.'

'Oh, so we're agreed on Ragnhild, then?'

'Yes,' Johanne said.

Adam put his arms round her.

'Ragnhild is a perfectly healthy eight-day-old baby,' he whispered. 'She wakes up three times a night for milk and then goes straight back to sleep. Just like she should. Do you want some coffee?'

'OK, but be quiet.'

He was about to say something. He opened his mouth, but then imperceptibly shook his head instead, picked up a sweater from the floor and pulled it on as he went out to the kitchen.

'Come and sit down in here,' he called. 'If you absolutely must stay awake all night, let's at least do something useful.'

Johanne pulled up a bar stool to the island in the middle of the kitchen and tightened her dressing gown. She absent-mindedly picked through a thick file that shouldn't be lying in the kitchen.

'Sigmund doesn't give up, does he?' she said and rubbed her eyes behind her glasses.

'No, but he's right. It's a fascinating case.'

He turned round so quickly that the water in the coffee jug spilt.

'I was only at work for an hour,' he said defensively. 'From the time I left here until I got back was only . . .'

'OK, OK, don't worry. That's fine. I understand that you have to go in every now and then. I have to admit . . .'

On the top of the pile was a photograph, a flattering portrait of a soon-to-be murder victim. The shoulder-length hair with a middle parting made her narrow face look even thinner. Not much else about Fiona Helle was old-fashioned. Her eyes were defiant, her full lips smiled confidently at the lens. She was wearing heavy eye make-up, but somehow managed to avoid looking vulgar. In fact, there was actually something quite captivating about the picture, an obvious glamour that contrasted sharply with the down-to-earth, family-friendly programme profile she had so successfully built up.

'What do you have to admit?' asked Adam.

'That . . .'

'That you think this case is bloody interesting too,' smirked Adam, banging around with the cups. 'I'm just going to get a pair of trousers.'

Fiona Helle's background was no less fascinating than the portrait. She graduated in History of Art, Johanne noted as she read. Married Bernt Helle, a plumber, when she was only twenty-two; they took over her grandparents' house in Lørenskog and lived there without children for thirteen years. The arrival of little Fiorella in 1998 had obviously not put any brakes on either her

13

ambition or her career. Quite the opposite in fact. Having gained cult status as a presenter for the arty *Cool Culture* on NRK2, she was then snapped up by the entertainment department. After a couple of seasons on a late-night chat show on Thursdays, she finally made it. At least, that was the expression she used herself, in the numerous interviews she had given over the past three years. *On the Move with Fiona* was one of national TV's greatest successes since the sixties, when there was little else for people to do other than gather round their TV screens to watch the one channel and share the experience of what a Saturday night was in Norway.

'You liked those programmes! A grown man sitting there crying!'

Johanne smiled at Adam, who had come back wearing a bright-red fleece, grey tracksuit bottoms and orange woollen socks.

'I did not cry,' Adam protested, pouring the coffee into the cups. 'I was touched, though, I admit that. But cry? Never!'

He moved a stool in closer to her.

'It was that episode about the war baby whose father was a German soldier,' he remembered quietly. 'You'd have to have a heart of stone not to be moved by her story. Having been persecuted and bullied throughout her childhood, she goes to the US and gets a job cleaning floors in the World Trade Center when it was first built. Then she took her first and only day off sick on the eleventh of September. And she had always remembered the little Norwegian boy next door who . . .'

'Yeah, yeah,' said Johanne, wetting her lips with the steaming hot coffee. 'Shhh!'

She froze.

'It's Ragnhild,' she said tersely.

'It's not,' he started, trying to catch her before she ran into the bedroom.

Too late. She rushed across the floor without a sound and disappeared. Only her anxiety remained. A bitterness gripped his stomach and made him pour more milk in his coffee.

14

His story was worse than hers. But to compare was not only mean, it was impossible. Pain cannot be measured and loss cannot be weighed. All the same, he couldn't help it. When they first met one dramatic spring, nearly four years ago now, he had found himself getting irritated a little too often by Johanne's sorrow at Kristiane's strangeness.

She had a child, after all. A child that was alive and had a voracious appetite for life. Different from most, but in her own way Kristiane was a lovely and very alert young child.

'I know,' Johanne said suddenly. She had come round the corner from the hall without him noticing. 'You've had to deal with more than me. Your child is dead. I should be grateful. And I am.'

A quiver in his lower lip, barely visible in the dim light, made her stop. His hand covered his eyes.

'Was Ragnhild OK?' Adam asked.

She nodded.

'I just get so frightened,' she whispered. 'When she's asleep, I'm scared that she'll die. When she's awake, I think she's going to die. Or that something will happen.'

'Johanne,' he said, helplessly, and patted the chair beside him. 'Come here and sit down.'

She sank down beside him. His hand rubbed her back, up and down, just a bit too roughly.

'Everything's fine,' he said.

'You're angry,' she whispered.

'No.'

'You are.'

His hand stopped, and he squeezed her gently on the neck.

'No, I said. But now . . .'

'Can't I just be . . .'

'D'you know what?' he interrupted with forced jolliness. 'Let's just agree that the children are fine. Neither of us can sleep. So now we can take an hour or so to look at this . . .' He tapped Fiona Helle's face with his stubby fingers. 'And then we can see whether it's possible to sleep. OK?'

'You're so good,' she said and wiped her nose with the back of her hand. 'And this case is worse than you fear.'

'Right.'

He finished his coffee and pushed the cup out of the way before spreading the papers over the large counter. The photograph lay between them. He ran his finger over Fiona Helle's nose, circled her mouth and paused a moment before picking up the picture and looking at it closely.

'What exactly do you think we're worried about?'

'No clues *whatsoever*,' she said lightly. 'I skimmed through all the papers.'

She was looking for a document without finding it.

'To begin with,' she sniffed, 'the footprints in the snow are as good as useless. OK, there were three prints on the driveway that probably belong to the killer, but the combination of the temperature, wind and snow makes their value limited. The only thing that is certain is that whoever did it had socks on over their shoes.'

'Ever since the Orderud case, every bloody petty thief has used that trick,' he grumbled.

'Watch your language.'

'They're asleep.'

'The shoe size is between forty-one and forty-five, in other words the same as around ninety per cent of the male population.'

'And a small share of the female population,' he smiled. Johanne tucked her feet in under the bar stool.

'In any case, using shoes that are too big for you is another well-known trick. And it's not possible to gauge the killer's weight from the footprints. He was simply very lucky with the weather.'

'Or she.'

'Could be a she. But to be honest, you'd need to use quite a lot of force to overpower Fiona Helle. A fit lady in her prime.'

They looked at the picture again. The woman looked good for her age. Her forty-two years were apparent around the eyes, there were visible wrinkles around her mouth, and her lipstick had bled.

But there was still something vibrant about her face, the direct look in her eyes, the firm skin on her neck and cheeks.

'Her tongue was cut out while she was still alive,' Adam said. 'The theory so far is that she lost consciousness through strangulation and then her tongue was cut out. The bleeding was so heavy that she can't have been dead. Maybe the killer chose his method with care, or maybe . . .'

'It's almost impossible to say,' Johanne said and frowned.

'Strangled her until she lost consciousness rather than died, I mean. He must have thought she was dead.'

'Well, at least we know that the cause of death was strangulation. He must have finished her off with his hands. After he'd cut out the tongue.'

Adam shuddered and added: 'Have you seen these?'

He fished out a manila envelope and looked at it for moment before obviously changing his mind and leaving it unopened.

'Just a peek,' Johanne said. 'Normally pictures of the scene of the crime don't bother me. But now, since Ragnhild was born, I . . .' Tears welled up in her eyes and she hid her face in her hands. 'I cry for no reason,' she said in a loud voice, nearly shouting, before pulling herself together and whispering: 'Pictures like that really don't bother me. Normally. I've seen . . .'

She dried her eyes with abrupt, harsh movements and forced a smile.

'The husband,' she said, 'he's got a watertight alibi.'

'No alibi is watertight,' answered Adam.

Again, he put his hand on her back. The warmth spread through the thin silk.

'That's true,' Johanne said. 'But as good as. He was at his mother's with Fiorella. Had to sleep in the same room as his daughter, because his sister and her husband were also staying the night. And on top of that, his sister had a tummy bug and was up all night. And another thing . . .'

She brushed her hand under her right eye once more. Adam

17

smiled and ran his thumb under her nose and then dried it on his trouser leg.

'And another thing, there's nothing to indicate anything other than the ordinary marital problems,' she finished. 'No relationship problems and certainly no financial problems. They're fairly equal on that score. He earns more than her, she owns a bigger share of the house. His firm seems to be sound.'

She took his free hand. The skin was coarse and his nails were short. Their thumbs met and moved in circles.

'And what's more, eight days have passed,' she continued, 'without you finding anything. All you've done is rule out a couple of obvious suspects.'

'It's a start,' he said lamely, and pulled back his hand.

'A very weak one.'

'What are your thoughts then?'

'I've got lots.'

'About what?'

'The tongue,' she replied and got up to get more coffee.

A car snailed its way down the street. The slow throb of the engine made the glass in the corner cabinet rattle. The beam of light danced about on the ceiling, a moving cloud of light in the big, dark room.

'The tongue,' he repeated, despondently, as if she had reminded him of an unpleasant fact that he would rather forget.

'Yes, the tongue. The method. Hate. It was deliberate. The vase . . .' Johanne signalled quote marks with her fingers. 'It was made beforehand. There was no red paper in the house. I saw in your papers that it takes about eight minutes to make something like that. And that's when you know what you're doing.'

For the first time, she seemed to be really fired up. She opened a cupboard and took two sugar cubes from a silver bowl. The spoon scratched on the ceramic of the mug as she stirred.

'Coffee when we can't sleep,' she mumbled. 'Smart move.' She looked up. 'Cutting someone's tongue out is such a loaded

18

symbol, so aggressive and horrific that it's hard to imagine that it's motivated by anything other than hate. A pretty intense hate.'

'And Fiona Helle was loved by all,' came Adam's dry retort. 'I think you've stirred the sugar enough now, dear.'

She licked the spoon and sat down again.

'The problem is, Adam, that it's impossible to know who hated her. As long as her family, her friends, acquaintances, colleagues . . . everyone around her seemed to like the woman, you'll have to look out there for the murderer.'

She pointed out of the window. One of the neighbours had turned a light on in the bathroom.

'I don't mean them, specifically,' she smiled. 'I mean the general public.'

'Dear God,' groaned Adam.

'Fiona Helle was one of the most high-profile TV stars in the country. I doubt there's many people who don't have an opinion about what she did, and therefore also about who they thought she was, right or wrong.'

'Over four million suspects, you mean.'

'Yep.'

She took a sip of coffee before putting down her mug.

'You can forget everyone under fifteen or over seventy, and the million or so who really adored her.'

'And that leaves how many, d'you reckon?'

'No idea. A couple of million, maybe?'

'A couple of million suspects . . .'

'Who possibly have never even spoken to her,' she added. 'There doesn't need to be any direct link between Fiona and the man who killed her.'

'Or woman.'

'Or woman,' she agreed. 'Good luck. And, looking at the tongue . . . Shhh!'

A feeble cry could be heard from the freshly decorated children's room. Adam got up before Johanne had time to react.

'She just wants food,' he said and made her sit down. 'I'll get her. Go and sit down on the sofa.'

She tried to pull herself together. The fear was physical, like an adrenalin shot. Her pulse rose, her cheeks flushed hot. When she lifted her hand and studied her palm, she saw the light from the ceiling reflected in the sweat in her lifeline. She dried her hands on her dressing gown and sat down heavily on the sofa.

'Is my little munchkin hungry?' she heard Adam murmuring into the baby's hair. 'You'll get some food from Mummy. There, there . . .'

The half-open eyes and eager mouth made Johanne cry again, with relief.

'I think I've gone mad,' she whispered and adjusted her breast.

'Not mad,' said Adam, 'just a bit tense and frightened, that's all.'

'The tongue,' mumbled Johanne.

'We don't need to talk about that now. Relax.'

'The fact that it was split.'

'Shhhh.'

'Liar,' she sniffed and looked up.

'Liar?'

'Not you, silly.'

She whispered to the child before she met his eye again.

'The split tongue. Can really only mean one thing. That someone thought that Fiona Helle was a liar.'

'Well, we all tell a lie now and then,' Adam said, and gently stroked the soft baby's head with his finger. 'Look, you can see the pulse in her fontanelle!'

'Someone believed that Fiona Helle was lying,' Johanne repeated. 'That her lying was so blatant and brutal that she deserved to die.'

Ragnhild let go of the nipple. Something that could easily be mistaken for a smile flitted across her face and Adam knelt down and put his cheek against her damp cheek. The blister on her upper lip from sucking was pink and full of fluid. Her tiny eyelashes were nearly black.

'It must have been some lie, in that case,' Adam mumbled. 'A bigger lie than I could ever make up.'

Ragnhild burped and then fell asleep.

She would never have chosen this place herself.

The others, notorious cheapskates, had suddenly decided to treat themselves to three weeks on the Riviera. What you were supposed to do in the Riviera in December was a mystery to her, but she said yes all the same. At least it would be a change.

Her father had become unbearable since her mother died. Whining and complaining and clinging to her all the time. He smelt like an old man, a combination of dirty clothes and poor bladder control. His fingers, which scraped her back when he gave the most unwanted goodbye hugs, were now disgustingly thin. Obligation forced her to visit him once month or so. The flat in Sandaker had never been palatial, but now that her father was living on his own it had really gone downhill. She had finally managed, after many letters, furious phone calls and a lot of bother, to get him a home help, but it didn't help much. The underside of the toilet seat was still splattered with shit. The food in the fridge was still well past its sell-by date and you couldn't open the door without gagging. It was unbelievable that the local council could offer an old, loyal taxpayer nothing more than an unreliable girl who had could scarcely turn on a washing machine.

The idea of Christmas without her father tempted her, even though she was sceptical about travelling. Especially as the children were going too. It irritated her beyond reason that children today seemed to be allergic to any form of healthy food. 'Don't like, don't like,' they kept on whingeing. A mantra before every meal. Not surprising they were skinny when they were little and then ballooned out when they hit their amorphous puberty, ravaged by modern eating disorders. The youngest, a girl of three or four, still had some charm. But the woman with the laptop was not particularly fond of her siblings.

But the house was big and the room they thought she should

have was impressive. They had shown her the brochures with great enthusiasm. She suspected they were relying on her to pay more than her fair share of the rent. They knew that she had money, even though they had absolutely no idea how much.

Truth be told, she had chosen not to keep in touch with most of her acquaintances. They scurried around in their small lives, making mountains out of molehills, problems that in no way would interest anyone but themselves. The red figures in her social accounts, which she had eventually decided it was necessary to draw up, screamed out at her. Sometimes, when she thought about it, she realized that she had really only met a handful of people of any merit.

They wanted her to come with them and she could not face another Christmas with her father.

So she was standing at Gardemoen airport, with her tickets in her hand, when her mobile phone rang. The little one, the girl, had suddenly been admitted to hospital.

She was furious. Of course her friends couldn't leave their little girl, but did they have to wait until three quarters of an hour before the flight was due to depart to tell her? After all, the child had fallen ill four hours earlier. But she still had a choice.

She went.

The others would still have to pay their share of the rent, she made that absolutely clear to them on the phone. She had actually found herself looking forward to spending three weeks with the people who she had, after all, known since she was a child.

After nineteen days down there, the landlord had offered to let her stay until March. He hadn't managed to find any tenants for the winter and didn't like the house to stand empty. Of course, it helped that the woman had tidied and cleaned just before he came. He probably also noticed that only one of the beds had been used, as he prowled from room to room, pretending to look at the electrics.

It was as easy to write on her laptop here as at home. And she had free accommodation.

The Riviera was overrated.

Villefranche was a sham town for tourists. In her opinion, any reality that might have been there had disappeared a long time ago; even the several-hundred-year-old castle by the sea looked as if it had been built from cardboard and plastic. When French taxi drivers can speak half-decent English, there has to be something seriously wrong with the place.

It annoyed her immensely that the police had got nowhere.

But then, it was a difficult case. And the Norwegian police had never been anything to boast about, provincial, weaponless eunuchs that they were.

She, on the other hand, was an expert.

The nights had closed in.

Three

Seventeen days had passed since Fiona Helle was murdered and it was now the 6th of February.

Adam Stubo sat in his office in the dreariest part of Oslo's east end, staring at the grains of sand running through an hourglass. The beautifully shaped object was unusually large. The stand was handmade. Adam had always thought it was made of oak, good old Norwegian woodwork that had darkened and aged over hundreds of years. But a visiting French criminologist, who had been there just before Christmas, had studied the antique with some interest. Mahogany, he declared, and shook his head when Adam told him that the instrument had been in his seafaring family for fourteen generations.

'This,' the Frenchman said, in perfect English, 'this little curiosity was made some time between 1880 and 1900. I doubt it has even been on board a ship. Many of them were made as ornaments for well-to-do people's homes.'

Then he shrugged his shoulders.

'But by all means,' he added, 'a pretty little thing.'

Adam chose to believe in the family story rather than some wayward passing Frenchman. The hourglass had stood on his grandparents' mantelpiece, out of reach of anyone under twenty-one. A treasured object that his father would turn over for his son every now and then, so he could watch the shiny grains of silver-grey sand in the beautiful, hand-blown glass as they ran through a hole that his grandmother claimed was smaller than a strand of hair.

The files that were piled up along the walls and on the desk on both sides of the hourglass told another, more tangible story. The story of Fiona Helle's murder had a grotesque start, but nothing that resembled an end. The hundreds of witness statements, the endless technical analyses, special reports, photographs and tactical observations seemed to point in all directions but led nowhere.

Adam could not remember another case like it, where they had absolutely nothing to go on.

He was getting on for fifty. He had worked in the police force since he was twenty-two. He had trudged the streets on the beat, hauled in down-and-outs and drunk drivers as a constable; he considered joining the dog unit out of sheer curiosity, had been extremely unhappy behind a desk in ØKOKRIM, the economic and environmental crime unit, and then finally ended up in the Criminal Investigation Service, by chance. It felt like a couple of lifetimes ago. Naturally, he couldn't remember all his cases. He had given up trying to keep a mental record a long time ago. The murders were too numerous, the rapes too callous. The figures were meaningless after a while. But one thing was certain and irrefutable: sometimes everything went wrong. That's just the way it was, and Adam Stubo didn't waste time dwelling on his defeats.

This was different.

This time he hadn't seen the victim. For once he hadn't been involved from the start. He had limped into the case, disoriented and behind. But in a way that made him more alert. He thought differently from the others and noticed it most clearly in meetings, gatherings of increasing collective frustration, where he generally kept shtum.

The others got bogged down in clues that weren't really there. With care and precision, they tried to piece together a puzzle that would never be solved, simply because the police only found clear blue skies wherever they looked for dark, murky shadows. They had found a total of twenty-four fingerprints in Fiona Helle's house, but there was nothing to indicate that any had been left by the murderer. An unexplained cigarette stub by the front door didn't lead anywhere; according to the latest analyses it was at least several weeks old. They might as well cross out the footprints in the snow with a thick red pen, as they couldn't be linked to any other information about the killer. The blood at the scene of the crime gave no more clues either. The saliva traces on the table, hair on the carpet and greasy, faint red lip marks on the wine glass told a very ordinary story of a woman sitting at her desk in peace and quiet, going through her weekly post.

'A phantom killer,' Sigmund Berli grinned from the doorway. 'Buggered if I'm not starting to believe the grumblings of the Romerike guys, that it's suicide.'

'Impressive,' Adam smiled back. 'First she half strangles herself, then she cuts out her tongue, before sitting down nicely to die from blood loss. But before she dies, she musters up enough energy to wrap the tongue up in a beautiful red paper package. If nothing else, it's original. How's it all going, by the way? Working with them, I mean?'

'The guys from Romerike are nice enough. Big district, you know. Of course they like to throw their weight around a bit. But they seem to be pretty happy that we're involved in the case.'

Sigmund Berli sat down on the spare chair and pulled it closer to the desk.

'Snorre's been selected for a big ice-hockey tournament for ten-year-olds this weekend,' he said and nodded meaningfully. 'Only eight and he's being selected for the top team with the ten-year-olds!'

'I didn't think they ranked teams for such young age groups.'

'That's just some rubbish the sports confederation has come up with. Can't think like that, can you? The boy lives for ice-hockey, twenty-four seven – he slept with his skates on the other night. If they don't learn the importance of competitions now, they'll just get left behind.'

'Fair enough. He's your child. I don't think I'd . . .'

'Where are we going?' Sigmund interrupted, casting his eye over all the files and piles of documents. 'Where the hell are we going with this case?'

Adam didn't answer. Instead he picked up the hourglass and turned it round again.

'Adam, stop it. Are the sleepless nights getting to you, or what?'

'No. Ragnhild's lovely. Nine. Ten.'

'Where are we going, Adam?'

Sigmund's voice was insistent now, and he leant towards his colleague and continued: 'There isn't a single fucking clue. Not technical at least. Nor tactical, as far as I can tell. I went through all the statements yesterday, then again today. Fiona Helle was well liked. By most people. Nice lady, they say. A character. Lots of people reckon it was her complexity that made her so interesting. Well read and interested in marginal cultural expression. But also liked cartoons and loved *Lord of the Rings*.'

'People who are as successful as Fiona Helle always have . . .'

Adam tried to find the right word.

'Enemies,' Sigmund suggested.

'No. Not necessarily. But people who aren't friends. There's always someone who feels overshadowed by people like that. Outshone. And Fiona Helle shone brighter than most. But I still find it hard to believe that some NRK employee with ambitions to present a Saturday night show, who might feel that they've been wronged, would go to such drastic lengths as to . . .'

He nodded at the board, where a poster-sized picture of a bare-breasted, open-legged Fiona Helle screamed at them.

'I think the answer is possibly somewhere in here,' Adam said, pulling out a pile of letters which had been carefully placed in a red folder. 'I picked out twenty letters. At random, basically. To get an impression of what kind of people wrote to Fiona Helle.'

Sigmund furrowed his brow in response and picked up the letter that lay on top.

'*Dear Fiona,*' he read out loud. '*I am a 22-year-old girl from Hemnesberget. Three years ago I found out my dad was a salor from Venezuela. My mum says he was a shit who just left never got in touch again . . .*'

Sigmund scratched his ear. 'She can't bloody write,' he muttered before continuing to read:

'*When he found out I was dew. But there is a lady here at the Coop says Juan Maria was a nice man and it was my mum who wanted . . .*'

Sigmund inspected his fingertip. A small dirty-yellow lump seemed to fascinate him. He paused for several seconds before wiping it off on his trousers.

'Are they all as hopeless as this?' he asked.

'I wouldn't say it was hopeless,' Adam said. 'After all, she's shown some initiative. Just because she can't spell and has bad grammar doesn't mean that she can't do her own detective work. She actually knows where her father lives. The letter is a plea for *On the Move with Fiona* to take her quest one step further. The girl is terrified of being rejected and thinks there's a greater chance that her father will accept her if it's all on TV.'

'Jesus,' exclaimed Sigmund and picked up another letter.

'That one is of a completely different calibre,' Adam said while his colleague glanced down the page. 'An eloquent dentist who's approaching retirement. He was just a boy during the war and lived on the east side of Oslo. In 1945, he was sent to the country as a weedy, anaemic orphan to be fattened up. There he met . . .'

'Fiona Helle was playing with fire,' Sigmund interrupted, leafing through the other letters. 'This is . . .'

'People's lives,' Adam said lightly and shrugged his shoulders. 'Every single letter that woman received – and believe me, it wasn't just a couple – told stories of loss and grief. Despair. But she's also been criticized for it. The usual debate in the end. On the one side, intellectual snobs who patronizingly argued against the exploitation of the ignorant masses. And on the other side, the People . . .' He drew a capital P with his finger. '. . . Who thought that the snobs could just shut up and turn off the TV if they didn't like what they saw.'

'That's a fair point,' Sigmund mumbled.

'Both camps had valid points, but as usual the debate didn't result in much. Except shouting and screaming and of course even better ratings for the programme. It has to be said in Fiona Helle's defence that the vetting of people who eventually made it onto the programme was extremely rigorous. There were three psychologists in the production team and every participant had to go through a kind of screening. Quite thorough preparations as far as I'm aware.'

'But what about the ones who didn't make it, then?'

'Exactly. There are people out there who poured their lives into a letter to Fiona Helle. Many of them had never told their story to anyone before. It must've been very painful, then, to be rejected, as most people were. Especially as the production team didn't have the capacity to answer them all. Some of the critics have also claimed . . .'

Adam fished a matt aluminium cigar case out of his breast pocket. He opened it carefully, pulled the cigar out and ran it under his nose.

'. . . That Fiona Helle became God,' he sniffed. 'A God who answered the prayers of desperate people with silence.'

'Very dramatic.'

'Or rather, melodramatic. Yes.' He returned the cigar to its case with equal care. 'But just a tiny little bit true, as Kristiane says when we catch her lying.'

Sigmund burst out laughing.

'My boys just flatly deny it. Even if I catch them red-handed and the evidence is stacked against them. Tough little nuts. Especially Snorre.' He stroked his crown in a shy gesture. 'The youngest one,' he explained. 'The one that looks like me.'

'So there we have it,' Adam said, and sighed. 'An unknown number of people who might have good grounds for being, at least, *disappointed* with Fiona Helle.'

'Disappointed,' Sigmund repeated. 'That's hardly . . .'

They both looked up at the picture of the victim.

'No. That's why I've started a small investigation of my own. I want to find out what happened to the people who actually got help from Fiona. All of them had their fifteen minutes of fame

29

and met their biological mother in South Korea, or their father who disappeared in Argentina, their daughter who was put up for adoption in Drøbak and God knows what else . . . All of them had their lives turned upside down during prime-time viewing.'

'Is there nothing like that already?'

'No, in fact, there isn't.'

'But hasn't NRK followed up all those who . . .'

'No.'

Sigmund sank back in the chair. He stared at the cigar case that was back in place in Adam's breast pocket.

'Haven't you stopped?' Sigmund asked in a tired voice.

'What? Oh, you mean this. I only sniff them. Old habit. Don't smoke any more. If I want to, I have to go out onto the veranda. Especially if it's a cigar. It takes time to smoke one of these.'

'But Adam . . .'

'Yes?'

'D'you think that all the technical work is wasted?'

Adam gave a hoarse laugh and put his hand to his mouth as he coughed.

'Consequence,' he explained. 'Consequence of all my damned smoking.' He grimaced, swallowed and then continued. 'No, of course not. Technical investigations are never wasted. But as we don't seem to have come up with any results, not so far, I think we should start at the other end. Instead of working outwards from the scene of the crime, we should start out there and work in. If we're lucky, we may find a motive or two. A strong enough motive, I mean.'

'Are you leaving? This early?'

Adam had stood up and was already over by his coat, which was hanging unwashed and creased on the coat stand by the window.

'Yes,' he said seriously and pulled on his coat. 'I'm a modern father. From now on I have to leave work every day at three o'clock to spend quality time with my daughter. Every day.'

'What?'

'Just joking, you idiot.'

Adam slapped his colleague on the shoulder and shouted as he disappeared down the corridor: 'Have a good weekend, everyone!'

'What the hell am I doing here?' Sigmund muttered, and looked at the door that had just slammed shut behind Adam. 'It's not even my office.'

Then he looked at his watch. It was half past five already. He couldn't understand where the day had gone.

The blonde woman in the Armani suit and trainers felt good as she got out of the taxi. It was still a good half-hour until midnight and she was practically sober. In a portrait interview for tomorrow's *VG* newspaper, it said that Vibeke Heinerback had realized that she was grown-up when she started to leave parties and receptions early because she was thinking about her productivity the next day. *Tomorrow's productivity*. It was her own turn of phrase. It said something about her, both personally and politically.

Her trainers weren't quite right, given her attire. But with a broken toe the possibilities were limited, and fortunately the TV producers hadn't cut the part in the chat show where she commented on her own inelegance, flirtatiously saying that she was, after all, only twenty-six. And that she'd broken her toe while playing with her nephew. Not quite true, but white lies were allowed every now and then, when it was nothing serious. The studio audience had laughed and warmed to her. Vibeke Heinerback smiled to herself as she struggled to get her key in the front door.

It had been a good week.

Politically. Personally. In every way.

Despite the pain in her toe.

It was annoyingly dark. She looked up. The outside light was not working and she could just make out that the bulb had been broken. That made her a bit anxious and she looked over her shoulder. The light by the gate was broken as well. She tried to

31

keep all her weight on her good foot as she held her keys up to see if she'd got the wrong one.

She never did manage to find out.

The next morning, Vibeke Heinerback was found by her boyfriend, who had wound his weary way home from his brother's stag night, by bus and taxi.

She was sitting in bed. She was naked. Her hands were nailed to the wall above the head of the bed. Her legs were splayed and it looked as if someone had tried to stuff something up her vagina.

Vibeke Heinerback's boyfriend didn't see this detail at first. He tore her hands free, threw up violently all over the place and then pulled the body out onto the floor, as if it was the bed itself that had attacked her so brutally. It wasn't until half an hour later that he came to his senses and called the police.

Then he discovered the green book that was still stuck between Vibeke Heinerback's thighs.

The ensuing investigation would establish that it was a leather-bound copy of the Koran.

Four

The woman in seat 16A seemed to be nice. She was reading the British papers and obviously in need of a coffee. The steward found it difficult to guess where she was from. Most of the passengers were Swedish, though everyone was being disturbed by a noisy Danish family with small children in the second-last row. He had also registered several Norwegians. It was by no means the high season, but lots of people were more than happy to get on a direct flight to Nice when the prices were so ridiculously low.

He should really stop working as a steward. His weight had always been a problem and now his colleagues had begun to make comments. No matter how hard he tried or how little he ate, the bathroom scales threatened to tip over into three digits at any moment.

It was good to have people like the lady in 16A on flights like this.

She was darker than most Scandinavians. Her eyes were brown and she had no reason to be happy about her weight either. She was big and heavy, but the first impression was one of strength. Powerful, he thought after a while. She was an Amazonian woman.

And she certainly liked her coffee.

What's more, she had no children, thank goodness, and didn't complain about anything.

The body was still warm.

The attendant at the Galleria multi-storey car park reckoned that it couldn't be more than a couple of hours since the prostitute had said her goodbyes. Maybe he was wrong. He was no expert, he had to admit, though it was the second time in under three months that he'd had to call the police because some poor woman had chosen to inject what would be her last hit somewhere sheltered from the biting wind that whipped through winter streets of Stockholm, forcing everyone to dress like polar explorers. As it was quite warm in the stairwell, it was difficult to say.

But she couldn't have been lying there long.

If you can't see forwards and you can't look back – then look up in life.
The words of wisdom were written in red marker on the wall. The tart had obviously taken them literally. She was lying on her side, with her head on her right arm, legs bent, as if someone had put her in the recovery position so that death would come gently. But she was looking up, with open eyes and an astonished, almost happy expression.

Peace, the attendant thought to himself, and took out his mobile phone. The woman looked like she'd found peace. The man was tired of having to chase the prostitutes out of the huge car park, but deep down he felt for them. Their tiresome existence reminded him of the joys of his own life. His job was boring and monotonous, but he had a good wife and the children seemed to be turning out OK. He could afford a beer or two on Friday night and prided himself on always paying his bills before they were due.

The reception for mobile phones was terrible down here.

He recognized her. She was one of the regulars. She seemed to live down here, at the bottom of the stairwell, in a space that was barely five square metres. The blue and red stripes on the wall were no doubt meant to conjure up movement and light. A bag lay flung in the corner, and three papers and a magazine had been stuck underneath a rolled-up sleeping bag just under the stairs. A bottle of mineral water had fallen down behind her back.

The attendant trudged up the stairs. His asthma was bothering him and he had to stop for a minute to draw breath. Finally he got to the top and opened a drab door out onto Brunkebergs Torg.

The woman's colleagues were already at work. He spotted a couple of them, shivering and emaciated; one of them got into a BMW which immediately accelerated towards Sergels Torg.

He eventually got hold of the police. They promised to be there within half an hour.

'Sure,' he muttered and rang off. Last time he had been alone with the dead prostitute for over an hour.

He lit a cigarette. The other woman, in thin tights and mock fur coat, got an offer on the other side of the square.

The dead whore wasn't that small. Quite the contrary, he thought, and took a long draw on his cigarette. She was the plumper type. There weren't many of those. Prostitutes normally shrank over the years. They got smaller and skinnier for every shot they took, every pill they swallowed. Maybe this woman remembered to eat, in between tricks and drugs.

He should go back down to keep an eye on her.

Instead he lit another cigarette and stood out there in the cold until the police finally came. They took a few seconds to confirm what the attendant already knew, that the woman was dead. An ambulance was called and the body was taken away.

Katinka Olsson was cremated three days later, and no one bothered to erect a stone to mark the remains of the late thirty-something prostitute. The four children she had brought into the world before she was thirty would never know that their biological mother carried baby pictures of them in her otherwise empty wallet, faded photographs with worn, uneven edges; Katinka Olsson's only treasure.

She died of an overdose and no would ever ask after her. No one grieved for Katinka Olsson and no one wondered why the dead prostitute smelt fresh and clean and had on newly washed, if worn clothes.

No one.

Vibeke Heinerback's home surprised him.

Standing in the middle of the relatively large sitting room, he got the impression of a far more interesting person than the media had ever managed to portray.

When he thought about it, he couldn't remember having seen any features about Vibeke Heinerback's house. Adam Stubo had used the early hours of the morning to go through a large pile of interviews and other cuttings, sensational and glamorous tales of an apparently successful life.

When her boyfriend proposed to her, the couple travelled to Paris with *Hello!*. The pictures of the two of them, embracing in front of the Eiffel Tower, under the Arc de Triomphe, outside well-known shops on the Champs-Elysées and on the streets of Montmartre, reminded him of advertisements from the seventies. Vibeke and Trond were both bottle blondes and inoffensively well groomed. They had an aura of self confidence and matching pastel-coloured psychedelic shirts. Only the wine glasses that were raised in a couple of the photographs broke the illusion. They should have been Coca-Cola bottles.

When Vibeke Heinerback was elected as Norway's youngest party leader, members of the press had been invited to follow her to her room when she retired after the national conference. The papers and magazines were all in raptures about her evening bath. Vibeke raised a glass of champagne to the readers from a sea of pink bubbles, with her smooth, beautifully shaped left leg hanging over the edge of the bath. According to the picture captions, she was absolutely exhausted.

The setting for the photographs was a hotel room.

Vibeke Heinerback was the ultimate example of young Scandinavian success. She only managed to complete a couple of years at the Norwegian School of Management before politics completely took over her life. She walked through the winter slush down Karl Johan in high heels, but also let herself be pictured wearing wellies in the woods. She was always suitably dressed in the Storting. She adhered to a strict dress code when she participated in debates that were to be televised, but when she took part in programmes that were less important her style had earned her third place in a list of the country's best-dressed women. She has a real eye for sexy details, the jury said in admiration. Naturally, she was going to have children. But not yet, she smiled to the impertinent journalists, and carried on climbing up the ladder of a party that, on good days, gloried in being the country's leading party (just) in the opinion polls.

As he looked around the sitting room for the third time, Adam felt a twinge of guilt at his own prejudices. His eyes fixed on a beautiful lampshade in milky glass. The glass was held in place by three metal tubes and the whole thing looked a bit like a fifties B-movie UFO. It was an impressive room. A cream corner sofa behind a steel and glass table. The chairs were upholstered in an intense orange fabric that was mirrored in small speckles on a huge abstract painting on the opposite wall. All the surfaces were clean. The only ornament in the room was an Alvar Aalto vase on the austere sideboard, where a colourful bunch of tulips was dying of thirst.

The woven-steel magazine rack was overflowing with magazines and tabloid papers. Adam picked up a gossip magazine. Two divorces, a celebrity anniversary and a singer's tragic decline into alcoholism graced the front cover.

To the extent that Adam had ever paid attention to Vibeke Heinerback, he had admired, somewhat reluctantly, her instinctive understanding of people's need for easy solutions. On the other hand, he had never detected any real political understanding, or overriding moral conviction. Vibeke Heinerback believed that petrol prices should be cut and that the country should be ashamed of its care of the elderly. She called for lower taxes and more police. She thought that shopping in Sweden was a justified protest by the Norwegian people; if the politicians chose to have the highest alcohol prices in Europe, it was all they could expect.

He had seen her as simple, superficial and politically savvy. Not well read, he thought, and in one interview she seemed to think that Ayn Rand, who she claimed was her favourite author, was a man.

It must have been the journalist who got it wrong, Adam thought, as he looked around the sitting room in more detail. Certainly not Vibeke Heinerback.

He slowly ran his fingers over the book spines in the full shelves that lined two of the walls, from floor to ceiling. A worn and well-read copy of *The Fountainhead* stood beside a paperback copy of *Atlas Shrugged*. An extensive biography of Frank Lloyd Wright, the eccentric architect and author, was in such a sorry state that several of the pages fell out when Adam tried to check the Ex Libris label.

Jens Bjørneboe and Hamsun, P. O. Enquist, Günter Grass and Don DeLillo, Lu Xun and Hanna Arendt. New and old side by side, in something that vaguely resembled a system. In order of love, Adam suddenly realized.

'Look,' he said to Sigmund Berli, who had just come back in from the bedroom. 'She's got all her favourite books between hip and head level! The books down towards the floor or above are almost untouched.'

He stretched up and pointed to an anthology of Chinese authors he had never even heard of. Then he hunkered down, took out a book from the bottom shelf and blew the dust off before he read out loud:

'Mircea Eliade.' He shook his head and put the book back. 'That's the sort of thing Johanne's sister reads. But I would never have guessed that Miss Heinerback did.'

'There's a lot of crime here too.'

Sigmund Berli ran his fingers over the shelves closest to the kitchen door. Adam squinted at the titles. They were all there. The Grand Old Dames of British literature and the arrogant Americans from the eighties. And here and there a French-sounding name popped up. Judging by the covers, with big cars and lethal weapons in grey stylized strokes, they had to be from the fifties. She had classics such as Chandler and Hammett in American presentation copies, alongside an almost complete catalogue of Norwegian crime novels published in the last ten years.

'Do you think they're her boyfriend's books?' Sigmund asked.

'He just moved in recently. These have been here for a while. I wonder why she . . . Why she never mentioned this.'

'What? That she read?'

'Yes. I mean, I've gone through a pile of interviews today that all gave the impression of a rather uninteresting person. A political animal, true enough, but someone who is more interested in banal individual issues than in putting things into context. Even in the . . .' Adam drew a square in the air before continuing:

'. . . Boxes, is that what they're called? The frames with standard questions, she never said anything about . . . this. When they asked if she read, she said newspapers. Five newspapers a day and not much time for anything else.'

'Maybe she read more before. Before she became a politician, I mean. Just didn't have enough time any more.'

Sigmund had moved out into the kitchen.

'Wow! Take a look at this.'

The kitchen was a bizarre mix of old and new. The front-angled wall cupboards looked like they were made just after the war. But when Adam opened a door, it glided silently and easily on modern plastic and metal fittings. The sink was enormous, with taps straight out of a 1930s film. The porcelain buttons that showed warm and cold in red and blue calligraphy were unreadable with age. The worktops were dark and matt.

'Slate,' Adam said and rapped the stone with his knuckles. 'She's obviously restored a lot of the old features and mixed in some new.'

'Classy,' Sigmund hesitated. 'It's pretty cool, isn't it?'

'Yes, and expensive.'

'How much do they earn in the Storting, d'you reckon?'

'Not enough,' Adam said and pinched his nose. 'When were the police here?'

'About seven o'clock this morning. Her boyfriend, he's called Trond Arnesen, had destroyed any evidence at the scene of the crime. Had thrown up everywhere and moved things around. He

39

pulled her out of the bed and stuff like that. Have you seen the bedroom?'

'Mmm.'

Adam moved over to the kitchen window. Dusk was settling in the east, heavy clouds hung over Lillestrøm in the distance, with the promise of snow during the night. He shifted a curved kitchen table with great care and put his face right up to the window, without touching the glass. He stood like that for a while, lost in his own thoughts, without responding to Sigmund's comments, which sounded more distant and muffled as his colleague moved around the house.

He looked at the compass on his sophisticated watch. He drew a map in his mind. Then he took a step back, closed one eye and looked at the view again.

If you were to fell the three spruce trees at the bottom of the garden and demolish the small housing development a few hundred metres away, you could see the house where Fiona Helle was murdered, only a week ago.

There couldn't be more than one and a half kilometres between the two places.

'Is there any chance at all? I mean, that the cases are linked?'

Adam helped himself to a healthy portion of the fried potatoes before reaching for the Heinz bottle.

'Do you have to have ketchup on absolutely everything?'

'Do you think there is? A connection?'

'I'm going now,' Kristiane shouted from the hall.

'Shit,' Johanne exclaimed, and ran to the stairs with Ragnhild in her arms, 'she's not asleep.'

Kristiane's nose was squashed up against the front door. Her red down jacket was zipped up. Her scarf was wound tightly around her neck and her hat hung down over her eyes. She had her boots on the wrong feet. She was clutching a mitten in each hand. She leant her whole body against the locked door and announced: 'I'm going.'

'Not now, you're not,' Johanne called and handed the baby to Adam. 'It's too late. It's past nine o'clock. You were in bed and . . . Do you want to hold Ragnhild for a while? Isn't she sweet and funny?'

'Horrible,' hissed Kristiane. 'Horrible child.'

'Kristiane!'

Adam Stubo's voice was so sharp that Ragnhild started to cry. He rocked her in frustration and murmured into the soft blanket that was wrapped round her. Kristiane started to howl. She rocked from foot to foot and banged her forehead against the wood. Her howling changed into desperate, rasping sobs.

'Daddy,' she growled in between the sobs. 'My daddy. I'm going to my daddy.'

Johanne threw up her hands and turned round to face Adam, who was standing halfway up the stairs.

'It might be best,' she started. 'I think maybe . . .'

'No way,' Adam stopped her. 'She's been with Isak for a week. So now she's going to stay with us. It's important for her to feel included. That she's part of the family. That . . .'

The baby had finally stopped crying. Some gunk from her eyes ran down her rosy cheek. Her soft hair stuck to her skull. Suddenly she blinked her eyes, reluctantly, as if she had just woken up from a long, deep sleep. She pulled a face so you could see her gums.

'. . . That this is her sister,' he finished quietly, and his lips brushed the child's skin. 'Kristiane must stay here. She can go to Isak's again in a few days.'

'Daddy! I want to go to my daddy!'

Adam descended into the small porch that they had on the ground floor. He could feel the underfloor heating burning through his woollen socks. He was worried that the electricians had done something wrong when they were doing up the house. God knows when he would get time to check it. He carefully gave the baby back to Johanna.

'Here comes Tiddly the Wriggling Tadpole,' he said and threw

Kristiane over his shoulder in a fireman's lift, before marching back up the stairs.

'Don't,' giggled Kristiane, against her will, as he pulled one of her boots off and planted it in a flowerpot. 'Don't!'

'This will grow into a boot flower in a week or two. And this one . . .'

He threw the other boot into the wastepaper basket.

'Haven't got any use for this one,' he said, and manoeuvred her into a firm hold. 'Tadpoles don't need shoes.'

He kicked open the door to her bedroom with a bang. Then he pulled off her clothes quick as a flash. Fortunately she still had her pyjamas on underneath.

'Quick,' he puffed. 'Or the troll will sweat to death. I'm going to start counting now.'

'Don't,' shrieked Kristiane with delight and buried herself under the duvet.

'One,' he started. 'Two, three. The magic is working now. Tiddly the Tadpole is fast asleep.'

Then he pulled the door to and shrugged his shoulders.

'There!'

Johanne stood with a blank face and Ragnhild over her shoulder.

'That's what we usually do when you're not here,' he excused himself. 'Fast and effective. Do you think there's a connection? Between Fiona Helle's and Vibeke Heinerback's murders?'

'That's how you put the girl to bed?'

Johanne looked at him in disbelief.

'So what! Forget it! She's asleep now. Magic. Come on.'

He padded into the sitting room and started to clear the dinner table. Leftovers were scraped into the bin, apart from the fried potatoes, which he ate as he cleared. The grease ran down his fingers and when he tried to pour himself more wine the bottle nearly slid out of his hand.

'Ooops . . . do you want any? You don't need to worry any more, you know. I'm sure a small glass won't hurt Ragnhild.'

42

'No thanks. Actually . . .'

Gently, she lay Ragnhild down in her cot, which Adam had eventually agreed could be moved in and out of the sitting room, depending on where they were themselves. It was by the end of the sofa now.

'Maybe a small glass,' she said, and sat down at the empty table. 'Can you wipe the table with the cloth, please?'

With an everyday, almost casual expression on her face, she grabbed the papers that Adam had thrown down when he came home. It was a thin file. This time there were no pictures. A couple of police reports, two handwritten memorandums and a map of Lørenskog with a red cross over Vibeke Heinerback's address were stapled together. Johanne couldn't see if there was any system to it.

'I see that you haven't much to go on here, either.'

'The murder was only discovered this morning.'

'And you've censored the file. Did you want to spare me the photographs?'

'No.'

He seemed to be sincere, and sat down and scratched his head.

'They haven't made enough copies yet,' he added, yawning. 'But you're not missing anything. Horrible sight. Especially the . . .'

'Enough, thank you.' She shook her head and put up her hand. 'You gave me enough details on the phone. And there are certainly similarities. Brutal murders. Both bodies have been mutilated.'

Adam knitted his brows. He cocked his head and his mouth moved, as if he wanted to say something, but didn't know quite what.

'Mutilated,' he repeated in the end. 'Cutting out someone's tongue definitely qualifies as mutilation. But Vibeke Heinerback . . .'

Again, his expression was one of doubt. He narrowed his eyes, blinked and almost imperceptibly shook his head, as if the scenario of a killer on a deadly hunt for female celebrities was too much to take in. He glanced over at the cot.

43

'Do you think she can understand any of this?'

'She's only three weeks old.'

'Yes, but the brain's like a sponge, you know. Maybe she's subconsciously taking it all in and storing it. And it will affect her, later I mean.'

'Idiot.' She stretched her hand over the table and stroked his cheek. 'You're scared that the press is right, aren't you?' she said. 'Have you seen the special editions?'

He shook his head. She cupped his jaw with her hand.

'They're having a field day. It must be annoying for them that the murder wasn't discovered until this morning and only announced later on in the day. The special editions are botch jobs. Full of inaccuracies, incredible speculation, incorrect facts, from what I can see. They've dubbed him the celebrity killer.'

'Or her,' said Adam and grabbed her hand.

He lifted it to his lips and kissed it.

'Or her. OK. Don't be such a pedant. Fortunately they were more reserved on the news, but there's still speculation that there's a madman on the loose who's got it in for beautiful, successful women. *VG* even managed to get a well-known psychologist to outline a profile of a sexually frustrated womanhater with a disability who was rejected by his mother.' She laughed quietly and took a sip from her glass. 'You know, it's only now that I realize how good this actually is. Having not tasted wine for ten months, that is.'

'You are . . .'

'Lovely,' she concluded for him and her smile broadened. 'What do you think?'

'About you?'

'About there being a link. You must have given it some thought. You and Sigmund and several others are working on both cases. Both murders . . .'

'Took place in Lørenskog, both victims are women, both are well known, both are high-profile celebrities, both . . .'

'. . . Are good-looking. Were, at least.' She swivelled the glass in

44

her hand and continued: 'And in both cases, the killer left a message, a highly symbolic abuse of the body.'

She was talking more slowly now, and her voice was not so loud, as if she was alarmed by her own reasoning.

'The press don't know about the book yet,' he said. 'About the Koran. It was actually taped between her legs. It would appear that the intention was to stuff it up her cunt, but . . .'

'Don't use that word!'

'Sorry, vagina. The book was taped to her thighs, right up by the vagina.'

'Or anus.'

'Or anus,' he repeated, somewhat surprised. 'Hmm, that's probably what he meant. *Up yours*, or something like that.'

'Maybe. You want some more?'

He nodded and she poured the rest of the bottle into his glass. She had only taken a sip from her own.

'If you were to look for similarities, apart from the obvious ones, which could be pure coincidence, I think the power of the symbolism is one of the most striking features,' she said. 'Cutting out someone's tongue and splitting it in two is such an unambiguous statement, such obvious symbolism, that you could almost imagine that the killer read too many Red Indian books as a boy. The Muslim bible up your bum is hardly a divine message.'

'I don't think our new compatriots would appreciate you calling the Koran a bible,' said Adam, massaging his neck. 'Would you mind?'

With an exasperated smile she got up and stood behind him. She leant back against the island unit and took a firm grip of Adam's neck muscles.

He was so broad. So big. She could feel his muscles were knotted under the surprisingly soft skin. It was his size that had first attracted her, she was captivated by a man who must have weighed 115 kilos without actually appearing to be fat. Just after they moved in together, she had tried to put him on a diet. 'Just thinking of your health,' she said, and gave up after three weeks.

45

Adam didn't get irritable when he ate less, he got desperate. She had stopped her project one afternoon when he wiped away something that could have been tears when faced with a plate of boiled cod, not a trace of fat, one potato and a spoonful of steamed carrots. Then he disappeared into the bathroom and stayed there for the rest of the meal. He had butter with everything, sauces and gravy with most things, and believed that a proper meal should always be rounded off with a dessert.

'Obviously, it's too early to say,' Johanne said, and pressed her thumbs into the muscles between his shoulder blades and spine. 'But I would advise against assuming it's the same killer.'

'Of course we're not assuming anything,' he groaned. 'More. A bit further up. But the truth is, just the thought is enough to frighten the life out of me. I mean . . . Ow! There, right there.'

'You mean if there really is only one murderer, you can expect more,' Johanne said. 'Victims, that is. More murders.'

His muscles stiffened under her fingers. Adam straightened his back, pushed her gently away and rearranged his shirt. Ragnhild's light breathing and snuffles could be heard from the sitting room. A cat was obviously courting outside somewhere. The yowling cut through the evening quiet and Johanne was convinced she could smell cat spray all the way up to the first floor.

'I hate those semi-feral beasts,' she said and sat down.

'Can you help me?' Adam asked in an urgent voice, almost insistent. 'Can you get anything at all out of the papers?'

'There's too little. You know that. I need to look through . . . I need to have . . .' She laughed feebly and shrugged her shoulders. 'Good God, of course I can't help you. I've got a new-born baby to look after! I'm on maternity leave! Obviously we can talk about it . . .'

'There's no one as good as you in the country. There are no real profilers here and we . . .'

'I am not a profiler,' she said, agitated. 'How many times do I have to tell you? I'm fed up with . . .'

'OK,' he interrupted and held up his hands in a gesture of

peace. 'But you bloody well know enough about profiling to be one. And I don't know anyone other than you who has been taught by the FBI's best . . .'

'Adam!'

The evening before they got married, he had promised, with his hand on his heart, never to ask about Johanne's time with the FBI. They had argued, harsh and unfamiliar; she had used words he never imagined she could use and he was positively furious that such an important period of her life was to be a closed book to him.

But she would not share it. Never, not with anyone. As a naïve young psychology student in Boston, she had been given the opportunity to participate in one of the FBI's profiler courses. The head of the course was Warren Scifford, already a legend in his fifties, as much for his knowledge as his relentless bedding of promising young female students. They called him *the Chief*, and Johanne had trusted the man who was nearly thirty years her senior. In the end she started to believe that she was something special. That she had been chosen, by him and the FBI, and that of course he would divorce his wife as soon as the children were old enough.

It all went wrong and nearly cost her her life. She got on the first possible flight back to Oslo, started to study law three weeks later and graduated from university in record time. Warren Scifford was a name she had tried to forget for the past thirteen years. Her time in the FBI, the months together with Warren, the catastrophic event that resulted in the Chief having to work in an office behind a desk for half a year as punishment until it all blew over and he was one of the big boys again, was a chapter in her life that occasionally came to mind, but she only thought about it reluctantly. It made her feel sick and she never, no matter what, wanted to talk about it again.

The problem was that Adam knew Warren Scifford. In fact, they had met up again only last summer, when Adam went to an international police conference in New Orleans. When he came

47

home and mentioned Warren's name in passing over supper, Johanne smashed two plates in a sudden outburst of anger. Then she ran into the guest room, locked the door and cried herself to sleep. For three days, he only managed to get monosyllabic replies out of her.

And now he was dangerously close to breaking his promise again.

'Adam,' she repeated harshly. 'Don't even go there.'

'Take it easy. If you don't want to help, you don't want to help.' He leant back in the chair with an indifferent smile. 'After all, it's not your problem, all this.'

'Don't be like that,' she said, dejected.

'Like what? I'm only stating the obvious. It's not your problem that a couple of famous women have been killed and mutilated just outside Oslo.'

He emptied his glass and put it down, a bit too hard.

'I've got children,' Johanne said with feeling. 'I've got a demanding nine-year-old and a two-week-old baby and more than enough to keep me busy without taking on a major role in a difficult murder investigation!'

'OK, OK, I said it was all right.' He stood up suddenly and got two dessert bowls out of the cupboard. 'Fruit salad,' he said. 'Do you want some?'

'Adam, honestly. Sit down. We can . . . I am perfectly willing to discuss the cases. Like now, in the evening, when the girls have gone to bed. But both you and I know that profiling work is extremely demanding, and so far-reaching that—'

'D'you know what,' he interrupted, and banged a bowl of whipped cream down so hard on the table that the cream jumped. 'Fiona Helle's death is one thing. A tragedy. She was a mother and a wife and far too young to die. Vibeke Heinerback didn't have any children, but I still think that twenty-six is too young to die. But all that aside, people die. People get killed.' He stroked his nose, his straight, beautifully shaped nose with nostrils that quivered when he, on rare occasions, got really angry. 'For God's sake, people are killed every second day in this country. But what upsets me, what really frightens me . . .'

Alarmed by his own choice of words, he hesitated before repeating himself.

'Frightened. I'm frightened, Johanne. I don't understand these cases. There are so many similarities between them, that I can't help wondering . . .'

'When the next victim will be killed,' Johanne helped him, as he still couldn't finish the sentence.

'Exactly. And that's why I'm asking for your help. I know that it's a lot to ask. I know that you've got more than enough on your plate with Kristiane and Ragnhild and your mother and the house and . . .'

'OK.'

'What?'

'Fine. I'll see how much I can manage.'

'Do you mean that?'

'Yes. But then I need all the facts. About both cases. And I want it to be clear from the start, that I can pull out at any point.'

'Whenever,' he nodded in confirmation. 'Shall I . . . I can catch a cab down to the office and . . .'

'It's nearly half past ten.'

Her laughter was lame. But it was still laughter, Adam thought. He studied her face for signs of irritation, small twitches in her lower lips, a muscle that drew a shadow along her cheekbone. But all he could see was dimples and a long yawn.

'I'm just going to check the children,' she said.

He loved the way she walked. She was slim without being thin. Even now, only a couple of weeks after giving birth, she moved with a boyish lightness that made him smile. She had narrow hips, straight shoulders. When she bent down over Ragnhild, her hair fell across her face, soft and tangled. She pushed it back behind her ear and said something. Ragnhild was snoring gently.

He followed her into Kristiane's room. She opened the door with great care. The little girl was asleep with her head to the foot of the bed, the duvet underneath her and her down jacket over her like a duvet. Her breathing was steady and even. A faint smell of sleep and clean bed linen filled the room and Adam put his arm round Johanne.

'Well, it certainly worked,' she whispered. He could hear she was smiling. 'The magic worked.'

'Thank you,' he whispered back.

'For what?'

Johanne stood still. Adam didn't let go of her. A feeling of unease that she had tried to repress all afternoon overwhelmed her. She had first noticed it around one, when Adam phoned to explain why he would be so late, and she staved it off. She was always fretting. About the children, about her mother who had started to get confused after her father's third heart attack and didn't always remember what day it was, about whether she would ever get back to her research. About the mortgage and the bad brakes on the car. About Isak's easygoing attitude when it came to discipline and about the war in the Middle East. There was always something to worry about. This afternoon she had tried to find out in one of her many medical books whether the white flecks on Kristiane's front teeth might be symptoms of too much milk or any other imbalance in her diet. Anxiety, bad conscience and the feeling of never being good enough were all part of her normal frame of mind, and she had grown accustomed to living with it.

But this was different.

There in the dark, quiet room, with the heat from Adam's body against her back and the barely audible breathing of her sleeping daughter to remind her of everyday joys and security, she couldn't put her finger on what was making her uneasy, a feeling that she knew something she did not want to remember.

'What's the matter?' Adam whispered.

'Nothing,' she said quietly and closed the bedroom door again gently.

*

It was years since she had dared to drink coffee on a plane. But the tempting aroma of coffee had filled the cabin so quickly that she wondered if they had a barrista onboard.

The steward responsible for her row must have weighed well over a hundred kilos. He was sweating like a pig. Normally she would have been disgusted by the unsightly rings of damp that were visible on the pale shirt fabric. She had nothing against male stewards, but she would prefer the more feminine type, thought the large lady who was now standing and staring southeast from her panorama windows on the hills above Villefranche. Trousered stewards often had a slight gay twist of the wrist and chose aftershaves that were more like light spring perfumes than masculine musks. The red-haired boar was therefore an obvious exception. She would normally have ignored him. But the smell of coffee had undone her. She had asked for a refill three times and smiled.

And even the wine tasted good.

She had recently discovered that the prices the wine monopoly in Norway charged for goods that had been so carefully and expensively imported were in fact the same as in any old wine shop in the Old Town. Unbelievable, she thought, but true. That afternoon she had opened a twenty-five-euro bottle of wine and drunk a glass. She couldn't remember tasting a better wine. The man in the shop had assured her that the bottle could stand open for a day or two. She hoped he was right.

All these years, she thought, and stroked her hair. All the projects that had never given her more than money and a headache. All her knowledge that had never been used for anything other than entertaining other people.

This morning she had felt the edge of winter in the air. February was the coldest month on the Riviera. The sea was no longer azure blue. The dirty grey foam lapped tamely at her feet as she walked along the beaches and enjoyed the solitude. Most of the trees had finally lost their leaves. Only the odd pine tree shone green along the roads. Even the path to St-Jean, where noisy well-dressed children with willowy mothers and wealthy

51

fathers usually shattered the idyll, was empty and desolate. She stopped frequently. Sometimes she lit a cigarette, even though she had stopped smoking years ago now. A slight taste of tar stuck to her tongue. It tasted good.

She had started walking. The restlessness that had plagued her for as long as she could remember felt different now. It was as if she finally understood herself now, understood the feeling of existing in a vacuum of waiting. She had wasted years of her life waiting for something that would never happen, she thought to herself as she stood at the window, holding her hand up against the cool glass.

'For things just to happen,' she whispered, and saw a brief, grey hint of breath on the windowpane.

She still felt restless, a vague tension in her body. But the unease that had previously got her down and pulled her away had now been replaced by an invigorating fear.

'Fear,' she whispered with satisfaction, and caressed the glass with slow hand movements.

She chose the word carefully. A good, exhilarating, bright fear was what she felt. She imagined it was like being in love.

Whereas before she felt down but couldn't cry, tired but couldn't sleep, she now accepted her existence so fully that she often burst out laughing. She slept well, although she frequently woke up with a feeling that could be mistaken for . . . happiness.

She chose the word happiness, even though it was perhaps a bit too strong at present.

Some people would, no doubt, say she was lonely. She was certain of that, but it didn't bother her. If only they knew what she actually thought of the people who thought they knew her, or what she did. So many of them had allowed themselves to be blinded by her success, despite living in a country where modesty was considered a virtue and superiority the deadliest of all deadly sins.

An unspecific, unfamiliar anger flared up in her. Her skin crawled and she ran her cold hand down her left arm and felt how firm she was, how compact her flesh was on her body, hard and dense, as if her skin was slightly too small.

It was a long time since she had bothered to think about the past. It wasn't worth it. But things had changed so much in recent weeks.

She was born on a rainy Sunday evening in November 1958. Her mother died within twenty minutes of giving birth, and the way the state had treated the tiny half-dead child made it crystal-clear that Norway was not a country where you should believe you were worth something.

Her father was abroad. She didn't have any grandparents. One of the nurses had wanted to take her home to her family when she recovered a bit. She thought the baby needed more love and care than could be offered by a three-way shift at the hospital. But the egalitarian country of which the baby was now a citizen did not permit such special arrangements. So she was left in a corner of the children's ward, was given food, had her nappy changed at fixed times and was otherwise given very little attention until her father came to take her home three months later, to a life where her new mother was already installed.

'Bitterness is not in my nature,' the woman said out loud to her own diffuse reflection in the window. 'Bitterness is not in my nature.'

She would never have used the expression *burning rage*. But that was the cliché that came to her all the same as she turned her back to the view and lay down on the far too soft sofa so she could breathe more easily. Her diaphragm was burning. She slowly raised her hands to her face. Big square hands with sweaty palms and short nails. She turned them round and noticed a scar on the back of one of them. Her thumb looked as though it had been broken. She tried to recall a story that she knew existed some-where. She quickly pulled up the sleeves of her jumper, she pinched and touched her own skin. The heat was extreme now, she could barely swallow. Suddenly she sat up and observed her body as if it belonged to someone else. She ran her fingers through her hair and felt the grease on her scalp against her fingertips. She scratched herself with small sharp movements until her scalp started to bleed.

She sucked her fingers greedily. A vague taste of iron hung under the nails and she tore them off, bit her skin and swallowed. Everything was clearer now. It was important to reflect on the past; it was necessary to piece together her story, to make it whole.

She had tried once before.

She'd been thirty-five years old when she finally managed to argue her way to seeing a copy of the dry hospital report of her birth, full of terminology, and she couldn't face dealing with it then. She had leafed through the yellowing pages that smelt of dusty archives and found confirmation of what she had feared, hoped and expected. Her mother had not given birth to her. The woman she knew as Mummy was a stranger. An intruder. Someone she didn't need to feel anything for.

She had felt neither anger nor sorrow. As she folded the hand-written pages, she simply felt flat. Or perhaps it was a sense of vague and almost indifferent irritation.

She had never challenged them about it.

She couldn't be bothered.

The false mother died soon after anyway.

That was ten years ago now.

Vibeke Heinerback had always irritated her.

Vibeke Heinerback was a racist.

Though naturally she wasn't open about it and wouldn't acknowledge it. The woman was after all politically savvy and had an almost impressive understanding of how the media worked. Her fellow party members, however, were constantly dropping stupid and completely unintellectual clangers about immigrants. For them, Somalians and Chinese were cut from the same cloth. Well-integrated Chinese people were lumped together with lazy Somalians. Vibeke Heinerback's party believed that a conscientious Pakistani who ran his own corner shop was the same burden on society as a gold-digger from Morocco who had come to

Norway thinking he could just help himself to the women and government money.

Vibeke Heinerback was responsible for this.

The woman who was spending winter alone on the Riviera got to her feet suddenly and stood up. She was a bit unsteady, a wave of dizziness forced her to hold on to something.

It was all so perfect, everything. Everything was working.

She laughed quietly to herself, astonished by the force of her mood swings.

Inspecting someone's house can tell you more than a thousand interviews, she thought as the nausea ebbed away.

Evening was falling and she wanted to pour herself another glass of the good wine from the Old Town. The beam from the lighthouse at Cap Ferrat swept over her in a pulsing stroke when she turned to stare out over the bay. To the north, street lamps lit the roads that cut through the steep terrain.

She was a master of her art, and from now on she would not be judged by anyone other than herself.

Five

The visit to Vibeke Heinerback's flat had not made Adam any less judgemental, but he now didn't know what to expect from the memorial service. He parked some distance from the house. The cars stood nose to tail along the narrow road, making it almost impassable.

The former party leader had generously offered his house and home for the occasion. The colossal villa by the water, only a few hundred metres from the old airport at Fornebu, was no longer plagued by pollution and noise, following the long-awaited relocation of the main airport. The once beleaguered, uninhabitable timber house, with its scores of bay windows, large terraces and two Ionic pillars framing the front door, had risen like a phoenix from the ashes, though the garden that sloped down to the fjord was still no more than clay and loose stones, ashen and snow-white.

The number of mourners dressed in dark clothes was impressive.

Adam Stubo shook hands with a woman at the door and, just in case, mumbled his condolences. He had no idea who she was. He almost stumbled on an umbrella stand further down the hall. At least fifteen people were waiting to hang up their coats. Then he felt someone tug his sleeve and before he could turn round, a young man with a thin neck and badly done tie had taken his coat from him and given him a gentle push towards one of several public rooms.

Before Adam knew it, he was standing with a half-full glass in his hand. As he was driving, he looked around in desperation for somewhere to put it down.

'It's non-alcoholic,' whispered a voice.

He recognized the woman straight away.

'Thank you,' he said, bewildered, and squeezed in to the side so he wouldn't block the door. 'You're here too.'

'Yes,' said the woman in a friendly quiet voice that could be heard above the humming of the crowd. 'Most of us are. This is more than politics. It's a tragedy that's touched us all.'

She was wearing a tight black suit that contrasted with her short blonde hair and made her look paler than she did on TV. Adam looked down, self-conscious, and noticed that the funereal mood had not prevented the Socialist Left leader from choosing a skirt that was so short it would have been more appropriate for someone ten years younger. But her legs were well toned and he realized he should look up.

'Were you a friend of Vibeke's?' asked the woman.

'No.' He cleared his throat and held out his hand. She took it. 'Adam Stubo,' he said. 'NCIS. Pleased to meet you.'

Her eyes were blue and alert and he registered a hint of curiosity in the way she tilted her head as she passed her glass from one hand to the other. Then she stopped herself with a quick nod.

'I just hope that you get to the bottom of this,' she said before turning into the room, where the newly retired party leader, Kjell Mundal, had positioned himself by a rostrum, presumably borrowed from a nearby hotel.

'Dear friends.' He coughed to get everyone's attention. 'I would like to welcome you all warmly on behalf of Kari and myself. We felt that it was not only right, but also very important to mark this sad occasion.' He coughed again, but this time more. 'Sorry,' he apologized and continued. 'It is only two days since we heard the terrible news that Vibeke had been so brutally taken from us. She . . .'

Adam could have sworn there were tears in the older man's eyes. Real tears, he thought, astonished. In public. Real, salt tears were wetting the weathered face of a man who for three decades had proved to be the toughest, most cunning and most resilient politician in Norway.

'It is no secret that Vibeke was . . .' The man stopped and took a deep breath before continuing. 'I don't want say "like a daughter to me". I have four daughters and Vibeke was not one of them. But she was someone who meant a lot to me. Politically, of course, as we worked together for many years, despite her young age, but also personally. To the extent that it's possible in politics . . .'

He stopped again. The silence was intense. No one touched their glasses. No one scraped their feet or chair on the dark cherrywood floor. People hardly dared to breathe. Adam glanced round the room, without moving his head. Over by one of the other rooms, squeezed between a couple of imposing armchairs and two men that Adam didn't recognize, was the chairman of the Standing Committee on Foreign Affairs, with his hands inappropriately deep in his pockets. His brow furrowed in expectation, he stared out of the window, as if he hoped that Vibeke Heinerback would surprise them all by waving from the deck of a small boat approaching the jetty just below the house. One of the Labour party's youngest MPs was standing weeping openly and silently beside an arrangement of white lilies in a huge Chinese vase. She sat on the Standing Committee for Finance and Economic Affairs and therefore knew Vibeke Heinerback better than most, Adam assumed. The Minister of Finance was standing next to the rostrum, with his head bent. He discreetly adjusted his glasses. The Storting's President was holding a woman by the hand. Adam looked down and concluded that the villa in Tveistveien must be one of Europe's least guarded terrorist targets right now. He shuddered. On his way out here, he had only seen one uniformed police car, just outside the house.

'. . . And to the extent that politics is a friendly place,' concluded the elderly man. 'And it can be. I am glad that . . .'

Adam nodded lightly to the blonde with the good legs, who gave a brief, sad smile back. He slowly withdrew from the room, while the man in front continued his speech.

'Excuse me,' he whispered to irritated faces as he made his way towards his goal. 'Excuse me, I just . . .'

At last he was out in the hall. It was empty. He carefully closed the double doors and sighed.

Perhaps it wasn't such a good idea to come. He had had a reason for coming, thinking that the memorial service would give him a better picture of Vibeke Heinerback. She was obviously not the person he had taken her to be. She was more. Even though he never for a moment imagined that the pictures of public figures drawn with broad strokes in the press were in any way genuine, real or exhaustive, his visit to the scene of the crime two days ago had made a deeper impression on him than he was prepared to admit. Earlier on, while he was rummaging around looking for a clean, white shirt, he had hoped that the people close to Vibeke Heinerback might give more of themselves and say more about her at an impulsive memorial service, held so soon after the young woman's death. But even now, twenty minutes into the service, he realized that he should have known better. This was a day for praise. For good thoughts and happy memories, a shared grief across party-political divides.

Adam stood with his back to the reception rooms and wondered where he would find his coat. The former party leader's speech, with frequent pauses and a cough here and there, filtered through the wood of the solid doors as a muffled murmur.

Then he heard another voice to his left, through a door that was ajar to what might be the kitchen. The sibilant, urgent whispers of a woman who sounded like she actually wanted to shout, but felt that it might be inappropriate, given the occasion. Adam was about to make his presence known, when he heard:

'Don't you worry about that.'

A man's voice, deep and aggressive.

The sound of a glass being banged down on a table, followed by what was obviously a sniff from the woman. Then she said something. Adam could only make out a few individual words that meant nothing to him. He took a couple of cautious steps towards the half-open door.

'Be careful,' he heard the woman say. 'You had better watch it now, Rudolf.'

She came out in to the hall so suddenly that Adam had to step back.

'Jesus,' he said, and smiled. 'You really gave me a fright. Adam Stubo.'

The woman let a man out after her, closed the door with care, took Adam's hand and returned his smile. She was smaller than he'd imagined, almost strikingly petite. She had a slim waist, something she emphasized with a tight, fitted black skirt that stopped just below the knee. The grey silk blouse had ruffles at the neck and down the front. She reminded him of a miniature Margaret Thatcher. Her nose was big and hooked and her chin was pointed. Her eyes were worthy of the iron lady. Icy blue and sharp, though her face was relaxed and welcoming.

'Kari Mundal,' she said quietly. 'Pleasure. You are very welcome here, despite the occasion. Perhaps you've already met Rudolf Fjord?'

The man was twice her height and half as old. He was obviously less practised at hiding his feelings. His hand was sweaty when he held it out, his eyes darted here and there for a few moments, before he finally managed to pull himself together and smile. At the same time he nodded, half bowed, as if he realized that his handshake was not particularly impressive.

'Were you looking for something?' Kari Mundal asked. 'The toilet? Just down there.' She pointed. 'When the service is over,' she added, 'there will be a bite to eat. Of course, we hadn't expected so many people. But a little something is better than nothing. Vibeke was such . . .'

She smoothed her hair.

Kari Mundal was as close as you could get to the icon of a good old-fashioned housewife; she had stayed at home with her four daughters and three sons, and her husband was the first to admit that his stamina on the political front was entirely due to his loyal wife.

'Everyone should have a Kari at home,' he often said in interviews, blissfully unaffected by the complaints of younger women. 'A Kari at home is better than ten in the workplace.'

Kari Mundal had looked after the house and children and ironed his shirts for more than forty years. She was happy to appear in magazines and on Saturday night TV, and since her husband had retired from politics she had become a sort of national mascot, a politically incorrect, friendly and sharp little granny.

'Were you looking for the toilet?' she asked and pointed again.

'Yes,' Adam replied. 'Sorry to have to miss some of your husband's speech . . .'

'When you have to go, you have to go,' interrupted Kari Mundal. 'Rudolf, shall we go in?'

Rudolf Fjord bowed again, stiff and obviously ill at ease. He followed behind the older woman, who opened the door to the reception room. It closed silently behind them.

Adam was alone.

The voice on the other side of the door sounded as if it was giving a service now. Adam wondered whether the gathering would soon start to sing. Vibeke Heinerback's body would not be released for a funeral for a long time, so in a sense there was nothing odd about holding a memorial service, but it struck him for the first time since he arrived that there was something vaguely distasteful about holding it here, in a private house, a sudden, but obviously well-planned event.

When he looked into the room where Rudolf Fjord and Kari Mundal had been having their whispered contretemps, his suspicion was confirmed. The kitchen was massive, as if it had been planned with occasions like this in mind. Silver platters of sandwiches, finger food and elegant hors d'oeuvres stood lined up on the worktops and table, between bowls full of colourful salads. Cases of mineral water were stacked against the wall. On the windowsill, which was at least half a metre deep and two metres long, the hostess had lined up bottles of red and white wine. Some had already been opened.

Adam carefully lifted the clingfilm on one of the trays and stuffed three bits of chicken in his mouth.

Then he left the kitchen again.

He noticed a wardrobe at the end of the hall. As he chewed whilst trying to find his coat among all the other coats, jackets, hats and scarves, it struck him that Mrs Mundal had not even asked who he was and why he was there. It wasn't likely that she knew him from before. Adam had only ever had one interview in the national media. The following day he had promised himself and his superiors that it would never happen again.

He eventually found his coat. He went out.

An argument, he mused, as the raw sea air hit him.

Arguing on a day like today. Little Mrs Mundal and Rudolf Fjord, second in charge of the party and, according to the papers, Vibeke Heinerback's obvious successor as party leader. The disagreement was obviously important, as they had not been present during Kjell Mundal's speech in the main room.

A gust of wind made his coat tails flap against his legs. Adam looked up at the sky and then ran with heavy steps over the gravel.

Of course it didn't have to mean anything.

When he got to the car, he heard the helicopters. There were two of them, one over a hill to the east, the other low over the water a few hundred metres from the shore. He also now saw that the small boat down by the jetty was a police boat. He counted five uniformed men along the road, all armed.

The gathering indoors was safe.

To the extent that anyone was, he thought and got into the car.

He spat out some parsley and had to reverse fifty metres before it was possible to turn.

The physical pain was not the worst thing. She was used to it. Her body had been ravaged by multiple sclerosis for more than twenty years now. Even though she was only sixty-seven, she knew that she was nearing the end. Nothing worked any more. Her bedsores leaked and were painful. Yvonne Knutsen's body was a shell round what could barely be called a life. She lay flat in a bed in a bland room in an institution that she had never liked. Grief drained what remained of her life force.

Bernt was wonderful. He came every day with little Fiorella. Stayed with her for a long time, even though Yvonne was constantly falling asleep. Her medicine was stronger now.

She wanted to die. But God refused to come and get her.

The worst thing about just lying like this was time. Time grew when you weren't able to do anything. It went in circles, in loops, in great big arcs, before returning back to where it started. She didn't want this any more. Her time on this earth should be over, it should have been over long ago, and her grief made the fact that her body was clinging on to life even more unbearable.

Fiona had been a good daughter. Naturally they had argued, like every mother and daughter. Their relationship had been cool now and then, but was it reasonable to expect anything else? It never took more than a few weeks before everything was the same as before. Fiona was kind. Yvonne's friends had always said so, in the days when she could still make and serve coffee, or even a meal on a good day.

'You're lucky, Yvonne.'

Fiona had never let her down.

They shared a secret, the two of them.

Just as time warped beyond recognition when it had no meaning, so secrets could grow to be so enormous that they were invisible. To begin with it had been like a thorn between them. But as there was no turning back, they had managed to agree with surprising ease.

We'll forget this.

Yvonne Knutsen could still hear her own voice back then, firm and maternal with an edge of determined protection:

'We will forget this.'

And they had forgotten.

Now Fiona was dead and loneliness gave the secret new life. It haunted her, particularly at night, when she thought she could see a shadow by the window, a silent figure seeking revenge that had now found reason to plague her, now when she had no one to help her forget.

If only God would let her follow Fiona.

'Dear God,' she whispered into the room.

But her heart went on beating stubbornly in her emaciated chest.

Daylight was disappearing fast. It was four o'clock in the afternoon of Monday the 9th of February. A thirty-seven-year old man was about to climb a crane without permission. It was yellow and over twenty metres high, towering above a confusion of construction materials and machinery. He was only a few metres from the ground and he could already feel the cold wind blasting through his clothes. His gloves were too thin. His friend had warned him. The metal felt like ice. But he had not dared to choose anything warmer, it was after all better to have more control over your fingers. He wasn't going fast enough. His friend was already halfway up. But he was younger and well trained.

Vegard Krogh tried to be positive.

He didn't really have the energy for this sort of thing any more. He was reluctantly approaching forty and had never received the recognition and publicity he deserved. He thought his writing was accessible, and the literary sarcasm was of a high quality. The critics all agreed, but Vegard Krogh's work was seldom given more than a passing comment in the local paper from his home town. Vegard Krogh had a distinct voice, a critic once said, an original and ironic pen. He was described as a talent. But since then he had not only got older, he had also become an author of some note. He knew it: he had important things to tell. His talent had blossomed, he should be established by now, a force to be reckoned with. A review of his third novel from *Morgenbladet* hung on the notice board at home. Not particularly impressive, just two columns, worn and yellow after several years in the kitchen, but the phrase 'strong, vital and at times technically brilliant' was written there.

The readers, however, had totally let him down.

64

Don't think. Climb.

He should have worn overalls. There was a gap between the waistband of his trousers and his sweater. The cold cut into his back like icicles. He tried to stuff his woollen vest into his trousers with one hand. It helped for a few seconds.

He would just have to manage. He didn't know where he got the energy. Without thinking about the cold, without worrying about his increasing height above the ground, without thinking about how dangerous the project was that he was now determined to carry through, he simply concentrated on lifting one leg after the other. Lifting one hand up a step while the other clung to the metal. Again and again. Keeping pace. Iron will.

He was up.

The wind was so strong that he could feel the crane swaying. He looked down. Closed his eyes.

'Don't look down,' his friend shouted. 'Don't look down yet, Vegard! Look at me!'

His eyelids were stuck to his irises.

He wanted to look but didn't dare. A violent wave of nausea washed over him.

'You've done this before,' he heard his friend's voice saying, much closer now. 'It'll be fine, just wait.'

A hand gripped his lower arm. A firm grip.

'It's exactly the same as this summer,' the voice said. 'The only difference is the weather.'

And the fact that it was illegal, thought Vegard Krogh, and tried not to look back.

His job at the left-wing paper, *Klassekampen* had been a dead end. He had stayed there too long. Maybe because he was, after all, allowed to write what he wanted. *Klassekampen* was important. It took sides. Papers should take sides, politically and on principle. And Vegard Krogh was allowed to rant as much as he liked. As long as his aggression was targeted in the right direction, as the editor put it. As *Klassekampen* and the young Vegard Krogh had more or less the same views on Norwegian cultural life, the paper fully supported his vitriolic, well-written reviews, angry analyses and highly libellous remarks. He carried on for several years, until he was exhausted and finally had to admit that practically no one read *Klassekampen*.

He was never actually sued.

When he got the job working in the culture department of TV2, everything looked set to improve. For a brief year he achieved a sort of cult status among the angry young men who voiced their views about the state of the nation and what direction Norway should take. Vegard Krogh was one of them, even if he was a bit old, he was one of them. He had first become known as a stunt reporter for *Young and Urban* and was given his own irate ten-minute slot on *Absolute Entertainment* every Thursday.

Then after one too many legal suits, which never made it to the courtroom thanks to the jolly and apologetic executive director, he lost the slot. TV2 was not as open as *Klassekampen* to what they ignorantly called shit in an internal review. Vegard Krogh was actually glad, when he thought about it. TV2 was a totally commercial channel, just like the worst American ones.

Finally he dared to look down.

'Can you see it?' his friend shouted. 'On the orange target?'

Vegard Krogh looked down. The wind had blown his anorak up into a balloon, a great big bubble that made it difficult to see.

'OK, let's go,' he spluttered.

'We have to go further out on to the arm,' his friend shouted and let go of him. 'Can you do it?'

He finally managed to get to where he was supposed to be. He tried to relax. Ignore the cold. Forget the height. Fixed his eyes on the book down there, an almost invisible rectangle on a large orange target. Tears streamed down his face. He blamed the wind and tried to muster his own inner strength. The camera had been positioned to the left on a pile of foundation blocks. The photographer had pulled a hood over his head. Vegard Krogh raised his arm as a signal. A bright light blinded him and it took him a few seconds to fix his eyes on the target.

The harness was properly fixed. His friend checked one last time.

'There,' he said loudly. 'You can jump.'

'Are you sure the bungee rope will hold?' Vegard Krogh shouted back, even though he didn't need to.

'To the last gram,' shouted his friend. 'I weighed you three times before choosing the bungee rope, for God's sake! And I measured this crane only yesterday! Jump! I'm fucking freezing!'

Vegard Krogh shot a glance at the photographer one last time. His hood, with its wolfskin trim, covered half the camera. The lens was focused on the two of them up there. He could hear sirens in the distance. They were getting closer.

Vegard Krogh took aim for the book. It was his latest collection of essays, an almost invisible speck on a round orange disc.

He jumped.

The fall was too slow.

He had time to think. He thought about the fact that he would soon be forty. He thought that his wife didn't appear to be very fertile. They'd been trying to have children for three years now, without any results other than the monthly disappointment, which they didn't talk about any more. He thought about the fact that they still lived in a one-bedroom flat in Grønland and that they never managed to save anything more than a pittance.

When he was halfway through the fall, he stopped thinking.

It was happening too fast.

Far too fast, thought the photographer, his lens following the man's descent towards the ground.

The book grew in front of Vegard's eyes. He couldn't blink, couldn't see anything other than the white cover that just kept growing. He stretched his arms down and out, he was plummeting towards the ground and at last thought: this is happening too fast.

The wind pulled off his hat and his fair hair, which was stuck to his sweaty forehead, brushed the orange target at the same moment that Vegard Krogh realized it was over. With great care, as if he had all the time in the world, he picked up his book and pressed it to his heart; his forehead brushed the ground, his fringe kissed the wood of the target.

The bungee rope recoiled. The movement rippled through his body, a powerful jolt from the soles of his feet, an oppressive pulse through his calves to his legs. It felt like his spine was being stretched by the tension.

He laughed.

He roared as he bounced up and down, from side to side. The laughter caught in his throat when the police car turned into the building site and the photographer tried to pack away all his equipment as he ran towards the hole in the fence that protected the area.

Vegard Krogh had never felt so alive. As long as the film was OK, this would be perfect. The jump had been just as he had wanted, just like the book, just like Vegard Krogh believed he had always been: daring, dangerous and provocative, bordering on what was permissible.

He didn't die that Monday in the middle of February. On the contrary, he felt immortal as he hung there, upside down below a bright-yellow crane, above an orange target, in the sharp blue light of the police car that howled towards him on the ground. Vegard Krogh swung between two bright colours that grey, windy afternoon, clutching the first copy of his new book:

Bungee Jump.

Vegard Krogh's death was postponed by one week and three days, but he didn't know that himself, of course.

No matter how hard she tried, Johanne could not get herself to like Sigmund Berli. The man was disgusting. He openly picked his nose, he farted constantly without even apologizing, he cleaned his ears and bit his nails in front of everyone. Right now he was sitting there tearing a dirty serviette to shreds without even thinking that the pieces would be caught on a draught and blown to the floor.

'He's a good lad,' Adam usually said, exasperated by Johanne's cool attitude. 'Just doesn't have many manners. Sigmund was the only one who actually spoke to me after Elisabeth and Trine died.'

She couldn't argue with the last statement. The terrible death of his first wife and daughter had nearly finished him off. He was about to drop out of working life and disappear into a serious and destructive depression when Sigmund, with a mixture of sudden authority and touching care, had managed to pull him back to a form of normality, but which didn't really take shape until he met Johanne two years later and started over again.

'You can't measure a bit of snot on someone's trousers against true loyalty,' Adam said. Consequently the man was now sitting on a bar stool in Johanne's kitchen, having just enjoyed three helpings of Stange chicken and rocket salad.

'You make great food,' he said and smiled broadly.

He was looking at Adam.

'Thank you,' Johanne said.

'I made the dressing,' laughed Adam. 'The dressing is the most important part. But you're right. Johanne is the cook in this house. I'm just a gourmet. I take care of the details. Everything that makes an ordinary meal more . . .'

He laughed when she hit him with the kitchen towel.

'Can't take being teased,' he said and pulled her to him. 'But good at heart.'

He kissed her and didn't want to let go.

'That argument in the kitchen,' Sigmund started, self-consciously folding the serviette before pushing it away from him, not knowing what he should do with the torn remains. 'It could've been about anything.'

'Yes,' Adam said, and let go of Johanne. 'But I still think we should make a note that there might be something to it. Not only were Kari Mundal and Rudolf Fjord at loggerheads, but the argument was so important that they also missed Kjell Mundal's well-prepared speech. It's not like Kari to miss an opportunity to praise and support her husband. And Rudolf Fjord was pretty worked up.'

'Politics,' Johanne said, '. . . is no Sunday school, as you know. If angry disagreements on the political sidelines were grounds for suspecting murder, you'd have your work cut out.'

'Yes, but . . .'

Adam pulled another bar stool up to the island unit and made himself comfortable. With his legs apart and his arms leaning on the counter.

'There was just something about the whole situation,' he said quietly. 'Something . . .' Then he shook his head. 'It has been noted,' he said lightly. 'But we'll leave it at that. We've got plenty else to do. Certainly at the moment.'

'At the moment we've got next to nothing,' Sigmund sulked. 'In either of the cases. *Nada*.'

'You're exaggerating a bit,' Adam said. 'We have got some leads.'

'Some,' muttered Sigmund.

'But nothing that fits together,' Adam continued. 'Nothing that leads anywhere. I agree with you there. We established almost straight away that there weren't any links between the two women, other than the obvious. And we've been over it a thousand times. The brutality of the murder. The sex of the victims. The fact that they were both in the public eye. Where they lived.'

He gave a long yawn and continued:

'But it's doubtful that we're looking for a killer who's got something against Lørenskog. Vibeke and Fiona didn't know each other, had no mutual friends or acquaintances other than what is normal in such a small country. They weren't involved in any of the same work. They lived very different lives. One was single and loved parties and the other had a family and a young child. To me, it seems . . .'

'. . . That we're looking at two separate cases, all the same,' Johanne said. She was holding the kettle under the tap. 'But both murderers must have been strong. Vibeke was killed outside her house and lifted into the bedroom. Fiona was overpowered.'

'Do you often talk like that?' Sigmund asked.

'Like what?'

'Finishing off each other's sentences. Like my sister's twins.'

'We are of course spiritual twins,' said Johanne, and smiled when Sigmund didn't pick up on the irony. 'Think the same, feel the same. Coffee?'

'Yes please. But if . . .' He put his hand in front of his mouth and tried to muffle a deep burp. '. . . If this really is two cases, is it possible that the second killer, the one who killed Vibeke Heinerback, wanted to make it look like the work of a serial killer?'

'Hardly, when there's only been two murders,' Adam said. 'That's almost pathetic. But first we have to agree that it isn't the work of one killer.'

'But that's obviously not possible,' Johanne said. 'Not yet. But I agree, even though there are many similarities, the character of the similarities is not such that . . . well, the murders don't exactly look like a series.'

'I wondered,' Sigmund started, and then blushed like a boy with his head full of sex.

He scratched his thigh and cocked his head awkwardly. At that moment Johanne thought he was sweet. She poured the boiling water into the cafetière, filled a jug with milk and put out a bowl of brown sugar.

'I just wondered,' Sigmund tried again. 'About how the whole profiling . . .'

He couldn't decide whether to use the Norwegian or English pronunciation and pinched his nose between his thumb and forefinger.

'Just say it in Norwegian,' Johanne said. 'It sounds like some sort of detective film when you say it in English. Don't you think?'

He filled his cup with too much coffee and had to put his lips to the rim and sip the boiling-hot liquid first before he dared to lift it up.

'Ow. Ow.' He rubbed his upper lip and snuffled on: 'We know quite a bit ourselves. A lot, in fact. But as you've actually trained with the FBI and all that, with that top guy, well, I thought—'

'Milk?' interrupted Adam, and filled up Sigmund's cup with cream without waiting for an answer. 'Sugar? Here.'

'Profiling can mean so much,' said Johanne, and handed Sigmund a cloth. 'Any murder will generally involve elements that point to some of the killer's characteristics. In that sense, profiling is used in all investigations. You just don't use the term.'

As he aimlessly wiped the surface in front of him, the milky coffee going everywhere, Sigmund said: 'You mean, when we find a man in his own filthy home with a knife in his groin and the guy who called the police is standing in the corner pissed and snivelling, then we make a profile? The kind of "killer who's drunk and argued with a close relative and the knife just happened to be there but he didn't mean to kill him and is really sorry now and would have rung for help later" type profile?'

Johanne burst out laughing and wiped away the remains of the coffee with kitchen roll.

'I couldn't have put it better myself,' she said. 'And the profile you just gave is so usual and easily constructed that it takes no more than thirty seconds to establish that the drunk in the corner is guilty. But you and Adam don't deal with many cases like that. The NCIS deals with much worse cases.'

'But Johanne,' Sigmund said, eager now. 'I assume that you analyse each case by picking it to pieces . . .'

'You analyse the *modus operandi*,' Johanne said helpfully. 'Take it to pieces, as you put it, look at all the elements of the crime. Then we make deductions based on the various factors and the overall impression. When we're analysing, we give a lot of importance to the victim's background and behaviour prior to the crime, both subjective and objective, as well as the actual killing. A massive amount of work. And . . .' The steam from her cup clouded her glasses. '. . . It would be hard to find a science that is more uncertain, more difficult or unreliable than profiling.'

'What you're describing is basically the same as tactical investigation,' Sigmund said, with a cynical frown.

'It's very similar,' Johanne nodded, and added: 'The main

difference is that tactical investigation, much more than profiling, deals with . . . how should I put it . . . undisputed fact. Profilers are often psychologists. A tactical investigator's purpose is to find the killer, whereas a profiler's job is to build up a psychological picture of the killer. So in a way, profiling is just a tool in the tactical investigation.'

'So if you were going to say something about Fiona Helle's murder alone,' said Sigmund, whose cheeks were flushed with excitement, 'forget Vibeke Heinerback for the moment, what would you say?'

Johanne looked at Sigmund over the rim of her cup.

'I'm not quite sure,' she said slowly. 'The whole thing seems very . . . un-Norwegian. I don't like the expression, as it's no longer possible to protect ourselves from gruesome murders like these. But all the same . . .'

She took a deep breath and then drank some coffee.

'I would say,' she started after a few moments, '. . . that it's possible to see the outlines of two very different profiles. Starting with the similarities: Fiona Helle's murder was well planned. It was obviously premeditated, so we're looking for someone who's capable of planning someone else's death in detail. The little paper basket can have had no other function than to hold the severed tongue. It was a perfect fit. We can more or less dismiss the idea that someone might think about cutting their victim's tongue out without killing them. The time of the killing was also right. Tuesday evening. Everyone knew that Fiona Helle was on her own on Tuesday evenings. And in several interviews she boasted that Lørenskog was "a peaceful oasis away from stresses of the city" . . .'

With two fingers, she drew quote marks in the air.

'Quite a statement,' Adam said.

'And very stupid to tell the whole world that she didn't need to lock her door in the little cul-de-sac where she lived, as everyone looked out for their neighbours and no one was nasty.'

Sigmund snorted and added: 'The Romerike boys got in touch with her to warn her about saying things like that, afterwards. But she still left the door open. She said something about "not giving in to evil". Jesus . . .'

He mumbled something incomprehensible into his cup of coffee.

'In any case,' Johanne said, and pulled over a pad of paper that Adam had found in Kristiane's red play chest. 'The murder was premeditated. So we've already come quite a long way.' She leant her elbows on the counter. 'There are also grounds for drawing another relatively given conclusion. I would say that the killing shows signs of intense hate. The fact that it was premeditated, the killer's determined, criminal intention, and the method . . .'

There was a short silence. Johanne wrinkled her brow, not noticeably, and turned her left ear towards the hall.

'It was nothing,' Adam said. 'Nothing.'

'To strangle someone, tie her up, cut out her tongue . . .' Johanne was talking quietly now, tense, still listening. 'Hate,' she concluded. 'But then the problems start. The drama of it, the split tongue, the origami . . . the whole thing, in fact . . .'

Her red pencil was drawing slow circles on the paper.

'It could be a cover. An act. Camouflage. The symbolism is so blatantly obvious, so . . .'

'. . . Childish?' suggested Sigmund.

'Exactly. So simple, in any case, that it could almost appear to be a cover-up. The intention was possibly to confuse people. And then we're talking about an unusually cunning person. Who must have hated Fiona Helle intensely. And then we're no further forward than . . .'

'Back where we started,' Adam said with resignation. 'But what if the symbolism was sincere?'

'Goodness . . . Didn't the Native Americans use it literally? "White man speak with forked tongue"? If we assume that the killer mutilated her body to tell the world something, it must be that Fiona Helle was not what she pretended to be. She was a liar. A traitor. According to him, that is. The murderer. Which in this

74

rather flimsy and therefore totally unusable profile would verge on . . . utter madness.'

'Shame,' Sigmund said, yawning loudly, '. . . that we can't find any problems in her life. No major conflicts. A bit of jealousy here and there, she was a successful lady. A dispute with the tax authorities a couple of years ago. And one with a neighbour about a spruce that blocked the light from Fiona's study. Of no consequence. The tree was chopped down, by the way. Without the case going to court.'

'Strange that there isn't anything,' Johanne started and then stopped. 'Now?'

Her anxiety was obvious when she looked at Adam.

'It's nothing,' he said again. 'Relax. She's asleep.'

Johanne had agreed that Ragnhild should sleep in her bedroom, at least when they had guests.

'It's strange,' she repeated hesitantly, 'that you can't find anything, nothing that even resembles dirt in Fiona Helle's life. Very strange indeed. After all, she was forty-two. You must've missed something.'

'Look yourself, then,' Sigmund said, obviously offended. 'We've had fifteen men on the job for several weeks now and come up with a big fat nothing. Maybe the woman really was a paragon of virtue.'

'There is no paragon of virtue.'

'But what about the profile then?'

'Which profile?'

'The one you were going to make,' Sigmund said.

'I can't make a profile of the person who killed Fiona Helle,' Johanne said, and drank the rest of her coffee in one gulp. 'Not of any consequence, at least. No one can. But I can give you a tip. Look for the lies in her life. Find the lie. Then you may not even need a profile. You'll have the man.'

'Or woman,' said Adam with a faint smile.

Johanne didn't even bother to answer. Instead she tiptoed out to the bedroom.

'Is she always so nervy?' Sigmund whispered.

'Yes.'

'Would drive me nuts.'

'You hardly see your family.'

'Shut up. I'm at home more than most people I know.'

'Which doesn't say much.'

'Jessie's blouse.'

'Idiot,' Adam smiled. 'More coffee?'

'No thanks. But some of that . . .'

He pointed towards the other end of the table, where a bottle glinted yellow and brown in the light of the candle on the windowsill.

'Are you not driving?'

'The wife's got the car. Parents' evening, or something like that.'

'See what I mean.'

Adam got down two outsized cognac glasses and poured some in.

'Cheers,' he said.

'Not a lot to raise our glasses to,' said Sigmund, and took a drink.

Jack's claws clacked over the parquet. The animal stopped in the middle of the floor where he stretched and gave a long yawn.

'Looks like he's bloody laughing,' mumbled Sigmund.

'I think he is,' Adam replied. 'At us, maybe. Our worries. All he thinks about is food.'

The dog wagged his tail and padded out to the kitchen. He whined a bit by the rubbish bin. He sniffed around on the floor and greedily licked the bits of grease and breadcrumbs.

'Your food's in the dish,' Adam said. 'Woof!'

Jack yapped and growled at the cupboard door.

'Don't wind him up. Stop it, Jack!'

Johanne had come back with an awake Ragnhild in her arms.

'I knew I heard something,' she said without trying to disguise the triumph in her voice. 'She's wet. You can change her. Jack, go and lie down!'

'Daddy's little daisy,' Adam babbled and gently took his daughter.

'Baby daisy's wet.'

'Completely ga-ga,' Sigmund said.

'It's called being a good father.'

Johanne smiled and followed Adam with her eyes as he disappeared into the bathroom. Jack followed with his tail between his legs. He stopped by the dividing wall to the sitting room and sent Johanne another pleading look.

'Lie down,' she said and the dog disappeared.

Muffled music could be heard from the ground floor. Half the soundscape got lost in the floor insulation. The thumping of the bass was all that reached them and Johanne wrinkled her nose before putting on the dishwasher.

'It's quite noisy here,' Sigmund observed, without showing any sign of moving. 'D'you mind?'

He pointed at the bottle of cognac.

'No, no. Not at all. Help yourself.'

The music got steadily louder.

'Must be Selma,' muttered Johanne. 'Teenager. At home alone, I should think.'

Sigmund smiled and poked his nose into the glass. He was relaxed here, he found himself thinking, to his surprise. There was something about the atmosphere here, the tone, the light, the furniture. There was something about Johanne. People at work whispered about her being so stern. They were wrong, Sigmund thought, and dipped his sore lip into the alcohol. The burn stung in a nice way and he took a sip.

Johanne wasn't stern. She was strong, he thought, even though she was obviously over-anxious about the baby. Not so surprising, really, when you thought about her strange oldest daughter, odd little thing who looked like she was three years younger than she actually was. Adam had taken her to work a few times and she would frighten the life out of anyone. One minute she behaved like a three-year-old and then the next minute she would say something that could well come out of a student's mouth. Evidently there was something wrong with her brain. They just didn't know what.

Sigmund had always liked Adam. He enjoyed the older man's company. But they seldom spent time together out of work. Sigmund had, of course, done as much as he could after the accident, when Adam's daughter fell down on top of her mother while trying to clean the gutters, killing them both. He remembered the low sun through the trees and the two bodies in the garden. Adam hadn't said anything, hadn't cried, hadn't spoken. He just stood there with his crying grandson in his arms, as if he was holding on to life itself, and was in danger of crushing it.

'Do you still have Amund here at the weekend?' he asked suddenly.

'In principle, we have him every other weekend,' Johanne said, taken aback by the question. 'But now, with the baby and all that, well . . . Originally the arrangement was to help give Adam's son-in-law a break.'

'No,' said Sigmund.

'Sorry?'

She turned towards him.

'That wasn't why it started,' he said calmly. 'I talked to Bjarne a lot at the time, I did. The son-in-law, that is.'

'I know what Adam's son-in-law is called.'

'Of course. But . . . Well, that arrangement was really to help Adam. To give him something to live for. We were really worried, you know. Extremely worried, Bjarne and I. It's good to see . . .'

He downed the rest of the cognac in one go and cheerfully looked around.

'You've got a good home,' he said with unexpected formality in his voice; his eyes were moist.

Johanne shook her head and chuckled. She stood with her hands on her hips, cocked her head and followed his hands with her eyes. He poured a generous amount into his glass before putting back the cork with a dramatic thump.

'There, that's enough for today. Here's to you, Johanne. I have to say you're a great lady. I wish I could come home every day to the wife and know that she was interested in what I did at work. Knew something about it. Like you. You're a great girl. Cheers.'

'And you're a strange one, Sigmund.'

'No, just a bit tipsy. Hi!'

He raised his glass to Adam, who lifted his arms in triumph and clapped his hands above his head.

'One baby, one nine-year-old and one canine sleeping like stones. Dry and happy, all of them.'

He plumped down on the bar stool.

'Are you celebrating, Sigmund? On a Monday?'

'Yes, there hasn't been much of that recently,' Sigmund answered. He had started to hiccup. 'But Johanne . . .'

'Yes?'

'If you were going to imagine the worst possible . . . the most difficult serial killer . . . To catch, I mean. If you were to draw a profile of the perfect serial killer, what would it be?'

'Don't you two have enough with the criminals who actually exist?' she said, and leant over the counter.

'Go on,' Adam smiled. 'Tell us. Tell what he'd be like.'

The candle on the windowsill was about to burn down. There was a violent hissing. Bits of soot floated around in front of the reflection in the dark glass. Johanne got out a new candle, pushed it down into the candlestick and lit the wick. She stood for a few seconds, studying the flame.

'It would be a woman,' she said slowly. 'Simply because we always imagine it to be a man. We find it difficult to imagine evil incarnate in the shape of a woman. Strangely enough. History has definitively shown that women can be evil.'

'A woman,' Adam said and nodded. 'What else?'

Johanne turned towards them and counted quickly on her fingers:

'Knowledgeable, of course, and insightful, intelligent, cunning and unscrupulous. At least, that's what they normally are. But the worst, the worst thing would be . . .'

Suddenly she looked like she was thinking about something else, as if trying to catch a thought that had just passed through her head. The two men sipped their cognac. A gang of boys could be heard shouting out on the street. A light was switched off in the neighbours' house. The darkness outside the kitchen window became denser, the reflections sharper.

'It's just as if,' she started and straightened her glasses with her forefinger. 'It's as if . . . This case gives me a feeling of . . . déjà vu. But I just can't think . . .' She studied the candle flame again. It danced in the draught from the window they couldn't afford to replace. A fleeting smile passed over her face. 'Forget it. Probably just rubbish.'

'Carry on,' Sigmund said. 'So far you've just given us the obvious list. What else would make it impossible for us to catch this lady of yours? Aren't they always basically mad?'

'Not mad.' Johanne gave a convinced shake of the head. 'Disturbed, perhaps. Twisted. I would guess that she suffered from some kind of personality disorder. But she's definitely not mad. Murderers are seldom not accountable, or insane, in a legal sense. But what would make it really difficult . . . What would make it almost impossible to catch her, if she wasn't caught the first time, that is . . .'

'Which this superwoman wouldn't allow to happen,' Adam interjected, and rubbed his neck.

'Precisely,' said Johanne, and fell silent.

The boys out on the street had moved on. Lights were being switched off all the way down Haugesvei. It was finally quiet in the flat downstairs. One of the blasted cats was howling in the garden again, but then it disappeared. Johanne realized that she was enjoying the peace, the safety of the house. For the first time since they had moved in, she really felt at home. She stroked the surface of the counter in surprise. Her finger ran over a dent. Kristiane had played with a knife in an unobserved moment. Johanne's eyes travelled over the sitting room to the west. The skirting boards were covered in Jack's eager claw marks, the parquet was damaged by the runners on Ragnhild's cot. A red felt-tip drawing of a sky-scraper rose up crookedly from the floor to the windowsill.

She sniffed. It smelt a bit stuffy, of food, clean babies and dirty dogs. She bent down to pick up a colourful baby's toy from the corner by the dishwasher and noticed that Kristiane had written her name along the bottom in strange, crooked letters.

The house was well lived in now, Johanne thought. It was home.

'The worst thing,' she said, and played with a smiling lion with teething rings and multicoloured ribbons round its head, 'the worst thing would be a murderer with no motive.'

She took a deep breath, put down the toy and took off her glasses. She tried to wipe away the grease from food and children's fingers with a corner of her shirt. Then she turned her short-sighted gaze on Sigmund and repeated:

'The most difficult murderer to catch would be one who killed without a motive. A qualified, intelligent killer who isn't out to get even with his victim at all. All modern tactical investigations are based on the assumption that there is a motive for the crime. Even the most seriously mentally disturbed serial killer can be caught, as the most absurd and apparently random selection of victims will have some kind of hidden pattern, connections. When there is nothing, no reason, no connection, no logic – no matter how twisted that sounds – we're just stuck. A murderer like that could keep playing with us . . . for ever.'

The candle on the windowsill flickered violently and then went out. Johanne put her glasses on and closed the window properly.

'But I've never heard of any monsters like that,' she added lightly. 'I have to go to bed. Any more questions before I go?'

There were no questions.

Rudolf Fjord was washing the bathroom.

It was three o'clock on Tuesday morning. The lanky man was down on all fours scrubbing the grouting between the floor tiles, with a toothbrush and ammonia. The smell ripped at his nose. He coughed, scrubbed, swore and rinsed it with water that was too hot for his bare hands. He was almost there. The tiles from the sink to the toilet bowl were now framed by light, pale-grey grouting against steel-blue ceramic. Strange that a bathroom could get so dirty in less than six months. He wanted to do the walls as well, he thought, and wiped his nose on his sleeve. He should empty the cupboards, wash the drawers. And give the inside of the cistern a going over. It was still hours until he had to go to work.

He couldn't sleep.

Maybe he could empty the bookshelves, vacuum the books, one by one. That would certainly get the time to pass.

The relief he had felt when Vibeke died, the physical, jubilant relief on Saturday morning, had lasted for exactly twelve minutes. Then he had realized that, paradoxically, Vibeke Heinerback was a better insurance in life than in death, and he was literally overwhelmed. He had tried to get up from the sofa, but his legs had given way. The sweat poured off him, but it felt cold. His thoughts were racing. Eventually he managed to get into the shower and then put together a suitable outfit for the extraordinary meeting of the Steering Committee.

They had looked at him.

Scowled.

Rudolf Fjord picked up the toothbrush.

The brush was flat and grey. Unusable. He staggered to his feet and rummaged around at random in the rubbish bin, looking for another one. Couldn't find one. The lump in his throat grew. He pulled open a drawer in the bathroom cabinet, cut himself badly as he tried to get a new brush out of the stiff plastic packaging. The stench of ammonia was unbearable now. He couldn't find a plaster.

They had really scowled.

'Good party comrades,' Vibeke had smiled, somewhat stiff, when inquisitive journalists had tried to delve deeper into their relationship. 'We work very well together, Rudolf and I.'

He tried to breathe deeply.

Straightened his back. Lifted his chest, tightened his stomach, as he had on the beach, last summer, that fantastic summer when the weather was great and nothing had been settled. When he was still certain he would be the next party leader as soon as the old man decided it was time for a change.

He simply couldn't breathe.

Red stars danced in front of his eyes. He was about to faint. With his hands against the wall, he stumbled out of the bathroom. It was better in the hall. He gagged without throwing up, staggered on into the sitting room, towards the doors to the balcony. They were locked. He tried to stay calm, there was something wrong with the hinges, he just had to lift it, like this. The blood drew funny patterns on the door frame. The door opened.

The ice-cold air brought him to round.

He opened his mouth and breathed in.

They had looked at him in an odd way.

Strange, they had no doubt thought. Strange that Rudolf Fjord was the one who was most obviously affected by Vibeke Heinerback's brutal murder.

Kari Mundal was the worst.

People really had no idea what she was like. Everyone thought she was a funny, tiny, sharp housewife.

She was certainly sharp.

At best, nothing will happen, Rudolf Fjord thought to himself, and gulped in the clean air. He was calmer now and buttoned his shirt with shaking hands. The blood had already started to clot. He carefully sucked his finger.

He realized that he had to dilute the ammonia.

At best, absolutely nothing would happen.

Six

The house at the edge of the woods was of its day. A boxy wooden house with vertical panelling and a bay window in the middle of a symmetrical façade. It was about the size of a cottage. The porch was small, with a bench on either side. The steps were of concrete and the middle step was in need of repair. Otherwise the building was well maintained. Adam Stubo stood on the road by the fence. He noticed that the roof was new and the external red paint so oily that the moon was reflected in it.

The light on one of the gateposts was broken. As any evidence had long since been secured, he leant over the broken light and lifted the wrought-iron casing to get a better look at the bulb. Smashed to smithereens. Only a small jagged piece of glass was left in the fitting. He ran his finger over the base of the light. Minute shards of fine, matt glass stuck to his skin. In the beam of his Maglite he could see that the filament was untouched. He turned off the torch, pulled on his glove and stood there for a few moments while his eyes adjusted to the dark.

There was another light just below the porch roof, above the front door. It was broken too. The evening was clear and cold. The moon hung above the bare trees at the bottom of the garden, a perfect half, as if someone had sliced it in two. It made it possible to see the details of the house, the gravel path and overgrown garden, although there was no other light nearby except for a street lamp some fifty metres up the road.

'It's rather dark here,' Trond Arnesen said, unnecessarily.

'Yes,' Adam said. 'But it was darker a week ago, as there wasn't even any moonlight.'

Trond Arnesen sniffed. Adam put a hand on his shoulder.

'Listen,' he said in a quiet voice. His breath hung in blue-white clouds between them. 'I know that this is incredibly difficult. I just want you to know, Trond . . . Is it all right if I call you Trond?'

The man nodded and wet his lips with his tongue.

'You're not a suspect in this case. OK?'

Another nod and this time he bit his lip.

'We know that you were out on a stag night the night she was killed. We know that you and Vibeke had a good relationship. I understand you were going to get married this summer. In fact, I could go as far as to say . . .'

He looked around, very furtively.

'We never let things like this out,' he whispered, not letting go of the other man's shoulder. 'No one in Vibeke's family is a suspect. Her parents, her brother. You. You were actually the first person we struck from the list. The very first. D'you hear?'

'Yes,' mumbled Trond Arnesen and brushed his eyes with his gloved hand. 'But I'm inheriting . . . I get the house and everything. We had a . . .'

His words were stopped by his crying, a strange, soft crying. Adam let his hand slide down his back. He held him tight. The boy was a head shorter than Adam and he leant in towards him as he raised his hands to his face.

'The fact that you had a cohabitation agreement only shows that you were sensible young people,' Adam said quietly. 'You must stop being so frightened, Trond. You have nothing to fear from the police. Nothing, d'you understand?'

Vibeke Heinerback's fiancé had been so terrified during the hearings that the officer present found it difficult not to laugh, despite the tragic circumstances. The fair man in the pink Lacoste shirt, good-looking and well groomed, had gripped the edge of the table and drunk litres of water, as if he still had an almighty hangover, three days after the stag night. He was barely able to give his date of birth and address when asked.

'Relax,' Adam said again. 'We'll go calmly into the bedroom now. It's been cleaned up. The blood has been removed. OK?

Everything is more or less as it was before ... Do you hear what I'm saying?'

Trond Arnesen pulled himself together and straightened up. He coughed lightly into his hand and then smoothed back his hair. A couple of deep breaths later, he gave a faint smile and said:

'I'm ready.'

The gravel, mixed with ice and snow, crunched under their feet. Trond stopped again by the steps, as if he needed to galvanize himself. He stood there for a moment, rocking on the balls of his feet. Then he stroked back his hair again, a helpless, vulnerable gesture. He straightened his scarf and pulled down his jacket before mounting the steps. A uniformed policeman guided him into the bedroom. Adam followed. Nothing was said.

The bed was empty, apart from two pillows. The room was tidy. A huge reproduction of Munch's *History* hung above the head of the bed. Three neatly folded duvet covers, some towels and a couple of colourful cushions were stored in a shelving unit along one wall.

The mattress was clean, without a trace of blood. The floor was newly washed and there was still a faint smell of floor soap in the air. Adam took some photographs out of a manila envelope. He stroked his nose thoughtfully while he studied the photographs for a few minutes in silence. Then he turned to Trond Arnesen, who looked deathly pale in the bright light from the ceiling, and asked in a friendly voice:

'Are you ready, Trond?'

He swallowed, nodded and stepped forwards.

'What do you want me to do?'

Bernt Helle had been a widower for twenty-four days. He kept a close track of time. Every morning he drew a red cross over the previous day's date on the calendar Fiona had hung up in the kitchen to help Fiorella understand the concept of days, weeks and months. There was a Moomin character above each date. This morning he had crossed off Snufkin, who had the number twelve on a silver chain round his neck. Bernt Helle didn't know why he did it. Every morning another cross. They said that time heals all wounds, and every hour was a step closer.

Every night an empty double bed.

'Today is Friday the thirteenth,' he thought, and stroked his mother-in-law's hair.

Fiona was always so superstitious. Frightened of black cats. Gave ladders a wide berth. Had lucky numbers and believed that the colour red made you restless.

'Are you still here?' Yvonne Knutsen said and opened her eyes. 'You must go now, really you must.'

'Don't need to. Fiorella is at Mum's tonight. It's Friday, you know.'

'No,' she said confused.

'Yes, it's Fri . . .'

'I didn't realize. One day is like the next, lying here. Could you get me some water?'

She drank greedily with a straw.

'Have you ever thought that Fiona had something . . .' he asked suddenly, without having really thought about it. '. . . that it was as if she . . .'

Yvonne had fallen asleep again. Or at least, her eyes were closed and she was breathing regularly.

Bernt had never understood Fiona's leaning towards religion. It might have been different if it was the Church, the normal Norwegian State Church, which he had grown up with and where he felt comfortable attending weddings, funerals and the odd service. But Fiona had no Church. No sect, either, thankfully. No parish, no spiritual home other than herself. She slipped in and out of something she would never share with him. When they were young, he thought it was fascinating that she read so much. About other religions, Eastern philosophy, the great thinkers and great thoughts. For a while, probably at the start of the nineties, maybe even earlier, she had flirted with New Age. Luckily that didn't last very long. But then, at the end of what seemed to be a search for a theological anchor that had lasted more than a decade, she was even more distant. Not always, and certainly not in every area of her life. When Fiorella was born, their feeling of togetherness was so strong that they arranged a second wedding, fifteen years after the first.

'An incurable loneliness of the soul' is how she explained her need, on the rare occasions when he asked. She would close down, smile without warmth in her eyes, and her face would be inscrutable.

Sometimes he wondered if she had a secret. But that was hard to imagine. They had always known each other, their childhood homes were barely a couple of hundred steps apart. They didn't see much of each other when they were teenagers, they were too different. So he couldn't believe his luck when they accidentally met in a café in Oslo, when they were twenty. He had just finished his apprenticeship and started to work in his father's plumbing business. Fiona had long blonde hair and was studying at the University of Oslo. He had hoisted his trousers up properly at the bar so she wouldn't realize that he was starting to get a builder's arse. They got together that evening and Bernt Helle had never been with another woman since.

She was strangely restless and yet she clung on to anything and everything that was fixed and lasting.

'I shouldn't have done it,' Yvonne said suddenly and opened her eyes. 'We shouldn't have done it.'

'Yvonne,' he said and leant over her.

'Oh,' she exclaimed weakly. 'I was dreaming. Water, please.'

She's starting to lose it, he thought flatly.

She fell asleep again.

It was no longer possible to have a proper conversation with Yvonne, he realized. But it didn't matter. They shared a great sorrow. That was enough.

He got up and looked at the clock. It was nearly midnight. He quietly put on his jacket and pulled the duvet over Yvonne. She obviously didn't want to carry on. They were each dealing with the loss in their own way; she was using what little strength she had left to shrug off this life.

He, on the other hand, hoped that he would be able fight his way back into it one day.

The reconstruction was over. Most people had gone. Only Adam Stubo and Trond Arnesen were left in the bedroom. The young man couldn't pull himself away. He looked around the room, again and again, he walked about stroking things, as if he needed reassurance that they still existed.

'Do you think it's strange that I want to move back?' he asked, without looking at Adam.

'Not at all. It's perfectly natural, if you ask me. This was your house. It's still your home, even if Vibeke is dead. I understand that you helped her do it up.'

'Yes. This room too.'

'Is this how you remember it?'

'No.'

'You must try. This is what the bedroom looks like.'

Adam opened his arms and then hesitated before he continued:

'Our people have done nothing except . . . clean. Unfortunately, the duvet and the bedclothes were beyond saving. Otherwise, everything is as it was, as far as I know. And this is how you should remember it. You're going to live here, Trond. You may live here for many years. In some way or another you have to let go of that evening just over a week ago. I know exactly what you're going through. And I can assure you, it gets easier. I've been there, Trond. It passes.'

The younger man looked directly at him. His eyes were blue with specks of green. Only now did Adam notice the hint of red in Trond Arnesen's thick blond hair and a shadow of freckles over his nose, despite his winter pallor.

'What do you mean?' he said indistinctly.

'I found my family dead in the garden,' Adam replied slowly, looking at Trond squarely. 'An accident. I was convinced that I would never be able to go near the place again. I wanted to move, but didn't have the energy. Then one day, it must've been a couple of months later, I opened the terrace door and went out. I didn't dare to open my eyes, but I started to listen.'

Trond sat down on the bed. His body was stiff and tense, as if he didn't believe that the bed would hold him. He put both his hands on the mattress to support himself.

'What did you hear?' he asked.

Adam fumbled around in his breast pocket and found the cigar case. He let it slide between his thumb and forefinger, backwards and forwards, again and again.

'So much,' he said in a hushed voice. 'I heard so much. The birds were still there. Just as they had been long ago when we first moved in, straight after we got married. We were only twenty. Rented at first, then bought it later. They were singing.'

Suddenly he gasped for breath.

'They were singing,' he repeated, louder this time. 'The birds were singing as always. And through the birdsong, and in amongst all that bloody twittering, I heard . . . Trine. My daughter. I heard her shouting for me when she was only three, bawling her eyes out because she'd fallen off the swing. I heard the clinking of ice cubes in glasses when my wife came out with juice. Trine's laughter as she played with the neighbour's dog was suddenly so clear. I swear I could hear the hissing of evening barbecues. Suddenly I could smell them both. My wife. My daughter. I opened my eyes and there was the garden. A garden full of the best memories I have. Of course I couldn't move.'

'Do you still live there?'

Trond was more relaxed now. His back was bent and he was leaning on his elbows.

'No, but that's another story.'

Adam gave a short laugh and dropped the cigar case back into his pocket.

'You'll get new stories,' he said. 'New stories happen all the time, Trond. That's life. But in the meantime, you have to take ownership of this room again. The house. The whole place. This is your home. And it's full of happy memories. Remember them and forget that terrible evening.'

Trond got up, stretched his body, rolled his head from side to side, and straightened his trousers. Then he gave a weak smile.

'You're a nice policeman.'

'Most policemen are nice.'

The boy went on smiling. He looked around for a last time and then walked towards the door.

Trond Arnesen was at last ready to leave.

Halfway across the floor, he stopped, hesitated, took another step forward, before turning and walking back to the bedside table on the left of the bed. He opened the small drawer with a slow, cautious hand, as if he expected to find some nasty in it.

'Did you say that nothing else had been done here?' Trond asked. 'That you'd just washed the place? Nothing was removed?'

'Yes. Not in here. We took some papers and the PC, obviously, but we told you we were going to do that and . . .'

'But nothing from here?'

'No.'

'My watch. It was lying on the bedside table. And my book.'

'OK?'

'I've got a diving watch. A great lump of a thing. Can't sleep with it on, so I always leave it here in the evening.'

He tapped the bedside table with his fingers. Then he pressed them to his lips in concentration.

'But you didn't go to bed. You were at your brother's . . .'

'Exactly,' Trond interrupted. 'I was dressed up. We were all wearing tuxedos and a great big black plastic watch doesn't exactly match. So I left it here . . .'

'Are you sure?' Adam inquired, with an edge to his voice.

Trond Arnesen turned towards him and Adam could hear the irritation in his voice when he answered:

'My book and watch were lying here. On the bedside table.

Vibeke was . . .' When he mentioned her name, the aggression in his voice disappeared. 'Vibeke had a slight allergy,' he muttered. 'She didn't want books in the bedroom. I was only allowed to have the one I was reading at the time. Bencke's latest. I was halfway through. It was lying here.'

'OK . . . I'll ask you once more, are you certain about it?'

'Yes! My watch . . . I mean, I really liked that watch. Got it from Vibeke. I would never have . . .'

He stopped himself. A faint blush was visible along his hairline. He tugged his ear in discomfort.

'Of course, I could be wrong,' he said feebly. 'I don't know, I . . .'

'But you remember . . .'

'As I remember . . . Maybe I did leave the book somewhere else. But I only read in bed, I . . .'

He stared at Adam, obviously upset. This had nothing to do with the book, Adam thought to himself. Trond Arnesen had for a moment allowed himself to believe that everything could be as it was. Adam had, for a moment or two, convinced him that the image of the crucified Vibeke in bed could be erased and disappear.

'I wouldn't have . . . Not the book. The watch perhaps, that might have been left somewhere else, but I . . .'

'Come on,' Adam said. 'I'll find out what's happened. They've probably just been put somewhere else. Come, let's go.'

Trond Arnesen opened the drawer again. It was empty. Then he went over to the other side of the bed. But he didn't find anything there either. He had a slightly crazy look in his eyes as he stormed out into the bathroom. Adam stayed where he was. He heard the sound of drawers and cupboards being opened and shut, the banging of what could be the lid of the rubbish bin.

Then the boy was there again, in the doorway, holding out his empty hands.

'I must've made a mistake,' he said in a hoarse voice.

His eyes were downcast as he followed Adam out of the bedroom.

'Vibeke was always saying that, that I was an airhead.'

Evil is an illusion, she thought.

She was standing by the bronze bust of Jean Cocteau. In her opinion it was slapdash with running features, as if a child had been playing with melted wax and suddenly decided to make a bust and dedicate it to someone. The sculpture stood on the edge of the quay, a short distance from the small chapel that Cocteau himself had decorated. You had to pay to get in, so she only caught a glimpse of the frescos at Christmas when she had been overwhelmed by a nostalgic desire to visit a church. St-Michel, the church on the hill behind her, had been unbearable with all its Catholic kitsch and the monotonous mumblings of the priest. She had backed her way out.

But paying to meet a God she had never believed in was even worse. She had had the urge to remind the fat old woman inside the door to Cocteau's chapel of Christ's rampage in the temple. The sour-faced old witch sat behind a table of simple but outrageously overpriced souvenirs and demanded an entrance fee of two euros. It was irritating that her French didn't stretch to anything more than mild swearing under her breath.

It was now late in the day on Friday the 13th of February. The spring tides that afternoon had caused considerable damage. The panorama windows of restaurants along the promenade had been broken by the high seas. Shivering young men in white shirts ran backwards and forwards with plywood that they nailed up without much skill, temporary protection against the wind and weather. Chairs had been smashed to kindling. A table was floating some metres from the quay. Most of the boats in the bay were loosely moored and had survived the storm, but four or five dinghies that had been moored by the jetty had fared worse, and now only driftwood and the remains of some rope could be seen in the turbulent, murky waters.

She leant towards Jean Cocteau and once again thought to herself: 'Evil is an illusion.'

The dark side of humanity was her bread and butter. She was

never sloppy. To the contrary. She knew more about betrayal, malice and spiritual bankruptcy than most.

She had once felt some pride in that.

To begin with, nineteen years ago, when she was still in her twenties and had newly discovered how easy it was for her to use this hidden and surprising talent, she had been excited by it. Enthusiastic. Even happy. At least, that is how she remembered it. She wasn't even bitter about all the years of education she would never use, all the conscientious effort at university that had only helped to pass the time. It was all a waste. But that didn't matter any more, once she had found her niche in life at the age of twenty-six.

The cliché made her smile.

One March evening in 1985, she sat with a copy of her bank balance in front of her, a beer in her hand, and tried to imagine what her niche was, that special place on an imaginary bookcase of life. This niche would make her special and valuable, completely unique. She had laughed at the well-worn metaphor and imagined everyone creeping around, searching for their niche on some vacant corner.

The sea was calmer now. The air temperature was no more than a few degrees and what little warmth there was was cut through by the gusts of wind that continued to blow from the south. The boys in shirts had managed to patch up the worst holes and obviously couldn't be bothered to do any more. A young couple in dark clothes walked towards her. They giggled and whispered something she didn't understand as they passed. She turned round and followed them with her eyes as they slipped on the wet cobbles and then disappeared into the dark.

They looked Norwegian. He had a rucksack on.

Fortunately, the last photograph of her had been taken twelve years ago. Almost exactly. She was slimmer then. Much slimmer and she had long hair. The picture, which she sometimes looked at by mistake, looked like someone else. That was what she had to think. She wore glasses now. Long hair didn't suit her any more.

When she looked in the mirror, she saw that life had shown no mercy in leaving its mark on what was once a very ordinary face. Her nose, which was as small back then as now, looked like a button. Her eyes had never been big, but they were brown and therefore not like everyone else's. They were now almost entirely hidden by her glasses and a fringe that was far too long.

The idea that anyone was unique was an illusion.

People were so damned alike.

She didn't know when the truth had dawned on her. She reckoned it must have been a gradual realization. She became impatient with the repetitiveness of her work, without really knowing what she wanted to change. Every plan was of course special, every crime had its own value. The circumstances varied, the victims were never the same. She put in tremendous effort. She was never sloppy in her work. But she still couldn't think of it as anything other than an enervating, endless repetition.

She could no longer get time to pass.

It just happened, of its own accord.

Until now, she thought and drew breath.

Everyone was the same.

Time, which everyone was so keen on 'filling', was a meaningless concept, created to give false meaning to what was meaningless: simply being alive.

The woman pulled her hat down over her head and slowly climbed the steps that were squeezed in between the old stone houses. The narrow alleys were unusually dark. Maybe the storm had damaged the electricity supply.

By studying people's behaviour, she had at some point understood that consideration, solidarity and goodness were no more than empty expressions. Virtues of model behaviour, as given by God and set in stone, extolled by aged monks and in the prophecies of an Arab warrior, in the musings of philosophers and tales from the mouths of persecuted Jews.

Evil was true human nature, she thought.

Evil was not the work of the devil, or the result of original sin, nor was it a dialectical consequence of material need and injustice. If a lioness abandoned a sick cub to a painful, loveless death, no one would say she was evil. The male alligator was not judged in zoological terms because he sired more children than he instinctively knew the environment could support.

She stopped in the alley by the insignificant door into St-Michel's church. She hesitated for a moment. She was breathing heavily after climbing all the stairs. She gently put her hand on the door handle, but then pulled back and carried on. It was time to get home. It had started to rain again, a fine light rain that covered her skin in a moist film.

There was no point in stigmatizing natural behaviour, she thought. That was why animals were free. Humans were likely to exterminate themselves if there was no culture, no order, bans or threats of corrective punishment, so it might possibly be expedient to brand anyone who deviated from the norm and followed their true nature with the mark of Cain.

'It's still not evil,' she whispered, and gasped for breath in the Place de la Paix.

The Pharmacie's bright-green cross winked at the deserted, closed café over the street. She stopped in front of the estate agents.

Her thighs ached, a dull pain, even though she had not climbed more than a couple of hundred steps. She could taste the sweat on her upper lip. A blister was stinging on her left heel. It was a long time since she'd known the pleasure of physical exercise. The dull pain gave her a sense of being alive. She lifted her face to the sky and felt the rain run down the inside of her collar, over her skin and down her shoulder: she felt her nipples harden.

Everything had changed. Life taken on a palpable, tangible intensity that she had never experienced before.

At last, she was unique.

Seven

I t was too big a job.

Johanne Vik wrinkled her nose at her tea. It had stewed for too long and was dark and bitter. She spat the yellowish brown liquid back into the cup.

'Ugh,' she muttered. She was glad she was alone, as she put down the cup and opened the fridge.

She should have refused. The two murder cases were hard enough to crack for professional policemen working in a team, with access to modern technology, advanced data programs, a full overview and all the time in the world.

Johanne had none of that. She had bitten off more than she could chew. The children ruled her days. Sometimes she felt she moved on autopilot, from the washing machine to Kristiane's homework, making food and trying to snatch a few moments' peace on the sofa while feeding a baby. Even when her oldest daughter wasn't at home, there was plenty to do.

But the nights were long.

They passed slowly, the hours that she spent poring over the copies of documents that Adam took home with him every afternoon, which was highly irregular. It was as if the clock also felt it deserved a rest after a tiring day.

She grabbed a mineral water, opened it and drank straight from the bottle.

'*Perineal rupture*,' she said to herself as she sat down at the table again and looked through the final post-mortem report in the Fiona Helle case.

A rupture was some kind of tear or another.

'Periscope,' she mumbled, chewing her pencil. 'Periphery. Peri . . .'

She slapped her forehead lightly. A good thing she hadn't asked anyone. It was embarrassing for a grown woman not to know what it meant immediately. Even though both her children had been born by Caesarean, Johanne had plenty of friends who had described the problem to her in great detail.

Little Fiorella had left her mark.

OK.

She lay the document to one side and focused on the reconstruction report. It told her nothing that she didn't know already. She carried on leafing through the papers impatiently. As the case had already generated several hundred, if not more than a thousand documents, she obviously didn't have access to them all.

Adam selected and prioritized. She read.

Without finding anything.

The papers contained nothing but endless repetitions, a round dance of the obvious. No secrets were uncovered. There was no contradiction, nothing surprising, nothing to spend more time on in the hope of seeing things from another angle.

Exasperated, she slapped the covers together.

She had to learn to say no more often.

Like when her mother rang earlier in the day and invited the whole family to lunch next Sunday. With Isak, of course.

It was nearly six years since their divorce. Although she often worried and was irritated by Isak's leniency with regard to Kristiane, with no set bedtimes, fast food and sweets on weekdays, it made her genuinely happy to see them together. Kristiane and Isak had the same physical build and were on the same wavelength, even though the girl suffered from an inexplicable handicap that had never been diagnosed. She found it harder to accept that her ex-husband still spent time with her parents. More than she did, if she was honest.

That hurt, and she blamed him for her shame.

'Get a grip!'

Without knowing why, she pulled out the post-mortem report again.

Strangulation, it stated.

She already knew the cause of death.

The tongue was described in clinical terms.

Nothing new there.

Abrasions on both wrists. No sign of sexual interference. Blood type A. A tumour in her mouth, on the left cheek, about the size of a pea and benign. Scars, in several places. All old. From an operation on the shoulder, the removal of four moles and a Caesarean. And a five-pointed, relatively big but almost invisible mark on her right upper arm. Probably a cut from way back. One earlobe was inflamed. The nail on her left index finger was blue and about to come off at the time of death.

The report, for all its precise details, still told her nothing. She was just left with the vague feeling that there was something important there, something that had caught her eye, the impression that something didn't add up.

Her concentration was failing. She was annoyed by Isak, by her mother, by their friendship.

A waste of energy. Isak was Isak. Her mother was the same as she had always been, scared of conflict, ambiguous and extremely loyal to those she cared for.

'Stop letting it bother you,' Johanne thought, exhausted, but couldn't stop all the same.

'Focus,' she said out loud to herself. 'You have to fo . . .'

There.

Her finger stopped at the bottom of the page.

It didn't make sense.

She swallowed, then lifted her hand to go through the report, furiously looking for something that she had just read in passing. She noticed that her hand was shaking. Her pulse was racing and she was breathing through her mouth.

There.

She was right. It couldn't be right. She grabbed the phone and discovered that her hand was sweaty.

*

On the other side of Oslo, Adam Stubo was babysitting for his grandson, who was nearly six. The boy was asleep on his grandfather's lap. The grandfather buried his nose in the dark hair. The smell of baby soap was soft and warm. The boy should really be in bed. His father was an easygoing, flexible sort of bloke, but he was adamant that the boy should sleep on his own. But Adam couldn't resist his round, dark eyes. He had smuggled one of Ragnhild's bottles from home. The look on Amund's face when he realized that he was going to be allowed to sit on his grandfather's knee with a bottle was priceless.

Strangely enough, the boy had never been jealous of Kristiane. Quite the contrary, he was fascinated by the strange girl who was four years older than he was. But it was very different when he was told that his grandfather was going to be a daddy again. He had clearly decided to ignore Ragnhild's arrival three weeks ago.

The telephone rang.

Amund didn't wake up. His grip on the baby bottle loosened when Adam carefully leant over to the table to answer the phone.

'Hallo,' he said quietly, holding the telephone between his chin and shoulder as he reached for the remote control.

'Hallo, my dear. Are you boys having a good time?'

He smiled. The eagerness in her voice gave her away.

'Yep. We've had a great time. Played a silly card game and made some Lego houses. But that's not why you phoned.'

'I won't keep you long if you're . . .'

'Amund's asleep. I've got all the time in the world.'

'Could you . . . tomorrow, or as soon as possible, could you check a couple of things for me?'

'Of course.'

He pressed the wrong button on the remote control. The newsreader shouted out that four American soldiers had been killed in Basra before Adam managed to find the right button. Amund grunted and buried his head in his grandfather's arm.

'I'm sitting a bit . . . Hang on a moment.'

'I'll be quick,' she insisted. 'You have to get me Fiona Helle's journal, about Fiorella's birth. From when her daughter was born.'

'OK,' he said. 'Why exactly?'

'I don't like talking about this sort of thing on the phone,' Johanne said with some hesitation. 'As you're staying at Bjarne and Randi's, you either have to come home first thing tomorrow morning so we can talk, or . . .'

'I won't have time. I promised Amund I'd take him to nursery.'

'Trust me then. It might be important.'

'I always trust you.'

'And with good reason.'

Her laughter rattled down the phone line.

'What about the other thing?' he said. 'You wanted me to do two things?'

'You have to let me . . . From the papers it's clear that Fiona's mother is very ill, and . . .'

'Yes, I questioned her myself. MS. Clear as a bell upstairs, but wasting away otherwise.'

'So she was all there?'

'As far as I know, the brain is not affected by multiple sclerosis,' he said.

'Don't be like that!'

Amund stuck his thumb in his mouth and turned in towards Adam again.

'I'm not like that,' he said and smiled. 'I'm just teasing you.'

'I need to talk to her.'

'You?'

'I'm working for you, Adam.'

'Very unofficially and without any form of recognition. It's bad enough that I have to sneak around with the documents. The boss has given a kind of silent consent to that. But I can't really give you . . .'

'But surely no one can prevent me from visiting an old lady in a nursing home as a private individual?' she said.

'Why are you asking me then?'

101

'Ragnhild. I don't think it would be a good idea to take her with me. Is there any chance of you coming home early tomorrow?'

'Early,' he repeated. 'What's that?'

'One, two?'

'I might be able to tear myself away around half past two. Would that be OK?'

'It'll have to be. Thank you.'

'Are you sure that you can't tell me anything? I have to admit I'm dying of curiosity now.'

'And I'm dying to tell you,' she said, and took a drink of something. Her voice almost vanished. 'But it was you who taught me to be careful on the phone.'

'I'll have to contain myself then. Until tomorrow.'

'Now put Amund to bed,' she said.

'He is in bed,' he said, crestfallen.

'He's not, he's sleeping in your lap with Ragnhild's baby bottle.'

'Rubbish.'

'Put the boy to bed, Adam. And sleep well. You're the best in the world.'

'You are . . .'

'Wait. If you get time, could you check one more thing? Could you try to find out whether Fiona was away from school for any long periods of time while she was in secondary?'

'What?'

'If she went on an exchange or something like that. Language course, or a long-lasting illness, or if she visited an aunt in Australia, for that matter. It should be easy enough to find out.'

'You can ask her mother,' he sighed. 'As you're going to see her anyway. She's probably the best one to ask.'

'I'm not sure that she'd answer. Ask the husband. Or an old friend or someone. Will you do it?'

'Yes, yes. Go to bed.'

'Good night, darling.'

'I mean it. Go to bed. Don't sit up reading those documents. They're not going to run away. Good night.'

He put down the receiver and got up as carefully as he could from the overly soft sofa. He struggled to find his balance and hugged Amund too tight. The boy whimpered but continued to lie in his arms like a rag doll.

'I don't know why everyone assumes that I spoil you,' Adam whispered. 'I just don't understand it.'

He carried the boy into the guest room, put him down in the middle of the bed, undressed quietly, put on his own pyjamas and lay down with his back to the child.

'Gramps,' the boy murmured in his sleep. A hand stroked Adam's neck.

They slept soundly for nine hours and Adam got to work nearly an hour late.

Trond Arnesen had made sure that the lights by the gate and in the porch were both working before he moved back to the small house that he would now inherit. His brother had offered to stay with him for the first few days. Trond said no. He didn't want to make the transition to a life alone in stages. It was his home, even if he'd only moved in a couple of months ago. Vibeke was quite old-fashioned and had not agreed to living together until a date had been set for the wedding.

He tried to avoid the windows. He drew the curtains before it got really dark. The gaps threatening, black strips of emptiness.

The TV flickered but there was no sound. Vibeke had bought him a 42-inch plasma screen for his birthday. Far too generous, they couldn't afford it after all the work on the house. 'So you can watch the football,' she smiled, and opened an expensive bottle of champagne. He turned thirty that day and they had decided to make babies in the autumn.

He didn't feel like watching TV, he was far too restless, but the silent people on the screen were a friendly presence. He had wandered from room to room for several hours now, sat down, touched some object or other, got up, moved on, anxious about what he might find behind the next door. He felt safe in the bathroom. It

103

had no windows and was warm, and at around six o'clock he had locked the door and stayed in there for about an hour. In desperation, he had taken a bath, as if he had to legitimize his need to feel secure in a house that he, at that precise moment, half past ten on Monday the 16th of February, did not think he would be able to live in.

He heard a noise from outside.

It came from the back of the house, he thought, from the slope down to the small stream, fifty metres down the garden, where a picket fence marked the boundary to a disused scrap yard.

He froze, listening.

The silence was overwhelming. He couldn't even hear the usual clicking of the thermostat on the heater under the window.

Just his imagination, no doubt.

A grown man, he thought to himself in irritation, and took down a random book from the shelf.

He looked at the title page. An author he'd never heard of. Must be new. He put it back, horizontally across the top of the other books. It struck him that that sort of thing always annoyed Vibeke, so he took it out again to put it back properly between two books.

The noise had sounded like something breaking, now he heard it again.

His brother had always called him a coward. That wasn't true. Trond Arnesen wasn't a coward, he was just cautious. If his fifteen-month-younger brother had climbed past him on trees, it was simply because common sense told him that to climb any further was stupid. When his brother was seven and jumped from the roof of a four-metre-high garage with a parachute made from a sheet and four bits of rope, Trond stood on the ground and advised him not to do it. His brother broke his leg.

Trond was not a coward. He always assessed the consequences.

The fear that gripped him now had nothing to do with the future. The unfamiliar taste of iron clung to his tongue, which immediately felt dry and too big. When the fear reached his eardrums, he had to shake his head if he wanted to hear anything other than the blood pumping round his body.

He looked quickly round the room.

Vibeke's furniture.

Vibeke's things here and there. A copy of *Her* magazine with a Post-it to mark an article about young families struggling to find enough time to get everything done. A steel and plastic lighter he had given her for Christmas to show that she didn't need to hide her cigarettes from him any more.

Vibeke's things.

His home.

He was no coward. Although the sound had come from behind the house, he now ran towards the front door without even looking out of the sitting room window to check if it was an animal, a confused elk or one of the many skinny feral cats.

Without a moment's hesitation, he pulled open the front door.

'Hallo,' said an obviously startled Rudolf Fjord. 'Hallo, Trond.'

He was standing with his foot on the first step up to the porch.

'Hi,' he said again, pathetically.

'Idiot,' hissed Trond. 'What the hell do you think you're doing sneaking around in the garden like that? What the fuck are you . . .'

'I just wanted to see if anyone was home,' Rudolf Fjord said. His voice was louder now, but still feeble, as if he was trying to pull himself together without succeeding. 'May I offer my condolences.'

Trond Arnesen threw out his hands and went forward onto the steps.

'Condolences? You've come here at . . .'

With a swift movement he pulled up his left sleeve. His diving watch had still not reappeared.

'. . . Bloody late on a Monday night,' he continued furiously, '. . . to give your *condolences*? Again! You've already done it! What the hell . . . You frightened . . . Just go!'

'OK, OK, calm down.'

Rudolf Fjord had managed to pull himself together. He put out his hand in a conciliatory gesture, but Trond showed no signs of taking it.

'I was just checking whether you were at home,' Rudolf tried again. 'I didn't want to disturb you if you were already asleep. That's why I went round the house. But you've blacked out all the windows, so it was only when I saw a chink of light from the sitting room that I knew you were at home. I was just about to ring the bell when . . .'

'What d'you want? What the hell d'you want, Rudolf?'

Trond had never really liked Vibeke's colleague. Nor had she. The few times that he'd asked her about the man, she got a closed look on her face and said that he wasn't to be trusted. She wouldn't say any more. Trond didn't know whether Rudolf Fjord was trustworthy or not, but he didn't like the way the guy treated women. Trond reckoned he was good-looking, tall, well built with a prominent chin and rather intense blue eyes. Rudolf used women. Exploited them.

'Like I said, I just wanted . . .'

'I'll give you one more chance,' Trond was shouting now. 'People don't turn up to give their condolences in the middle of the night. You can't pull the wool over my eyes. What do you want?'

'I'd also thought,' Rudolf Fjord started, and then looked as if he was literally trying to catch a word on the tip of his tongue. His eyes darted aimlessly round the garden. 'I just thought I would ask you if I could look for some important papers Vibeke took home with her from the office. She was going to bring them back on the Monday, the one after she was murdered that is. I think . . .'

'For God's sake!'

Trond Arnesen was laughing now, a loud, joyless laughter.

'Are you completely . . . stupid? Are you soft in the head or what?'

He laughed again, in desperation.

'The police have taken all the papers. Are you . . . Don't you understand anything? D'you have no idea of what happens when someone is murdered? Hm?'

He took a step forward and remained standing at the top of the steps. He covered his ears with his hands, as if trying to block out a catastrophe. Then he lowered his arms, took a deep breath and said:

'Talk to the police. Good night.'

He went back into the house and was just about to shut the door when Rudolf Fjord leapt up the steps. He put his foot in the door to stop it from closing, his lower leg caught between the door and the frame. Trond stared at it. He was surprised by his own outburst of rage when he slammed the door shut with all his might.

'Ow, shit, Trond! Ow. Listen . . . listen . . . ow!'

'Move your foot,' Trond said, and let go of the door for a moment.

'My laptop,' Rudolf said and stuck his leg in the door a bit further. 'And . . . and . . .'

Trond Arnesen didn't back down. He had both his hands on the door handle.

'Your leg will break soon,' he said very calmly. 'Move.'

'I need those papers. And the laptop.'

'You're lying. The laptop was her own one. She got it from me.'

'But the other one, then . . .'

'There wasn't another one.'

'But . . .'

Trond gathered all his strength and pushed hard.

'Ow! *Oooowww!* She'd also borrowed a book from me.'

His leg was badly twisted now. Trond stared at the black boot with fascination. The door was cutting into the leather just by the ankle.

'Which book?' he asked without looking up.

'The latest one by Bencke,' Rudolf groaned.

That at least was true. Trond had noticed the Ex Libris label and had been surprised that the two of them borrowed books from each other.

'It's disappeared,' he said.

'Disappeared?'

'Jesus, Rudolf! The book's not here and right now that's the least of my worries. And yours for that matter! Buy a paperback.'

'Let me go.'

Trond gave him a few centimetres slack. Rudolf Fjord edged his leg out. He let out a pathetic whimper as he carefully tried to massage the blood back into his lower leg.

'Good night,' he said weakly.

He limped down the steps. Trond stood in the doorway and watched him. The man nearly collapsed on the gravel driveway. Rudolf Fjord looked pathetic as he limped out to the road, despite his broad shoulders and his expensive camel-hair coat. His car was parked some distance away. Trond could just see the roof, a silver disc under the street lamp, at the top of the hill. For a moment he felt sorry for him. But he didn't know why.

'Pathetic man,' he said to himself, and realized that he was no longer scared of being alone.

Rudolf Fjord sat in the car until the windows steamed up. Everything was quiet. His foot ached intensely. He didn't dare take off his boot to see if there was any real damage, in case he couldn't get it back on again. He tried to push down the clutch. Luckily the pain was bearable. He'd been afraid he wouldn't be able to drive.

At best, nothing would happen.

The police had the papers. They wouldn't find anything. It wasn't what they were looking for.

Rudolf Fjord wasn't even sure that there was anything to find. Vibeke had never told him what she had seen. Her hints were subtle, her threats vague. But she must have found something.

Rudolf Fjord had hoped he would find the house empty. He couldn't understand why, because now the whole venture seemed absurd. Breaking in was out of the question. He was neither dressed nor equipped to break in to a house. Maybe he had hoped that they could have a rational conversation. That Trond would give him what he asked for, without asking any questions. That it would be possible to draw a line under the whole thing, the whole depressing, aggravating affair would be over for good.

He could feel the tiredness behind his eyes, which were dry from lack of sleep.

He had never known that it was physically painful to be frightened.

Maybe she just made it up.

Of course she hadn't, he argued with himself.

His foot was getting steadily worse. He had cramp in his calves. Frustrated, he wiped the condensation from the front screen and started the car.

At best, nothing would happen.

Three dull meetings were finally over. Adam Stubo sank into his chair and looked despondently at the pile of post. He quickly flicked through the letters and memorandums. Nothing urgent. His hourglass was standing perilously near to the edge of the desk. He carefully pushed it to a safer place. The grains of sand formed a silver peak in the bottom glass. He set the sand in motion and more and more grains moved faster and faster.

Time was running out.

That was becoming increasingly apparent with each day that passed. No one said much. They all still had a false confidence and people still accepted overtime without any protest, but with waning enthusiasm. There were still moments of optimism among the investigators. After all, new discoveries were made every day, even though they proved to be insignificant later.

It couldn't go on like this much longer.

Three weeks or so, Adam reckoned. Dissatisfaction would spread fast once it took hold. He knew the score from earlier cases when no tangible evidence was forthcoming. Today it was exactly four weeks since Fiona Helle was murdered. After twenty-eight days of intense investigation, they should at least have an idea of a possible suspect, an indication of a possible killer, a hint, a direction to follow.

But there was nothing in the folders that lay on Adam Stubo's desk. And soon people would get fed up. Despondency was seeping into the most recent case too, as if they all, despite repeated warnings not to, just assumed that Vibeke Heinerback had been killed by the same person as Fiona Helle and that the man had quite simply got away with it.

The cases wouldn't be shelved. Of course not. But grumblings about resources, insufficient results and too much overtime would gradually turn into sharp protest. Everyone knew what no one dared to say: for every hour that passed, the solution to the murders was slipping away.

The NCIS probably had the most motivated staff in the country. There was no doubt that it was the most competent. All of the investigators involved were therefore painfully aware of the depressing time-to-solution ratio.

Adam was dying for a cigar.

He picked up his phone and punched in a number that was written on a scrap of paper at the bottom of the case board.

The urge for a cigar was stronger than it had been for a long time.

'Bernt Helle? This is Adam Stubo from the NCIS.'

'Hi,' said the voice at the other end of the line.

Then it was quiet.

'I hope that everything's going well, given the circumstances.'

'Yep.'

More silence.

'I rang because there's something I want to ask you, but I won't keep you long,' Adam explained, and pressed the conference call button before putting the receiver down and patting his breast pocket. 'Just a minor detail, really.'

'OK,' Bernt Helle said and coughed. 'I was actually just on my way out . . .'

Scraping. A loud cough.

'Fire away,' he said eventually. 'What's it about?'

His cigar tube had dents in it.

'I don't really know whether it's of any significance or not,' Adam said, and tried to remember how long he'd been carrying the same tube around. 'But could you tell me . . . Was Fiona ever an exchange student?'

'Exchange student?'

'Yes, you know, programmes where . . .'

'Yes, I know what an exchange student is,' Bernt Helle said indignantly, and coughed again. 'Fiona didn't go abroad in secondary school. I'm fairly sure of that. Even though I didn't know her particularly well at the time. She was at secondary school and I was at poly. But, you know . . .'

Adam knew.

And he felt like an idiot. If he had waited until the next day, he would know why he was phoning him. But Johanne had insisted.

With great care, he pulled the cigar out of its aluminium tube.

'Yes,' Adam said. 'If she had spent any time studying abroad, she would of course have talked about it later.'

'Yeah, I'm certain she would.'

There were some silver scissors on the shelf behind Adam, a miniature guillotine. When he cut the end of the cigar the noise made his mouth water. He took his lighter and rotated the cigar slowly over the flame.

'Not abroad at all,' he summed up. 'No language schools in England? Summer holidays? Long stays with friends or family abroad?'

'No . . . listen . . .' A terrible coughing fit rattled in the receiver. 'Sorry,' Bernt Helle sniffed.

The cigar tasted better than Adam had ever dreamt it could. The smoke was blue and dry on his tongue and not too hot. The smell stung his nose. Bernt Helle continued:

'Obviously I can't know everything Fiona did when she was at school, in detail that is. Like I said, we didn't hang around together then. We only really met later, after . . .' A loud sneeze. 'Sorry.'

'No problem. You should get to bed,' Adam said.

111

'I run a business. And I've got a little girl who has just lost her mother. I don't really have time to go to bed.'

'Now it's my turn to say sorry,' Adam apologized. 'I won't keep you any longer. Hope you feel better soon.'

Adam hung up. A delicate, light-grey fog was starting to fill the room. He smoked slowly. A drag every half-minute or so allowed the taste to settle and stopped the cigar from getting too hot.

He would never manage to stop. He had breaks, long periods when he didn't enjoy a good cigar, the taste of pepper and leather, with perhaps an undertone of sweet cocoa. He often wondered whether the masculine aroma on the odd Friday night would really do the children any harm. Cuban cigars were best, of course, but he could also enjoy a mild Sumatra, after dinner on a Friday evening, with his cognac or preferably a good calvados.

But those days were over.

He ran his finger over his lower lip. The cigar was a bit dry after lying in his breast pocket for weeks. It didn't matter. He already felt lighter and leant back in his chair and blew out three perfect smoke rings. They floated slowly up to the ceiling and then vanished.

'Weren't you going to go home early?'

Adam's feet, which had been crossed on his desk, now slammed to the floor.

'What's the time?' he asked, putting out the cigar out carefully in a mug with some coffee still in it.

'Half past two.'

'Shit.'

'It smells all the way down the corridor,' Sigmund Berli commented, and sniffed the air disapprovingly. 'The boss'll be pissed off, Adam. Didn't you read the last circular about—'

'Yeah. Have to dash.'

He felled the coat stand as he tried to get his coat off the hook.

'I should've been home by now,' he said, and rushed past Sigmund without bothering to pick the coat stand back up. 'Far too late.'

'Wait,' shouted Sigmund.

Adam slowed down and stopped as he tried to get his arm into a twisted sleeve.

'This just came in,' Sigmund said, and handed him an envelope.

'Oh for Christ's sake,' hissed Adam between clenched teeth, his coat half on while he fumbled with the rest. 'Has this bloody thing gone to pieces?'

Sigmund laughed. He patiently straightened the sleeve, as if he was helping a stroppy, overgrown schoolboy, then he held the coat by the collar and helped Adam put in his arm.

'There,' Sigmund chuckled, and thrust the envelope under Adam's nose. 'You said it was urgent.'

'You can say that. Express delivery.'

Adam gave a fleeting smile, stuffed the envelope in his pocket and made a dash. Sigmund could feel the floor heaving under his heavy steps.

'One day you'll get into trouble about all these papers you keep dragging backwards and forwards,' Sigmund said to himself. 'It's not right.'

The smell of Adam's cigar hung heavy in the air, sour and unpleasant.

Vegard Krogh drank the flat beer and felt happy.

There must be something wrong with the taps at Coma, the only decent lunch restaurant in Grünerløkka. He held the glass up towards the window. The froth was thin and pathetic. The afternoon light barely managed to filter through the tepid beer. Golden-brown reflections played on the table in front of him, and he grinned before taking another drink.

The bungee-jump stunt had been a disaster.

The film was fine until about halfway through the jump. Then Vegard Krogh disappeared from the picture. The lens wavered around up to the sky. Slipped past a crane. Tipped back towards the ground. Suddenly, for a split second, it caught Vegard Krogh on the rebound. Straight up. With the background music of sirens

113

and the photographer's desperate attempt to get away from the place, the rest of the film showed only earth, stones and building materials.

But it didn't matter now.

The invitation arrived yesterday.

Vegard Krogh had hoped and waited. At times he was absolutely certain. It would come. He thought about the invitation in the evenings. His last conscious image before he fell asleep was of a beautiful card with a monogram and his name, written in neat calligraphy.

Then it came.

His hands were shaking as he opened the envelope, thick, stiff egg-shell coloured paper. The card was just as he'd imagined it. A dream card waiting for him in his post box, just when he needed it most.

Vegard Krogh had finally arrived.

He was now someone who mattered. From now on he would be one of them. One of the chosen few who answered, 'No comment' when the tabloids rang, as they did, to the couple's friends, relentlessly.

'I'm going to be hounded,' he mumbled to himself, drowning his euphoric grin in the pint glass.

The young royals in Sweden surrounded themselves with the upper classes, aristocracy and decadence. It was completely different in Norway. In Norway, it was culture that mattered. Music. Literature. Art.

It was six years now since he had first bought wine for a dandy young man with doe eyes and feminine clothes. The boy was sitting in a corner, surrounded by girls. Vegard was shitfaced, but had always had a nose for where the girls were. The man thanked him politely and chatted away, until Vegard pulled a brunette and left.

They bumped into each other, every now and then. Had a drink. Shared stories. Until his circle of friends was purged a couple of years ago, for obvious reasons, and Vegard was dropped.

Bungee Jump must have made an impression.

114

He had sent a signed copy. Not one review of the book had been written yet, eight days after publication. But it had had an impact on the most important critic of all.

From one bungee jumper to another. To dare! From your friend, Vegard.

It had taken him an hour to find the right words. It was important not to be too pushy.

Vegard Krogh downed the rest of his beer in one, a great satisfied draught.

The glass of cheap Merlot was finally starting to kick in.

Dress: casual & sharp, it said on the invite.

He would have to swallow his pride and borrow money from his mum.

She wouldn't be angry this time.

'You say this Stubo guy's OK.'

Bård Arnesen leant over the table and gave his brother an encouraging slap on the shoulder. Then he scratched his head, before saving a lettuce leaf from drowning in dressing at the bottom of the glass bowl.

'Lying to the cops isn't very clever, Trond.'

Trond didn't answer. He just stared straight ahead without looking at anything. His plate was half empty. He moved the leftovers from side to side, meat and fried potatoes. He listlessly picked up a piece of asparagus and put it in his mouth, then chewed it slowly without swallowing.

'Hallo, planet earth calling. You look like a cow.'

Bård waved a hand in front of his brother's face.

'It'll be much worse if they find out themselves,' he said earnestly. 'In fact, it's pretty strange that they haven't . . .'

'Don't you understand?' Trond exclaimed. '. . . I can't say anything to Stubo. For a start, I'd blow a hole in my alibi. And then I'm in shit up to here . . .' His hand made an aggressive cut across his forehead. '. . . Just for having lied. They'd pull me in straight away, Bård. Straight away.'

'Yeah, but you said that they knew that you were innocent. That Stubo bloke said you were the first one they struck from the list. You said that . . .'

'Said! What the fuck does it matter what I *said*!'

His fist hit the table. He was struggling to hold it together, his lower lip was trembled, his nostrils flared and his eyes had nearly receded into his skull. He pushed the plate away, then pulled it back, balanced his knife on the fork and folded the serviette so many times that he couldn't fold it any more.

Bård kept quiet. The smell of his brother's fear added a sweet edge to the greasy, heavy fried potato air that filled the kitchen. Bård had never seen his brother like this before. He had been a scaredy cat as long as Bård could remember. Wary of everything. A real Mummy's boy. Cried whenever he got hurt, which he seldom did.

But now he wasn't worried or nervous.

His brother was terrified and he couldn't swallow the piece of asparagus.

'Hey,' Bård said in a friendly voice, and gave him another gentle push. 'There's no one who would seriously believe you murdered Vibeke. For Christ's sake, she was a real catch. Good-looking, fun, with money and a house and things like that. Can't you just . . . hallo, Trond!' He clicked his fingers in resignation. 'Listen to me at least!'

'I'm listening.'

'Spit out that bloody stuff.'

Trond spat it out. A grey-green lump of mulch dropped onto the leftovers on his plate.

'You trust me, don't you, Trond?'

The question got no reaction.

'You're my brother, Trond.'

Still no reaction.

'Oh for fuck's sake!'

Bård got up suddenly and the chair fell back. It slammed into the fridge door and scraped off some of the paint. Perplexed, he put his finger on the green patch in the middle of all the white.

116

'I'll sort that out,' he said in a flat voice. 'I'll paint it later, some-time.'

His brother still didn't react. He just brushed his hand over his eyes quickly.

'What did you do in those hours?' Bård asked. 'Can't you at least tell me? Eh? I'm your brother, for fuck's sake!'

'It was an hour and half.'

'Whatever.'

'You said hours. It wasn't several hours. It was an hour and a half. Barely one and a half hours.'

Trond Arnesen had managed to forget that tiny bit of secret time. It had been easier than he'd expected. Surprisingly easy. He left the whole episode behind on the way home. When the taxi that picked him up from the bus stop at twenty past six in the morning on Saturday the 7th of February stopped so he could throw up by the roadside, he'd tried to focus on the vomit in the snow. Bent double, with his hands on his knees, he recognized an undigested peanut in all the red-wine redness. When he saw the shreds of meat, he threw up again. The taxi driver shouted impatiently. Trond stood there. That was the last time, he thought to himself in a haze. He studied his own spew, fascinated, the revolting remains of everything he had consumed in the past twenty-four hours. And it was out now. Gone. Done with.

Never again.

He scraped the snow with the tip of his boots, wanting to cover the puke, but he lost his balance. The taxi driver helped him into the car. Took him home. Everything was forgotten and it was the last time ever.

Since then, no one had asked.

The stag night, from which he eventually crawled home, had grown during the course of the night. At six o'clock on Friday evening, nineteen men dressed immaculately in tuxedos had headed into town. Then they met Bård's football team, with dirty red shirts and a victory to celebrate. The party grew a tail. Things started to warm up. Ten or twelve of Bård's colleagues appeared at around eight o'clock, when the bridegroom was selling French kisses from a stall on Karl Johan for fifty krone a shot. By the time his brother slurred that Trond had to help him to the toilet to release the pressure at around half past ten, the stag night had turned into a blind drunk, random, rowdy bunch of men: the Skeid team, some economists from Telenor, a gang of bowlers from Hokksund that had tagged along since about nine, and the odd drunk who they didn't know from Adam.

At least fifty people, Trond thought.

And no one had noticed.

No one had told the police anything other than that Trond was at his brother's stag night from six o'clock on Friday evening until someone put him on the first bus to Lørenskog the next morning.

Everyone had said that. Everything was forgotten.

'What makes you say that?' he finally asked.

'Can't you just tell me where you were?'

His voice was no longer impatient. His brother was pleading with him now, a whining, demanding little-brother voice that Trond recognized from childhood and that still annoyed him.

'What makes you say that and why are you asking me now?'

After all, he was the oldest.

Bård shrugged his shoulders.

'What with everything that's happened . . . I've had other things to think about. But now, now that . . . You just disappeared! I looked for you everywhere. After I'd been for a slash. You helped me? D'you remember?'

Trond nodded but said nothing.

'You were the only who wasn't absolutely trashed. I wanted to borrow some money. Used over three thousand krone. Think I bought rounds for everyone. You weren't there. Couldn't find you anywhere.'

'Did you ask anyone where I was?'

'Everyone was asking where everyone was all the time! Don't you remember? We just about had the run of the place. It was mad.' He grinned, then pulled himself together. 'The next time I saw you, it was three minutes past twelve. And I know that fine well, because you made such a big thing about your watch, the one you got from . . .'

'My watch? I didn't have my watch on.'

'Yeah you did, cut the crap. When we had that beer-drinking competition, you stood on the bar and took the time with that monstrosity on your arm.'

Trond flushed. And then got hotter. He could smell his own body odour, sharp and bitter. His bladder was bursting. He wanted to get up. He wanted to go to the toilet, but his knees refused to help him.

'Why did I admit it?' he thought. 'Why didn't I just deny it? Bård was shitfaced. He might have made a mistake. Muddled up the times. There were so many people there. Everyone said that I was just mingling and drinking. Showing off. I should have denied it. I had every chance to deny it. I'll deny it.'

'You're getting it all confused,' he said, and clutched the table with both hands. 'I didn't go anywhere. You fell asleep on the bog. Don't know how long you . . .'

'What the hell are you saying? I know I didn't fall asleep! I didn't get to bed until eight the next morning. I was pretty pissed that night, but not enough not to notice . . .'

Trond forced himself out of the chair. He took a deep breath. Pushed out his chest and held his shoulders back. He was the big brother. The biggest, nearly ten centimetres taller than his brother.

'I need a piss,' he barked.

'Right?'

'You're my brother. We're brothers.'

'Right,' Bård repeated with a puzzled, slightly irritated look, as if Trond was wasting his energy trying to convince him that the world was round and circled the sun. 'And?'

'You're wrong. I was there all the time.'

'Do you think I'm a complete idiot, or what?'

He slipped round the table and stood in front of Trond, his fists

119

balled. Bård was shorter than his brother, but much stronger. Their faces were barely a hand apart.

'You admitted it ten minutes ago,' he hissed, his eyes narrowed. Trond felt a fine shower of spit on his skin.

'I admitted nothing.'

'You said that you couldn't say anything to Stubo. You said that you'd lied. Isn't that admitting, or what?'

'I really need a piss.'

'Admit it.'

Bård punched his brother on the shoulder. Hard, with his fist. 'Admit.'

Suddenly, without warning, Trond grabbed him round the waist. Bård struggled to keep his balance, holding on to his brother's shirt with his left hand as he tried to find something solid to hold on to with his right. A bit too late, he noticed that Trond's foot was in the way as he tried to take a step sideways. They fell over. As they went down, Bård got caught on the cord of the mixer. A survival instinct made him move his head when he saw the heavy Kenwood. The steel edge caught his ear. He howled and tried to lift his hand to feel the wound. His arms were pinned down. Only his head was free and he threw it from side to side as he shouted.

Trond punched him.

Trond sat with a knee on each of his brother's arms and let rip. He closed his eyes and laid into his brother.

When he was exhausted, he got up quickly. He smoothed down his hair, as if he couldn't quite believe what had just happened and wanted to pretend that nothing had. His brother groaned. Blood was pouring from his ear. One eye had already started to swell up. His upper lip was split. His shirt was torn. His upper groin was soaking, a dark butterfly-shaped patch on the khaki material of his trousers.

'You've pissed yourself,' Bård slurred, holding his ear. 'You've bloody pissed on me.'

He sat up, stiff and unsure if anything was broken. He studied his bloody hand and then put it over his ear again.

'Is the lobe still there?' he asked. His voice was hoarse and he spat some blood. 'Have I lost my earlobe, Trond?'

His big brother crouched down and looked at the wound.

'No. Nasty cut. The ear's all there.'

Bård started to laugh. At first Trond thought he was crying. But his brother was laughing, he laughed until he coughed, holding his knees roaring with laughter and spitting blood.

'What the hell's wrong with you?' he groaned. 'You've never beaten me up before. You've never even managed to tackle me to the ground. Have you ever had a fight before?'

'Here,' Trond said and gave him a hand.

'Wait. Hurts everywhere. Have to do it myself.'

It took him a few minutes to get to his feet. Trond stood help-lessly by watching him, hands hanging by his side. He scratched his thigh uncertainly.

'Worst thing is the piss,' Bård said and carefully shook a leg. 'In any case, you've still got an alibi.'

'What?'

'An hour and a half,' Bård said and gently tested one of his front teeth.

'What?'

'I can swear on the Bible that you were in the centre of Oslo at half past ten and around midnight. You wouldn't make it out here and back. Not without anyone seeing you, anyway.'

'I could've taken a taxi.'

'The driver would've told the police ages ago.'

'I could've driven.'

'Your car was at Mum and Dad's. All the boys know that, they picked us up there.'

'I might've stolen one.'

'Aw shit, this ear,' Bård said, and closed his eyes as he tried to move one of his shoulders. 'It's bloody sore. Do I need stitches?'

Trond bent down closer.

'Maybe. I'll drive you down to A&E.'

'You still have an alibi, Trond.'

'Yes, I was at Smuget. All evening.'

Bård bit himself gently on his split lip.

'OK,' he said and nodded.

They looked at each other. It's like looking into my own eyes, thought Trond, even though his brother was beaten and bloody. The same slightly slanting left eye. Green specks in the blue iris. The Mongolian fold in the corner of the eye, which his mother always said was so unusual in this country. Even their eyebrows, which were so fair that their foreheads almost looked naked, were the same. He had beaten up his brother. He couldn't understand why. And he found it even harder to believe that he'd managed it, Bård was stronger, faster and much bolder.

'OK,' Bård said, and wiped his nose on the back of his hand. 'You were at Smuget. All night. Fine.'

He limped towards the sitting-room door.

'I won't say any more,' he said and stopped. 'But . . .'

He turned around and took a breath.

'No one is going to think you killed Vibeke, Trond. I think you should tell the police everything. I can come with you, if you want.'

'I was at Smuget all night,' Trond repeated. 'So it's not necessary.'

Bård shrugged and limped on.

He was on his way to the bedroom to lay claim to Trond's most expensive trousers. Theresa, his fiancée, could take them up. He had a right to take at least his best trousers.

'You gave me a good bashing,' he muttered, impressed.

The visit to Yvonne Knutsen was not a success. Johanne had already been warned in the corridor. The nurse whispered that she was suffering from severe MS and refused to see most people. Only her son-in-law and granddaughter were always welcome.

The woman in white was right. Yvonne Knutsen clammed up the minute Johanne walked into the room. She lay rigid in her bed, which stood in the centre of the room. Otherwise the room was more or less empty. A faded lithograph hung askew in a broken frame on one wall and there was a wooden chair by the bed. Through the dirty, streaked windowpanes, the sharp light of the low sun that had blinded Johanne as she drove the last stretch to the nursing home had been reduced to a matt disc above the horizon. Johanne got nothing out of Yvonne Knutsen other than 'Please go away,' before the sick woman turned her head and pretended to fall asleep.

'I'm so sorry,' the nurse had said, and rested a comforting hand on her shoulder when she came out, as if it was Johanne's mother who lay there motionless, waiting to die.

The journey home was awful. One of her tyres punctured on the E18 on the way back to Oslo. It took a while to find a lay-by where she could pull in and the tyre was frayed to shreds. It was bucketing down and stormy, and by the time she got the jack out, she was soaked to the skin.

She finally got home, an hour late.

'MS is a horrible disease,' she muttered, and rearranged the cushions to get more comfortable. She was sitting on the sofa in her tracksuit, with Ragnhild half asleep at her breast.

'You think all illnesses are horrible,' replied Adam.

'No, I don't.'

'Oh, yes you do.'

He put a large spoon of honey in her tea and stirred it.

'Drink up. I've put some ginger in, so that should help.'

'It's too hot. What if Ragnhild moved suddenly and I spill . . .'

'Here,' he said with determination, and took up the baby. 'She's full. Drink up so you don't catch anything. Do you want a dram of something?'

'No thank you. It was so awful to see.'

'I agree. I had to talk to her just after the murder.'

Johanne lifted the cup to her mouth.

'Tell me about it,' Adam said, and sat down on the sofa facing her.

She pulled up her feet and tucked the cushions behind her back.

123

'Fiona has two children,' she said.

'Fiona, she's . . . she's got a daughter.'

'Yes, but she definitely gave birth to two children.'

Ragnhild burped. Adam put her over his shoulder and stroked her tiny back.

'I don't get it,' he said.

'Nor do I, in fact,' she retorted.

She reached out for the papers he had given her when she got home, soaking wet and grumpy. The bottom page was still damp and soft.

'In the journal of Fiona's pregnancy and birth, she is constantly referred to as a first-time mother. And I can assure you . . .'

She dropped the papers back onto the table and made herself more comfortable.

'A doctor or a midwife can easily identify whether a woman has had a child before or not. It's routine. But nothing like that is written in the papers. Fiorella was born by Caesarean and it was planned. As far as I can tell from Fiona's journal, she suffered from anxiety in connection with giving birth, which they obviously took seriously. A Caesarean on a set date, for no reason other than the psychological.'

'Yes, but . . .'

Adam put Ragnhild down in the cot, which had been moved back into the sitting room. He was rocking it gently with his feet.

'I don't understand.'

'Not so strange. Everyone thinks that Fiorella was Fiona's first child. The doctors too, even though they must have known it wasn't so.'

'But you,' Adam's brow was wrinkled with scepticism, 'you know better than everyone else.'

'Not me, the pathologist.'

She went out into the kitchen and came back with the teapot in one hand and the autopsy report in the other.

'*Perineal rupture*,' she read out loud.

'Which means?'

'Think about it.'

'I'm thinking. What does it mean?'

'Listen to the words,' she said impatiently, and helped herself to more tea and honey. 'I'm coming down with a cold.'

'Oh give over,' Adam said. 'Tell me what you're getting at. How can you . . .'

'Perineum,' she interrupted, '. . . is the medical term for the area between the vagina and the anus. A perineal rupture can occur during childbirth, when you get torn from . . .'

'Enough,' he said and pulled a face. 'I understand. But why the hell haven't we seen that? If it's there in black and white . . .'

He was put out and leant over the coffee table, grabbed the autopsy report from her and started to read.

'You just didn't get what it meant,' Johanne said. 'You simply ignored it. You were blinded by looking for some sort of sexual motive, so . . .'

'Ignored it,' Adam shouted. '*Ignored it?*'

'You're in good company. It's been revealed that in the Knutby case, the Swedish police shelved a possible murder because they didn't know what "toxic mass" meant. Don't you read the papers?'

'Preferably not,' he retorted, leafing frantically through the report trying to find something. 'But these new . . . What about that journal there?'

He tapped the other papers with his finger.

'Why would the doctors lie? Is the journal a fake?'

'Probably not. I rang my cousin Even – the doctor you met . . .'

'I remember Even. What did he say?'

Adam sat down in the sofa opposite her again.

'There can be only one reason why the journals don't include details that are so relevant for doctors and midwives, and so easy to verify,' Johanne explained.

'And that is?'

'That it would cause considerable distress to the patient if they were included. Considerable distress, Even said. And as far as I understood, great importance is attached to that.'

They sat in silence. Adam scratched his neck. The desire for a cigar had returned. He swallowed and stared out of the window, distracted. The rain was drumming on the windowpane. A car had stopped. 'Youths,' he thought. The engine revved up again and again. Someone shouted something, the others laughed. A door slammed and the car jangled down the road and vanished.

Ragnhild was fast asleep. Jack trotted in from the hall. He stood for a moment with his head to one side, ears pricked, as if he couldn't quite believe how quiet it was. Then he buried his snout in Adam's lap and pawed his thighs.

'Not the sofa,' Adam mumbled. 'Lie down on the floor. Down, boy.'

The dog appeared to shrug his shoulders and then crept lithely under the table and jumped up on to the other sofa, beside Johanne.

'Can you get that kind of injury from rape or something like that?' Adam eventually asked, without commenting on how badly trained the shitty-brown dog was.

'Adam, really.'

'But . . .'

'Imagine a birth. A child's head. Why do you think women get torn?'

Adam stuck his fingers in his ears.

'The answer is no,' Johanne said. 'Not from rape.'

'But,' Adam tried again and swallowed. 'Wouldn't a man . . . Wouldn't Bernt have noticed if . . .'

'No,' Johanne replied. 'At least, that's what Even said. Not necessarily. Not during intercourse or . . . other such pleasure.'

He smiled.

'Strange.'

She smiled back.

'But it's the truth.'

Jack growled in his sleep.

'So, to sum up,' Adam said and stood up again. He stroked his chin with his thumb and index finger. 'We can confirm the following: Fiona Helle was pregnant twice. The first child was born

126

under circumstances which meant that she tore badly. It must have been a long time ago, as there is nothing to indicate that Bernt Helle knows anything about the child. And nor does anyone else. Fiona publicly expressed her delight at being a late first-time mother. She would hardly have dared to say something like that if there was anyone out there who knew . . .'

He went over to the window. He could feel the draught. He ran his finger around the window frame.

'Damn me if it's not blowing straight through the wall,' he muttered. 'We'll have to get that fixed soon. Can't be good for the kids.'

'A bit of draught just makes it cooler and fresher indoors,' Johanne said, and waved her hand. 'Carry on.'

'No . . .'

He pulled and fiddled with the old-fashioned insulation tape that was about to fall off.

'I just can't believe that Bernt is a liar,' he said slowly, and turned to face her again. 'The guy's behaviour has been fine throughout the investigation. Even though he's no doubt sick and tired of our constant questions that never seem to come to anything, he always answers and does what we want him to. Answers the phone. Comes to us when ask him to. Seems to be well adjusted and intelligent. So I'm sure he would have understood that information like that would be relevant for us. Wouldn't he?'

Johanne wrinkled her nose.

'Um, yes,' she said. 'He probably would. I think we can at least assume that the child wasn't born after they became a couple. Gossip is rife in small places. They married quite quickly too, and I can't imagine that a normal, if very young, couple would have any reason to hide a pregnancy. In fact, I think the answer to this mystery is simple. It must have been a very unwanted pregnancy, when she was very young.'

'Please don't say it was incest,' Adam warned. 'That's all this case needs now.'

'Well, it certainly couldn't have been Fiona's father. He died

127

when she was nine. And I think we can safely say that she wasn't that young. But she must have been young enough to disappear or be sent away for a while without it causing a stir. Fiona was a teenager in . . .' She mouthed the numbers as she calculated. '. . . At the end of the seventies,' she finished. 'She was sixteen in seventy-eight.'

'That late,' Adam said disappointed. 'It wasn't exactly a catastrophe to be a teenage mum then.'

'Huh,' exclaimed Johanne and rolled her eyes. 'Typical man! I was terrified of getting pregnant before I was sixteen, and that was in the mid-eighties.'

'Sixteen,' Adam said. 'Were you only sixteen . . .'

'Forget it,' Johanne swiftly interposed. 'Can we just concentrate on the case?'

'Yes . . . But sixteen . . .' He sat down and scratched Jack behind the ear. 'Fiona didn't go abroad,' he said. 'Not for any length of time, anyway. I checked with Bernt. And I guess he would have known that. Even though not everyone I know likes to talk on and on about time spent studying abroad, I doubt that Fiona would have kept her mouth shut about—'

'Stop it,' Johanne said, and leant over to him.

She kissed him lightly.

'So, a child was born,' she continued. 'It isn't necessarily relevant to the investigation, but, on the other hand, it does bear an uncanny resemblance to her programme . . .'

'. . . That she presented so successfully for several years, and that gave her such a high profile.'

'Adopted children and grieving mothers. Reunited or rejected. That sort of thing.'

Jack lifted his head and pricked one ear. The house groaned in the strong wind. The rain was hurled against the window from the south. Johanne bent down over Ragnhild and tucked the blanket more snugly around the child, who slept on undisturbed. The stereo clicked on and off by itself several times and the main light above the table flickered.

Then everything went dark.

'Damn,' said Adam.

'Ragnhild,' said Johanne.

'Take it easy.'

'That's why I went to see Yvonne Knutsen,' Johanne said in the dark. 'She knows what happened. You can be sure of that.'

'Presumably,' Adam replied. His face was covered in great flickering shadows as he struck a match.

'Maybe that's why she didn't want to speak to me,' Johanne mused. 'Maybe the child has turned up, maybe . . .'

'A lot of maybes there now,' Adam pointed out. 'Hold on a minute.'

He finally managed to find a candle.

She followed him with her eyes. He was so lithe, despite his size. When he walked, he stepped heavily, as if he wanted to make a point of being so big. But as he crouched in front of the fireplace, tearing newspaper into strips, then reaching out for wood from the metal basket and building a fire, there was something light and easy about his movements, a fascinating softness in his solid body.

The flames licked the paper.

She clapped quietly and smiled.

'I'll cheat a bit, just to be on the safe side,' he said, and pushed in a couple of firelighters between the wood. 'I'll just go down to the cellar for some more wood. Power cuts can last a while in weather like this. Where's the torch?'

She pointed to the hall. He went out.

The flames crackled warmly and threw a golden-red light out into the sitting room. Johanne could already feel the heat on her face. Once again she tucked the blanket in around her daughter and was grateful that Kristiane was at Isak's. She took the woollen blanket that was lying over the back of the sofa and wrapped it around her legs, then leant back and shut her eyes.

Adam should talk to the doctor who was there at the birth. Or the midwife. They would both cite the duty of confidentiality, but

129

would give in in the end. They always did in cases like this.

It would take time though, Johanne realized.

If there was actually a living adult descendant of Fiona Helle, they might be getting close to something that resembled a clue. A pretty flimsy one, to be sure, and it might lead to nothing. He or she wouldn't be the first child in history born out of wedlock and adopted into a loving family. Probably a perfectly normal twenty-something person – maybe a student, or a carpenter with a Volvo and two snotty children. Not a cold-blooded murderer with a need to avenge the rejection a quarter of a century earlier.

But when she died, Fiona's tongue had been split and cut out.

The child was Fiona's great lie.

Vibeke Heinerback had been nailed to the wall.

Two women. Two cases.

An illegitimate child.

Johanne sat up suddenly. She was just about to nod off when a feeling of déjà vu ran through her again, the uncomfortable feeling that there was something important she couldn't grasp. She lifted Jack closer and laid her face on the dog's fur.

'Can we talk about something else?' she asked when Adam came back with his arms full of wood.

He put down the wood.

'Of course we can,' he said, and kissed her on the head. 'We can talk about whatever you want to. The fact that I want a new horse, for example.'

'New horse? I've said it a thousand times: no new horse.'

'We'll see,' Adam laughed as he went out to the kitchen. 'Kristiane's on my side. And I'm sure Ragnhild is too. And Jack. That's four against one.'

Johanne wanted to respond to his laughter, but the feeling of unease still clung to her body, the remnants of a fleeting premonition of danger.

'Forget it,' she said. 'You can just forget the horse.'

Eight

The storm had died down. The wind was still blowing strong, but the clouds had opened to reveal light-blue stripes to the south. Old dirty snow lay compacted and rotting in gardens and by the roadside after the rain. Johanne tried to avoid the worst puddles as she manoeuvred the pram on the narrow pavement along Maridalsveien. Heavy traffic and buses thundered past. She didn't like it, so she crossed the road at Badebakken to cut down to the Aker River. Jack was pulling at the leash and wanted to sniff at everything.

The temperature was dropping and snow was forecast for the evening. Johanne stopped and tightened her scarf, then carried on. Her nose was freezing. She sniffed. She should have put a hat on. At least Ragnhild was warm enough, snug in her Baby Grobag with a sheep fleece under her and extra woollen blankets on top. When Johanne gently pulled back the edge of the bag, she could only just see her little face tightly tucked in. Her dummy was pulsing and Johanne could tell from the movements behind the thin, fine eyelids that Ragnhild was dreaming.

She sat down on a bench just by the nursery at Heftyeløkka and let Jack off the leash. He shot off down to the river and barked at the ducks, which paid no attention to him. They just swam around in the open channels in the ice. The King of America whimpered and barked and stuck an adventurous paw in the water.

'Stop it,' she muttered, scared of waking Ragnhild.

The cold wind ripped through her duffel coat, but she liked sitting here, on her own, rocking the pram, back and forth, back and forth with one hand. It was Tuesday the 17th of February. She could call at midday. In eight minutes, she discovered when she looked at her mobile phone. Fiona Helle's best friend had said that she would be back in the office by then. She seemed puzzled, but happy to talk. Johanne had not introduced herself as a police-woman, but her vague phraseology might have given Sara Brubakk the impression that her inquiry was of an official nature.

Not good.

It wasn't like her. In fact, she wanted to pull out of the case, not get in any deeper, and certainly not using methods that verged on unacceptable.

Johanne blew her nose. She was getting a cold, as expected.

There were no people around. Then a jogger came puffing by in a cloud of condensation. He nodded and smiled, but then jumped when Jack came tearing out of some bushes and snapped at his heels.

'Keep your dog on a leash,' he shouted and raced on.

'Come here, Jack.'

He wagged his tail as she tied him to the pram. Then he lay down.

It was twelve o'clock. She dialled the number.

'Hi, this is Johanne Vik,' she started. 'We spoke earlier this morning and . . .'

'Oh yes, hallo again. Just a minute while I sit down. I've just got in the door and . . .'

Scraping. Scratching. A bang.

'Hallo?'

'I'm still here,' Johanne confirmed.

'There. That's me ready. Now, how can I help you?'

'I've just got a couple of questions about Fiona Helle's time in secondary school. You were in her class, weren't you?'

'Yes. As I said when I was questioned, Fiona and I were at school together from primary one. We were inseparable. Always friends. It's just been so awful since . . . I couldn't face coming back to work until a week ago, in fact. Got compassionate leave. My boss is so . . .'

'I understand,' Johanne assured her. 'And I definitely won't keep you long. I just wanted to find out if Fiona was ever . . . away from school? For a long period of time, I mean.'

'Away from school . . .'

'Yes. Not just for a few days because she had a cold, I mean, something longer.'

'She was away at Modum Bad in first year. For quite a long time.'

'Sorry?' Johanne wasn't cold any more. She switched the phone to her right hand and asked again. 'Sorry, what did you just say?'

'Fiona had some kind of nervous breakdown, I think. It was never really talked about. We were about to go back to school after the holidays. I remember I'd been in France all summer with my family, so I was really looking forward to seeing Fiona again. We . . . She didn't come. She was in hospital.'

'At Modum Bad?'

'Well . . . to tell the truth, I'm not sure. I've always just presumed it was Modum Bad because I didn't know of anywhere else you could go for that sort of thing. Breakdowns, I mean.'

'How do you know it was a breakdown?'

Silence.

More scraping, not as loud this time.

'Now that you ask,' Sara Brubakk said slowly, '. . . I'm actually not sure about any of it. Except that she wasn't there. For a long time. I seem to remember that she wasn't back until after Christmas. Or no . . . she came back just before. We always had a school show and started rehearsals at the beginning of December.'

'School show? Right after a nervous breakdown?'

Jack growled at an over-confident drake. It puffed out its feathers and tried to take a piece of bread that was only a couple of metres from the dog's snout.

'Quiet,' Johanne said.

'Excuse me?'

'Sorry. I'm talking to the dog. So, did Fiona take part? Did she tell you why she'd been away?'

'Yes. Well, not . . . Oh, it was all so long ago.'

Her voice sounded slightly apologetic. But it also sounded as if she really wanted to help.

'Like I said, we were best friends. Talked about everything and anything, like best friends do. But I remember that I was a bit put out, hurt, that Fiona didn't really want to tell me where she'd been and what was actually wrong with her. That I'm sure about. I remember my mother said I should just let it lie. That kind of . . . sickness was never easy.'

'But Modum Bad and the nervous breakdown could easily be your own conclusions, not necessarily something you knew or are certain about,' Johanne summarized.

'Yes, I'm afraid so.'

'Could you just give me an idea of what she was like when she came back?'

'No . . . what she was like? Just normal, really. Like before. I hadn't seen her for, well . . . five months, it must have been. From midsummer until the end of November. And at that age you grow up so fast. But we were best friends. Still, I should say.'

A group from the nursery walked by, two by two, hand in hand, waddling down the path in their oversized winter clothes. A little fellow with his hat down over his eyes and a snotty nose was crying. A woman took him by the arm and called:

'Not far to go now, children. Come along!'

'Do you think she might have been pregnant?' asked Johanne.

'Pregnant? *Pregnant?*'

Sara Brubakk laughed lightly.

'No, you can forget that. Goodness, time showed that it was extremely difficult for her to get pregnant at all. You know that Fiorella was a test-tube baby?'

Johanne didn't know. In fact, there was a bit too much about Fiona Helle's life that hadn't found its way into the NCIS investigation files.

'In any case,' Sara Brubakk added, '. . . I'm a hundred per cent certain that Fiona would've told me if it was anything like that. We were like Bill and Ben. Pregnant? No, never.'

'But you didn't see her for five months,' Johanne argued.

'No. But pregnant? Absolutely not.'

'OK. Well thank you very much for your time.'

'Was that all?'

'For the moment, yes. Thank you.'

'Are you getting anywhere with the case?'

'We generally manage to solve them,' Johanne said evasively. 'It just takes time. I realize that it must be very difficult for you all. Family and friends.'

'Yes. Just give me a call if there's anything else I can do. I am more than willing to help.'

'Thank you, I understand. Goodbye.'

The crocodile of children had turned into Mor Go'hjertasvei and disappeared between the blocks of flats. The ducks had settled down. They were sitting in groups on the ice, their legs underneath them and their beaks tucked into the heat of their breast feathers.

Johanne started to wander up the path along the river.

'For a long time there were no secrets in this case,' she thought to herself. Jack lolloped obediently along beside her. 'It was remarkably free of hate and secrets. But then they popped up. As they always do, in all cases, after all murders. Lies. Half-truths. Veiled facts and forgotten, hidden stories.'

Ragnhild started to cry. Johanne looked into the pram. Her toothless gums were bared in a furious howl. Her mother filled the gaping hole with the dummy. All was quiet.

She had pondered on it for a long time. Why both cases, Fiona's and Vibeke's, were so strangely free of contradictions and underlying conflicts.

She picked up speed. The wind was bitter and biting. Ragnhild would wake up properly soon. They had to get home.

'Maternal rejection has ended in murder before this,' she mused as she struggled with the pavement edge in Bergensgate. 'But why nearly twenty-six years later? Had the child, now an adult, only just found out the truth? Could the revelation of a past betrayal have stirred such hate? Could it be the driving force behind a murder like this, a gruesome, symbolic execution? Or . . .'

She stopped. Jack looked at her in surprise, with his tongue hanging out of his slavering mouth. A bus drove past. The exhaust made Johanne cough and turn away.

Maybe the rejection wasn't that long ago.

The thought had struck her the night before, when Adam warned her against unfounded speculation. Maybe Fiona Helle's secret child had only recently traced its biological mother. Ironic, she thought to herself, if Fiona herself had become an object of desire, like those she had exploited for entertainment, on which she had built her career.

'Don't speculate. Adam's right. This is too vague. And if the child really does exist . . .'

'What the hell would that person have to do with Vibeke Heinerback?' she asked herself aloud, and then shook her head.

It had to be two murderers.

Or maybe not.

Yes, two. Or one.

'I've got to stop,' she thought. 'This is madness. Unprofessional. A profiler uses sophisticated data programs. Works in a team. Has access to archives and know-how. I am not a profiler. I'm an ordinary woman out walking with her baby and dog. But there's something, there's something that . . .'

She started to run. Ragnhild was screaming in the pram, which rattled and shook and nearly turned over when Johanne slid on some ice as she turned the corner into Haugesvei.

When she finally got home, she locked the door and put on the security chain before taking off her coat and boots.

Trond Arnesen couldn't sleep. It was two o'clock on Wednesday morning. He had been up a couple of times to get water, his mouth felt like sandpaper, but he didn't know why. There was nothing on TV. At least, nothing that caught his interest, or at least stopped him from worrying, gave him some minutes' respite from his brain that was churning things over and over and keeping sleep at bay.

He gave up. Got up for the fourth time. Got dressed.

He thought he could take a walk, get some air.

The snow had started to fall at around eight. It lay like a clean, light blanket over the ground, over the rotting leaves and winter remains, dirty-grey snow banks and sludgy roads. The gravel crunched under his feet and the gate squealed when he opened it. He walked aimlessly up the hill, as if lured by the lamplight.

There was no way he could tell the truth.

He couldn't even have told the truth straight away, at the time, when he still had a chance, in that sweaty room with the policeman who looked like he was about to burst out laughing.

It had definitely been the last time that Friday, and it had been so easy to forget.

Then Bård came.

Idiot.

Trond thrust his hands deep into the pockets of his down jacket. He walked fast. There was no else around at this time of night and people had gone to bed in the dark houses along the road, hours ago. A cat darted across the road, stopped for a moment and stared at him with yellow, luminescent eyes, before disappearing between the trees on the other side.

He missed Vibeke. There was a vacuum behind his ribs, a longing that he couldn't remember ever having felt before, but it was like missing his mum when he went to camp as a boy.

Vibeke was so strong. She would have sorted things out.

The tears left frozen tracks on his cheeks.

He sniffed, blew his nose on his fingers, and then stood still. This was where the taxi had stopped for him to throw up. He prodded the snowdrift with the toes of his boots. It was lighter up here, with lamp posts every five metres or so. The snow shimmered like blue-white diamonds when he kicked it.

His watch suddenly appeared.

Puzzled, he bent down.

It was his watch. He blew on it and shook off the snow, held it up to his eyes. Ten past three. The second hand ticked loyally on and the date showed the 18th.

When he put the watch on, the plastic burnt ice-cold against his skin.

He was glad and smiled. The watch reminded him of Vibeke and he put his hand round the black watchstrap and squeezed it.

He should tell them.

He'd made such a fuss about the diving watch that he should let Adam Stubo know that he'd found it. Trond had simply been mistaken. He hadn't left it at home, but had worn it to the party and it'd fallen off when he was bent double puking up his guts.

The policeman might have moved heaven and earth to try and find the watch. And Trond didn't want heaven and earth to be moved. He wanted peace and quiet, and to have as little as possible to do with the police.

He could send a text message. That was the solution. Stubo had given him his number and assured him that he could phone whenever he wanted. Texting would be safest. It was ordinary and undramatic, the modern way to communicate trivial messages and minor events.

Found my watch. Had dropped it in the snow. Sorry about the fuss! Trond Arnesen.

There, it was done. He turned around. Couldn't wander the streets all night. Maybe he could find a DVD to kill time. He could take one of Vibeke's sleeping pills. He'd never tried one before. It would probably knock him out completely. The idea was very appealing.

He didn't care about the book that had disappeared. Rudolf Fjord could buy a new copy.

'Adam.'

She prodded him.

'Hmmm.'

138

'I'm scared.'

'Don't be scared. Go to sleep.'

'I can't.'

He gave a demonstrative sigh and pulled the pillow down over his face.

'We have to sleep sometimes,' was Adam's muffled response. 'Every now and then.'

He peeped out from behind the pillow and yawned.

'What are you frightened of now?'

'I woke up because your phone was beeping and then . . .'

'Did my phone ring? Bugger, I should've . . .'

His hands fumbled around trying to find the light switch on the bedside table. He knocked over a glass of water.

'Shit,' he groaned. 'Where . . .?'

The light exploded in his face. He squinted and sat up in bed.

'It didn't ring,' Johanne explained quickly. 'Just peeped. And then . . .'

'Jesus,' he mumbled. 'Great time to send a text. Poor boy. Guess he can't sleep either. Seems a bit weedy, to tell the truth.'

'Who?'

'Trond Arnesen. Forget it. Nothing important.'

He got out of bed and pulled on his boxer shorts.

'It's good that you've finally agreed to let Ragnhild sleep in her own bed. Otherwise we'd all be going round like zombies. As if we don't already.'

'Don't be angry. Where are you going?'

'Water,' he grumbled and pointed. 'Have to get a cloth.'

'Just leave it. It's only water.'

He hesitated for a moment. Then he shrugged his shoulders and crept back under the duvet. He turned down the light and held out an arm towards Johanne. She snuggled up to him.

'What are you frightened of?' he asked again. 'Ragnhild's just fine.'

'It's not that. It's these cases . . .'

'I knew it,' he sighed, and made himself more comfortable.

The light still hurt his eyes.

'Should never have got you involved in this mess. I'm an idiot. Can I turn off the light?'

'Mmm. I just don't think you've got much time.'

'What d'you mean?'

'What I say.'

'We all know that time is our worst enemy,' he said, and gave a long yawn. 'But then again, as we haven't even found one hot lead, it's better to be painstaking. Build stone by stone.'

'But what if . . .'

He suddenly pulled himself away and sat up.

'It's nearly three in the morning,' he groaned. 'I want to sleep! Can't we leave this until the morning?'

'What if the murderer was only out to get one of the victims?' she said slowly. 'If, for example, it was Fiona he wanted to get and then Vibeke was killed to camouflage his real motive.'

'Hallo,' Adam exclaimed and filled his cheeks with air. 'We're living in Norway. Camouflage killings! Have you ever even *heard* about that sort of thing?'

'Yes, lots of times.'

'But not here!'

His hands hit the duvet with a dull thud.

'Not in the tiny kingdom of Norway, where people generally kill each other with knives in drunken brawls! And in any case, one more murder is a pretty pathetic camouflage, I must say! *But now we have to go to sleep!*'

'Shhh,' she whispered.

'I will talk as loud as I like.'

'I agree that one killing is a poor camouflage. But that's why you haven't got much time.'

He stood up abruptly. The floorboards creaked under his weight. The water spilt and he swore under his breath. The glass rolled slowly under the bed. He pulled off the duvet and walked towards the door.

'You seem to get by on remarkably little sleep,' he snapped.

She could have sworn that his voice trembled, as if he was holding back the tears. 'But I can't. If you're frightened . . .'

His shoulders sank. He struggled with the bedclothes. Then he took a deep breath and continued:

'You can wake me, of course. But then you have to be really frightened. Absolutely terrified. I'm going to sleep in Kristiane's bed. Good night.'

The door slammed and Ragnhild started to cry.

'No,' she heard a groan from the hall. 'Dear God, noooooo!'

Vegard Krogh had never liked the woods that he had to go through to get to his mother's house. When he was little, he never dared to take the path unless it was broad daylight, and then preferably with someone else. There was a story that a ghost lived there. Supposedly the place had once been a graveyard. It had been levelled in the eighteenth century, with no respect for the dead. The poltergeists were taking their revenge, that was what the children in the neighbourhood said, and would hound anyone who dared to go into the woods after dark.

Total rubbish, of course, and Vegard Krogh couldn't be bothered to walk all the way round. It was late in the evening on Thursday the 19th of February. The snow that had fallen over the past couple of days still lay on the bare branches and covered the ground in a thin blanket between the trees, and thankfully gave off some light. He could at least see his feet in front of him.

He was carrying two desirable designer bags. His mother had lent him fifteen thousand krone without any hesitation and without the usual complaints that he was grown up now and a married man, so he had to sort out his own finances. Quite the opposite, she had handed him the money with a twinkle in her eye. In return, he had promised to spend a couple of evenings with her. Which was easy enough, with good food on the table and free wine in his glass.

Fifteen thousand didn't go far. But he was happy. When he was writing the day's blog, he was tempted to say something about the invitation. But he didn't. Discretion, he thought to himself, and stuck to giving an account of his shopping trip. It was an ironic epistle about shops where there were only five garments and two assistants who seemed so bored with life that they might at any moment put a gun to their head.

The most important readers would perhaps understand why he, who normally only wore jeans and hooded sweatshirts, had suddenly spent a fortune at Kamikaze and Ferner Jacobsen, the shops where he had eventually found something that he believed was both *casual* and *sharp*.

He had released three of the essays from *Bungee Jump* on his website. He hadn't asked the publishers about it. They didn't make any effort to get the material distributed anyway, so what did it matter? He'd release another two tomorrow morning. People had devoured them. It was only a couple of hours before the first discussions started. The piece about established popular culture, in particular, had generated debate. He used the milk carton as a metaphor for the welfare state's excessive mass production. They tasted of nothing, were of no benefit to anyone and were to be found everywhere in easily recognizable branded packaging, and were politically correctly recycled ad nauseam. The essay was called 'Skimmed Culture', and once he added a link on *Dagbladet*'s literature pages, things really took off.

Vegard Krogh walked with a light step. His new boots fitted him like a glove. The solid soles meant that it was no problem to walk on the muddy path.

Maybe he should do a bit more to get a freelance contract with NRK television. *Big Studio* was not exactly his thing. Too fluffy, obviously, and far too superficial. But the show was fast, and at times could be quite hard-hitting and urban, and Anne Lindmo was a babe.

He would push harder for the job.

Soon he would be out of the woods. He just needed to go round the bend, over the brow of the hill where he had once built a tree-house in an old oak tree, and then he would be at his old childhood home by the edge of the woods. His mother had promised to make him food, even if he was late.

Someone was walking behind him. Fear constricted his throat; he recognized the terror he had felt as a boy, when he ran through the woods, out of breath, with ghosts at his heels.

He turned round slowly. He noticed he was gripping his bags even harder, as if the worst thing that could happen to him was to be robbed of his new clothes.

He realized now that the person wasn't behind him. The person emerged from the woods, from between the trees, where there was no path, leaving a necklace of black, uneven footsteps in the new snow. It was difficult to see anything other than the outline of the body. Vegard Krogh was nearly blinded by the beam from a powerful torch.

Unusual outfit, he noticed.

A white boiler suit.

It rustled quietly.

His fear receded somewhat.

'Bloody hell,' Vegard Krogh said, holding up his arm to shield his eyes from the bright light. 'You'll scare people sneaking round like that.'

The torch was lowered and turned; now it lit up the other person's face. From below, like the big boys had done when they tried to frighten the younger kids on those dusky summer nights, when they dared each other to make a terrifying dash over the living dead.

'You?' Vegard Krogh said in surprise and irritation; he squinted and looked at the face more closely. 'You? Is this . . .?'

He leant forwards, furious now.

'What are you . . . you've got a bloody . . .'

He didn't die when the two-kilo torch hit him with great force on the temple. He simply collapsed and sank to his knees.

The torch struck him again, this time on the back of the head, with a cracking, fleshy sound that would possibly have fascinated him had he been able to hear. But Vegard Krogh was deaf to it. He died before his body hit the freezing, muddy ground.

Nine

The first thing that struck Adam Stubo as he followed Sigmund Berli and Bernt Helle in through the glass doors of the yellow nursing home just outside Oslo, on the morning of the 20th of February, was the institutional smell. He could not fathom why people in need of nursing care should be forced to live with the reek of overcooked fish and strong detergents. The public sector might well be struggling, but fresh air was free, after all. When he came into the room where Yvonne Knutsen lay immobile in bed for the third year running, he could hardly resist the urge to open the window.

'Yvonne,' Bernt Helle said. 'It's me. I've got the police with me today. Are you asleep?'

'No.'

She turned her face towards her son-in-law. Her smile was reserved. Bernt Helle laid his hand on her lower arm and gave her a quick peck on the cheek. Then he pulled the only chair in the room over to the bed and sat down. Adam and Sigmund stayed standing just inside the door.

'I know that you don't like talking to anyone,' Bernt Helle said, and wrapped his great hand round Yvonne Knutsen's emaciated hand, with blood vessels that traced blue just under the skin. 'Apart from me and Fiorella, that is. But this is quite important. You see . . .'

He ran his hand over his hair and gave an audible sigh.

'What is it?' Yvonne asked.

'You see, something has happened . . .'

Again he faltered. He fiddled with a tape measure that was poking out of one of the pockets in his khaki dungarees.

Adam approached the bed.

'Adam Stubo,' he said, and raised his hand in greeting. 'I've been here before. Just after . . .'

'Yes, I remember that,' Yvonne Knutsen said. 'Unfortunately I'm not senile yet. As far as I can remember, you promised not to bother me again.'

'Yes, that's true,' Adam nodded. 'But I'm afraid the situation has changed.'

'Not for me,' Yvonne replied.

'There's been another murder,' Adam told her.

'I see,' said the paralysed woman.

'And once again, the victim is a celebrity.'

'Who?'

'Vegard Krogh,' Adam said.

'Never heard of the man.'

'Well, there's famous and there's famous. It's all relative. The point is that we . . .'

'The point is that I'm lying here waiting to die,' Yvonne Knutsen said in a very calm voice, without a trace of hysteria or self-pity. 'The sooner the better. And while I'm waiting, I don't want to be disturbed. Or to talk to anyone. A modest request, if you ask me. Given my condition.'

Adam glanced swiftly up and down the quilt. Not even the slightest movement to indicate that the person lying there was alive; not even her chest rose visibly beneath the covers. Only her face showed the traces of what had once been a beautiful woman, high forehead and big almond eyes. Her mouth was reduced to a slit between sunken cheeks. But there was still enough information in the pale death mask for Adam to catch a glimpse of Yvonne Knutsen as she must once have been, straight-backed, confident and attractive.

'I understand,' he said. 'Really I do. The problem is that I unfortunately can't comply with your wish. The situation is now so serious that we have to follow what leads we have.'

'As I said, I don't know anyone called Vegard Krag and can . . .'

'Krogh,' Sigmund corrected from where he was standing in the middle of the floor. 'Vegard Krogh.'

'Krogh,' she repeated weakly without even looking in Sigmund's direction. 'I don't know anyone by that name. So I don't see how I can help you.'

'I've got some questions about Fiona's children,' Adam said quietly.

'Fiorella?' asked the woman in the bed, surprised, looking from Adam to Bernt and back. 'What about her?'

'Not Fiorella,' Adam explained. 'Her first child. I'd like to know a bit more about the baby Fiona had when she was a teenager.'

Yvonne Knutsen suddenly changed. Her nose reddened. Colour spread quickly, like butterfly wings, over her grey skin. Her breathing was faster and deeper and she made a vain attempt to sit up in bed. Her mouth grew. She licked her lips and they became redder and plumper. Her eyes, which only a moment ago had looked like they'd died already, now sparked with great distress.

Bernt carefully laid his hand on her chest.

'Take it easy,' he said.

'Bernt,' she gasped.

'It's all right.'

'But . . .'

'Relax.'

Adam Stubo moved even closer. He leant against the high bedframe and bent down over the sick woman.

'I realize that this must be very distressing . . .'

Bernt Helle pushed him away. For the first time during the long, fruitless investigation into Fiona's murder, his behaviour was aggressive. He didn't relent until Adam was standing about a metre from the bed. Then he stroked Yvonne's hair.

'Actually, hearing this has been a relief for me,' he said in a quiet voice, as if the police were no longer there. 'Fiona was so . . . always searching, you know. I often wondered why. I don't under-

146

stand why it would've been so hard to tell me, though, after all these years, so many . . .'

There was an edge of repressed anger in his voice, which he heard himself and swallowed. Adam noticed that the grip on his mother-in-law's hand was firmer when he continued:

'I accept that there's a lot of this I don't understand. We have to talk. Properly, I mean. But right now you have to answer Stubo's questions. It's important, Yvonne. Please.'

She was crying silently. Her tears were as big as raindrops. They gathered in the corners of her eyes for a moment before overflowing and running down her temples into her hair.

'I didn't want . . . We thought . . . It was . . .'

'Shhh,' Bernt comforted. 'Take it easy.'

'Her life would have been ruined,' Yvonne whispered. 'She wasn't even sixteen. The baby's father . . .'

Speech failed her. A fine stream of transparent fluid escaped from her left nostril and she wiped the back of her hand over her face.

'He was a good-for-nothing,' she said loudly. 'And Fiona was just about to start upper secondary. The boy ran away and it was too late to . . . I should have noticed, of course, but who would . . . Teenagers have a right to a private life too. And a bit of puppy fat . . . I . . .'

'Yvonne,' Bernt Helle said firmly, trying to look her in the eyes. 'Listen to me. Just listen to me for a minute!'

She had turned away from her son-in-law. She was trying to pull her hand from his firm grip.

'Listen to me,' he repeated, as if he was talking to a rebellious daughter. 'The two of us can take all the time we need to talk about this later. But what is important right now, is that the police get some answers.'

No one said anything. Yvonne had given up the fight with her reluctant muscles. She lay there helpless once again, bereft of energy. Even her hair looked lifeless, spread out grey and thin across the pillow.

'He's called Mats Bohus,' she said suddenly, the same old voice, dismissive and indifferent at the same time.

'Sorry?'

'Mats Bohus. He was born on the thirteenth of October 1978. I don't know any more.'

'How can you . . .' Bernt Helle started, but couldn't finish the question.

Once again, Adam approached the bed.

'And this Mats got in touch with Fiona recently,' he stated, as if he didn't need confirmation from Yvonne.

She mumbled in agreement all the same, without looking at Adam.

'Before or after New Year?' he asked.

'Before Christmas,' Yvonne whispered. 'He was . . . he is . . .'

Her nose would not stop running. Bernt Helle fished out a handkerchief from a drawer in the bedside table and gave it to her. She had just enough energy to lift her left hand and put the hanky to her nose.

'I sent her away,' she said. 'I sent Fiona to my sister in Dokka. Far enough away. Secluded enough to prevent any questions.'

Adam shuddered when the woman laughed. She sounded like a wounded crow; her laugher was hoarse, grating and joyless.

'Then she gave birth prematurely,' Yvonne continued. 'I wasn't there. No one was there. They just about died, both of them. Then . . .'

She gulped as she breathed in and then coughed so much that Bernt sat her up in bed. When the coughing eventually subsided, he carefully wiped around her mouth and lowered her back down.

'There was something wrong with the boy,' she said, her voice hard, 'but it was no longer our problem.'

'Something wrong with the boy,' Adam repeated. 'What exactly?'

'He was too big. Slow, heavy and unbelievably . . . ugly.'

For a split second, Adam envisaged Ragnhild just after she had been taken from her mother's womb, red, slimy and helplessly un-beautiful. He put his hand to his mouth and coughed. His eyes narrowed. Yvonne Knutsen didn't appear to notice his disapproval.

'What happened then?' Bernt Helle asked almost inaudibly.

'We forgot,' Yvonne replied. 'We had to forget.'

'Forget . . .'

Adam took a silent step away from the bed.

'The boy was given away,' said the woman. 'Adopted. Obviously I don't know by who. It was best that way. For him and for Fiona. She had her whole life in front of her. If only we managed to forget.'

'And did you manage? Did *you* manage to forget, Yvonne?'

Bernt Helle had let go of her hand now and was sitting on the edge of the chair, as if he was about to make a break. His left leg was twitching and the heel of his boot was tapping on the linoleum.

'I forgot,' Yvonne said. 'Fiona forgot. It was best. Don't you understand that, Bernt?'

Her fingers clawed the sheets, where his hand no longer was. His gaze was fixed on the crooked, faded lithograph. He leant back in the chair and cocked his head. His eyes did not leave the picture. He stared, blinked, and squinted at the abstract composition of discoloured cubes and cylinders.

'Please try to understand,' Yvonne pleaded. 'Fiona was too young. It was the best thing to do, to send her away, put the child up for adoption once it was born, and then forget the whole thing. Carry on as if nothing had happened. It was absolutely necessary, Bernt. I had to think about Fiona. And her alone. She was my responsibility. I was her mother. The boy would have a better life with mature parents, with people who could . . .'

'We're not exactly talking about the 1930s,' Bernt exclaimed, and pulled away from the bed even more. 'It was the late seventies! The age of feminism, Yvonne! Gro Harlem Bruntland and eco-activism, abortion and positive discrimination for women in the workplace, for Christ's sake, it was . . .'

149

He got up suddenly. He stood over her with his balled hands raised in a manner that was at once threatening and desperate. Then he lifted his face to the ceiling and ran his open hands over his head.

'For years and years we struggled to have children! We went abroad, to all kinds of clinics, we tried and tried and . . .'

'I think,' Adam interrupted tersely, 'that we should stick to your own wise words, Helle. These are obviously issues you need to talk about, but that can wait until later.'

The big man looked at him in surprise, as if he had just registered that the policemen were there.

'Yes,' he said in a feeble voice. 'But then I think I'll . . .'

He moved slowly over to the other side of the bed. The air in the room was stale. Adam could feel the sweat dripping from his armpits, cold trickles down to the waist of his trousers. He wiped his finger under his nose.

'What are you going to do?' he asked cautiously.

Bernt Helle didn't answer. Instead he straightened the picture. Gently pushed it to one side, then a fraction to the other.

'I understand that you need answers,' he said, still facing the wall. 'And I really want to help. But right now there's actually not a lot I can do. I shouldn't be here. So I'll go.'

Sigmund blocked the door.

'I'm not under arrest,' Bernt Helle said. He was at least a head taller than the compact policeman. 'Out of the way.'

'Let him go,' Adam instructed. 'Of course he's got the right to do exactly as he pleases. Thank you for your help, Mr Helle.'

The widower didn't answer. The door closed slowly behind him and they could hear his steps, hard rubber on polished linoleum, fading down the corridor. Adam took Bernt Helle's place on the chair.

'So now it's just us.'

The sick woman seemed to be even sicker now. Her flush had died down. Her face was not as grey as when they arrived, but it now had a frightening bluish-white tint. Her eyelids slid shut. Her lower lip was trembling, the only indication that Yvonne Knutsen was still alive.

'I understand that this is difficult,' Adam tried. 'And I won't bother you for much longer. I just want to know what happened . . .'

'Go away.'

'Yes, I just want . . .'

'Go away.'

Her voice broke.

'What did he want?' Adam asked. 'Mats Bohus. What happened when he turned up?'

'Go away.'

'Does he live in . . .?'

'Please, leave me alone.'

Her hand fumbled for the alarm button that was taped to the side of the bed. He got up.

'I do apologize for all this,' he said. 'Goodbye.'

'But,' Sigmund Berli protested when Adam grabbed him by the arm and led him out into the corridor. 'We have to . . .'

'The man is called Mats Bohus and we know his date of birth,' Adam said, and looked over his shoulder.

Yvonne Knutsen was gasping for breath and pushing the alarm button again and again.

'How difficult can it be to find him when we already know that much?' Adam whispered and remained standing in the doorway.

When a coated man in his thirties appeared in response to the frantic alarm, Adam took Sigmund's arm again and started to walk away.

'It can't be that difficult,' he said again, as if he was trying to convince himself.

He glanced at his watch.

'Quarter past twelve already. We don't have much time.'

The air outside was cold and sharp, with a scent of spruce and burnt wood coming from a nearby house. Adam stood still for several minutes before sitting down with heavy movements in the passenger seat.

'You drive,' he said to Sigmund, who took his place behind the wheel in surprise and put the key in the ignition. 'We don't have much time.'

He didn't find it hard being on his own any more. In fact, he did whatever he could to stop people from coming. They were queuing up. His parents, especially his mother, rang several times a day. He hadn't seen hide nor hair of his brother since the inexplicable fight, but friends, colleagues and acquaintances all seemed to think that Trond Arnesen had none of the qualities required for living alone. Yesterday, two old friends from school had turned up on his doorstep with homemade lasagne. They were put out when he wouldn't let them in.

He had read that normally it was the opposite.

He had read in the glossy women's magazines that he hadn't got rid of yet that normally the nearest and dearest were left in peace and quiet following a tragic death in the family. He had read how the death of a child often left behind an emptiness that the parents' friends and acquaintances avoided in silent embarrassment.

It wasn't like that for him. People were elbowing their way in. His boss at work had said that he should take it easy. Take the time he needed to grieve, was the expression he'd used on the morning he laid his arm around Trond's shoulders and offered to drive him home. As Trond accepted, it was difficult not to invite him in. The man was in his fifties, balding with a comb-over and a snub nose in the middle of his round face. His boss had sent stealthy glances in every direction, as if storing impressions that he could expand on when he got back to work. Finally he was satisfied and left.

Another celebrity had been murdered.

Trond put the newspaper down and went out into the kitchen. He had everything he needed for the weekend in the fridge. His mother had insisted on shopping for him. He opened a beer. It wasn't even one o'clock yet, but he had locked the doors, taken the battery out of his home phone and turned off his mobile. He wanted to be alone, right until Monday. The very thought gave him a boost. For the first time since Vibeke had been killed, he felt something that resembled peace.

The clandestine one and a half hours were nearly forgotten. He drank half the can in one go before sitting down in an armchair with the day's newspapers.

Even *Aftenposten* was making a big thing of it. The greater part of the front page and two whole inside pages were dedicated to the murderer who, according to the paper's grim comments, was a killing machine the likes of which Norway had never seen. Six columns were taken up drawing a speculative profile. They imagined that it was a man, obviously, with heavy features and unruly hair. The news desk had superimposed pictures of Fiona Helle, Vibeke Heinerback and Vegard Krogh across his chest. There was no more talk of a woman hater who had been rejected by his mother. Rather, they veered towards the idea of an unsuccessful wannabe. The underlying implication of a major opinionated interview with three well-known psychologists and a retired policeman from Bergen was that the murderer was probably to be found among the ranks of people voted out of the Big Brother house, unsuccessful Pop Idol contestants or Eurovision Song Contest finalists who hadn't won. The brutal killer had probably experienced his fifteen minutes of fame and couldn't cope with the withdrawal symptoms when the spotlight was suddenly turned off. That's what the experts believed.

Vegard Krogh was described as a rising talent, an uncompromising artist.

He was found with a pen stabbed in his eye.

Trond laughed so much that the beer sprayed out of his mouth.

Vegard Krogh was the world's biggest tosser.

The guy had hated Vibeke and everything she stood for. Lots of people did, but Vegard Krogh had not been satisfied with mere discontent. After one of Vibeke's harangues about culture's inability to adjust to market forces, Vegard had approached them at

Kunstnernes Hus. It was late on a Friday night and everyone was there. In a loud voice, he'd picked an argument with her. Then, when Vibeke turned her back on him with her little finger bent like a pathetic penis for all the others round the table to see, he had poured his beer over her head. Quite a scrum followed. Trond wanted to report him to the police.

'That'll just make him more important than he is,' Vibeke said at the time. 'He wants attention and I can't be bothered to give it to him.'

Since then, they had neither seen nor heard from Vegard Krogh, except for the odd barbed comment in articles that the *Observer* sent to Vibeke. She didn't care, but Trond got rattled every time he came across one of Krogh's rotten pieces. When the guy was given a short guest appearance on *Absolute Entertainment*, Trond stopped watching TV2.

A wanker of the highest calibre, he thought.

Vegard Krogh wanted to be a celebrity at any cost and had now finally succeeded.

Trond drank the rest of the beer and went to get another can.

He was going to be alone all weekend and decided to get drunk. Maybe he would have a bath. Watch a film. Take a couple of the pills in Vibeke's medicine cabinet and sleep for twelve hours.

The clandestine one and a half hours were nearly forgotten.

'A pen,' Sigmund Berli said lamely.

'Mont Blanc,' replied the pathologist. 'Type, Boheme. Appropriate, according to what I've read in the papers. I didn't want to remove it till you'd had a look.'

'How is it . . .?'

Adam broke off and bent down over the body. He studied the exposed face. The mouth was half open. The nose was covered in scratches. The unscathed eye stared at a point on the ceiling. Poking out of the other eye was a stubby pen. When Adam walked round the metal table, he could see that the writing instrument had been thrust into the corner of the eye. It went deep, he assumed, as only about five or six centimetres of the black pen could be seen, perfectly positioned at right angles to the cheekbone. A small jewel in the clip shone ruby red in the harsh light.

'Has the eyeball itself not been perforated?' Adam asked, and leant even closer.

The deceased's right pupil looked alarmingly alive, as it squinted towards the alien body in the corner of the eye. It looked like Vegard Krogh had realized that his favourite pen was on its way into his brain.

'Well,' the pathologist said. 'The eyeball has in all likelihood been destroyed, naturally. But he . . . the killer didn't stab the pen into the eye itself.'

'But he may have tried to,' Adam suggested.

'Yes. The pen may have slipped on the eyeball and then penetrated here . . .' He used a light pen and made the red dot dance around the corner of the eye. '. . . Where it is of course easier to get in.'

'Interesting,' Adam mumbled.

Sigmund Berli said nothing. Unnoticed, he had retreated a couple of steps from the metal table.

'So he was actually dead before this was done?' Adam asked.

'Yes,' the pathologist replied. 'Possibly. What killed him was the blow to the neck. As I said, I haven't done a detailed investigation yet, because I understood that you wanted to see him first. However, it seems to be reasonably clear that he was hit here . . .'

The red dot vibrated just above Vegard Krogh's left temple. His hair was matted and dark.

'Knocked out, more than likely. Then this blow to the neck . . .' The pathologist scratched his cheek and then hunkered down, so that his face was at the same level as the head of the victim. '. . . Killed him. It's a bit difficult to show you without turning him over and I don't want to do that before I've taken out the pen and . . .'

'That's fine,' Adam said. 'I'll wait for the final report. So it was a blow to the neck. Having been knocked out first by a blow to the left temple. With what?'

'Something heavy. Probably something metal. My initial bet would be a solid bar. When we have a closer look we'll no doubt find particles in the wounds, which will give us more precise information.'

'Then we can assume that the murderer is right-handed,' Adam said. 'Not that that's much help.'

'Right-handed?'

'Left temple,' Adam explained, distracted. 'Hit with the right hand.'

'Only if they were facing each other,' Sigmund said. He had gone over to the door and was sucking a sweet. 'If the murderer came from behind, he might . . .'

'They were facing each other,' Adam interrupted. 'At least, that's what the team who examined the scene have concluded. From the tracks. Thanks for your help.'

He held his hand out to the pathologist, who took it and then sat down at a desk in the corner.

'What's the matter with you?' Adam teased Sigmund once the door to the post-mortem room had closed behind them. 'You usually cope with worse things than that!'

'Fucking hell. A pen in your eye, come on!'

'Don't know what's worst,' Adam said, and groped for his notebook in his coat pocket. 'Pen in the eye, tongue in a nice bag or the Koran stuffed up your fanny.'

'Pen in the eye,' muttered Sigmund. 'A bloody posh pen shoved into your brain is the worst thing I've seen.'

A passer-by stopped for a moment outside the impressive building down towards the central station. He was in a hurry. If he didn't make the bus, he would have to wait a whole hour until the next one. But he still stopped. He heard clapping coming from inside. The applause was so loud that he imagined that he could feel vibrations in the ground, as if the enthusiasm contained by the solid brick walls was so great that it set the whole of Oslo in motion. The man looked up. He had passed this place, on his way to and from work, five days a week for five years. He had passed the building, which had stood derelict for a long time, and the neighbours had called for it to be pulled down, nearly two and a half thousand times.

He had watched new life being breathed into the building over the past four seasons. Last winter it had been wrapped in scaffolding and plastic, which shivered and flapped in the gusts of wind from the fjord. During the spring, the building had been reduced to a façade with nothing behind it, like a Hollywood stage set. And before the summer was over, the empty space once again became a four-storey building, with grand stairways and hardwood floors, beautiful doors and carefully restored leaded windows on the ground floor. Throughout the autumn, Polish and Danish swearwords could be heard from the scaffolding and the openings that still gaped in the walls, twenty-four seven. The papers wrote about overspends, delays and open conflicts about money.

The new party headquarters was finally unwrapped just before Christmas. Bang on time. The building was officially opened with a new Christmas play for children, performed in the beautiful, elegant auditorium.

The man looked at the façade.

Passing this building gave him inexplicable pleasure. The colours were an exact replica of what had been chosen at the end of the 1800s when the building was built as a residency and office for the town's richest entrepreneur. When his grandchild died in 1998, ancient and childless, the property was gifted to the party. As they barely had the means to pay the municipal charges, it had stood empty until yet another new liberal capitalist, appreciative of the party's high-profile tax policy, gave them an astonishing donation that allowed them to create the grandest party headquarters in the whole of Scandinavia.

The clapping seemed to be unstoppable.

The man smiled. He pulled his coat tighter and ran for the bus.

If, however, he had instead gone up the stone steps to the huge, heavy oak door, he would have discovered that it was open. And if he had gone into the hall, he would no doubt have admired the floor. Pieces of hand-turned solid wood spiralled out from a case in the middle of the floor, where the party's motto was engraved in pure gold, behind glass:

Mankind – market – moral.

The man who was now getting onto the bus three blocks further west was a loyal social democrat, so he would probably have been antagonized by the banal message. But the beauty of the entrance hall, with its hand-painted dome and crystal and silver chandeliers, might possibly have drawn him on up the stairs. The thick carpets would have felt like summer pastures under his feet. Perhaps he would have let the endless clapping lure him into the auditorium. Behind the double doors at the end of the wide corridor, on the opposite side of the room, he would have seen Rudolf Fjord behind a lectern, with his hands raised above his head in victory.

The man who was sitting on the bus, dreading admitting to his partner that he had forgotten to buy wine, might possibly have been astonished by the overwhelming display of jubilation at the extraordinary national congress, such a short time after their young leader had been murdered.

A new party chairman had just been elected.

If the passer-by, who was leaning his forehead against the bus window, trying to decide which of his friends might have three bottles of red wine he could borrow, had instead slipped into the back rows of the auditorium, he would have seen something that only Rudolf Fjord had noticed until now.

In amongst all the whooping, clapping and whistling delegates, there was one person who neither smiled nor laughed. Her hands moved slowly towards each other, in a demonstrative silent protest.

The woman was Kari Mundal. The man on the bus would have seen her turn her back to the stage and leave the auditorium, quietly and calmly, before Rudolf Fjord had had a chance to thank the delegates for their overwhelming confidence in him.

A sharp observer would have seen all of this.

But the passer-by had a bus to catch. And now he was fast asleep, with his head on a stranger's shoulder.

It was one o'clock on Friday night. Kristiane was back. She was always over-excited when she'd been away from her mother, and hadn't fallen asleep until around midnight. Adam had gone to bed about the same time. He didn't even try to convince Johanne to come with him. They had barely managed to talk in all the commotion. Isak had stayed until it was quite late.

Johanne knew that she shouldn't let herself be irritated by Isak. And yet she felt that she would never succeed. It was his naturalness that annoyed her most, the nonchalant assumption that it was always fine for him just to sit down, that they had nothing better to do than serve up food and small talk every time he took Kristiane home. Even now, only a month after Ragnhild was born, he ran boisterously round the house playing Superman, with Kristiane on his back and not a thought for Ragnhild who was sleeping.

'Just be glad,' Adam had said before he went to bed, with some exasperation in his voice. 'Kristiane has a good dad. He may be a bit . . . He takes liberties, but he does love that girl. Give him some credit.'

Maybe it was actually Adam's fault that she had no patience with Isak. He was the one who should protest. It was Adam, her husband, who should put his foot down, take the intruder to task, her skinny ex-husband who always cheerfully slapped his successor on his twice-as-broad back and offered him a lukewarm beer from the six-pack he usually brought every other Friday, along with a bag of Kristiane's dirty clothes. Always dirty clothes. He never remembered her toiletries.

'I've got some cold beer,' Adam always smiled.

Johanne refused to see it as a sign of weakness.

Compliancy.

She got up from the sofa abruptly.

159

'What's wrong now?' Adam asked.

She stopped and shrugged her shoulders.

'Nothing. Go back to bed.'

He was dressed. The sloppy fleece and grey tracksuit bottoms irritated her. She had given him a dark-blue Nike set for Christmas, to use at home. It still lay unused in the cupboard.

'Go to bed,' she snapped and went out into the kitchen.

'This has got to stop,' he said. 'You can't be angry with me every second Friday. It's not on.'

'I'm not angry with you,' Johanne retorted, and let the tap run. 'If I'm pissed off with anyone, it's Isak. But we'll just let it lie.'

'No, we can't . . .'

'Let it lie, Adam.'

And they let it lie. He wandered into the sitting room. He heard her filling a glass with water. She took great gulps. The thump of the glass on the work surface was harder than necessary. Then it was quiet.

'What about doing some work?'

His smile was timid. He grabbed her hand as she passed to go and sit on the other sofa. She let him hold it for a moment before pulling her arm into her body.

'A pen in the eye,' she said slowly as she relaxed into the cushions. It was as if she had to concentrate on showing any interest at all. 'Certainly very symbolic.'

'You can say that,' Adam nodded, still not sure where he had her. 'And for the first time we can safely say that the victim had enemies. Vibeke Heinerback had people who objected to her and she had fallen out with some politicians. There were people who were jealous of Fiona Helle and who talked behind her back. Vegard Krogh, on the other hand, had fallen out with everyone. Because of his behaviour and what he wrote. But mainly the latter, perhaps.'

'People like that are awful,' Johanne burst out. 'All cocky and hard when they're sitting at home behind their computer, but pathetic and cowardly when standing face to face with the person they're ripping to shreds. Unless they've drunk themselves stupid, that is.'

'Quite an outburst,' Adam mumbled under his breath. 'Is there any more wine left?'

She nodded and pulled the blanket more tightly round her.

'I think hotheads like that are OK,' he said, and put his generously filled glass down on the coffee table. 'Do you want some?'

She shook her head.

'Honestly,' she said with unusual passion. 'People like that ruin any kind of public debate. It's *impossible* in this country to . . .'

Her voice gave her a fright and she was quieter when she continued:

'There's no point in discussing anything any more. Certainly not in the papers. People are more interested in making extreme statements and elegantly crucifying their opponent to make themselves look good, rather than discussing an issue properly. Elucidating the matter. Being non-judgemental. Gaining insight. Sharing knowledge.'

Adam picked up the glass and leant back. He looked at her. Her hair was tousled and she had bags under her eyes. She was pale, like everyone else at this time of year, but he thought that there was also something transparent about her skin, a vulnerability that she was trying to hide behind the unfamiliar anger.

'Come over here,' he said softly. 'Don't take it all so seriously. People can be outspoken if they like. They generally don't mean to hurt people. Exaggerating things, arguing, a bit of passion, it's just entertaining. You mustn't take it too seriously.'

Johanne pulled in her legs and ran her fingers through her hair. Her lower lip trembled.

'Come to me,' Adam said. 'Come here, love.'

'I just get so angry,' she said quietly. 'I'd rather sit here by myself.'

'OK. That's fine.'

'Mats Bohus,' she started.

'That's his name.'

161

'Have you found him?'

'No.'

'Why not?'

Adam ran his hands through his fair hair, which was getting too long. He knew it looked stupid, thinning on top with a bit of a mullet at the neck and by the ears. He normally had short hair, which made it look thick and youthful.

'His home address is in Oslo,' he explained. 'In Bislett. Louisesgate. But he's not there. The neighbours have described him as being slightly odd. The woman across the corridor said he was away a lot. Never any trouble with the boy, but he's often away for long periods. Doesn't talk to anyone, apart from saying hallo on the stairs. And we get the impression that he looks a bit strange. Can you cut my hair tomorrow?'

'I can cut it now, if you like.'

He laughed and drank some more wine.

'Now?'

'Yes, this is when we have time.'

Jack wagged his tail joyfully when Adam shrugged his shoulders and got up to get the clippers.

'No walkies,' he said sternly. 'Lie down.'

The dog padded over to a corner, turned round a few times and then lay down on the parquet with a thump.

'Not too short,' Adam warned, and tied a towel round his neck. 'Not a crop, that is. I want some hair.'

'OK, OK. Sit down.'

He felt like a sheep as the clippers cut their way through the hair on his neck. The vibrations resounded in his skull.

'It tickles my ears,' he smiled, and brushed the hair off his chest.

'Sit still.'

'The killer really has had so much luck,' he said thoughtfully. 'If it really is one and the same man who is making his way through a list of Norwegian celebrities, he's either planned it meticulously or has a golden egg.'

'Not necessarily,' Johanne said and moved the clippers steadily over Adam's left temple.

'Yes,' he said stubbornly. 'Yet again, he has managed to get to and from the scene of the crime without being seen. As things stand now – and we've got thirty men from Asker and Bærum doing a major door-to-door inquiry. There's plenty of evidence at the scene and a lot of it is good enough to get a fairly detailed picture of what happened in the minutes before the murder. The murderer was waiting in the woods, let Vegard Krogh walk past on the path, then followed him, got him to turn around and then knocked him down. But there's nothing . . .'

The clippers cut into his skin.

'Ow! Be careful! And I said I didn't want a crop!'

'You'll look great. What were you going to say?'

'We're still pretty blank. No organic evidence. Difficult to conclude anything from the weight and size of the foot, except that the killer isn't the lightest of people. He's been lucky.'

She turned off the clippers. She stood behind him for a moment, thoughtful, without really focusing on anything.

'You don't necessarily need to have luck. If you're clever and careful, that might be enough. All the victims are public figures, more or less, and it is surprising . . .'

There was silence. The children were fast asleep. The neighbours had gone to bed. There wasn't a sound from the garden or the street. No cats. No cars or drunk youths on the way to another party. The house was silent; the new extension had finally settled and no longer creaked at night. Even the King of America was sleeping soundly and silent.

'I was at Lina's today,' she said eventually. 'Our computer is hopeless, and Lina's got broadband. It only took me a few minutes to find out that these victims, these . . .' She put down the clippers and squatted down in front of him. 'These public figures really are public,' she said, and put her elbows on his knees. 'Truly. Vibeke Heinerback's homepages have remained unchanged since her murder, it's . . .'

'Her family have no doubt had other things to think about.'

'I don't mean to criticize,' she interposed. 'The point is that her brother-in-law's stag night . . .'

'Brother-in-law to be.'

'Don't interrupt. There was a bit about the stag night with a link to Trond's homepages, where the reader had access to a detailed programme! Anyone who wanted to could have found out that Vibeke was likely to be at home alone that evening. Most people knew that she went to bed early, as she made such a fuss about it in all her interviews.'

'I'm not quite sure what you're getting at. My hair must look pretty strange.'

'It'll be fine.'

She stood behind him again and turned on the clippers.

'Fiona Helle was also pretty generous with her private life. She had told the whole world that she was alone every Tuesday. Vegard Krogh kept a blog, one of those incredibly self-centred things that the author thinks are interesting for the rest of the world. Yesterday he told his readers that he had to have supper with his mother because he owed her money. The revolting man really was a great . . .'

'What are you doing?' Adam turned round with a subdued cry. 'I said not a crop!'

'Ooops,' Johanne said. 'A bit short, maybe. Hang on a minute.'

She quickly took a few strokes with the machine from his neck up and over to his forehead.

'There,' she said with some doubt. 'Now it's even, at least. Can't we just say it's a summer cut?'

'In February? Let me see.'

She reluctantly passed him the mirror. His expression changed from disbelief to desperation.

'I look like a loaf of bread,' he wailed. 'My head looks like a big loaf of white bread! I said you weren't to cut it all off!'

'I didn't cut it all off,' she said. 'You look great. And now we have to concentrate.'

'I look like Kojak!'

'Do you think they lie a lot?' she asked, trying to sweep all the hair into a dustpan.

'Who?' he muttered.

'Celebrities.'

'Lie?'

'Yes. When they're interviewed.'

'Well . . .'

'I've heard some people admit it. Or boast about it, depending on how you look at it. I fully understand if that's the case. They create a pretend life that we can all be part of and then keep the real one to themselves.'

'You just said that they write everything about their lives on the Internet.'

'Bits of it. The safe things. It makes the lie more effective, I presume. Don't know. Maybe I'm talking rubbish.'

She emptied the hair into a plastic bag, tied it up and put it in the bin. Adam stayed sitting on the stool, with the towel round his neck. The mirror was lying on the floor, back up. There was a thin line of blood on his neck from a cut just behind his ear. Johanne moistened one of Ragnhild's cloths and pressed it to the wound.

'Sorry,' she whispered. 'I should have concentrated more.'

'What do you mean when you say you don't necessarily need to be lucky?' Adam asked. 'That this killer hasn't just been lucky as hell?'

'A murder in itself doesn't need much planning,' she said. 'Unless you're someone who will immediately be suspected, that is. If I want to kill someone who everyone knows I bear a grudge against, I would have to think about it. Make sure I have an alibi, for example. That's the biggest challenge.'

'A enormous one,' Adam nodded in agreement. 'That's why so few succeed.'

'Exactly. But bank robbery . . . then we're talking about planning! Money is far better protected than people. A successful armed robbery depends on prior knowledge and meticulously planned logistics. Expertise. Modern weapons and other cutting-edge equipment. But humans, we're so . . .'

She put her hand on his head. The cropped hair felt lovely against her palm.

'. . . So vulnerable. A thin layer of skin. And inside we're vulnerable too. A blow to the head, a knife in the right place. A push down the stairs. In fact, it's strange that it doesn't happen more often.'

'For a woman who I know has a good heart and who's just had a baby, you're painting a bloody grim picture,' he said, and got up. 'D'you really think that?'

'Yes. I said it just the other day. When Sigmund was here. The worst thing would be a murder without a motive. If we can't catch him red-handed, or he doesn't slip up, he gets away with it.'

'I completely disagree with you,' Adam said, spitting out some hair while trying to scratch his back. 'A murder also needs to be planned. Prior knowledge.'

She looked over at the bottle of wine. About a third full. She got a glass and poured herself some.

'Of course,' she agreed. 'You're right. It takes some skill. But that's all. You don't need much equipment, for example. None of the three victims have been killed with a gun, which you would have to get hold of, and also leaves interesting traces. The most important thing is that you can pull out. Right up until the last second. If something goes wrong, something unexpected happens or disturbs you, you can calmly walk away without killing the person. Especially as you don't need anyone else with you to commit murder. That's a huge advantage. What one person knows, no one knows, what two people know, everyone knows.'

'Your mother,' Adam laughed, and plumped down into the sofa.

'Mmm. Not everything she says is stupid.'

She followed suit and this time she sat next to him.

'It frightens me to think about the possibility that this person knows what they're doing. A . . . professional.'

'Do they actually exist?' Adam asked. 'Professional killers? I mean here, in Norway, in this part of the world?'

She tilted her head and sent him a look as if he had asked whether it was ever winter in Norway.

'OK,' he muttered. 'They exist. But would they not have a motive? A cause to fight for? Or some distorted reason, be it money or God's will?'

For a moment their eyes met. Then she leant against him. He held her tight.

'What do you think about Mats Bohus?' she asked in a quiet voice.

'We have to find him.'

'But do you think he's got anything to do with the murders?'

Adam sighed loudly. Johanne made herself more comfortable, pulled her legs up onto the sofa and took a sip of her wine. He ran his fingers up her under arm.

'It's easy to imagine that he might have been involved in Fiona Helle's murder,' he said. 'At least he has a motive. Possibly. We don't really know enough about what happened when he contacted her. But what the hell would the guy have against Vibeke Heinerback and Vegard Krogh?'

'Nemo,' said the nine-year-old in the doorway. 'Me and Sulamit want to watch Nemo.'

'Kristiane,' Johanne smiled. 'Come here. It's night time, poppet. We don't watch films in the middle of the night.'

'Yes we do,' Kristiane said and climbed up onto the sofa, forcing herself in between them. 'Leonard says that Sulamit isn't a cat.'

She hugged the fire engine to her body and kissed the ladder, which was broken.

'It's up to you whether Sulamit is a cat or not,' Adam told her.

'Only me,' Kristiane nodded.

'But I do think that Leonard will think Sulamit is a fire engine. Is that OK with you?'

'No, cat.'

'Cat for you, fire engine for Leonard.'

'And cat for you,' Kristiane said and held the sad, wheel-less toy up to Adam's face. He kissed the bonnet.

'Now you have to go back to bed,' Johanne said.

'With you,' Kristiane replied.

'In your own bed,' Adam said. 'Come along now.'

He lifted up the child and the fire engine and disappeared. Johanne stayed in the sofa. Her joints ached with fatigue. She felt weaker than she had done for ages. It was as if all the energy had drained out of her; the greedy baby's mouth sucked out what little she had left after the birth, every four hours, all day and all night; the little bundle made her anxious and weak. Of course she should spend more time with Kristiane. But there wasn't more time to be had.

Not even the nights were her own any more.

Mats Bohus could feasibly have killed his biological mother.

But could he have killed the other two?

She should really get some sleep.

She drank some more wine. She held it in her mouth, let it run over her tongue, tasted it, then swallowed.

If Mats Bohus wanted to camouflage his mother's murder, he had made a big mistake. He killed Fiona Helle first. The actual murder in a series of camouflage killings should never come first.

Elementary, she thought to herself. A beginner's mistake. No skill.

The murderer was professional. Had insight.

Maybe not.

She had to sleep.

There was another case. Something similar. Somewhere in her brain's hard disk was a story that she couldn't locate.

All was quiet. She was missing something without knowing quite what.

Johanne fell asleep and was not disturbed by dreams.

Sigmund Berli emptied his fourth cup of bitter coffee in three hours. Not only was it bitter, it was also cold. He wrinkled his nose. A bag of jelly babies lay on the desk beside his screen. He popped three in his mouth and chewed slowly. The missus wasn't happy that he was putting on weight. She should try sitting here at four in the morning, in front of a bloody computer that didn't want to tell him anything. The woman should try staying awake for twenty-four hours and then try to find some meaning in the columns, names, numbers and flickering letters on a bright square screen that made his eyes water.

It was sometimes hard to find a wanted person. Even in a small country like Norway, there were plenty of hiding places. The Schengen Agreement meant that they now worked with police forces in Europe, which helped when they were looking for someone. But then the Agreement also made it easier to cross borders and thus the number of hiding places had mushroomed. A wanted person could escape. But an ordinary Norwegian, a Mats Bohus, a pure-blooded Norwegian with no criminal record, with a permanent address and personal identity number – they should be able to trace him in a couple of hours.

They'd been looking for nearly twenty-four hours.

Gone. The man had simply vanished.

When they finally managed to confirm that he had been last seen at his flat in Louisesgate on the 20th of January, the whole NCIS went into action. Adam was probably the only person who was allowed to go home. New baby and all that.

A stab of envy. A wisp of desire; Sigmund saw Johanne's face reflected on the screen. He filled his mouth with three red jelly babies. The sugar crunched on his teeth. His tongue stuck to the roof of his mouth. He grabbed his cup, even though he knew it was empty.

Foreigners, all these bloody foreigners, they just came and went, in and out of Norway, as they pleased, as if they just came here for a dump. They played with the police. If only people knew. Some people were starting to realize. Luckily. Foreigners.

But Mats Bohus?

Fiona Helle had been murdered on the 20th of January. And since then no one had seen him. Where the hell was he?

'Hallelujah, Sigmund!'

Lars Kirkeland was standing in the doorway with his shirt tails out and red eyes. He had a stupid grin on his face and thumped the doorframe with his fist.

'We found the guy!'

Sigmund burst out laughing and clapped his hands a couple of times before stuffing the rest of the jelly babies in his mouth.

'Mmmm,' he said and chewed furiously. 'We have to phone Adam.'

She should have chosen another hotel. The SAS hotel, for example, with its Arne Jacobsen design and discreet, cosmopolitan staff. Almost everything you needed was there under one roof, so she wouldn't have needed to go out. Copenhagen was a Norwegian town, far too Norwegian, haunted by beer-drinking men in stupid hats and women with carrier bags and cheap sunglasses. Like shoals of fish they streamed backwards and forwards over Rådhusplassen, driven by instinct, between Tivoli and Strøget, always Tivoli and Strøget, as if Copenhagen consisted entirely of a big park with a bar at one end and a dirty shopping street at the other.

She stayed in her room. Even now in February, with an ice-cold wind blowing in from Øresund, Copenhagen was full of Norwegians. They shopped and drank and flocked together in the brown cafés, ate *frikadeller*, and couldn't wait for their next visit, in spring, when they could enjoy their beer outside and Tivoli would be open for the season once again.

She wanted to go home.

Home. To her astonishment, she realized that Villefranche was home. She had never liked the Riviera. Never. But that was before.

Everything was new now.

She had been reborn, she thought to herself, and smiled at the cliché. Her fingers stroked her stomach. It was more toned now, certainly flatter. She was lying naked on the bed, on top of the

170

duvet. The heavy velvet curtains were open and only the thin, semi-transparent curtain hung between her and anyone who might be outside. If anyone wanted to look in, if someone on the first or second floor on the other side of the street was looking in, if someone really wanted to see her, she was visible. There was a draught from the window. She stretched. She could feel the goosebumps under her fingertips when she ran her hands up her arms. Braille, the woman thought. Her new life was written in Braille on her skin.

She knew that she was taking chances now. No one knew that better than she did and she could have chosen a safer path.

The first one was perfect. Flawless.

But safety soon became too safe. She had realized that as soon as she was back in the villa at the Baie des Anges.

The constraints of boredom, the numbness of a life without risk, were something she had never thought about before and therefore never been able to do anything about. Not until now when she had finally woken up, broken out of an existence that was protected and padded by routines and passive obligations, where she never did more than she was paid for. Never more, never less. The days slowly accumulated. Became weeks and years. She got older. And better and better at her work. She was forty-five years old and about to die of boredom.

Danger gave her a new lease of life. Terror kept her awake now. Fear made her pulse leap. The days waltzed by, enticing her to give chase, happy but scared, like a child running after an elephant that has escaped from the circus.

'And you're dying so slowly that you think you're alive,' the woman thought to herself, and tried to remember a poem. 'It's about me. It was me he was writing about, the poet.'

The Chief claimed that Vik was the best. He was wrong.

'I am the base jumper, testing equipment that no one else dares to try. And she is the one standing on the ground, not knowing whether it will hold or break. I dive down where no one has been before, while she sits up in the boat and calculates how long it will take for my lungs to explode. She is a theoretician, as I once was. Now I take action. I am the practitioner and finally I exist.'

She slid her fingers down between her legs. She looked over at the windows on the other side of the road. There was a light on and a shadow was moving around in one of the rooms. Then it disappeared. She was cold. She turned her body towards the window. With open legs. The person who was casting a shadow didn't come back.

She could lead Johanne Vik a merry dance for ever.

But there was no fun in that.

No tension.

Ragnhild burped. A pale white liquid ran down her chin into the deep folds on her neck. Johanne wiped it off carefully and laid the baby back over her shoulder.

'Are you asleep?' she whispered.

'Mmm.'

Adam turned over heavily and pulled the pillow down over his head.

'I just thought of something,' she said quietly.

'In the morning,' he groaned and turned around again.

'Even though all the victims had strong links with Oslo,' she continued, showing no consideration. '. . . they were all murdered outside Oslo. Have you thought about that?'

'Tomorrow. Please!'

'Vegard Krogh lived in Oslo. He just happened to be out in Asker that night. Fiona and Vibeke both worked in Oslo. And they worked long hours. They spent most of their time in the capital. But they were killed outside town. Strange, isn't it?'

'No.'

He hauled himself up onto one elbow.

'You've got to stop,' he said, earnestly.

'Has it ever struck you that there might be a *reason* for that?' she asked, unaffected. 'Have you ever asked yourself what happens when a murder takes place outside town?'

'No, I've never asked myself that.'

'The Criminal Investigation Services,' she stated, and put Ragnhild gently down in her cot. She was asleep.

'The NCIS?' he repeated, in a daze.

'You never help the Oslo Police with murders.'

'Yes, we do.'

'But not with tactical investigations.'

'Well, I . . .'

'Listen to me, then!'

He lay back down on the bed and stared at the ceiling.

'I'm listening.'

'Maybe the killer wants to take on more? A stronger opponent?'

'Jesus, Johanne! Your speculation knows no bounds! And we still don't know that there's only one murderer. And another thing, we are *so* close to a possible suspect. And, and . . . Oslo Police are good enough. I would've thought that the most infamous villains would find them challenging enough.'

'After that Wilhelmsen woman stepped down, there's been rumours that everything's going to pieces and . . .'

'Don't listen to rumours.'

'You just don't want to even consider it.'

'Not at ten past four in the morning, no,' he said, and hid his face in his hands.

'You're the best,' she murmured.

'No.'

'Yes. They write about you. In the papers. Even though you never give interviews after that fiasco . . .'

'Don't remind me about it,' he said in a strangled voice.

'You are portrayed as a great tactician. The big, wise, strange outsider who didn't want to move up the ladder, but who . . .'

'Oh come on.'

'We need to get an alarm installed.'

'*Please* stop being so frightened, love.'

His arm was lying heavy on her stomach. She was still half-sitting up in bed. She wrapped her fingers round his. The telephone rang.

'Fuck!'

Adam fumbled around on the bedside table in the dark.

'Hallo,' he barked.

'It's me, Sigmund. We've found him. Are you coming?'

Adam sat up straight. His feet hit the ice-cold floor. He rubbed his eyes and felt Johanne's warm hand on his lower back.

'I'm coming,' he said and rang off.

He turned round and stroked his unfamiliar, naked head.

'Mats Bohus,' he said quietly. 'They've found him.'

Ten

The medical director of the psychiatric department greeted them in a friendly but rather restrained manner. He too had been pulled out of bed at an ungodly hour. It was still pitch-dark outside the windows of his office when he asked Adam Stubo and Sigmund Berli to sit down on the grey sofa. A woman with red lips and green hospital overalls brought them some coffee. When she went out, she left behind a smell of spring that made Sigmund smile at the door, which closed silently behind her. The office was tidy and quite cosy. On a shelf behind the doctor's chair was a sculpture that reminded Adam of Africa, masks and fat, headless goddesses. A framed child's drawing in vibrant colours brightened the room.

'I understand,' said the doctor, when Adam had explained why they needed to talk to him. 'Just fire away. I'll answer as best I can. Now that all the formalities are in place.'

Adam sipped his coffee. It was scalding hot. He looked at Dr Bonheur over the rim of his mug. The man was probably around forty and in good shape. His hair was even shorter than Adam's. He had swarthy skin and brown eyes. His name could indicate that he was foreign, but he spoke Norwegian without an accent. He was slim and moved gracefully when he went over to a small fridge, poured some milk into a jug and offered it to them. They both declined.

'Need the kick,' Adam said and chuckled. 'At this time in the morning.'

Sigmund yawned without putting a hand over his mouth. Tears sprang to his eyes and he shook his head vigorously.

'Been up all night,' he explained.

'I see,' the doctor nodded, his close-set eyes sparkling. Adam had the uncomfortable but distinct feeling that he was weighing them up.

'Mats Bohus,' Adam started. 'What's wrong with him?'

'Just now?'

'Well . . . I get the impression that he's in and out of here quite a lot. I'm not too sure about psychiatric terminology, so I don't know whether these illnesses . . . does he have a diagnosis?'

'Yes. He suffers from a bipolar disorder. He's a manic depressive. And yes, he's been coming here for quite a while. Mats Bohus has never been scared of asking for help. In that sense, he's a model patient. It's just a shame that he often comes here a bit too late.'

'Born 13 October 1978,' Adam read from his notebook, and then leafed on. 'Is that correct?'

'Yes. He came here for the first time when he was eighteen. He had been referred to us by his GP, who had been struggling to help him for some months. Since then, well . . . he's been here relatively frequently.'

'Does he come when he's manic or depressed?' Sigmund asked.

'When he's down,' Dr Bonheur smiled. 'It's unusual for people to feel the need for help when they're in a manic phase. Then they generally feel like they can take on the world. You should be aware that he . . .'

Once again, Adam felt the doctor looking at him, watching him, weighing him up.

'Mats is a very intelligent boy,' Dr Bonheur said. 'But as a child, he was not very good at school. His parents were wise enough to move him to a smaller school. A private school. Not that I want to press an opinion . . .'

He raised his hands with a smile. Adam noticed that the pinkie on his right hand was missing. There was only a stump, pink against his otherwise dark skin.

'. . . But the Steiner school was perfect for Mats. He's a . . .'

Again, there was some hesitation. It seemed as though he was weighing every word.

'He is an exceptional young man. Very knowledgeable. Plays chess like a professional. And he's good with his hands too.'

Adam had noticed the chessboard just by the door. It was free-standing and the squares looked as if they were made from ebony and ivory, in a hardwood surround. The pieces had been left in the middle of a game. Adam got up and went over to the table. The white knight on c3 was foaming at the mouth, its hoofs rearing above the pawn beside it, a hunchbacked man in a cloak with a staff.

'The opening move at Reykjavik,' Adam said and smiled. 'When they finally started to play after all the setbacks. Spassky played white.'

'You play chess?' asked Dr Bonheur in a friendly voice and came over to the table.

'Played. Don't get time any more. You know . . . But the world championships in Iceland were something else. Great moves. Followed it all the way. Then.'

Adam picked up the queen.

'Beautiful,' he murmured, and admired the cloak of blue stones and the crown with a band of crystals.

'But totally unpractical to play with,' the doctor said, and laughed. 'I prefer a classic wooden board. I got this for my fortieth birthday. I don't really use it. But it's decorative.'

'I thought one of the symptoms of bipolar depression was the inability to concentrate,' Adam said, and put the queen carefully back in place. 'Doesn't really tally with chess.'

'You're right.'

The doctor nodded.

'I repeat: Mats Bohus is an exceptional and special young man. He can't always play. But in his good periods, he enjoys a game. He's better than me. He sometimes just drops by for a game, even when he's not sectioned. Perhaps he gets particular pleasure from beating me.'

They laughed a little. Sigmund Berli yawned and yawned.

'What is this actually about?' asked Dr Bonheur, his tone suddenly very different. Adam straightened up.

177

'I would rather not say yet.'

'Mats Bohus is in a very vulnerable position.'

'I fully understand and respect that. But we're also in a . . . vulnerable situation. A completely different one, of course.'

'Has this got anything to do with the death of Fiona Helle?'

Sigmund suddenly woke up.

'Why do you ask?' he said.

'I'm sure that you know that Mats was adopted.'

'Yes . . .'

Adam drew it out.

'He loved her programme,' Dr Bonheur continued, and gave a fleeting smile. 'Videoed them all. Watched them over and over again. He didn't know he was adopted until he was eighteen. His mother decided to tell him the truth when his adoptive father died. He could at times be quite obsessed with stories similar to those on *On the Move with Fiona*. His mother died as well, about a year ago now. Mats talked constantly about trying to find out where he came from. Who he was, as he put it.'

'Did he manage?' Adam asked.

'To find out who he was?'

'Yes.'

A brief smile swept over Dr Bonheur's face as he said: 'I tried to get him to realize that the key to understanding himself lay in his life with his adoptive parents. Not in looking for someone who accidentally brought him into the world.'

'But did he find his biological parents?'

'Not that I know of. Evidently one of the social workers gave him some guidelines on how to trace his parents. But I don't think he ever got any further.'

'Why did you ask if our visit was anything to do with Fiona Helle, then?' asked Sigmund, and rubbed one of his eyes with his knuckles.

The doctor held Adam's eyes when he answered.

'I see I've hit the nail on the head.'

He picked up a pawn, thought for a moment, and then put it back where it was before. Adam picked up the same piece.

'How does his illness manifest itself?' he asked as he gently fingered the staff.

'Over the past twelve months, the intervals between phases have been shorter,' Dr Bonheur explained. 'Which is, of course, exhausting for him. He was very manic for a period before Christmas. Then he had a relatively good period. On . . .'

He crossed the floor and leant over his desk. Looked through a pile of papers. He ran his finger down a page and then stopped.

'He came here in the morning of the twenty-first of January,' he finished.

'Early?'

The doctor turned the page.

'Yes. Very early. He got here around seven, in fact. In a very bad way.'

'Do you think he's . . .' Adam put the pawn down again and looked at his watch. '. . . Awake yet?'

'I know that he is,' the doctor replied. 'He normally wakes up about five o'clock. Sits alone in the common room until the others turn up. Likes to be on his own. Especially when he's as down as he is now.'

'Could we . . .?' asked Adam, and raised an arm towards to the shut door.

Dr Bonheur nodded and led the way. He locked the door behind them and went over to the lift. No one said anything. They went in.

'I should let you know . . .'

The lift stopped. Halfway down the corridor, the doctor turned and finished his sentence:

'I should let you know that Mats Bohus has a . . . very special appearance.'

'I see,' said Adam, perplexed.

'He has problems with his metabolism, so he's very large. Heavy. And he was born with a harelip, which was operated on, though obviously not very successfully. We have offered him another operation several times, but he has refused.'

179

Without waiting for a response, he walked on. He opened a door and went in.

'Hi Mats. You've got visitors.'

Mats Bohus was sitting on a wooden chair by a Formica table in the middle of the room. His buttocks oozed over the edge of the seat and it looked like the man had problems getting his thighs under the table. He was dressed in a shapeless training suit. In front of him was a row of beautiful animals. Adam could make out a swan as he got closer. A giraffe. Two lions with glorious manes and open mouths. The elephant was shiny and golden, with a raised trunk and big, see-through ears.

'What are you making?' Adam asked quietly. He was right up by the table; the other two men were still by the door.

Mats Bohus didn't answer. His fingers were nimble, working fast with something that looked like tissue paper. Adam stood beside him and watched a horse being created, with great anatomical detail, down to the hoofs and raised tail.

'Adam Stubo,' he finally said. 'I'm from the police.'

Mats Bohus got up. Adam was astonished by the ease with which he pushed back the chair, put the horse with the lions and the giraffe, took a step to one side and turned towards him.

'I knew you would come,' he said, without smiling. 'But you took your time.'

The scar on his upper lip was angry and red. It pulled. You could see one of his front teeth, even though his mouth was shut. He had a small nose and his chin was invisible in the folds of skin that ran down his neck.

But his eyes were like Fiona Helle's. Slightly slanting and clear blue, with long, dark lashes.

'I don't regret it,' Mats Bohus said. 'Don't for a moment think that I'm sorry.'

'I understand,' Adam Stubo said.

'No,' Mats Bohus retorted. 'I don't think you do. Shall we go?'

He was already halfway to the door.

Eleven

Lina Skytter padded into her study. Her slippers were too big. The dressing gown must have been bought for someone else. The turn-up on the sleeves was at least twenty centimetres wide.

'Even though you're my best friend,' she said, and sat down on the guest bed, 'I hope you're not going to get in the habit of turning up at half past seven on a Saturday morning to borrow my computer. Don't you have Kristiane at the moment? What've you done with her?'

'With the neighbours,' mumbled Johanne. 'At Leonard's.'

A battered notebook lay by the keyboard. She hadn't opened it for years, but she had always known where it was. Thirteen years, she calculated. She had moved three times since then. Three times she had found the notebook in a shoebox of small secrets: a brass ring from when she was a child – she had been engaged to the best-looking boy on the street when she was five. The plastic name tag that Kristiane had round her arm in the maternity ward. *Johanne Vik's girl.* A love letter from Isak. Her grandmother's brown cameo.

The notebook.

Three times she had decided to throw it away. Each time she had changed her mind. The yellow notebook, with a spiral binding and a tiny heart on the second-last page, continued to accompany her through life. Once upon a time she had written W inside the heart. Childish. But then she *was* a child, she argued with herself. A girl of twenty-three.

'What are you looking for?' Lina asked.

'You'd rather not know. But thanks for letting me come again. Our computer is just hopeless. Virus-ridden and slow.'

'My pleasure. I hardly see you these days.'

'It's only a month since I gave birth, Lina! For the sixteen weeks before that I was waddling round like a duck, with pelvic dysfunction and insomnia.'

'You've always had sleeping problems,' replied Lina cheerfully. 'Can't you just stay here today? We could go into town when you're finished. Do a bit of shopping. Go to a café. It's no smoking almost everywhere now, so it wouldn't be a problem with Ragnhild.'

She looked out of the window. The pram was just below.

'They just sleep all the time at that age, anyway.'

'In fact they don't,' Johanne told her friend. 'Thank you for asking, but I have to go home.'

'Where's Adam? How are you getting on at the moment? Is he completely potty about Ragnhild? I bet . . .'

Johanne groaned loudly and looked at Lina over her glasses.

'I'm very grateful that I could come here,' she said slowly. 'But when I actually dare to disturb my childless, party-going friend early on a Saturday morning, it's because I actually have something quite important to do. Do you think you could leave me to work uninterrupted for a while, then we can talk afterwards?'

'Of course,' muttered Lina and got up. 'Jesus, you are . . .'

'Lina!'

'Fine. I'll put on some coffee. If you want any, you'll have to say.'

The door slammed a bit too hard. Johanne looked over at the pram. Not a movement. Not a sound. She sat back in her chair with relief.

In the olden days, she would still have been confined to bed after the birth. She needed peace and quiet, she thought every time Lina rang or her sister pestered her or Adam made cautious noises about how nice it would be if people came to visit. Just a light supper, maybe, or Sunday tea? As soon as he mentioned it, he could see her shoulders rising, and let it drop. Talked about something else. Then she forgot. Until the next time the phone rang, and someone went on and on about seeing Ragnhild, about coming to see them all.

She had to find a way to normalize her sleeping pattern.

She had to sleep.

Her fingers danced on the keyboard.

www.fbi.gov

She clicked her way to the history, mainly because she didn't really know what she wanted. Under a picture of a fluttering Stars and Stripes, J. Edgar Hoover was portrayed as an excellent and democratic boss: a model of neutrality, in political terms, for nearly half a century. Even now, well into a new century, over thirty years after the perverted director had died, he was still patriotically hailed as the responsible and visionary innovator of the modern FBI, the world's most powerful police organisation.

She smiled. Then she burst out laughing.

Enthusiasm. Self-confidence. The indomitable American superiority that was so infectious. She was young, in love, and she nearly became one of them.

The notebook was still closed.

She clicked on the link to the Academy. The picture of the building, surrounded by a beautiful park full of autumn colours, made her stomach turn. Johanne didn't want to remember Quantico, Virginia. She refused to remember Warren striding round the classroom, she didn't want to see his thick grey fringe that fell over his eyes whenever he leant over one of the students' shoulders, usually hers, as he recited Longfellow and winked his right eye with the last line. Johanne heard him laugh, coarse, vigorous and infectious, even his laughter was American.

The notebook was still unopened.

Opening the notebook with all those addresses loaded with memories would turn back the clock. For thirteen years she had banished the months in Washington, weeks in Quantico, nights with Warren, picnics with wine and skinny-dipping in the river, and the catastrophic, unspeakable turn of events that had ruined everything and nearly broken her.

183

She didn't want to do this.

She picked up the yellow book. It smelt of nothing. She touched the spiral binding with the tip of her tongue. Cold, sweet metal.

The picture of the Academy covered half the screen.

The auditorium. The chapel. Hogan's Alley. Demanding days, beers in the evening. Dinner with friends. Warren, always late, unfocused as he poured a pint of beer down his throat. They always left the others separately, with some minutes in between, as if no one knew.

The notebook would remain unopened. It wasn't necessary.

Because she remembered.

Now she knew what she had been looking for since Adam had come home in the evening of the 21st of January, exactly one month ago, and told her about the body without a tongue in Lørenskog. The story had touched something in her, light and diffuse, like a cobweb in a dark attic. The feeling had bothered her again when Vibeke Heinerback was killed and had been frighteningly intense when Vegard Krogh had been found a day and a half ago, dead, with a designer pen stuck deep in his eye.

But now she knew.

A glimpse of the secret, forgotten chamber was enough.

Ragnhild was crying. Johanne dropped the notebook into her bag, speedily exited the websites she had visited, logged off and pulled on her jacket as she was leaving.

'Oh,' Lina said, now fully dressed. 'Are you leaving already?'

'Thanks for your help,' Johanne kissed her on the cheek. 'Have to dash. Ragnhild's crying!'

'But you can . . .'

The door shut.

'Jesus,' Lina Skytter muttered and wandered back into the sitting room.

She had never seen her friend in such a state.

Calm, kind, predictable Johanne.

Boring Johanne Vik.

*

Mats Bohus had been in hospital for a month now. Exactly a month. He liked numbers. Numbers didn't argue. Dates followed one after the other, neat and orderly, without any discussion. He had come here four weeks and three days ago. It was five to seven in the morning by the time he finally made it to the entrance. He had walked and walked around Oslo all night. A cat had accompanied him the last part of the way, from Bislett, where he had stood looking at his own flat for a while. There was no one there. It was completely dark. Of course there was no one there, it was his flat and he lived alone. He was completely alone and the cat was grey. It miaowed. He hated cats.

Of course they would come.

He didn't read the papers.

Not the way things had turned out. It seemed as if the snow was never-ending. At night, when everyone else was asleep, he often sat watching the snowflakes dance in the night light. They weren't really white. More grey, or luminescent blue. Every now and then someone popped in to check up on him. They said that it wasn't snowing. They just couldn't see it.

'Mats Bohus,' the large man said to him. 'This is your lawyer, Kristoffer Nilsen. You know Dr Bonheur. My colleague is called Sigmund Berli. Do you need anything?'

'Yes,' he replied. 'I need quite a lot.'

'I mean, would you like a coffee or something like that? Tea?'

'No, thank you.'

'Water, perhaps?'

'Yes, please.'

Stubo poured him a glass of water from the carafe. It was a big glass and Mats Bohus gulped it down in one go.

'This is not an ordinary hearing,' the policeman said. 'OK? You've not been charged with anything for the moment.'

'Right, I see.'

'If we do find it necessary to charge you later, we'll certainly take your . . . illness into account. You'll be looked after. I just want to talk to you now. Get some answers.'

185

'Understand.'

'That's why your doctor is here and, just in case, we asked Mr Nilsen to attend. If you don't like him . . .' Adam Stubo smiled. '. . . You can have someone else. Later. If necessary.'

Mats Bohus nodded.

'As far as I understand, you were quite old when you discovered that you were adopted.'

Mats Bohus nodded again. The man who called himself Stubo was sitting opposite him, in the doctor's chair. Behind the doctor's desk. He thought it was impertinent. It was a personal desk, with a picture of Dr Bonheur's wife and three children in a silver frame. Alex Bonheur was sitting on the windowsill. It looked uncomfortable. Behind him, through the window, Mats Bohus could see the day dawning, a grey, matt light.

'Can you tell us a little bit about it?'

'Why d'you ask?'

'Because I'm interested.'

'I don't actually believe that.'

Mats Bohus had picked up the rook from the chessboard on the way in. He was hiding it in his right hand.

'Well, I am, in fact.'

'OK. I'm adopted. Didn't know anything about it until I was eighteen. Then my father died. On that day. My birthday. There's isn't much more to tell.'

'Were you . . . shocked? Surprised? Sad?'

'Don't really know.'

'Try.'

'Try what?'

'Try to remember. How you felt.'

Mats got up. The men's eyes were burning into his body, the same look that branded him wherever he went. They were all staring, except Alex, who gave a slight smile and nodded. Mats pulled at his sweater.

'I don't know how much you know about my illness,' he said, and crossed the floor. 'But for your information, it's hard enough for me to deal with the feelings I have already, now. More than enough. I have to say that I'm not very impressed with you.'

'Right, fine. Is there anything in particular that you're upset by?'

'Don't know that I can be bothered to stay here any longer.'

He had reached the door now. He put one hand on the handle and slowly opened the other. He studied the black rook.

'Tactics are nothing new to me,' he said. 'Your tactics suck.'

Stubo smiled and asked:

'Any suggestions as to how I can improve?'

'Stop treating me like an idiot.'

'That was certainly not the intention. If I've treated you like an idiot, I apologize.'

'You're doing it again.'

'What?'

'That attitude. That "poor monster" attitude.'

'Cut it out.'

Stubo got up. Came over to the chessboard. The policeman was as tall as him. He moved the bishop.

'That's wrong,' Mats said.

'Wrong? I'll decide that.'

'No, it's a set game. The opening of the . . .'

'Nothing is set in stone, Mats Bohus. That's what's so fascinating about all games.'

Mats let go of the door handle. His head hurt. He tended to get headaches about this time of day. When the place came alive and there were too many people. The room was overcrowded. The lawyer was standing in a corner with his hands behind his back. He rose up on his toes and then down again. Up. Down. He reminded Mats more of a stressed policeman than a person who was there to help him.

'I know what you're playing at,' Mats said to Adam Stubo.

'I'm trying to have a conversation.'

'Bullshit. You're trying to build up trust. Talking about harmless things. To begin with. You want to create a relaxed atmosphere.

187

Make me feel safe. Make me think that you're actually trying to help me.'

'I am trying to help you.'

'Really. You're going to arrest me. You think this pandering helps. Eventually you'll get to the point. That guy there . . .'

He pointed a stubby, fat finger in Sigmund Berli's direction. Sigmund was sitting on a chair, repressing yawn after yawn.

'. . . he'll probably turn out to be the bad guy. If your nicely-nicely tactics don't work. Pretty obvious really.'

The policeman had a small cut just behind his ear. The scab looked like an A, as if someone has started to carve his name on his scalp, but then changed their mind.

'This is just a waste of time,' Mats Bohus said.

The rook's embrasures were framed with silver. A minute miniature figure with a crossbow was kneeling down, aiming, in one of them. Mats poked the tiny soldier carefully.

'Do you not remember what I said when you came?'

'Yes.'

'What? What did I say?'

Adam Stubo looked long and hard at the young man. It didn't look as if he was thinking of leaving any more. The door was still closed and Mats Bohus was standing with his back to the others.

'You said that you didn't regret it.'

'Exactly. And how do you interpret that?'

'As a confession.'

'Of what?'

'I'm not quite sure yet.'

'I killed her. That's what I was talking about.'

The lawyer opened his mouth and took a step into the room, as he raised his arm in warning. Then he stopped suddenly, his jaw shutting with an audible snap. Dr Bonheur was sitting with his arms crossed, his face devoid of expression. Sigmund Berli looked as if he was about to get up, but changed his mind and sank back onto the chair with a grunt.

No one said anything.

Mats Bohus crossed the floor and sat down in the deep visitor's chair. Adam followed him with his eyes. There was a strange aesthetic in the way the young man moved. He rolled. His flesh rolled forwards, streamlined in waves, like a whale in the depths of the sea.

'I killed my mother.'

His voice was different now. His whole appearance was of a man who had just expended a huge amount of energy. The scar on his upper lip looked redder, tighter, he licked it with his tongue. His arms hung heavy on either side of the chair.

Everyone was still silent.

Adam sat down as well. He leant over the desk.

Mats Bohus seemed younger than his twenty-six years. There was hardly any sign of stubble. His skin was smooth. No spots, nor scars apart from the broad red stripe above his mouth. His eyes filled with tears.

'She didn't want me,' he said. 'She didn't want me when I was born and she didn't want me now. In her programmes . . . In interviews, she always said that nothing bad could come of families being reunited. Everyone else got Fiona Helle's help. She only turned her back on me, her own son. She lied. She didn't want me. No one wants me. I don't want myself either.'

'Your mother wanted you,' Adam said. 'Your real mother and father. They wanted you.'

'But they weren't real. As it turned out.'

'You're too intelligent to actually believe that.'

'They're dead.'

'Yes, that's true.'

Adam hesitated for a second before continuing:

'The others, what about them?'

Mats Bohus was crying. Big, round tears hung on his lashes before breaking and running down his nose. He leant slowly forwards, brushed the papers and family photos from the desk and buried his face in his arms. The glass of water fell on the floor without breaking.

'The others,' Adam Stubo repeated. 'Vibeke Heinerback and Vegard Krogh. What had they done?'

'I don't want myself,' cried Mats. 'I . . . don't . . . want . . .'

'I don't quite understand,' said Alex Bonheur, his voice sharp. 'First of all, I must insist that this . . . hearing ends immediately. Continuing is not advisable. And . . .'

He put his hand gently on Mats Bohus's back. The young man responded with some loud sobs.

'I don't see how there can be any connection between . . .'

'I'm sure you understand,' Adam said calmly. 'Even though Mats doesn't read the papers, I'm sure you do. As you know, there have been several murders with similar features and . . .'

'There's no question,' Dr Bonheur said, and sent a reproachful look to the lawyer, who was still standing there with his mouth open, not knowing what to say. 'Mats Bohus has been here since the twenty-first of January.'

Sigmund Berli was trying to think. His brain cells were asleep. He was so tired that he barely managed to get up, but he had to think and he burst out:

'But the man's here voluntarily. So he must be allowed to come and go as he pleases? Sometimes . . .'

'No,' Dr Bonheur said. 'He's been here all the time.'

An uncomfortable silence followed. The lawyer had finally managed to close his mouth for good. Sigmund held his hand up, as if to protest, but didn't manage to say anything. Adam closed his eyes. Even Mats Bohus had stopped crying. Earlier they had heard footsteps going up and down the corridor, people talking, a very loud scream, on the other side of the closed door. Now there wasn't a sound.

It was Sigmund who finally ventured to ask the question:

'Are you absolutely sure? One hundred per cent sure?'

'Yes. Mats Bohus came to the hospital on the twenty-first of January at seven in the morning. And he has not been out since. I can vouch for that.'

Sigmund Berli had never felt so awake.

The TV was appalling on Saturday night, which suited Johanne rather well. Every now and then she drifted off, but was woken abruptly by her own thoughts that mutated into strange dreams as she dozed.

Kristiane was staying with the neighbours. It was the first time she had stayed the night with a friend. Leonard had turned up with a written invitation on a piece of red A4, with big, bold letters. Kristiane's bedwetting, the fact that Sulamit had to be a cat before she could fall asleep, went through Johanne's mind. She hesitated.

'The fire engine can be a cat for tonight if that's what matters,' Leonard said.

Gitta Jensen, who was standing halfway up the stairs, smiled.

'That's true,' she said. 'Leonard would really love Kristiane to stay. And what with Ragnhild and having to get up every night . . . we thought it might be nice for you too.'

'I want to,' Kristiane decided. 'I'm going to sleep in the bunkbeds. On the top one.'

Kristiane was allowed to go, and now Johanne regretted it.

The girl could get so frightened. She was so wary of change. It had taken her months to get used to the new house. For a long time, she had woken up every night and looked for the grown-ups' room where it had been in the old flat, only to be confronted with a wall. Her disconsolate cries did not stop until she was allowed to sleep on a small mattress beside Adam's bed.

Kristiane would wet the bed. Then she would be ashamed and sad. She had started to register what was going on around her recently and was more aware of her differentness. It was a step forward, but also incredibly painful.

For Johanne, at least.

Adam had rung. He was brief. Said that he would be home late.

Johanne turned off the TV. But then it was too quiet so she turned it on again. She strained to hear sounds from the flat below. They must have gone to bed already. More than anything, she wanted to go down and get Kristiane. To have her on her lap, chatting

191

about strange, harmless things. Put a night nappy on the nine-year-old, which was invisible as no one apart from Mummy knew. They could play chess, according to Kristiane's rules, which meant that the knight was allowed to charge wherever it liked and it was the only one that was allowed to eat pawns for dinner. They could watch a film. Stay awake together.

Johanne was shivering. It didn't help to snuggle up in a blanket. That morning, in a home that wasn't her own, she had finally dared to peek into a room that had been closed for so long. She had been forced to do it. She didn't want to. She felt humiliated and pathetic, and she was cold.

If only Adam would come home soon!

She held Ragnhild to her chest. She weighed nearly five kilos now and her skin lay in small folds over her plump hands. Time passed so quickly. Her first dark baby down had almost disappeared and it looked like she would have fair hair. She could hold her gaze now, and even though everyone said it was too early to tell, Johanne was sure that she would have green eyes. There was a shadow of Adam's cleft in her chin.

If only he would come home. It was eleven o'clock already.

They were going to her parents for a family meal tomorrow. Johanne didn't know whether she'd be able to leave the house.

The noise of a door downstairs made Johanne instinctively hug Ragnhild closer. Her mouth slipped from the nipple and she howled.

The rattling of keys. Heavy steps on the stairs.

At last she could tell Adam what they were up against.

One murderer.

A murderer who had killed and mutilated Fiona Helle, Vibeke Heinerback and Vegard Krogh. There was a monster out there. The incomprehensible outlines of a plan that for the moment told her little other than that the murders were carried out by one and the same man.

Adam stood in the doorway, his shoulders sloping under his coat.

'It was him. Mats Bohus. He's confessed.'

'What?'

Johanne got up from the sofa. She was shaking and nearly dropped her daughter. Slowly, she sank back into the sofa.

'So . . . but . . . What a great relief, Adam!'

'He killed his mother.'

'And?'

'Fiona Helle, that is.'

'And . . .'

'There is no and. No more.'

Adam pulled off his coat and dropped it on the floor. He went out into the kitchen. Johanne heard the fridge door opening and closing. A can of beer being opened.

Adam was wrong and she knew it.

'He killed the others as well, didn't he? He . . .'

'No.'

Adam crossed the floor and stood behind the sofa, with one hand on her shoulders and the other round the beer can. He drank. His swallowing was audible, almost demonstrative.

'There is no serial killer,' he said, and dried his mouth with the back of his hand, before finishing the can. 'Just a series of bloody killings. Must be contagious. I'm going to bed, love. Exhausted.'

'But,' she started.

He stopped in the door and turned round.

'Do you want a hand with Ragnhild?'

'No, it's not necessary. I'll . . . But, Adam . . .'

'What?'

'Maybe he's lying? Maybe he's . . .'

'He's not lying. So far, everything he's told us matches the evidence we found at Fiona's house. We managed to question him again this evening. Probably not advisable, in terms of his health, but . . . He knows details that haven't been released. He had a clear motive. Fiona didn't want anything to do with him. Like you said. She simply rejected him. Mats Bohus said she was repulsed by him. Repulsed, he repeated it again and again. He's even . . .' Adam rubbed his face with his left hand and let out a great sigh.

'. . . kept the knife. The one he used to cut out her tongue. He killed her, Johanne.'

'But he might be lying about the others! He might have confessed about murdering his mother but lied about . . .'

Adam was still clutching the empty beer can.

'No,' he said. 'I've never heard a better alibi. He hasn't left the hospital building since the twenty-first of January.'

He stared at the beer can in exasperation, as if he had forgotten that he'd crushed it. Distracted, he looked up and asked:

'Were you going to say something?'

'What?'

Johanne put Ragnhild over her shoulder and pulled the blanket tighter round them both.

'You looked as if you wanted to tell me something when I came in,' Adam said, and gave a great yawn. 'What was it?'

She had waited for him for hours, watched for him from the window, stared at the phone, looked the clock. She had been impatient and anxious, longing to share the burden of what she had seen and remembered. But now it was only a coincidence, everything.

It couldn't be a coincidence.

'Nothing,' she said. 'It was nothing.'

'OK, I'm off to bed then,' he said, and left the room.

Sunday the 22nd of February had barely dawned. The streets were unusually quiet. Scarcely a pedestrian was to be seen on the main drag of Karl Johan, even though the clubs and the odd pub would be open for a few hours yet. A snowstorm was blowing in from the fjord, thick and furious, discouraging people from looking for a new watering hole. Even the taxi rank by the National Theatre, which normally generated its fair share of fights and arguments, was almost empty. Just one young woman in far too short a skirt and bad shoes was leaning into the wind. She was stamping her feet and talking angrily into her mobile phone.

194

'It's easiest to drive down Dronning Maudsgate,' said one of the policemen and put a piece of paper in his pocket.

'Isn't it better to . . .'

'Dronning Maudsgate,' he repeated crossly. 'Have I been driving these streets for years, or what?'

The younger one backed down. It was his first shift with the big man in the passenger seat. Rumour had long since told him that it was best just to keep your mouth shut and do as you were told. There was silence for the rest of the journey.

'Here we are,' said the younger policeman, and he parked the car in a snowdrift on Huitfeldtsgate. 'Can't find anywhere better to park.'

'Fucking hell,' muttered the other man as he unfolded himself out of the tightly parked car. 'If we have problems getting out again, you can sort it out. I'll get a taxi. Just so that's clear. I'm damned if I'm . . .'

The rest of what he said was lost in a mumble and the wind.

The young man followed behind his colleague.

'That's a bit of luck,' said the older man, having managed to pick the lock on the door in a matter of seconds, sheltered by his broad back. 'The door was open. Don't need a fucking blessing from any crappy lawyer. C'mon, Constable Kalvø.'

Petter Kalvø was twenty-nine and still clung to some of his childhood beliefs. He had thick, cropped hair and was well dressed. Compared with the unkempt man in jeans and worn-down Doc Martens who marched over to the lift in front of him, Petter Kalvø looked as if he had just been accepted at West Point. By the stairs, he took on a stern posture and put his hands behind his back.

'This is highly irregular,' he said, his voice breaking. 'I can't . . .'

'Shut up.'

The lift doors opened. His colleague walked in, Petter Kalvø followed with some hesitation.

'Trust me,' laughed the older man. 'Can't survive in this job without taking shortcuts here and there. We have to take them by surprise, you know. Otherwise . . .'

He winked at him. His eyes were frightening, one blue and brown, like an ice-cold husky.

They came to the third floor. The bald policeman pounded on a green door with his fist before even looking at the name which was written in clumsy letters and attached with a drawing pin.

'Ulrik Gjemselund,' he read. 'Right place then.'

Suddenly he took two steps back. With considerable force he rammed his shoulder against the door. There was a shout from inside. The policeman aimed and ran at the door again. The door gave way, torn from its frame and hinges. It fell into the hallway in slow motion.

'That's the way we do it,' the policeman grinned, and went in. 'Ulrik! *Ulrik Gjemselund!*'

Petter Kalvø stayed out in the corridor. He was sweating under his Burberry coat. 'He's mad,' he thought to himself, dazed. 'The man is raving mad. The others said I should just do what he says. They said just to obey and keep my mouth shut. No one can stand working with the guy after his suspension. A loner, they said. Someone who's got nothing to lose any more. But I have got something to lose. I don't want . . .'

'PC Kalvø,' his colleague yelled from somewhere inside the flat, 'Come here! Get your arse in here, for fuck's sake!'

Reluctantly, he went in. He could see a TV in what was probably the sitting room. He crept closer.

'Get a look at this whippersnapper,' his colleague said.

A man in his early twenties was standing in the furthest corner, beside a sound system, under a shelf of books that ran right round the room, just below the ceiling. He was naked and clutching his sexual organ. His back and shoulders were hunched and his half-length hair was standing out in all directions.

'Got 'im under control there,' the older man said to Kalvø. 'Now you stay here and keep an eye on our lad while I have a look around. He's got such a grip on his dick you'd think he was scared of losing it. But we ain't going to steal it. Relax.'

This was directed at the young man who lived in the flat, who was still cowering in the corner.

'Take what you want,' he stammered. 'Take what . . . I've got money in my wallet. You can just take . . .'

'Relax,' Petter Kalvø said.

He took a step towards the naked man, who raised his arm to protect his face.

'Didn't you say?' Kalvø asked, surprised at the force of his anger. 'Fucking hell, didn't you tell him we're from the police?'

The boy sobbed.

His colleague hissed:

'Take it easy. Of course I did. The guy must be bloody deaf. Don't let him go anywhere.'

PC Petter Kalvø tried to think clearly. He straightened his collar, tightened his tie, as if it was more important than ever, during this alarmingly unlawful search, to be correctly dressed. He should do something. Stop it. He should stand up to his much older colleague. Phone someone. Raise the alarm. Protest. He could for example, go out to the car and call a patrol.

'Just relax,' he whispered instead and tried to force a smile. 'His bark's worse than his bite.'

His voice was weedy and lacked any conviction. He could hear it himself. He took another step towards the boy, who had at last let his arm drop.

'Bloody amateur,' his colleague complained by the door. 'Ulrik Gjemselund is obviously a novice!'

In his hand he had a small plastic bag of white powder.

'In the cistern,' he said, smacking his lips. 'That's the first place we look, Ulrik. The very first place. Take me to a flat where I think there's drugs and I walk blind out to the bog, lift the cistern lid and have a look. God, that's boring.'

He stroked his rust-red, peppered moustache. He shook his head from side to side as he open the plastic bag, stuck his pinkie into the white powder and then tasted it.

'Cocaine,' he said and pretended to look surprised. 'And here's me thinking it was cornflour you kept in the bog. Or heroin or something like that. But instead it's a nice amount of posh shit. Dear oh dear. *Stand fucking still!*'

The boy in the corner straightened up, terrified. He had been about to sink down to a sitting position, with his hands still holding his balls. He was crying without shame now.

'Take it easy, little boy. Just stay there. Don't you go anywhere.'

The policeman opened cupboards and drawers. He ran his hands under all the shelves and behind all the books. Round all the picture frames and under all the cushions. He stopped by a computer desk in the kitchen. Four IKEA storage boxes were stacked on the printer. He opened the top one and emptied the contents onto the floor.

'Now, what have we here?' he said contentedly. 'Let me see. Five condoms . . .'

He tore open one of the packets and held it up to his nose.

'Banana,' he sniffed. 'If that's what turns you on.'

He picked through the pile on the floor and pulled out a trumpet-shaped cigarette.

'Look and you'll find,' he said. 'A secret little joint.'

He smelt the contents.

'Shit quality,' he wrinkled his nose. 'You obviously don't know much about weed. Shame on you.'

Another box was emptied.

'Nothing of interest here,' said the policeman, and flicked through a pack of cards before he emptied the third box.

It was empty, apart from an envelope.

'Trond Arnesen,' he read out loud. 'That's a familiar name.'

The boy in the corner forgot himself. He took four steps out onto the floor, stopped abruptly and put his hands to his face.

'Please don't,' he wept. 'Please don't touch it. It's not drugs. It's . . . nothing. Nothing . . .'

'Interesting,' said the policeman, and tore open the envelope. 'You've made me curious.'

There were five smaller envelopes inside, held together with an old hairband. They were all addressed to Ulrik Gjemselund, in neutral capital letters that sloped slightly to the left. No sender's details. The policeman pulled a letter out of the top one and started to read.

'You don't say,' he murmured, and put the letter carefully back in the envelope. 'Trond Arnesen. Trond Arnesen . . . Where do I know that name from?'

'I beg you,' the young boy pleaded; he wasn't crying any more. 'Please just leave them. They're private, OK? You've got no bloody right to just burst in here and . . .'

The policeman was astonishingly fast and nimble. Before Petter Kalvø even realized what was happening, his colleague had crossed the floor in four strides and lifted the naked man with a firm clasp round his waist and dumped him back in the corner. His index finger was thrust deep into Ulrik Gjemselund's left cheek.

'Now you listen to me,' he said in a low voice, and pressed his finger in even harder. He was about a head and a half taller than the boy. 'It's me who decides what's interesting around here. All you have to do is stay put and do as I tell you. I've been wading through the shit that you and your kind make for nearly thirty years. And that's a long time. A bloody long time. And I'm fucking bored of posh . . .'

It looked like his finger was about to go through the boy's cheek and into his mouth.

'I think we should . . . now . . .' Petter Kalvø started. 'I think perhaps . . .'

'You shut the fuck up,' hissed his colleague. 'Trond Arnesen is the prick that was going to get married to Vibeke Heinerback. I'm pretty sure that the boys at Romerike and the NCIS will want to have a butcher's at these letters.'

He let go. Ulrik Gjemselund sank to the floor. The rank smell of faeces filled the room.

'You've shat yourself now,' said the policeman with some resignation. 'Go and wash yourself. Find some clothes. You're coming with us.'

'Should I go with him?' Petter Kalvø asked. 'So that he . . .'

'He won't jump out from the third floor. He'd die. He's not that stupid.'

Ulrik Gjemselund kept his legs apart as he left the room. He left a trail behind him and Petter Kalvø stepped to one side without thinking as the boy passed on his way to the bathroom. They heard the sound of muffled sobs and running water.

'Now let me just make one thing clear, Petter.'

The older policeman put his hand on his partner's shoulder, a gesture that was in part threatening and in part friendly.

'The door downstairs was open,' he said quietly. 'OK? And as to why it was necessary for us to break in here . . .' He nodded at the hallway. '. . . Well, we heard shouting and screaming, as if some-one was being attacked. Raped, maybe. OK?'

'But he . . . he was alone!'

'We didn't know that beforehand. The shouting was really alarming, don't you remember? You do, don't you? In fact, the guy was sitting here wanking and screaming, but how were we to know that?'

'I don't know how . . .'

'You don't need to know anything, Petter. We found what we were looking for, didn't we? We've got a good bag of cocaine, a pathetic joint and a pile of letters that might be worth their weight in gold.'

Ulrik Gjemselund came out of the bathroom with a towel round his waist.

'My clothes are in the bedroom.'

'Well, we'd better go there then, hadn't we?'

'But listen! Trond had nothing to do with . . . Trond doesn't do drugs. I swear. He doesn't know that . . .'

'Come on now. Get dressed.'

They followed Ulrik into a chaotic bedroom and waited while he put on some underpants, a T-shirt, a red woollen sweater, jeans and socks. The older policeman found a pair of boots on the shoe rack and flung them across the floor.

'Here,' he said. 'Put these on.'

'I need to go to the loo again,' said Ulrik and clutched his stomach.

'Well, go then, lad.'

The boy shot past them.

It was quiet. The policemen studied the destruction in the hallway. The hinges on one side of the door had been torn away from the doorframe. It would be pointless to try screwing the door back in place.

'We can't leave the flat open,' Petter Kalvø said.

The other man shrugged.

'We'll take any valuables with us,' he said. 'We can put the door back in place and then leave it like that.'

'But . . .'

'Only joking,' chuckled the older man. 'Call a patrol car. Ask them to get a locksmith or joiner or whatever the fuck they need to repair this.'

The toilet flushed. They heard the sound of a cabinet being opened and shut.

'Go on, tell me,' Petter Kalvø whispered, looking over at the bathroom. 'What were the letters about?'

His colleague slapped his breast pocket.

'Love letters,' he whispered back with a grin. 'Judging by what's written here, these two were at it like rabbits. And Trond, who was about to get married this summer. Tut tut.'

'What are you going to do with the door?' Ulrik complained when he came out of the bathroom with his boots on. 'We can't just . . .'

'Come on,' said the policeman and grabbed him by the arm. 'You've got more to worry about than a broken door. And don't think that I don't know what you did just now. In the bathroom. You don't open a cabinet when you're having a shit, you know.'

'I . . .'

'Shut up. You deserve a few pills to calm you down. And it'll be a while before the next ones.'

He gave a loud laugh and pushed the prisoner out towards the lift.

They had survived the meal and Johanne had to admit somewhat reluctantly that it had even been a success. Her mother had been on her best behaviour, warm, happy and utterly wrapped up in the children. Her father seemed to be healthier than he had been for a long time. He ate well and for once didn't touch the wine. It irritated her that Isak was so familiar with everyone and everything, but Kristiane was, as always, delighted to have them all together.

'My family,' she said, and lay down on the floor with her arms in the air in the middle of the meal. 'Fy mamily. Dam-di-rum-ram. I didn't pee in Leonard's bed.'

Even Marie, Johanne's three-years-younger and childless sister, had managed not to pass comment on Johanne's homemade sweater and worn velvet trousers. She came to the table in a deep-green suit that didn't look as if it had been bought in Norway, and her hair must take at least an hour to style and curl every morning and evening. However, Johanne's glasses had not escaped her sister's ambiguous remarks.

'I'm sure you'd really suit smaller glasses,' Marie had smiled as she tucked a loose lock of hair back in place. 'Have you tried?'

'I think her glasses are fine,' Adam said, and helped himself to more beef, for the third time. 'And in any case, it's a waste of money buying designer glasses when Ragnhild will soon be pulling them off. Solid frames, just what she needs.'

Isak had played with Ragnhild and claimed that she laughed. Adam didn't say much, but patted Johanne's knee every now and then. Her father shed a couple of tears when he said a few words after the meal. Things were just as they had always been. Not one of them had noticed that Johanne checked the driveway outside the house several times during the meal and that she jumped when the telephone rang.

It was nearly midnight.

It was as if the mere thought that it was close to bedtime made her wake up. She had yawned and dozed the whole day, but as soon as it was dark it was impossible for her to find any rest. Her anxiety had been justified in the first couple of weeks after she'd given birth: she thought of Kristiane every time she saw the baby. She remembered the strange baby with eyes that never looked at anything or anyone. When Ragnhild was feeding, Johanne was reminded of the listless little bundle that didn't want to eat, with fists that were always balled and lips that turned blue when she had one of her breathless, alien crying fits.

But Ragnhild was healthy. She screamed and was a glutton, she waved her arms and legs around and slept as she should. There was nothing wrong with her.

But healthy children could also die. Suddenly, without reason or explanation.

'I need help,' Johanne thought to herself, and picked up an arch-lever file. 'You can go mad if you don't get enough sleep. I don't smoke, I barely drink. I have to pull myself together. She's not going to die. I won't find her lifeless and limp in bed. She uses a dummy and sleeps on her back. Like they said she should.'

Adam had given up. When he went to bed, he didn't ask any more if she was coming. Sometimes he got up at night, sat with her for a while on the sofa, yawning, and then went back to bed.

'Something's wrong,' Johanne thought. 'Not with Ragnhild. There's nothing wrong with her. But there's something that isn't right. Someone is playing with us. Coincidences like that don't happen. It's too close to be a coincidence.'

She turned the pages in the file about the three murders, but without any real interest. The dividers were red. She resolutely ripped out the pages about Fiona Helle. Then she regretted it and tried to put them back in. And didn't manage. The holes were torn. She went to fetch some Sellotape from a drawer in the kitchen. With dogged determination, she set about repairing the damage she'd done, but then she threw the tape on the floor and put her face in her hands.

'I can't take any more. There's someone out there.'

Aloud, she hissed with clenched teeth: 'Pull yourself together. Get a grip, Johanne.'

'I agree.'

Adam was up again. Without saying another word, he went out into the kitchen. The smell of coffee spread through the flat and Johanne closed her eyes. Adam could stay awake and be on guard. If only she could keep Ragnhild in bed beside her, she was sure she would sleep then. But the baby might die if she let her sleep with them. That's what the latest research had shown. She'd read about it in all the publications on her bedside table, medical periodicals and magazines for concerned parents. Ragnhild had to sleep on her own and Johanne had to stay awake and watch over her, because there was someone out there, someone who wanted to harm them.

She fell asleep.

'I fell asleep!'

She got a fright when he tried to put a blanket over her.

'Just you carry on,' he whispered.

'No. Awake now.'

'You need help.'

'No.'

'The risk of cot death is not . . .'

'Don't say that word!'

'Strictly speaking the risk isn't over until Ragnhild is two,' Adam said drily.

He sat down heavily beside her. There was only one cup of coffee on the table and he pushed it away when she reached for it.

'And you bloody well can't stay awake every night for two years!'

'I've discovered something,' she said.

'Well, I would be very happy to hear about it in the morning,' he said, and ran a hand over his hair, still unused to the short cut. 'When the children have gone to bed and there is still a decent amount of time left of the day.'

She pulled the mug over. He shook his head and lay back in the sofa in resignation. She drank. He closed his eyes.

'This series of killings has absurd similarities to something else,' she started, hesitant, tentative, '. . . something that I . . .'

The sofa was full of Adam. His arms were resting along the back of the sofa and his legs were wide apart. His head fell back with his mouth open, as if he was fast asleep.

'Stop it,' she said. 'I know you're awake.'

He opened his eyes. He squinted at the ceiling. But didn't say a word.

'A lecture,' Johanne said quickly and drank some more coffee.

'What?'

'I heard about these murders in a lecture. Thirteen years ago.'

He struggled to sit up properly.

'You heard about these murders thirteen years ago,' he repeated, his voice expressionless. 'Right.'

'Not the actual murders, obviously.'

'I guessed that.'

His voice was alert now.

'But ones that were very similar,' she finished.

'Could I get my coffee back, love?'

He smiled reassuringly, as if she wasn't all there and needed to be grounded in reality by a normal, simple act. She got up, keeping the cup firmly in her hands.

'I was at Lina's yesterday,' she said. 'That computer of ours is . . .'

'I know,' he interrupted. 'I promised I'd get it fixed. One of the boys at work . . . It's just that . . .'

'I went on a kind of sentimental journey, if you like. Only it wasn't that sentimental.'

Three clear furrows appeared in his brow as he leant forwards.

'What d'you mean?'

'For a long time, I've had a nagging feeling that there's something familiar about the cases. The murders of Fiona Helle, Vibeke Heinerback and Vegard Krogh. I just wasn't able to grasp it. The feeling that is. The memory. But it had to be something that . . .'

She took a sip of coffee. The steam clung to her face.

'Something what?'

'It had to be something that I'd come across in Washington. Or Quantico. It was very distant. So . . . forgotten and long ago. And I was right. I didn't need to look very far. When I saw . . . Just a picture of . . . Forget it.'

She tucked her hair behind her ear and didn't want to let go of the warmth from the mug of coffee. She clutched the cup in both hands and turned her back on Adam.

'My darling.'

'*Sit down.*'

'OK,' he said reluctantly.

'All I needed to see was the picture of the Academy,' she said so quietly that he had trouble hearing. 'Then I remembered. I remembered the class. I remembered the long days, the tiring, demanding, fun . . .'

She approached her reflection in the window, as if it was easier to talk to herself.

'Now I even know which lecture series it was, Behavioural Science. Warren amused us with a lecture he called "Proportional Retribution".'

For a moment, Adam thought he saw the reflection smile.

'Amused us,' she repeated. 'That was actually what he did. We laughed. Everyone laughed when Warren wanted us to laugh. It was towards the end of June. Almost the holidays. It was warm. Very humid and warm. The air conditioning in the auditorium was broken. We were sweating. But not Warren. He always so cool – in every sense.'

Slowly she turned around. She lowered her cup. It was empty and hung by the handle from her finger.

'I expend so much effort on trying to forget,' she said without looking at him. 'Maybe it isn't that strange that I found it so hard to remember. Although . . .'

Her eyes filled up. She leant her head back to prevent the tears from running. Adam started to get up again.

'Don't,' she said harshly.

She smiled suddenly through the tears and wiped her left eye lightly with the back of her hand.

'The lecture was about revenge, people with a strong sense of "eye for an eye, tooth for a tooth",' she said. 'About criminals with an exaggerated need for the punishment to fit the crime. At least symbolically. Warren loved things like that. He loved anything that was violent. Clear. Exaggerated.'

'Sit down, Johanne.'

He patted the cushion next to him on the sofa.

'No, I'd rather stand. I have to tell you this. While I still have the energy to do it. Or rather . . .' Another fleeting, thin smile. '. . . When I don't have the energy not to,' she added.

'To be honest, I have no idea what you're talking about, Johanne.'

'He told us about five cases,' she continued, as if she hadn't heard him. 'One was . . . It was about one of those eccentrics that you only find in the States. A slightly twisted, intellectual type. With green fingers. He had a beautiful garden, which he protected, tooth and nail. I can't remember how he made a living, but he must have had money, because the garden was the jewel of the neighbourhood. Then a neighbour sued him in connection with a boundary dispute. The neighbour claimed that the fence was a few metres too far into his property and the court ruled in his favour, having gone through several instances in the judicial system. I don't remember all the details. The point is that . . .'

She froze, with the tip of her tongue on her lips and her head cocked.

'Did you hear something?'

'No. Can't you . . .'

She swallowed and sighed deeply before carrying on.

'The point is that the neighbour was found dead just after the final judgement. His tongue had been cut out and was lying in a folded envelope, made from the cover of *House & Garden*. A magazine. About . . .'

207

'Houses and gardens,' said Adam, exasperated. 'Can you please sit down. You're freezing. Come here.'

'Are you listening?'

'Yes, but . . .'

'His tongue had been cut out! And beautifully wrapped! The most banal, vulgar symbol . . .'

'I am sure,' he interjected in a quiet voice, 'that there are examples of bodies that have been dismembered in that way all over the world, Johanne. Without it having anything to do with the death of Fiona Helle. You said it yourself, it was a long time ago and you don't remember all . . .'

'The worst thing is that I do *remember*,' she burst out. 'I remember everything now. Please try to understand, Adam! Don't you know how . . . *hard* it is to force yourself to remember something that you have desperately tried to forget? How . . . how much it *hurts* to . . .'

'It's difficult for me to understand something I don't know about,' Adam retorted and immediately regretted it. 'I mean . . . I can see that it's painful for you. That's not difficult to . . .'

'Don't push it,' she almost screamed. 'I will never, I will *never* talk about what happened. I'm just trying to explain to you why this story got hidden. It's so painfully close to . . .'

He got up. He grabbed her by the wrists and felt how thin she had become. Her watch, which had been too tight to wear in the last months of pregnancy, was now in danger of slipping over her hand. Without any resistance, she let him hold her. He stroked her back. He could feel the sharp vertebrae through her sweater.

'You need to start eating,' he said, with his face buried in her lifeless and matted hair. 'You need to eat and sleep, Johanne.'

'And you need to listen to me,' she cried. 'Can't you just listen to my story? Without asking what . . . Without mixing everything . . .'

With a sudden angry movement she straightened up and put her hands on his chest.

'Can't you just stop asking about things that are my business, and my business alone? Can't you forget that and just listen to what I'm saying?'

'It's difficult. At some point you're going to have to . . .'

'Never. OK? Never. You promised not . . .'

'We were getting married the next day, Johanne. I was frightened that you'd cancel the whole wedding if I didn't go along with your demands. It's different now.'

'Nothing is different.'

'Yes it is. We're married. We've got children. You're about to . . . You're upset, Johanne. You're suffering because of something you refuse to let me in on. And I won't accept that.'

'You have to.'

He let go of her. They stood there for a while, close, but not touching. He was nearly a head taller than her. Johanne lifted her face. There was a darkness in her eyes that he didn't recognize, and his heart started to race when for a moment he saw something that he thought might resemble . . . hate.

'Johanne,' he whispered.

'I love you,' she said quietly. 'But you *have to* let it lie. Maybe one day I will be able to tell you about what happened between Warren and me. But not now. Not for a long time, Adam. I have spent the last few weeks trying to find my way back to that memory and it's been a tough journey. I can't take any more. I want to leave it behind. To come back. To my life here. To you and the children. Us.'

'Of course,' he said in a hoarse voice. His heart was still pounding.

'But I took a story back with me that I really need to tell. I put a lid on the rest. And it will be there for a long time, maybe for ever. But you must . . . you must listen to what I have to say.'

He swallowed and nodded.

'Shall we sit down?' he said, his voice still raw.

'Don't be like that,' Johanne said and stroked his cropped head. 'Can't you . . .'

'You frightened me,' he said, keeping his eyes locked in hers.

They were normal again. Friendly. Johanne's own normal friendly eyes.

'I didn't mean to.'

'Can we sit down?'

'Can you please stop . . .'

'What?'

'I'm sorry that I frightened you. But you don't need to treat me as if I'm a casual guest.'

For a moment her eyes were hostile. Not full of hate, as he had felt before, but aggressive and hostile.

'Rubbish,' he said and smiled. 'OK, let's just drop you and . . . you and Warren. Now tell me the rest.'

He got another cup and poured them both coffee, then sat down in the sofa and patted the cushion beside him.

'Come on,' he said with strained cheerfulness.

'Are you sure?' she asked, and took the fresh cup of coffee without sitting down.

'Absolutely.'

His smile still hadn't reached his eyes.

'OK,' she said slowly. 'The other case was a small-town murder in California. Or . . . yes, it was California. A local politician was literally suffocated with Bible quotations. Nailed to the wall with his mouth full of wet paper. Pages from the poor sod's own bible.'

Johanne's eyes wandered round the room, as if she needed to find comfort in the security and familiarity it offered, before she could continue. Darkness enveloped the house like an insulating cape. It was so quiet that Adam thought he could hear the whirring of his own thoughts. They were careering round in his head, confused and unstructured. What was this? What kind of absurd story was she telling him? How could three murders in Norway in 2004 be connected to a repressed and forgotten lecture in the States thirteen years ago?

Bible then, Koran now.

Beautifully wrapped tongues. Then and now.

'Why was he killed?' was all he could think of to say.

'A pastor who had his own wacky following believed that this local councillor deserved to die because he had encouraged ungodly racism. He got one of his followers to carry out the murder. A simpleton. Who just grinned throughout the court case, told them everything . . . or so we were told.'

'Racism,' thought Adam.

Vibeke Heinerback was not a racist. Vibeke Heinerback worked primarily with economics. They had hardly paid the issue any attention. They had looked for political motives: unpopular cuts and brutal power struggles. Racism was quickly dismissed as a motive, despite the Koran. The young party leader had avoided the issue and was clever enough to answer questions generally and harmlessly whenever forced into a corner by journalists who were not satisfied with platitudes about immigration costs and resource issues.

'But Vibeke Heinerback did have several fellow party members,' Adam hesitated, 'who might be accused of not liking our new countrymen.'

He hadn't touched the coffee. He leant forwards over the coffee table. His hand was shaking.

'That's two cases,' he said, and left the cup where it was. 'You said there were five.'

'A journalist was beaten to death,' continued Johanne. 'He had uncovered a financial mismanagement case in a company on the east coast, I can't remember what it was about. The story cost him his life.'

'But he wasn't killed by a . . . *pen*?'

'No.'

She gave a wan smile.

'A typewriter. A Remington, a huge, old-fashioned . . .'

Adam wasn't listening any more.

'A typewriter to the head,' he thought. 'A pen in the eye. Two journalists, then and now, killed by the tools of their trade. Two politicians, then and now, crucified and desecrated with religious scripts. Two tongues. Two people accused of lying.'

211

'Jesus Christ,' he whispered.

Johanne picked up a red rag doll from the shelf by the TV. It was missing an arm. Its face was dirty grey and its red hair was as faded as its dress, almost pink after countless spins in the washing machine.

'I heard all this on a warm day in early summer many years ago,' she said, and ran her fingers down the doll's absurdly long legs. 'Each case individually is not that interesting. America's criminal history is full of far more spectacular stories than that.'

All of a sudden, she threw the doll down into the toy box.

'What's interesting for us is that someone in this country is trying to emulate the series again. But we mustn't get bogged down in the past, we have to focus on . . . on Fiona Helle, Vibeke Heinerback and Vegard Krogh. On today. Our own murders. Don't we?' Johanne paused.

He wanted to nod. He really wanted to smile and agree. What she had told him was useful enough, sketchy and imprecise though it was. It was sufficient.

They both knew that it was impossible.

She had told him an important story and at the same time had driven a wedge between them. He would use the next few days to put the heavens in motion, to trace every detail of the cases. He would get international organizations involved. They needed transcripts, judgements, hearings. They needed names and dates.

They needed Warren's help.

'I think,' he said, and hesitated for a moment before continuing: 'I think that's enough for this evening. Tomorrow's going to be a long day.'

'I know,' she said, and hunkered down. Jack had woken up and was rubbing against her. 'We can't do much good now. Go to bed.'

'Come with me.'

'There's no point, Adam. Go to bed.'

'Not without you.'

'I don't want to. Can't.'

212

'Are you hungry?'

'I know that you're going to talk to Warren. I understand that you need to.'

'Should I make an omelette?'

'You're just like Mother. Think that food solves everything.'

She buried her nose in the warm, acrid smell of dirty dog and mumbled:

'Don't act as if I'm stupid, Adam.'

Again, he didn't know what to say.

'Of course I realize what you have to do with the information I've given you,' she continued. 'I'm not asking for fanfares for having dived back into a past I wanted to forget, but I would like some kind of respect. Just pretending that everything is fine and I've just told you a goodnight story, I think that's . . . unfair.'

She lifted up the dog and hid her face in his fur.

'We should be happy,' he thought. 'We should be delighted about Ragnhild. About Kristiane's development. About each other. We get on well together, the two of us. The four of us. That morning, a month ago, feels like an age now, when Kristiane thought we'd got an heir to the throne, wasn't I happy then? Satisfied? The baby was healthy. You were a bit anxious and very happy. I want to turn back time and forget everything that is alien and secret, that opens up this chasm between us. Your eyes were hostile and now you're slipping away from me.'

'Just keep me out of it,' Johanne said. 'Do what you must, but keep me out of it. OK?'

He nodded.

Jack wriggled in her arms and wanted to get down.

'He doesn't like being held,' Adam said.

'Is Mats Bohus definitely out of the question?'

'What?'

'Are you one hundred per cent sure that Mats Bohus is not behind all the murders?'

'Yes.'

The King of America made a leap for it and landed on the floor

213

with a dull thud. He whimpered a bit and then shot off into a corner with his tail between his legs.

'What can it be?' Johanne said, and sat down on the other sofa.

'You mean who, don't you'?' he said in a flat voice.

'Well, both who and what.'

'I can't bear this,' he said.

'What?'

'Your coldness.'

'I'm not being cold.'

'Yes, you are.'

'You're hopeless. You want me to be happy and warm and close all the time. That's impossible. Grow up. We're two adults, with adult problems. It doesn't mean to say that something's wrong.'

She said 'doesn't mean to say something's wrong'. He wanted to hear 'nothing's wrong'. He folded his hands and studied his knuckles, which were white now. In fourteen months he would be fifty. The signs of age were getting clearer, the dry loose skin on the backs of his hands, even when he curled his fingers.

'Do you think someone might be setting this up?' she asked, doubtfully.

'Oh come on,' he mumbled and opened his right hand.

She looked at Jack, who was still turning in circles on his cushion, trying to settle down.

'Maybe there's someone else outside who's manipulating others to commit murder,' she said, mostly to herself, as if she was thinking out loud. 'Someone who knows about these old stories and who, for some reason, is trying to recreate . . .'

The dog finally lay down.

'I'm going mad,' she murmured.

'We're going to bed,' Adam stated.

'Yes,' she said.

'You mentioned five,' he said.

'Five what?'

'Five murders. The lecture was about five murders. All examples of what Warren called . . . proportional revenge?'

214

'Retribution.'

'What were the last two cases?' he asked, without looking up from his hand.

Johanne took off her glasses. The room became fuzzy and she cleaned her glasses with half-closed eyes.

'Who was killed?' he asked. 'And how?'

'An athlete.'

'What happened to him?'

'He got a javelin through the heart.'

'A javelin . . . Like the ones you throw?'

'Yes.'

'Why?'

'The killer was a competitor. He felt he'd been overlooked when one of the Ivy League schools awarded an athletics grant. Something like that. I can't remember exactly. I'm exhausted.'

'So now all we can do is just sit tight,' he started. 'Completely helpless . . . and wait for an athlete to be brutally murdered.'

She was still polishing and rubbing her glasses with the corner of her shirt, without purpose or reason.

'And the last one?' he asked, almost inaudibly.

Johanne held her glasses up to the standard lamp and closed one eye. She squinted into the light through both lenses, several times. Then she slowly put the glasses back on. Shrugged her shoulders.

'D'you know what, I think I might actually try to get some sleep. It's been . . .'

'Johanne,' Adam stopped her, then drank the rest of his coffee in one go.

The mug thumped down on the table.

A sharp light appeared on the ceiling. The beam wandered slowly from the kitchen to just above the door out to the south-facing balcony. The throb of an engine made the windowpanes vibrate.

'Rubbish men,' Adam said quickly. 'So?'

If he hadn't been so tired, he might have noticed that Johanne

215

was holding her breath. If he had looked at her instead of going over to the window to check who was letting their engine idle in a residential area in the middle of the night, he might have noticed that her mouth was half open and her lips were pale. He would have seen that she was sitting tensely, with her eyes on the front door, then the children's room.

But Adam was at the window, with his back to Johanne.

'Sixth-formers partying,' he said, peeved. 'It's only February. They don't have their exams until May. They start earlier and earlier.'

He hesitated for a moment, before going back to sit in the sofa opposite Johanne.

'The last one,' he insisted. 'What happened in the last case?'

'He didn't succeed. Warren included the example because . . .'

'Who did he try to murder, Johanne?'

She reached out for both cups and got up. He caught her as she passed.

'It doesn't matter,' she said. 'He didn't manage it.'

The movement with which she broke free was unnecessarily harsh.

'Johanne,' he said, without following her. He heard the cups being put in the dishwasher. 'You're just being difficult now.'

'I'm sure.'

'Who did he try to kill?' Adam repeated.

He was surprised to hear the noise of the dishwasher. He pulled up his sleeve and looked at his watch. Nearly half past one. Johanne was rummaging around in the drawers and cupboards.

'What are you doing?' he muttered, and went out into the kitchen.

'Tidying,' she replied tersely.

'Well,' he said and pointed at the clock, 'I see that you're getting used to living in a semi-detached house.'

The cutlery drawer fell to the floor with a crash. Johanne bent down on her knees and tried to gather up the knives and forks, spoons and other gadgets.

'It was a family man,' she sobbed, 'who was being investigated for insurance fraud in connection with a house fire. He . . . he set light to the policeman's home. The investigator's home. While all the family were sleeping.'

'Come here.'

He held her by the arms, firm and friendly, pulled her up. She resisted.

'No one is going to set this house on fire,' Adam said. 'No one is ever going to set our house on fire.'

Twelve

For hundreds of years, people had walked the narrow streets between the low, crooked houses that clung together. Steps wound up narrow passages. Feet had trodden on the stone steps, in the same place, year after year, leaving behind a smoothly polished path that she crouched down to touch, several times. The shiny hollows were cold against her fingers. She put her fingers in her mouth and felt a sting of salt on the tip of her tongue.

She leant over the wall to the south. A greyish-blue mist fused sea and sky. There was no horizon out there, no perspective, only an endlessness that made her dizzy. There was no wind, not even up here on the hilltop. A dank humidity swathed the medieval town of Eze. She was alone.

In summer this place must be unbearable. Even with shuttered windows and unwelcoming shop doors, closed for the winter, the signs of the summer season were obvious. Souvenir shops stood wall to wall, and on the few small squares that opened out in the heart of the town she saw the scars from scraping chairs and countless cigarettes that had been stubbed out on the cobbles. As she walked by herself along the wall facing the sea, she imagined the sound of the summer hordes, chirruping Japanese and loud redcheeked Germans.

She was a veritable wanderer now. She had gradually discovered the old paths and found ways to avoid the main roads that were dangerous, with no pavements and a steady flow of roaring traffic.

Her new duffel coat was warm without being completely windproof. She had bought it in Nice along with three pairs of trousers, four sweaters, a handful of skirts and a suit that she wasn't really sure she would dare to use. When she came to France, just before Christmas, she only had with her two pairs of shoes. They were now in the rubbish container down on the street. Yesterday evening she had resolutely put them in a plastic bag and dropped them into the container, even though one pair was barely half a year old. They were brown and solid. Sensible shoes, best suited for a middle-aged housewife.

The duffel coat was beige and her Camper shoes were comfortable to walk in. The lady in the shop hadn't so much as raised an eyebrow when she asked to try them on. A young boy sat beside her on one of the bright yellow pouffes and tried on the same shoes. When he caught her eye, he gave a friendly smile. Nodded in appreciation. She bought two pairs. They were very comfortable.

She walked.

Walking made it easier to think. It was during her long, slow walks along the sea, in the mountains and across the steep hillsides between Nice and Cap-d'Ail that she felt most acutely that her life had been injected with new vigour. Sometimes, often when she came home at night, she felt a tiredness in her muscles that was a wonderful reminder of her strength. She would take off her clothes and wander naked around the house, her reflection in the windows confirming the changes she was going through. She drank wine, but never too much. She enjoyed the food, whether she made it herself or went to a restaurant where she was recognized, always recognized now, by polite waiters who pulled out her chair and remembered that she liked to have a glass of champagne before her meal.

Over the past few days, she had been filled with a sense of gratitude.

She had driven directly from Copenhagen, where she had left her car in an anonymous car park before taking the ferry to Oslo and back. Ferry passenger lists between Denmark and Norway were a joke. She travelled as Eva Hansen and stayed in her cabin. Both ways. Then after one night in a hotel, she managed to sit behind the wheel for thirty-five hours, without ever really getting tired. She did feel a stiffness in her muscles and joints whenever she took a short break, small detours from the main road to fill the tank or to eat in a roadside café in a German village or along the Rhône. But she never felt the need for sleep.

She delivered the car back to the Moroccan waiter at the Café de la Paix. He was well rewarded for the bother of hiring the car in his name. He might perhaps not have entirely believed her explanation that she really needed a car but because she had a bad cold she wanted to avoid an unnecessary trip into Nice. As he was going back to Morocco and a newly opened restaurant owned by his father, he accepted the money with a smile and no questions.

Then she walked home. As soon as her head hit the pillow, she fell into a dreamless slumber that lasted for eleven hours.

She had derived no pleasure from all those years of meticulous planning, gathering detailed information and painstaking research, other than that it was her work. It was necessary if she was to do the job she was paid for. She was good and had never been caught out. No one could say that she made mistakes, was sloppy, or took shortcuts whenever she could.

Despite everything, she was grateful for those lifeless years.

They had given her knowledge and insight.

Even though the filing cabinet was in Norway, she could remember enough. The huge metal cabinet contained information about the people she had studied. Known and unknown. Famous people and celebrities, alongside the postman from Otta who always filled her postbox with junk mail, despite the clear notice that it was not welcome. She registered people's weaknesses and routines, observed their desires and needs, stowed their love lives, secrets and movements in files and stored it all in a huge grey metal cabinet.

She wasn't sloppy. The secret of her trade was knowledge. Her memory never failed her.

All those living-dead years were not wasted. She was grateful for them now. She could assemble an AG-3 blindfolded and hotwire a car in thirty seconds. It would take her less than a week to get hold of a false passport and she had an overview of the Scandinavian heroin market that the police would envy. She knew people that no one else wanted to know, she knew them well; but none of them knew her.

It had got colder. An insidious wind blew down from the hills, dispersing the mist out at sea. The duffel was not protection enough, so she hurried down the mountain path. It was too cold to walk all the way back home. If the bus came when it was due, she would take it. If not, she could always treat herself to a taxi.

She had become more generous recently.

Suddenly a splash of colour appeared in the sky to the north. A person swayed rhythmically from side to side under an orange paraglider. Another paraglider appeared over the top of the hill, red and yellow, with green writing that it was impossible to read. A sudden turbulence made the fabric flap. The glider lost its lift and dropped some fifty or sixty metres before the pilot managed to regain control and slowly cut down into the valley below her.

She followed him with her eyes and laughed softly.

They thought they were challenging fate.

Extreme sport had always provoked her, primarily because she thought the people who did it were pathetic. Of course, not everyone had been granted an exciting life. Quite the contrary. Most of the world's six billion people, the greater part of the inhabitants of Europe and probably all of the Norwegian population, lived uneventful lives. Their fight for survival consisted of getting enough food to live, taking care of their children, finding a better job or having the newest car in the neighbourhood. Human existence was and would always be a mere bagatelle. The fact that depraved, spoilt young people found it necessary to defy death by jumping and diving from sheer rock faces at great speed was an expression of Western decadence that she had always scorned.

Loathed.

They suffered from ennui because they believed they deserved

221

something else, something better than what life in fact was to most: an insignificant period of time between life and death.

'They think they can escape from the meaninglessness of life,' she thought to herself. 'By throwing themselves over the edge of Trollveggen with a parachute made from unreliable fabric. Or crossing one of the Poles. Climbing an unclimbable mountain. They want to go higher, further, and to more daring lengths. They don't notice the boredom that constantly shadows them, grey and sneering. They don't see it until they've landed, before they're safely at home. So they repeat the exercise, do something different, more dangerous, more daring, until they either understand that you can't outwit life or they meet their death attempting to prove the opposite.'

The paragliders were nearly down now, they were aiming to land on a slope with long rows of dwarf vines. She thought she could hear them laughing. Only imagination, obviously, as the wind was in the wrong direction and the bottom of the valley was far away. But she could see the two pilots slapping each other on the back and jumping up and down with excitement. Two women came running up the terraced slope. They waved happily.

She still felt disgusted by the way they played arbitrarily with death.

The only thing they risked was their lives.

Dying was nothing more than a pleasant end to the boredom. And dying also enhanced your reputation, as obituaries were full of praise, not truth. If you died young, life had not yet aged you, made you ugly, fat or skinny. A person who doesn't live to be old leaves behind a tragic memento: a glamorized, redeeming story where what was boring becomes exciting and what was ugly becomes beautiful.

She thought about Vegard Krogh and bit her tongue.

She didn't want to read about him any more. The articles were all lies. Journalists and acquaintances, friends and family all contributed to the image that was drawn of Krogh, the artist. An uncompromising and upright champion of what was genuine and true. A colourful spirit, a fearless soldier in the service of that great and incorruptible force, culture.

She swore out loud and started to run down the road. The bus was just pulling out from the bus stop down on the main road, but stopped when the driver saw her. She paid and plumped down into an empty seat.

She would be going back to Norway for good soon.

That is, she had to leave the house in Villefranche. The contract had been extended until the 1st of March, but not longer. In just over a week she would be homeless, unless she went home.

She pictured her flat, tastefully decorated and far too big for one person. Only the steel cabinet in the bedroom broke with the soft style she had copied from an interiors magazine. She'd bought most of the stuff at IKEA, but had also come across a couple of the more expensive items in the sales.

She somehow didn't fit in to her flat in Norway.

She seldom had guests and didn't need the space. When she was at home, she generally sat in the untidy study and therefore didn't really get much pleasure from the fact that the rest of the flat was so tasteful. In fact, she had never really felt at home there. It was more like living in a hotel. On her many trips to Europe, she had stayed in rooms that felt more personal, warmer and more comfortable than her own sitting room.

She didn't fit in in Norway at all. Norway was not for people like her. She felt suffocated by its grand egalitarian philosophy. Excluded by the narrow-minded, exclusive elite. Norway was not big enough for someone like her, she was not recognized for what she was and had therefore chosen to protect herself with the cloak of anonymity. Aloof. Invisible. They didn't want to see her. So she wouldn't show herself to them.

The bus rolled westwards. The suspension was French and not good enough. She had to close her eyes so as not to feel sick.

To risk dying was no great feat. The danger they exposed themselves to, these mountaineers and air acrobats, solitary rowers in fragile boats crossing the Atlantic and motorcyclists performing death-defying stunts in front of audiences charged with the hope that something might go terribly wrong, was limited to the journey they each took, whether it lasted three seconds or eight weeks, one minute or maybe one year.

She was taking a gamble on life itself. The suspense of never landing, of never achieving her goal, made her unique. The risk increased each day, as she hoped it would and wanted it to. It was constantly there, intense and invigorating, the danger of being caught and exposed.

She leant her forehead against the window. Evening was falling. The lights had been lit along the promenade below. A light rain darkened the asphalt.

There was nothing to indicate that they were getting closer. Despite the clues she had left, the obvious invitation in the pattern she had chosen, the police were still at a loss. It was so annoying and made her more determined to continue. Of course, the fact that the woman had just had a baby did upset the equation a bit. The timing was not optimal, she had already known that when she started, but there were limits to what she could control.

Maybe it would be a good thing to go home. To get closer.

Run a greater risk.

The bus stopped and she got off. It was pouring with rain now and she ran all the way home. It was the evening of the 24th of February.

Thirteen

'Maybe there's someone behind it all, who's manipulating the situation,' said Adam Stubo, and tucked into his chicken in yoghurt sauce. 'That's her latest theory. I'm not too sure.'

He smiled with his mouth full of food.

'How d'you mean?' asked Sigmund Berli. 'That someone's getting other people to do the killing, or what? Duping them?'

He broke off a piece of nan bread, held it between his thumb and finger and peered at it suspiciously.

'Is this some kind of bread?'

'Nan,' Adam replied. 'Try it. The theory isn't that stupid. I mean, it's pretty logical. In a way. If we accept that Mats Bohus actually killed Fiona Helle but none of the others, then it's plausible that someone is behind it all. Pulling the strings. An overriding motive, as it were. But at the same time . . .'

Sigmund chewed and chewed. Didn't manage to swallow.

'For Christ's sake,' whispered Adam, and leant over the table. 'Pull yourself together. There've been Indian restaurants in Norway for thirty years! You're behaving as if it's snake meat you're eating. It's bread, Sigmund. Just bread.'

'That guy over there's not an Indian,' his colleague muttered, and nodded in the direction of the waiter, a middle-aged man with a trimmed moustache and a kind smile. 'He's a Paki.'

The handle of Adam's knife came crashing down onto the table.

'Cut it out,' he hissed. 'I owe you a lot, Sigmund, but not enough to accept that kind of crap. I've told you a thousand times, keep that bloody . . .'

'I meant Pakistani. Sorry. But he *is* a Pakistani. Not an Indian. And my stomach can't cope with things that are too spicy.'

225

He pulled an exaggerated face as he clutched his belly dramatically.

'You ordered mild food,' Adam growled, and helped himself to more raita. 'If you can't eat this, you can't eat sausage and mash. Bon appétit.'

Sigmund put a tiny bit on his fork. Hesitated. Cautiously put it in his mouth. Chewed.

'I just can't get it to tally,' Adam said. 'It's somehow so . . . un-Norwegian. Un-European. That anyone would think of using some poor sod as a pawn in a killing game.'

'Now it's you that should cut it out,' retorted Sigmund. He swallowed and took some more. 'Nothing is un-Norwegian any more. In terms of crime, I mean. The situation is no better here than anywhere else. And it hasn't been for years. It's all these . . .' He stopped himself, thought about it and continued: '. . . Russians,' he ventured. 'And those bloody bandits from the Balkans. Those boys know no shame, you know. You can see the evil in their eyes.'

The expression on Adam's face made him raise a hand.

'Describing reality is not racism,' he protested fervently. 'Those people are just like us! Same race and all that. But you know yourself how—'

'Stop. There are no foreigners in this case. The victims are pure Norwegian. All of them fair, in fact. And the same is true of the poor sod we've arrested on one count. Forget the Russians. Forget the Balkans. Forget . . .'

He gave a sudden jerk and put his hand to his cheek.

'Sorry, bit my cheek,' he mumbled. 'Hurts.'

Sigmund pulled his chair in to the table. Put his napkin on his knee and picked up his knife and fork, as if he wanted to start the meal all over again.

'Have to admit, that lecture of Johanne's is pretty freaky,' Sigmund said, unscathed by Adam's reprimand. 'A bit *X-files*. Time warps and the like. What d'you reckon?'

'Not much,' Adam admitted.

'So what, then?'

'It could just be a coincidence, of course.'

'Coincidence,' Sigmund snorted. 'Right. Your wife sits over there on the other side of the world thirteen years ago and listens to a lecture about highly symbolic murders, and then the same method, exactly the same symbols, appear in Norway in 2004! *Three times!* Sod coincidence, I say. No way.'

'Well, then maybe you've got an explanation! I mean, you watch *The X-files*.'

'They've stopped making it. It got a bit too absurd towards the end.'

Adam helped himself to some more from the small iron pot. The rice stuck to the serving spoon. He shook it lightly. The white sticky mass fell into the sauce with a splash. Red spots appeared on his shirt.

'I think there's an evil bastard out there,' Sigmund said in a calm voice. 'An evil bastard who's heard the same lecture. And enjoyed it. And toyed with the idea of playing with us.'

Adam felt a chill down his spine.

'Right,' he said slowly and stopped eating. 'Anything else?'

'The symbolism's too clear. In the original cases, the killers were a bit simple, at least from what you've said. Idiots choose obvious symbols. But our man's certainly not an idiot. Our man's . . .' Sigmund's smile was almost childish now, he saw a new and unfamiliar acknowledgement in Adam's narrowed eyes and slight nod of the head. 'If we take it as given,' Sigmund continued, 'that Johanne is right, and that there's someone out there pulling the strings, getting other people to do the killing . . .'

A furrow appeared between his heavy eyebrows.

'. . . and gets them to do it in a very particular way, then we're definitely not talking about someone of limited capacity. Quite the opposite.'

There wasn't a sound. They were the only guests now. The waiter had disappeared into a back room. All that could be heard was the gentle oriental music coming from the speakers on the other side of the room. The loudspeakers vibrated on the higher notes.

'Hmm,' Adam said eventually, lifting his mineral water in appreciation. 'That's not bad. But if this Mr X has heard the same lecture, it must be someone who . . . someone who Johanne knows from . . .'

'No,' Sigmund interjected, and tried another piece of bread. 'It's been a while now since I went to police college, but I do remember one thing. The lectures were the same, year after year. The teachers just turned over the pile. I borrowed some notes from a friend who was in the year above me. A blueprint. This bread is actually quite nice.'

'Try the tandoori,' Adam suggested. 'But you're forgetting that we're not talking about any old teacher. Warren Scifford is a legend. He would hardly . . .'

'As if good teachers are any better than bad ones when it comes to that,' Sigmund exclaimed, looking at his fork before cautiously putting the meat in his mouth. 'The opposite, I'd say. If a series of lectures is successful, all the less reason to change it. Students come and go. Teachers stay. Have we managed to get hold of the guy?'

'Warren?'

'Yes.'

'No. If you don't want your food, I'll . . .'

'Help yourself.'

Sigmund pushed his plate across the table.

'The FBI's mandate was changed, to put it mildly, after Nine Eleven,' Adam said. 'Now it's all anti-terrorism and hush-hush. Finding Warren has proved to be harder than anticipated. Before, I could just pick up the phone and have him on the other end of the line within thirty seconds. But now . . .' He shrugged. 'My guess is Iraq,' he said lightly.

'Iraq? But the FBI has limited jurisdiction! Aren't they supposed to stick to their own territory? To the USA?'

'In principle, yes. In reality, well . . .'

Another slight shrug of the shoulders.

'I should think they could do with Warren's expertise down there in that hell hole.'

'What does he actually do?'

Adam guffawed and wiped his mouth with the starched napkin.

'Easier to say what he doesn't do. First he got a Ph.D. in sociology, then he trained as a lawyer. But most importantly, he's been connected to what's clearly the world's best police organization for more than thirty years. Star.'

'And now he's in Iraq.'

'I don't *know* that he's in Iraq,' Adam corrected. 'But looking at how the Americans are getting on down there, I wouldn't be surprised if they needed their best men there. Whether that's FBI folk or anyone else. But I haven't given up trying to find him yet.'

The waiter came back. He politely overlooked the fact that Adam had two plates in front of him.

'Would you like anything else to drink?'

'Water,' Sigmund said gruffly, and put his elbows on the table.

'Yes, please,' Adam smiled and praised the food. 'A sparkling mineral water, please.'

He poked the wound in his cheek with his tongue.

'Hurts,' he mumbled.

'Do you believe in my theory?' Sigmund asked. 'In Johanne's theory?'

Adam took his time.

'I can't quite . . . quite imagine how it's possible to manipulate people in that way. On the other hand . . .'

The waiter poured the water into their glasses, smiled and withdrew again.

'It may be because I don't dare,' Adam admitted, and took a drink. 'If you're right, it means that the investigations will be . . . even harder. Because among other things, it means that the real mastermind doesn't necessarily have any obvious connection with the victims. But the murderers do. And so far, we've only found one of them.'

'A raving loony in a nuthouse,' sighed Sigmund.

Adam's raised fork obliged him to quickly add:

'I mean, someone with mental health issues who's in an institution. What d'you think we should do? Should we pursue the . . . theory?'

'We should at least bear it in mind,' Adam said. 'As we have to carry on looking for connections between the three victims, it won't make much extra work if Mats Bohus is included in the picture.'

'Hmm? I don't understand. He hasn't been killed, he . . .'

'If you and Johanne really are on to something, he's the only one we've got. So while we carry on looking for links between Fiona Helle, Vibeke Heinerback and Vegard Krogh, we can also look to see if there are any hidden connections between Mats Bohus and the other two. Long shot, but why not. The problem is that we can't talk to Mats Bohus any more. Completely lost it. The hearing last Saturday was obviously too much. Dr Bonheur was right. And now we have to pay the price – put it like this, the man's in a closed ward, so it won't be easy to find out who he's had contact with.'

He snatched up the last piece of bread and popped it in his mouth.

'Full,' he mumbled. 'Shall we go?'

'What about coffee?' Sigmund suggested.

'I'd advise against that. The coffee here isn't exactly . . .'

His mobile started ringing. Adam got out his phone and signalled to the waiter that they'd like the bill.

'Stubo,' he said curtly.

When he rang off about a minute and a half later, without having said more than yes and no, he looked very concerned. His eyes were narrower than ever and his mouth was pursed with tiredness and worry.

'What's wrong?' asked Sigmund.

Adam paid and got up.

'What the hell is it?' Sigmund repeated impatiently as they came out on to Arendalsgate. A bus thundered past.

'Trond Arnesen was lying,' Adam replied, and started to walk towards Myrens Engineering Workshop, where the car was parked outside the old factory.

'What?' Sigmund bellowed, jogging along beside him.

A trailer was waiting at the red lights and the noise was deafening.

'Trond Arnesen is not as innocent as I thought,' Adam yelled back. 'He was having an affair on the side.'

The lights turned to green and the trailer accelerated and disappeared up to Torshov.

'What?'

'With a man,' Adam said and ran over the road. 'A young lad.'

'Isn't that what I've always said?' Sigmund said, speeding up to keep pace with his partner. 'You can't trust a faggot.'

Adam couldn't be bothered to react.

He had been absolutely convinced of Trond Arnesen's innocence.

Johanne was woken by someone coming up the stairs. Fear froze her limbs. Ragnhild was lying between her left arm and her body. She was fast asleep. It was still light outside. It must still be daytime. Sometime in the afternoon. How long had she been asleep? Someone came closer.

'Were you sleeping? That's good.'

Her mother smiled and came over to the sofa.

'Mother,' Johanne stammered. 'You gave me a fright! You can't just . . .'

'Yes, I can,' her mother replied firmly. Johanne suddenly realized that she hadn't even taken off her coat. 'I used the spare key you left with us. To be honest, I was afraid that you wouldn't open the door if I rang the bell and you looked out and saw it was me.'

'Of course I would've . . .'

Johanne struggled to sit up in the sofa without waking Ragnhild.

'No, dear. I don't think you would have opened the door. How long have you been asleep?'

Johanne looked at her watch.

'Twelve minutes,' she yawned. 'Why are you here?'

'Just relax,' her mother said, and disappeared into the kitchen.

She could hear drawers and cupboards being opened. The fridge door opened and closed. Johanne heard the clinking of bottles and the reluctant sucking noise of the freezer being opening. She managed to get up on her feet.

'What are you doing?' she muttered in irritation.

'I'm packing,' her mother replied.

'Packing . . .'

'Good thing you've got so much of your milk in the freezer. There . . .'

With a practised hand, she wrapped each of the frozen bottles in newspaper.

'What are you *doing*, Mother?'

'Can't you just be a good girl and get out some clothes? Her pyjamas. Some nappies. No, actually, your father has already bought some. *Libero*, that's what you use, isn't it? Just put a little bag together. And please remember to pack some extra dummies.'

Johanne tried to move the baby over to her other arm; her eyes opened and she started to whimper.

'You're not taking Ragnhild, Mother.'

'Yes, I most definitely am.'

Her mother was already putting the well-insulated bottles into a soft thermal bag with a Coca-Cola logo on it.

'No way.'

'Now listen to me, Johanne.'

With an angry movement, her mother zipped the bag shut and put it on the island unit. Then she ran her fingers through her grey hair, before catching her daughter's eye and saying:

'I will decide that.'

'You can't . . .'

'Be quiet.'

Her voice was sharp, but level. Ragnhild didn't react.

'I am fully aware that you think I'm generally pretty hopeless,

Johanne. And that we haven't always been the best of friends. But I am your mother and I'm not as stupid as you think. Not only could I see that you were absolutely exhausted during dinner on Sunday, but I also detected something that I can only interpret as . . . fear.'

Johanne opened her mouth to protest.

'Don't say a word,' her mother scolded. 'I have no intention of asking you what it is you're frightened of. You never tell me anything anyway. But I can help with the tiredness. So now I'm going to take my grandchild home with me and you are going to go to bed. The time is . . .' She looked over at the wall clock. '. . . half past two. I've asked Isak to pick Kristiane up from school. Adam said he'd be working late tonight. He'll stay over at ours, so you're not disturbed. You . . .'

Her finger was shaking when she pointed it at Johanne.

'. . . go to bed and get some sleep. You're no fool and you know perfectly well that Ragnhild is in the best hands. With me, with us. You can sleep for as long as you need. Or you can read books all night if that makes you any happier. But I think . . . oh, darling.'

Johanne hid her face in the baby's blanket. It smelt of clean clothes and she started to cry. Her mother stroked her hair and then gently loosened Ragnhild from her daughter's arms.

'You see,' she clucked. 'You're overtired. Go to bed, dear, I'll find what I need myself.'

'I can . . . You can't . . .'

'I've reared two children. I've got my home economics exams. I've looked after a house and home for as long as I remember. I can look after a baby for a night or two.'

Her mother's heels clicked on the parquet as she turned and walked resolutely towards the children's room. Johanne wanted to follow, but couldn't face it.

Sleep. Hours and hours of sleep.

She was almost ready to lie down on the floor. Instead she grabbed a half-full bottle of water from the worktop and drank it. Then she went into the bedroom. She barely had the energy to take off her clothes. The sheets felt cool and good to touch. The room was cold. The duvet was warm. She heard her mother mumbling in the children's room for a few minutes. Footsteps moving around, out into the bathroom, back to the kitchen, into Ragnhild's room.

'The cream,' Johanne murmured. 'Don't forget the nappy rash cream.'

But she was already asleep, and didn't wake up until sixteen hours later.

'I'm not like that,' Trond Arnesen said in desperation. 'I'm not really that way inclined!'

Five elegant envelopes lay on the table between him and Detective Inspector Adam Stubo, tied together with an old hairband. They were all addressed to Ulrik Gjemselund. The writing slanted to the left, just as it did in the Filofax that was lying beside them.

'Trond Arnesen,' Adam Stubo read, tapping his finger on the page. 'You've got very distinct handwriting. I think we can agree that there's no need to analyse the writing. Are you left-handed?'

'I'm not like that! You have to believe me!'

Adam tipped his chair back. He clasped his hands behind his neck, ran his thumbs over the folds of skin. His cropped hair brushed against his fingers. The back of the chair hit the wall rhythmically. He looked at the boy without saying a word. His face was blank and neutral, as if he was bored and waiting for someone or something.

'You have to believe me,' Trond insisted. 'I've never been with . . . any other guys. I swear to you! And that night, that night, was the *very last time*. I was going to get married and . . .'

Big tears spilled over down his cheeks. His nose was running. He used his sleeve to wipe his face, but couldn't stop crying. His sobbing sounded like a small child. Adam rocked on his chair and carried on rocking. The back of the chair hit the wall. Thump. Thump. Thump.

'Can't you stop that?' Trond pleaded. 'Please!'

Adam carried on rocking. He still didn't say anything.

'I was so drunk,' Trond said. 'I was already pissed by nine. It was a long time since I'd seen Ulrik, so . . . Then about half ten I went out to get some air. I went outside to clear my head. And he didn't live that far away. Huitfeldtsgate. So I . . .'

Adam's chair slammed back down to the floor. The young man jumped. The plastic cup from which he had just drunk some water was knocked over. The policeman retrieved the letters. He pulled off the hairband and looked at the envelopes again without opening any of them. Then he put the hairband back round them and dropped the pile into a grey file. There was nothing to remind Trond of the friendly policeman from the reconstruction. It was impossible to read his eyes and he said so little.

'It's been really hard,' he whined, and sobbed as he drew breath. 'Ulrik has been . . . He said he . . . I meant to tell. I wanted to tell the truth, but when I realized that you thought I'd been at Smuget the whole evening, I'm not sure why . . . I thought . . .'

He suddenly put his head back.

'Can't you say something?' he appealed. He pulled his head back up and slammed his palms down on the table. 'Can't you at least say something?'

'You're the one who's got something to say.'

'But I've got nothing more to say! I'm really sorry that I didn't tell you straight away, but I . . . I loved Vibeke! I miss her so much. We were going to get married and I was so . . . You don't believe me!'

'Right now it's not important whether I believe you or not,' Adam said, and pulled on his ear lobe. 'But I am very interested to know exactly how long you were away from the nightclub.'

'One and a half hours, I told you. From half past ten until twelve. Midnight. I swear. Just ask the others, just ask my brother.'

'They obviously made a mistake last time we questioned them. Or lied, all of them. They swore that you were there all night.'

'They thought I was there! Jesus, it was chaos and I was only away for a while. I should have told you straight away, but I was . . . embarrassed. I was about to get married.'

'Yes, we know,' Adam said, unrelenting. 'So you keep saying.'

'I should have told you,' the young man moaned again. 'It was just so . . . I thought . . .'

'You thought you could get away with it,' Adam Stubo said. His voice had an unfamiliar edge to it. 'Didn't you?'

He got up, put his hands behind his back and walked slowly round the room. Trond shrunk, he lowered his head and hunched his shoulders, as if he was afraid of being hit.

'What's interesting,' Adam said – his voice now had an exaggerated fatherly tone to it, both strict and friendly at the same time. 'What's interesting is that you just told me something we didn't know.'

The boy had stopped crying. He dried the snot and tears with a corner of his shirt and for a moment looked more confused than desperate.

'Don't know what you mean,' he said, and looked the policeman in the eye. 'You've obviously spoken to Ulrik and that night . . .'

'You're wrong,' Adam said. 'Ulrik refused to talk to us. He's sitting in a cell in Grønland station and keeping schtum. And he has every right to. Not talk, that is. So we actually didn't know that you'd lied about your alibi. Not until now.'

'In a cell? What's he done? Ulrik?'

Adam stopped about a metre away from the young man. He put his right elbow in his left hand and stroked his nose, thoughtfully.

'You're not that stupid, Trond.'

'I . . .'

'You what?'

'I really don't know what it's about.'

'Hmm. Fine. You want me to believe that you've had a relationship with Ulrik . . . you know him, well, intimately, as they say . . .'

Adam nodded at the file. The letters were sticking out from the top. Trond's face blushed red.

'. . . Without knowing that Ulrik was involved with illegal substances,' Adam continued. 'With all due respect, I find that very hard to believe.'

Trond looked like he'd seen the devil himself, with horns on his forehead and a burning tail. Wide eyes, open mouth and running nose, which he didn't wipe. He made nonsensical noises. Adam chewed his knuckles but made no attempt to help.

'Drugs,' Trond finally managed to say. 'I knew nothing about that. I promise!'

'I have a little girl at home,' Adam said, and started to walk again, taking long, slow strides backwards and forwards across the small interview room. 'She's nearly ten and has an enviable imagination.'

He stopped and smiled.

'She lies all the time. You say "I swear" more than she does. It doesn't exactly make you more believable.'

'I give up,' Trond muttered, and it looked like he really meant it. He leant back in the chair and repeated: 'I bloody give up.'

His arms hung loose by his body. He head fell back. He closed his eyes. His legs were apart. He looked like an overgrown teenager.

'Then you didn't know, either, that Ulrik was a rent boy?' Adam said calmly. His eyes did not leave the sprawling young man's face, so that he could catch every emotion.

Nothing happened. Trond Arnesen just sat there, his mouth half open, his knees wide apart, his hands moving in rhythm.

'Of the more exclusive type,' Adam added. 'But of course you didn't know that. Because I'm sure you never paid.'

The young man still didn't react. For a long time he didn't move at all. Even his hands were still. Just a twitch in his eyelids showed that he had heard at all. The only noise in the stuffy interview room was of Adam's even breathing and the barely audible buzz of the air conditioning.

'You shouldn't have written those letters,' Adam said quietly and maliciously, though he didn't know why. 'If you hadn't written those letters, everything would be fine now. You'd be sitting at home. In your house. You'd have everyone's sympathy. Life would have normalized again eventually. You're young. In six months or so the worst would be over and you could move on. But you had to write those letters. Not very smart, Trond.'

'Now I'm being mean,' Adam thought to himself and pulled a big aluminium cigar case out of his breast pocket. 'I'm punishing him for my own disappointment. What am I disappointed about? That he lied? That he had secrets? Everyone lies. Everyone has secrets. No one has a streamlined life without shame, without faults and stains. I'm not punishing him for being immoral, I've seen and understood too much for that. I'm disappointed that I've been fooled. For once I chose to believe. My whole working life depends on other people's lies and deceit, cowardice and betrayal. There was something about this boy, this immature man. Something innocent. Genuine. But I was wrong, and I'm punishing him for it.'

He could smell the cigar. Opened the case a little and inhaled.

Slowly, Trond straightened up on his chair. His eyes were full of tears. A fine dribble of spit hung from the left-hand corner of his mouth. He caught his breath in gasps.

'I never paid,' he said and put his face in his hands. 'I didn't know he took money from others. I didn't know that there were others . . . apart from me.'

Then he was overcome by tears. He was inconsolable. He didn't stop crying when Adam gently put a hand on his shoulder, when his mother hugged him after she had been called in, agitated and terrified, half an hour later, nor when his brother gave him an awkward brotherly embrace in the car park before helping him into the back of the car.

'He's well over the age of consent,' Adam replied to his mother's many questions. 'You'll have to ask him what it's about.'

'But . . . you must tell . . . is he . . . was it him who . . .'

'Trond didn't kill Vibeke. You can be sure of that. But he's a troubled man. Take good care of him.'

Adam stayed in the car park long after the red tail lights of Bård Arnesen's car had disappeared. The temperature fell a degree or two while he stood there, without a coat. It started to snow. He stood quite still, without acknowledging people who left the building and called out goodbye before getting into their cars, shivering, and driving home to their families and their own skewed lives.

It was times like these that he was reminded why the passion he once felt for his work was now no more than an occasional and subdued feeling of satisfaction. He still believed that what he was doing was important. His job still challenged him every day. He could draw on a wealth of experience and knew that it was valuable. His intuition had also become stronger and more precise over the years. Adam Stubo was a great old-fashioned champion of what is good and just and he knew he could never be anything other than a policeman. But he no longer felt a sense of triumph or overwhelming joy when he solved a case, as he had when he was younger.

Over the years it had grown harder and harder to live with the destruction that every investigation involved. He turned other people's lives upside down, changed destinies. Revealed secrets. Hidden parts of people's lives were pulled out of drawers and forgotten cupboards.

Next summer, Adam Stubo would turn fifty. He had been a policeman for twenty-eight years and he knew that Trond Arnesen was not guilty of murdering his fiancée. Adam had met many Trond Arnesens before, with all their weaknesses and foibles; ordinary people who unfortunately suddenly had floodlights trained on every dark corner of their lives.

Trond Arnesen had lied when he felt threatened and was deceptive when he thought it would help. He was just like everyone else.

The snow was getting thicker and the temperature was falling steadily.

Adam stood there and enjoyed the feeling of being bare-headed and thinly clad in an open space in bad weather.

Enjoyed the sensation of being cold.

Kari Mundal, the party's former first lady, stood for a moment, as she usually did, and looked up at the façade, before climbing the stone steps. She was proud of the party headquarters. Unlike her husband, who thought that he would be the stranger at the wedding if he didn't stay away, Mrs Mundal popped in several times a week. Generally she didn't have any particular errand and sometimes she just came in to drop off some bags on one of her frequent and extensive shopping trips in the centre of town. And she always paused for a few seconds to relish the sight of the newly renovated façade. She got great pleasure from all the details, the corniced string courses at each level, the statues of saints in the niches above the windows. She was particularly fond of John the Baptist, who was closest to the door and looked down at her with a very realistic lamb in his arms. The steps were wide and dark and she was out of breath when she put her hand on the door handle, opened the door and went in.

'It's only me,' she chirped. 'I'm back.'

The receptionist smiled. She stood up so she could look over the high reception desk and nodded approvingly.

'Beautiful,' she said. 'But should you be wearing them in this weather?'

Kari Mundal looked at her new boots, held her foot out provocatively in front of her, turned her ankle and clicked her tongue.

'I'm sure I shouldn't,' she said. 'But they're so elegant. You're here late tonight, my dear. You should get off home.'

'There's lots of meetings this evening,' the woman replied. She was big and heavy with unflattering glasses. 'I thought it would be best to stay a while longer, with people coming and going all the time. And not everyone is good at making sure the door is locked behind them. But if I'm here, it's not so much of a problem.'

'You truly are a loyal trouper,' Kari Mundal praised her. 'But please don't wait for me. I may well be very late. I'll be in the Yellow Room, if you want anything.'

She leant conspiratorially over the desk and whispered:

'I'd rather not be disturbed.'

With her hands full of shopping bags, she tripped over the spiral pattern on the floor. As always, she cast a glance at the gold shield bearing the party's motto, and smiled, before heading for the lift.

'Did you find everything I wanted?' she asked suddenly, turning back to the entrance.

'Yes,' replied the stout lady behind the desk. 'Everything should be there. Forms, vouchers, everything. Hege in accounts is working overtime today, so you just go in to her if you need anything. I didn't mention it to anyone else.'

'Thank you,' said Kari Mundal. 'You're an angel.'

Rudolf Fjord paused for a few minutes on the broad landing on the first floor that looked down into the foyer, where the chandelier had been lit, casting a soft yellow glow on the room below. Then he drew back into the shadows by the wall, by the impressive palm next to the door to his office. The fear that he had managed to repress, the anxiety he had buried on the day he received the party's unconditional acceptance, flared up again, as he had known it would, even though he had prayed to God that it would never haunt him again.

'I really appreciate your discretion,' he heard Kari Mundal call, before a click and nearly inaudible rush of air told him that the lift was on its way up.

Vegard Krogh's widow opened the door and smiled half-heartedly. Adam Stubo had rung in advance and found her voice unusually pleasant. He had pictured a dark woman. Tall, with a straight back, a large mouth and languid movements. But she was in fact small and blonde. Her thick hair was tied up in two tired pigtails. Her jumper looked like it had been pulled from a seventies time capsule; it was brown with orange stripes and a drawstring at the neck.

'Thank you for letting me come,' Adam said, giving her his coat.

She led him into the sitting room and gestured that he should sit down in a stained, light-coloured sofa. Adam moved a cushion, lifted up a book and sat down. He looked around the room. The shelves were crammed and chaotic. The newspaper rack was over-flowing, and he noted two copies of *Information* and a torn copy of *Le Monde diplomatique*. The glass table, between the sofa and the two armchairs that didn't match, was dirty and a wine glass with the remains of some red wine was standing unsteadily on a pile of magazines he didn't recognize.

'Sorry about the mess,' said Elsbeth Davidsen. 'I haven't exactly had the energy to tidy recently.'

Her voice didn't suit her body. It was deep and melodious and made her pigtails look like a joke. She had no make-up on and her eyes were the palest that Adam had ever seen. He smiled in understanding.

'I think it's homely,' he said, and meant it. 'Who's that by?'

He nodded at a lithograph above the sofa.

'Inger Sitter,' she mumbled. 'Can I offer you anything? Haven't got much in the house, but . . . Coffee? Tea?'

'Coffee would be nice,' he said. 'If it's not too much trouble.'

'Not at all. I made some half an hour ago.'

She pointed at an Alessi coffee thermos and went to get a cup.

'Would you like milk or sugar?' he heard from the kitchen.

'Both, please,' he laughed. 'But my wife doesn't let me, so I'll just take it black.'

When she came back, he noticed that she had a great figure under her shabby clothes. Her jeans needed a wash and her slippers must have once belonged to Vegard. But her waist was small and her neck was long and thin. Her movements, when she put down the mugs and poured the coffee, were graceful.

'I thought I was done with you lot,' she said, without sounding unfriendly. 'So I wonder what you want. A friend of mine, he's a lawyer, said that it's unusual for you to visit people at home. He said . . .'

Her smile was unreadable. A thin finger brushed her left eyebrow. Her eyes, when they met his, were almost teasing.

'. . . that the police call people in to make them feel insecure. You're at home in the police station, not me. But here I'm at home. Not you.'

'I don't feel particularly threatened where I'm sitting,' Adam said, and tasted the coffee. 'But your friend has a point. So you could draw the conclusion that I don't intend to make you feel insecure. It's more that I'm looking for . . .'

'To talk?' she observed. 'You're at a bit of loss and you're the kind of policeman who looks around, tries to get a better overall impression, a bigger picture. And then maybe you'll discover a new angle. Paths and evidence that you haven't noticed before.'

'Hmm,' he said, astonished. 'Not so far from the truth.'

'My friend. He knows you. You're quite well known.'

She gave a short laugh. Adam Stubo resisted the urge to ask who her friend was.

'I can't quite get a handle on your husband,' he said.

'Don't call him my husband, please. We only married for one reason, and that was that if we wanted to have children it looked like we'd have to adopt. Please just say Vegard.'

'OK, I can't quite get a handle on Vegard.'

Laughter again, deep and short.

'I don't think there were many who did.'

'Not even you?'

'Certainly not me. Vegard was many people. We all are, I suppose, but, he was worse than most. Or better. Depends on how you want to look at it.'

The irony was obvious. Again, Adam was struck by her voice. Elsbeth Davidsen used a wide range of expressions. Small, telling movements in her hands and face, and careful but obvious changes in her voice.

'Do tell.'

'Tell? Tell you about Vegard . . .'

She picked absent-mindedly at her knee.

'Vegard *wanted* so much,' she said. 'At the same time. He wanted to be obscure, literary and alternative. Innovative and provocative. Unique. But he also had a craving for recognition that was difficult to combine with writing essays and inaccessible novels.'

Now it was Adam's turn to laugh. As he put down his mug and looked around the room again, he realized that he liked this woman.

'Vegard had a great talent,' she continued thoughtfully. 'Once upon a time. I wouldn't exactly say that he . . . wasted it, but he . . . he was an angry young man for too long. When he was younger he was full of charm. Energy. I was fascinated by the uncompromising strength in everything he did. But then . . . he never grew out of it. He thought he was fighting against everyone and would never admit that as the years passed he was only fighting against himself. He lashed out, not realizing that whoever it was he was trying to hit had long since left. It was . . .'

Adam hadn't reacted to the fact that the woman, up to now, appeared to be untouched by her husband's brutal death just over two weeks ago. A sensible strategy, he thought, given the situation. She was talking to an unknown policeman. But now he could see that her lower lip was quivering.

'It was actually quite pathetic,' she said, and swallowed. 'And pretty bloody horrible to watch.'

'Who was he out after most?'

With a listless hand, she puffed up a dirty red cushion.

'Anyone who achieved the success that he felt he deserved,' she explained. 'Which he felt . . . robbed of, in a way. In that sense, Vegard was the classic cliché of an artist: he was misunderstood. The one who had been passed by. But at the same time . . . at the same time he tried to be one of them. More than anything, he wanted to be *one of them*.'

She leant forward and picked up a card that had fallen on the floor. She handed it over to him.

'This came a day or two before he died,' she said, and pulled at one of her pigtails. 'I've never seen Vegard so happy.'

The card was cream-coloured and adorned with a beautiful royal monogram. Adam tried to repress a smile and carefully put the card back down on the glass table.

'You may well laugh,' she sighed sadly. 'We had a terrible argument about that invitation. I couldn't understand why he felt it was so important to get in with that crowd. To be honest, I was worried. He seemed to be obsessed with the idea that he finally was going to "be someone", as he put it.'

She mimed speech marks in the air.

'Did you often argue?'

'Yes. At least latterly. When Vegard really started to get stuck and definitely couldn't be called young and promising any more. We've been soooo . . .' She held her thumb and her forefinger a millimetre apart. '. . . Close to splitting up. Several times.'

'But you still wanted to have children?'

'Don't most people?'

He didn't answer. There was a sudden commotion outside on the stairs. Something heavy fell on the floor and two angry voices bounced off the concrete walls. Adam thought they were speaking Urdu.

'Nice here at Grønland,' she said drily. 'Sometimes it can be a bit too lively. At least for those of us who can't afford to buy a flat in the new blocks.'

The voices out on the stair died down and then trailed off. Only the monotone drone of the city forced its way in through the dilapidated windows and filled the silence between them.

'If you could choose one,' Adam said in the end, 'one of Vegard's enemies . . . Someone who really had a reason to wish him ill, who would that be?'

'That's impossible,' she answered without hesitation. 'Vegard had offended so many people and threw his shit around so liberally

245

that it would be impossible to pick out one person. And in any case . . .'

She picked again at the hole on the knee of her jeans. The skin underneath was winter-white against the indigo blue.

'Like I said, I'm not really sure if he could cause that much damage any more. Before, he was hard-hitting and on target with his criticism. Recently it's just been . . . shit, like I said.'

'But would it be possible,' Adam tried again, '. . . to identify . . . one group, then . . . One group of people that has greater reason to feel they've been wronged? Tabloid journalists? TV celebrities? Politicians?'

'Crime writers!'

Finally, a broad and genuine smile. Her teeth were small and pearly white, with a slight gap between the upper front teeth. A dimple appeared on one of her cheeks, an oval shadow of forgotten laughter.

'What?'

'Some years ago, when all his antics still attracted attention, he wrote a parody of three of that year's bestsellers. Nonsense, really, but very funny. He got a taste for it. And in many ways it was his trademark, for years. Haranguing crime writers, that is. Also in situations where it was completely unjustified or inappropriate. A kind of personal version of "Moreover, I advise that Carthage must be destroyed."'

Again she mimed speech marks in the air. A car backfired outside the sitting-room window. Adam heard a dog barking in the back yard. His back was sore and his shoulders ached. His eyes were dry and he rubbed them with his knuckles, like a tired child.

'What are we doing?' he asked himself. 'What am I doing? Searching for ghosts and shadows. Getting nowhere. There's no connection, no common features, no where to go. Not even an overgrown, invisible path. We're flailing around in the dark, getting nowhere, without seeing anything except more new, impenetrable scrub. Fiona Helle was popular. Vibeke Heinerback had political opponents, but no enemies. Vegard Krogh was a

246

ridiculous Don Quixote who waged war with popular fiction authors in a world full of despots, fanaticism and threatening catastrophe. What a . . .'

'I have to go,' he muttered. 'It's late.'

'So soon?' She seemed disappointed. 'I mean . . . of course.'

She went to get his coat and came back before he had managed to struggle out of the deep sofa.

'I'm terribly sorry, on your behalf,' Adam said as he took his coat and put it on. 'For what has happened, and for bothering you like this.'

Elsbeth Davidsen didn't answer. She walked silently in front of him down the hall.

'Thank you for letting me come,' Adam said.

'It is I who should thank you,' said Elsbeth Davidsen seriously, and held out her hand. 'It's been a pleasure meeting you.'

Adam felt her warmth, the dry, soft hand, and dropped it a second too late. Then he turned and left. The dog in the back yard had got company. The animals were making a din that followed him all the way to the car, which was parked a block away. Both wing mirrors had been broken and a parting message from Oslo East had been scratched onto the nearside doors:

Fuck you, you fucker.

At least it was spelt correctly.

Fourteen

'If you don't mind me saying, Johanne, you look bloody great tonight. You really do. Cheers!'

Sigmund Berli lifted his glass of cognac. It didn't seem to bother him that he was the only one drinking. A red flush spread around his eyes like a rash and his smile was broad.

'Amazing what a good night's sleep can do,' Adam said.

'More like eighteen hours,' Johanne said under her breath. 'Don't think I've slept that long since I was in my last year at school.'

She was standing behind Sigmund's back asking Adam silently, with gestures and facial expressions, why he had invited his colleague home with him on yet another weekday.

'Sigmund's a grass widower at the moment,' Adam explained in a loud, cheerful voice. 'And the man doesn't have enough sense to eat unless the food is put on the table in front of him.'

'If only I got food like this every day,' Sigmund said, and swallowed a burp. 'I've never tasted such a good pizza. We normally have Grandiosa. Is it hard to make pizza? D'you think I could get the recipe for the wife?'

He grabbed the last piece as Adam started to clear the table.

'Would you rather have a beer?' Johanne asked in desperation, looking at the cognac bottle on the windowsill. 'If you're going to eat more, that is. Doesn't it, well . . . go better?'

'Cognac goes with most things,' Sigmund said happily, and launched into the last piece of pizza. 'It's bloody nice to be here. Thanks for asking.'

'You're welcome,' Johanne said flatly. 'Are you still hungry?'

'After this, I could only be hungry for life,' grinned the guest, rinsing down the pizza with the rest of the cognac.

'Dear God,' muttered Johanne, and went to the bathroom.

Sigmund was right, the sleep had done her the world of good. The bags under her eyes were no longer so dark, even though they were more obvious than Johanne liked in the sharp light by the mirror. This morning she had taken the time to have a proper bath, wash her hair, cut and varnish her nails. Put on make-up. When she finally felt ready to collect Ragnhild, she had lain down and slept for another hour and a half. Her mother had demanded to look after her grandchild again at the weekend. Johanne had shaken her head, but her mother's smile showed that she wasn't going to yield.

'What is it about mothers?' Johanne asked herself. 'Will I be like that too? Will I be just as hopeless, project my feelings on my daughters and irritate them, be equally good at reading their needs? She's the only person I can give my baby to without feeling worried or ashamed. She makes me feel like a child again. That's what I need, I need to have no responsibility, no demands, every now and then. I don't want to be like her. I need her. What is it about mothers?'

She let the cold water run over her hands for a long, long time.

More than anything, she wanted to go to bed. It was as if the previous night's long sleep had reminded her body that it was possible to sleep and now it was screaming for more. But it was only nine o'clock. She dried her hands thoroughly, put her glasses on and reluctantly went back to the kitchen.

'. . . Or what d'you reckon, Johanne?'

Sigmund's moon face smiled expectantly at her.

'About what?' she asked, trying to muster a smile.

'I was saying that surely it must be easier to make a profile of the killer now. If we take all your theories seriously, I mean.'

'All my theories? I don't have many theories.'

'Don't be a pedant,' Adam said. 'Sigmund's right, isn't he?'

Johanne picked up a bottle of mineral water and drank. Then she screwed the lid back on, thought about it, smiled fleetingly and said:

'We've certainly got a lot more to go on than before. I agree.'

'Come on then!'

Sigmund pushed a pen and some paper in her direction. His eyes were bright, like an excited child. Johanne stared at the sheets of paper in irritation.

'Fiona Helle's the problem,' she said slowly.

'Why?' asked Adam. 'Is she not the only one who's *not* a problem? We've got a murderer, a confession, and a perfect motive that underpins the murderer's confession.'

'Exactly,' Johanne agreed, and sat down on the empty bar stool. 'And for that reason she doesn't fit in.'

She took three pieces of paper and laid them side by side on the worktop. She wrote FH in felt pen on the first page, and pushed it to one side. Then she took the second and wrote VH in big letters and left it in front of her. She sat biting the pen for a while before she scribbled VK on the last piece of paper and put it in line with the others.

'Three murders. Two unsolved.'

She was talking to herself. Biting the pen. Thinking. The men were quiet. Suddenly she wrote Tuesday 20 January, Friday 6 February and Thursday 19 February under the initials.

'Different days,' she murmured. 'No pattern to the intervals.'

Adam's mouth moved as he calculated the days.

'Seventeen days between the first and second murders,' he said. 'And thirteen between the second and third. Thirty between the first and the last.'

'At least it's a round figure,' Sigmund tried.

Johanne moved the FH sheet to one side. Then pulled it back.

'Something's not right,' she said. 'There's something that just doesn't fit.'

'Can't we try to base ourselves on the assumption that someone is behind it all?' Adam suggested impatiently, and pushed the sheet over. 'Imagine that Mats Bohus has been influenced by someone. The same person who's manipulated someone into killing Vibeke Heinerback and Vegard Krogh. Let's . . .'

Johanne wrinkled her nose.

'But that's completely mad,' she said. 'I don't understand . . .'

'Let's just try,' Adam insisted. 'What does that conjure up? What sort of person could . . .'

'It has to be someone with an incredible insight into the human psyche,' she started. Again, she seemed to be talking to herself. 'A psychiatrist or a psychologist. Maybe an experienced policeman. A mad priest? No . . .'

Her fingers drummed on the sheet with Fiona Helle's initials. She bit her lip. Blinked and straightened her glasses.

'I'm afraid I just can't,' she said in a whisper. 'I can't see what the connection is. Not unless . . . what if . . .'

She stood up abruptly. A file of notes lay on the shelf by the TV. She flicked eagerly through it as she came back across the floor and found the photo of Fiona Helle. When she sat back down, she put the picture directly above the sheet of paper with the victim's initials on it.

'This case is actually completely clear-cut,' she said. 'Fiona Helle let down her son. She can hardly be blamed for what happened in 1978, when Mats was born and her mother made a decision that would affect the fate of three generations. But I'm sure that I'm not the only one who has some kind of understanding for Mats Bohus' extreme reaction to what happened. You can think what you like about some people's strange desire to discover their biological origins, but . . .'

Her eyes did not leave the photograph. Johanne took off her glasses, picked up the photo and studied it.

'It's all about dreams and great expectations,' she said in a quiet voice. 'Often, at least. When things go wrong and life is difficult, it must be tempting to think that there's something else out there, your true self, your real life. A kind of comfort. A dream that can sometimes become an obsession. Mats Bohus has had a harder life than most. His mother's final and absolute rejection must have been . . . crushing. This time she had everything to offer, but nothing to give. Mats had a motive for killing her. He killed her.'

251

Deep in thought, she put the photo on top of the sheet of paper and kept them together with a paper clip. She sat in silence as if the others were no longer there and stared at the photograph of the beautiful TV star with fascinating eyes, a straight nose and provocative, sensual mouth.

Sigmund stole a look at the bottle by the window. Adam nodded.

'What if,' Johanne began again; they could hear the enthusiasm in her voice. 'What if we assume that it's *not* three cases in a series?'

'Sorry?'

'Huh?' uttered Sigmund and filled his glass.

'We should perhaps . . .' Adam started.

'Wait,' Johanne said sharply.

She placed the sheets in a triangle, with her hand over Fiona Helle's face.

'This case has been solved,' she said. 'A murder. An investigation. A suspect. The suspect has a motive. He confesses. The confession is confirmed by other facts in the case. Case closed.'

'I have no idea where you're going,' Adam admitted. 'Are we back to square one? Do you think it's just coincidence and that we're talking about three unconnected—'

'But what about the symbolism?' Sigmund interjected. 'What about the lecture you heard thirteen years ago that . . .'

'Hang on a minute! Wait!'

Johanne stood up. She walked in circles around the floor. Every now and then she stopped by the window. Looked aimlessly out at the street, as if she had no expectation of seeing anyone there.

'It's the tongue,' she said. 'The severed tongue is the key. The starting point.'

She turned towards the two men. Two bright circles were growing on her cheeks, touching her glasses, which were steamed up. Adam and Sigmund sat quite still, in deep concentration, as if they were spectators about to watch a dangerous stunt.

'We had it already on day one,' Johanne said, excited. 'The very first day, when Fiona was found with her tongue cut off and all wrapped up. It was there. We said that it was so banal. Such simple, obvious symbolism that it could almost have been taken from a cheap book about Red Indians. You said it yourself, Adam, just the other day . . . You said that there must be countless examples of bodies with dismembered tongues throughout history. You were right. You're absolutely right. Fiona Helle's murder had nothing to do with the lecture I heard on that hot summer's day in an auditorium in Quantico. It's so . . .'

She put her hands to her face and swayed slightly from side to side.

'. . . clear,' she said, half stifled, 'so obvious. Jesus.'

Adam stared at her, bewildered.

'Don't touch me,' Johanne warned. 'Let me go on.'

Sigmund didn't drink. He was staring, his moist pink lips slightly open. His eyes moved from Johanne to Adam and back. Jack, the King of America, had come in from the sitting room. Even the dog stood stock-still, with his mouth shut and a twitching nose.

'These three cases,' Johanne finally said and dropped her hands, '. . . have a number of common features. But rather than looking for more, perhaps we should ask ourselves, what are the differences? What makes them different from each other? What makes the Fiona Helle case so different from the others?'

Adam hadn't taken his eyes off her since she started to wander round the room. Only now did he dare reach out for the bottle of water. His hands were shaking slightly as he unscrewed the top.

'It's been solved,' he quipped.

'Exactly!'

Johanne pointed at him with both hands.

'*Exactly! It's been solved!*'

Jack wagged his tail and it hit her legs when he came close. She stood on his paw by accident as she hurried back to the worktop. The dog howled.

'You found the answer in the Fiona Helle case,' she said, picking

253

up the photograph and paying no attention to the dog. 'You struggled, fumbled around and were lost for a while. But the answer was there. The post-mortem revealed details that led back to an old, sad story, which in turn led to Mats Bohus. To the murderer. Motive and opportunity. Everything was there, Adam. And it normally is. Murders are usually solved in this country.'

Sigmund grabbed his glass and took a drink.

'Hallo, I'm here too,' he complained.

'But now take the other two cases,' Johanne continued, and slid the photograph down to the end of the worktop, before grasping the other two sheets with the big letters VH and VK on. 'Have you ever, in all your working life, come across cases so devoid of suspects? So chaotic and full of false leads and distractions? Trond Arnesen . . .'

She spat the name out over the worktop.

'A boy. He certainly had things to hide, just like everyone else. But he obviously didn't kill her. His alibi is watertight, even with a one-and-a-half-hour interlude for a lovers' tryst.'

'Rudolf Fjord is a name that still interests me,' objected Sigmund.

'Rudolf Fjord,' she sighed. 'God, I'm sure he's no angel, either. Angels don't exist. So overall . . .'

Adam put his hand on hers; she was leaning against the worktop, clutching a sheet of paper in each hand. He stroked the taut skin.

'In these two cases,' she said and pulled away, '. . . you will never achieve anything, except upsetting people's lives, standing on their toes with spiked shoes. As the police never give up, you will turn people's lives upside down, in ever-increasing circles around the victims. And before you give up, before you finally admit that you will never find the murderer, you will have destroyed, derailed so many, so many lives . . .'

'OK, calm down now, Johanne. Sit down. I assume you want us to understand what you're trying to say, so you'll have to take it slower on the bends.'

She forced herself to sit down and unsuccessfully tried to tuck her hair back behind her ears. It kept falling forwards and her fringe was far too long.

'You need a drink,' Sigmund declared. 'That's what you need.'

'No thanks.'

'Wine would be better,' Adam said. 'I'm definitely going to have a glass.'

A car rattled past outside. Jack lifted his head and growled. Adam took a bottle out of the corner cupboard, held it at arm's length and nodded in satisfaction. He calmly put three glasses on the table, without comment, and opened the bottle. Then he poured a glass for himself and Johanne.

'I agree with the division you're making,' he said, and nodded. 'The Fiona Helle case is a more . . . normal case, you might say. Than the other two.'

'Normal and normal,' Sigmund said, and filled his own glass to the brim. 'There's nothing very normal about cutting tongues out of people's mouths.'

Adam ignored him, took a sip, put down his glass and crossed his arms.

'I just don't understand the connection you're making . . .'

He gave her a friendly smile, as if he was frightened he might annoy her. It annoyed her.

'Listen,' she said, in a voice that was higher than normal, with a mixture of fear, enthusiasm and anger. 'The first case triggered the other two. That's the only way it works.'

'Triggered,' Adam repeated the word.

'Triggered?'

Sigmund was more alert now and pushed his glass away a touch.

'It doesn't make sense any other way,' Johanne said. 'As I see it, the first murder happened more or less as we think it did. Fiona Helle destroyed Mats Bohus' dreams. He killed her and cut out her tongue, split it in two as a symbol of how he felt. She had lied about the most important things in life. Outwardly she appeared

255

to be a fixer of dreams, a saviour for those with difficulties. When her own son needed her, he discovered it was all a show. A huge lie, how could he feel otherwise?'

Jack barked. At the same time, as if it were cause and effect, the kitchen window slid open. A cold draught blew out the candle. Adam swore and got up.

'We've got to get these windows replaced,' he said, and bashed the frame into place before taking a match and relighting the candle.

'So there has to be someone out there,' Johanne said, as if nothing had happened. Her eyes were fixed somewhere on the wall. 'Someone who's heard Warren's lecture on Proportional Retribution. And who then decides to copy it. And is doing just that.'

An angel passed through the room.

The silence was prolonged.

The candle was still flickering in the draught. Jack had gone back to sleep. Sigmund was breathing through his mouth. A pleasant smell of cognac swathed the three people round the kitchen table.

'That has to be the case,' Johanne thought to herself. 'Someone was . . . inspired. Someone seized the moment, when they read about a murder where the victim's tongue had been cut out and wrapped up. The first piece was in place. Mats Bohus was an ignorant, arbitrary trigger.'

Still no one said a word.

'I've never heard anything like it,' Adam was thinking. 'In all my years on the job, with all my experience, and everything I've studied and read, I've never, never heard of a case like that. It can't be right. It just can't be true.'

The silence continued.

'She's a fantastic lady,' Sigmund thought. 'But she's lost it this time.'

'OK,' Adam said, finally. 'And what would the motive be for doing something like that?'

'I don't know,' replied Johanne.

'Try,' Sigmund encouraged her.

'I don't know the motive.'

'But what sort of . . .'

'He has to be of more than average intelligence. With more knowledge than most. He has . . .' She moved imperceptibly nearer to the table, closer to the others. 'It has to be someone who has unusual insight into police work. Investigations, both technical and tactical, procedures and routines. So far you haven't found a single biological trace of any significance. And my guess is that you won't. Tactically you're at a loss. This is obviously a man with no . . .'

She had a faraway look in her eyes when she took off her glasses.

'A man with no empathy,' she concluded. 'A damaged person, in some way. Personality disorder. But probably well adjusted. He won't necessarily have a criminal record. But I can't help . . .'

The look she sent Adam, unclear and searching, was one of growing desperation.

'He has to be a policeman,' she said, in despair. 'Or at least someone who . . . How can he *know* so much? He must have heard Warren's lecture. It can't be a coincidence that he's using the same symbolism?'

She held her breath. Then slowly she let it out again through clamped teeth.

'We're looking for someone who works professionally with crime,' she said without expression or tone. 'A twisted, clever and knowledgeable mind.'

'So he hasn't influenced others, made them kill?' Sigmund ventured. 'Have we dropped that theory now?'

'He's done it himself. Definitely.'

Johanne held on to Adam's eyes.

'He doesn't trust anyone,' she continued. 'He despises other people. He probably lives what we would call a lonely life, but without being a loner. People don't interest him. His actions are in

257

themselves grotesque and copying the symbolism is so sick that . . .'

She ran her hand slowly over the worktop and looked away.

'He doesn't necessarily have anything in particular against Vibeke Heinerback or Vegard Krogh.'

'That would make him the only one,' muttered Adam, 'regarding Vegard Krogh. If he has nothing against him, that is. But if you're right, what would the motive be? What the hell would the motive be for someone to . . .'

'Wait!'

Johanne gripped Adam's hand and crushed it.

'The motive doesn't need to have anything to do with Vibeke or Vegard,' she said, with renewed enthusiasm and vigour, as if catching a thought that had slipped away. 'They may have been chosen simply because they were famous. The killer wants the murders to attract attention, like the first one did, Fiona Helle's murder. This case has—'

'Vegard Krogh wasn't famous,' Sigmund cut in. 'I, for one, didn't have a clue who the guy was before he was killed.'

Johanne let go of Adam's hand. She put her glasses on again. Raised her wine glass and took a sip.

'You're right,' she said. 'You're absolutely right. I don't quite know how . . .'

'He was pretty well known in certain circles,' Adam said. 'He'd been on TV and . . .'

'Sigmund has a point,' Johanne insisted. 'The fact that Vegard Krogh was not more well known weakens my theory. But on the other hand . . .'

She broke off with a thoughtful expression on her face, as if trying to grasp some vague and undefined feeling, so she could share it with the others.

'But the motive,' Adam repeated. 'If the primary purpose was not to harm Vibeke or Vegard per se, what was it? To play with us?'

'Hush! Shhh!' Johanne was completely awake and alert now. 'Did you hear that? Is that coming from . . .?'

'It's only Kristiane,' Adam said and got up. 'I'll go.'

'No, let me.'

Johanne tried to be quiet when she got out into the hall. Ragnhild might still sleep for another hour before she needed food. Johanne heard sounds from Kristiane's room that she couldn't make out.

'What are you up to, sweetie?' she whispered as she opened the door.

Kristiane was sitting up in bed. She had put on some tights and a thick sweater. She had a felt hat on her head, a green Tyrol hat with a feather in it that Isak had once brought back from Munich. Four Barbie dolls lay strewn over the bed. The girl had a knife in her hand and was smiling at her mother.

'What . . . Kristiane! What are you . . .?'

Johanne sat down on the bed and carefully loosened her daughter's hand and took the knife.

'You mustn't . . . It's dangerous . . .'

Only then did she notice the dolls' heads. The Barbies had been decapitated. Their hair had been cut off and lay like old golden Christmas decorations on the duvet.

'What have you . . .' Johanne stammered. 'Why have you ruined your dolls?'

Her voice was angrier than she intended. Kristiane burst out crying.

'Don't know, Mummy. I was bored.'

Johanne put the knife down on the floor. She hugged her daughter to her, pulled her into her lap, pushed off the ridiculous hat, and held her tight. Rocked from side to side. Kissed her tousled hair.

'You mustn't do things like that, sweetie. You must never do things like that.'

'But I was so bored, Mummy.'

The window was open and the room was freezing. Johanne felt she was shivering all over. She threw the remains of the dolls into a corner, pushed the knife far in under the bed and lifted the

259

duvet. She lay down beside her daughter, with her stomach to her daughter's back. Johanne lay like this, whispering tender words to her, until the crying child finally fell asleep.

Kari Mundal didn't know the ins and outs of accounting, but she did have a sharp mind and robust common sense, and knew roughly what she was looking for. Not because anyone had told her, but because in the weeks since Vibeke Heinerback's death she had used her long morning walks to think, from exactly ten past six until she returned to her husband and freshly made coffee fifty minutes later.

Vibeke Heinerback had originally been Kari Mundal's project. It was the older woman who had discovered the girl's talent, when Vibeke was only seventeen years old. Potential successors to the throne had come and gone over the past fifteen years, but none of them had delivered what they once promised. A couple of them had even stabbed the old king, Kjell Mundal, in the back. Out they went. Others had fallen victim to extreme liberalism, which did not sit comfortably with the party's persistent efforts to become a new popular party, the people's party, with stringent state regulation in crucial areas of society. Such as immigration.

Out went the liberals as well, and behind them all stood Vibeke Heinerback.

It was Kari Mundal who found her. The seventeen-year-old from the suburbs, from Grorud, who chewed bubble gum and tied her bleached hair up in a ridiculous ponytail. But her eyes were blue and alert and she had a quick mind. And she was attractive once Kari Mundal persuaded her to get a new haircut and to ditch the pale-pink wardrobe.

And she was loyal to Kjell, unstintingly loyal. Always.

It wasn't easy to get close to Vibeke. Even though they had seen each other every day for years, Kari and Vibeke had never really been close. Not on a personal level. Maybe it was the age difference that made it difficult. On the other hand, Vibeke Heinerback was not open with anyone, as far as Kari Mundal knew. Not even with that show-off she was engaged to. Mrs Mundal thought the boy had no integrity, but was wise enough not to say it. They certainly looked good together. And that was something.

Politically, however, it was a different matter. Vibeke Heinerback was not forthcoming with her views about her own and the party's future, but when she did speak out, she always allied herself with Kjell and Kari Mundal. The three of them had long since laid down a long-term strategy for the party, aside from the manifesto and the other party members. The first milestone had been achieved when Vibeke had been elected by acclamation to succeed Kjell Mundal as party leader. The next would come after the parliamentary elections in 2005, when the party would, for the first time in history, be in a position where the old king could make a political comeback as a minister. Then by 2009, the country should be ready for another young female prime minister.

Rudolf Fjord might be a problem.

They had realized that already last summer during the leadership campaign, when the man was blessed with a wave of good will from the party apparatus. He was popular in the regions. He travelled a lot and local government was his forte. It was easy to promise millions to local government as long as the party was in opposition, and Rudolf was a master of the art. For a while it looked as though the race between the two leadership candidates might be closer than the Mundals cared for. But Kari knew what to do. She whispered a few well-chosen words in selected ears about Rudolf's relationships with women, and the desired results were achieved. The man seemed to be incapable of commitment. There was something suspicious about the way he always turned up at premieres and A-list parties with a new woman on his arm. It just wasn't appropriate for a man of his age.

Vibeke felt that Rudolf was necessary for the party and seemed to be quite happy to have him as deputy leader. But Kari Mundal, with her sharp nose, well trained and finely tuned from working as Kjell's closest adviser for over a generation, knew that Vibeke was hiding something. She became very alert whenever Rudolf was near. There was something in her eyes, a watchfulness that Kari never managed to grasp and that Vibeke avoided explaining the few times that she had mentioned it.

'Rudolf should be grateful that everyone is so happy about the new building that no one takes a closer look,' Vibeke had said the last time they spoke together. 'He has done a good job as chairman of the works committee, but he should tread carefully!'

Vibeke had been furious when she said it. Rudolf Fjord had taken part in a TV debate where he had openly broken a pact they had made. They had agreed to keep on a good footing with the government for a while, as it wasn't long until the revised national budget was to be announced. They had a plan. An agreement. He broke it and her eyes were dark when she repeated:

'That man should be careful. I could crush him. Like a louse, if I wanted to. He's walking on thin ice. But he should watch out what's coming from above, literally.'

And then she had to rush off to a meeting and Kari never found out what she meant. They never met again, as she was killed two weeks later. When she had confronted Rudolf about Vibeke's outburst, during the memorial service at the house on Snarøya, he had claimed that he didn't know what she was talking about. But the colour in his cheeks intensified, and he had been very uncomfortable when they met the policeman who was lost in the hall.

It was only three days ago, when she had gone to Rudolf's flat in Frogner to drop off some papers from Kjell, that she had finally discovered one possible explanation for Vibeke's outburst before she died. Rudolf was irritated by her being there, impatient for her to leave. She asked if she could use the toilet. He looked angrily at the clock, but couldn't say no. And it was there, as she let the warm water run over her thin, sinewy and soapy hands, that she realized where she should look.

The accounts department was situated right above Rudolf Fjord's office. The name was a misnomer, as it wasn't really a department, just a nice small room with cream wallpaper and cherrywood filing cabinets. The light flooded in through a large window facing the back and over the desk where Hege Hansen sat alone and kept the accounts for the party and the operations company, Kvadraturen Building Ltd.

Vibeke had said: 'He's walking on thin ice, but he should watch out for what's coming from above.'

It was late and the building was almost empty. Kari Mundal had drunk a whole thermos of tea. She wasn't used to figures and columns. She didn't even do her own tax returns. Kjell looked after things like that. But curiosity drove her on as she ploughed through the accounts for the extensive renovation project, from cover to cover, from the ledger down to the smallest receipt. Every now and then she stopped, straightened her glasses that were perched on the end of her sharp nose, squinted a bit longer at an invoice, before shaking her head and carrying on.

Then she stopped.

Div plumbing
PStark porcelain
Ft ++
Wk se ok 03
Tot NOK 342 293
VAT NOK 82 150 32
To pay NOK 424 443 32

She had been studying unclear and meaningless vouchers for five hours now, but this was by far the worst. The words porcelain and plumbing were easy enough, but it took a while before she realized that Ft had to mean fittings and that there were in fact spaces between s*e* and *ok* and *03*. Had someone inspected the work and said it was OK in 2003? What did PStark mean? Postscript tark? And why was there a PS at the top of the invoice?

The VAT had been invoiced and paid.

Se ok 03.

Se ok, pondered Kari Mundal.

263

September – October 2003, perhaps? Strange abbreviation.

She thought back to autumn last year, when it looked as if everything was going wrong with the building. It was primarily the cellar, roof and façade that were causing the problems. They had chosen the wrong kind of paint. The stone couldn't breathe and they had to repaint the whole thing. And there was something wrong with the drainage. Following torrential rain, the cellar flooded. The flooring on the ground floor had to be pulled up and replaced due to damp, which was an expensive and time-consuming operation that had nearly ruined all plans of a big opening Christmas party.

The toilets were already finished in June.

PStark.

Philippe Starck.

When they were doing up the big house at Snarøya, their youngest daughter had deluged her with interior design magazines. 'Think new, Mum,' she nagged, and pointed at jacuzzis that Kari Mundal couldn't bear and toilets that looked like eggs. She most certainly did not want to feel like a hen every time she went to the toilet, was how she dismissed her daughter's suggestion.

The big building in the Kvadraturen area of Oslo was renovated meticulously and with great care. The toilets were old-fashioned, with high-level cisterns and porcelain handpulls on gold chains.

But in Rudolf's flat, in his newly refurbished bathroom, everything was *du jour*. Philippe Starck. She had been there, she had seen it, and the realization of what she had just unearthed made her hands sweat. She resolutely drank what was left of the lukewarm tea.

Then she took the voucher out of the file and went to get the key to the photocopying room. When she opened the door, the silence in the corridor was like a dense wall. She hesitated for a moment, listening. She seemed to be alone.

Had Rudolf killed Vibeke?

Not for making a fuss about a bill for NOK 424 443 32. He couldn't have. Or could he?

Did he know that she knew? Had she threatened him? Was that why everything had suddenly gone so smoothly just before the election, when Rudolf unexpectedly withdrew his candidature and asked his supporters to vote for Vibeke?

Rudolf Fjord couldn't have killed Vibeke. Could he?

Kari Mundal put the copy in a small brown handbag before tidying away all the papers and quietly letting herself out of the building.

The woman who had wintered on the Riviera was on her way back to Norway. She was looking forward to it, in a way. At first she didn't recognize the feeling. It reminded her of something rare from her childhood, something unspecific and vague, and she wasn't even sure that it was pleasant. She felt restless, she had an uncomfortable feeling that time was passing too slowly. Only when the plane climbed steeply into the sky and she watched the wide Baie des Anges disappear under steel grey clouds, did she smile. Then she understood that it was anticipation she was feeling.

It was Friday the 27th of February and the plane was only half full. She had a whole row to herself, and when the air hostess asked if she would like some wine, she replied 'Yes, please.' It was too cold. She put the bottle between her thighs and leant back in her seat. Closed her eyes.

There was no way back.

Everything would be closer now. More intense.

More dangerous – and better.

Ulrik Gjemselund was petrified. The madman who had arrested him just under a week ago had come to get him from the prison cell. Ulrik had tried to protest. He would rather sit in his cell until he rotted than spend time with the oversized bald man who obviously didn't give a shit about anything or anyone. Particularly not Ulrik Gjemselund and his democratic legal rights.

'Jesus,' he thought to himself as he was shoved into a spartan interview room in Oslo's main police station. 'I only had some cocaine and a bloody joint. A whole week! One week! When are they going to release me? Why hasn't my lawyer done anything? She promised I would be out of custody by the weekend. I need to get a new lawyer. I want one of the top ones. I want out. Now.'

'I'm sure you're wondering why we've kept you in so long,' the policeman said in an unexpectedly cheerful voice, and pointed to a chair. 'I understand, believe me. But you see, we can generally get the judges to do what we want. When we're not happy with the trash we pick up. I once had . . .' He bellowed with laughter and closed the door behind him before sitting down on a chair that didn't look like it would take his weight. '. . . a real little shit. Not that unlike you. Pulled him in with three grams of hash in his pocket. Three grams, mind you. He was in custody for fourteen days, he was. Down in the back yard. Wasn't even room for him in a proper prison. Fourteen days he was inside. For three grams! Just because he couldn't understand that . . .' Suddenly he leant forward and smiled. His teeth were even and surprisingly white. '. . . that I'm really a good guy.'

Ulrik swallowed.

'A good guy,' the policeman repeated. 'Right now, I'm the best friend you've got. So you see, I get disappointed when . . .' He brushed his hand over his scalp, with a hurt expression on his face. '. . . when you just ignore me. Won't answer my questions or anything.'

Ulrik fiddled with the sleeve of his sweater. A thread had come loose. He wound it round his fingers, tried to push it in between two loose stitches.

'I'm sure that your lawyer's made loads of promises,' the policeman continued. 'That's what they do, you know. But for her, you're just one of many. She's got other things to do than . . .'

'I want a new lawyer,' Ulrik said loudly, and pulled back closer to the wall. 'I want the best, I want Tor Edvin Staff.'

The policeman laughed again.

'Tor *Erling* Staff,' he corrected him, and grinned. 'I'm sure he's got far more exciting things to do. But you just listen to me . . .'

He leant so far over the table that Ulrik could feel his breath on his face. Garlic and stale tobacco. The detainee pressed his head back against the wall and gripped the edge of the table.

'You're probably wondering why I'm keeping you here,' the man said, and again his tone was almost conciliatory, friendly. 'I quite understand, I do. You haven't exactly killed anyone, have you? But let me tell you something. It's what I call . . . *the delicate ecology of crime.*'

He sat back and straightened up again, at last. He looked puzzled, as if he didn't really understand what he'd just said. Ulrik let the chair down to the floor again and dared to breathe out.

'Smart,' the man said, pleased with himself. '*The delicate ecology of crime.* Not used that expression before. You know, everything's connected. Out there in the wild.'

He waved one of his massive fists at the wall, as if nature were pressing in through the plasterboard.

'If there's lots of midges, there's plenty of food for the birds. If there's food for the birds, they lay lots of eggs. Snakes and martens eat the eggs. If there are lots of martens, it's good for the fur trade . . . oh, hang on, they've got tame martens as well, haven't they? Minks, isn't that what they're called?'

For a moment he looked thoughtfully at Ulrik. The blue eye nearly closed, the brown one squinting. Then he shrugged and gave a quick shake of the head.

'You get the point,' he stated. 'Everything's connected. It's the same with crime. The smallest junkie creep is connected with the worst bank robber, the most brutal killer. Or maybe it's better to say . . . their actions are connected. It's a web, you see. An incredibly intricate web of . . .' He hunched his back, lifted his elbows and clawed his fingers, as if he was trying to frighten a child. 'Evil,' he hissed. 'You buy drugs. Someone has to smuggle them in. They get rich. They get greedy. They steal. Kill if they have to. Sell drugs. Kids get addicted. Attack old ladies on the street.'

He was still pretending to be an enormous crab. His fingers

267

were waving around in front of Ulrik's eyes. His nails were bitten to the quick.

'The man's a lunatic', Ulrik thought to himself. 'Does anyone else know that I'm here? He's locked the door. It's locked.'

'And that takes us back,' continued the policeman, who resumed his normal behaviour, 'to why I didn't just let a squirt like you back on the streets again, as soon as I'd got your details, last Saturday. D'you see why now?'

Ulrik didn't dare to answer. It obviously made no difference.

'Because when the name Trond Arnesen popped up, it suddenly became more than just the white lines and a spliff,' the policeman explained. 'Cos everything . . .'

He paused and made an encouraging, rotating movement with his right hand.

'. . . is connected,' mumbled Ulrik.

'Well done! Exactly! Now we're getting somewhere, son! And I'll show you what I found at your place the other day. Had to take an extra look round, you see. Round your lovely, expensive flat.'

He slapped the bum of his trousers. Then his face lit up and he pulled a notebook out of his breast pocket.

'Here it is,' he said, pleased with himself. 'So, I'm guessing that these are your accounts.'

Ulrik opened his mouth to protest.

'Shut it,' the man snarled. 'I've been banging up people like you since way before your dad got hairs on his dick. This is your book and these are your customers.' He tapped his finger on the initials in the margin of an open page. 'Telephone numbers and everything, so I've managed to identify lots of them already. Strange, really, the secrets that people carry around. But not a lot surprises me any more.'

He clicked his tongue and shook his head. He seemed to be completely engrossed in the little book.

'But not all of them,' he said suddenly. 'I'm missing three names. I want to know who AC is. And APL and RF. And Ulrik . . .'

He got up slowly. He scratched his moustache, stretched. Pulled on his ear lobe. Smiled and then was very serious. Both his palms smashed down onto the table. Ulrik jumped in his chair, quite literally.

'Now don't muck me around,' he snapped. 'Don't you even try. They're your customers and I want to know who they are, OK? We can sit here until the moon falls from the sky, but that would be bloody uncomfortable. For both of us. But mainly for you. So start talking. Now.'

His hand landed lightly on Ulrik's neck. And squeezed. Not too hard. He loosened his grip, but left his hand there. It was enormous and burning hot.

'Don't waste our time, son.'

'Arne Christiansen and Arne-Petter Larsen,' Ulrik forced out.

'RF,' the man barked. 'Who's RF?'

'Rudolf Fjord,' Ulrik whispered. 'But I haven't seen him for ages. A couple of years, at least.'

The hand gently stroked the back of his head and then withdrew.

'Good boy,' the policeman said. 'Now what did I say?'

Ulrik looked at him terrified, the blood was pounding in his ears and he was sweating.

'What did I tell you?' the man asked again in a friendly voice. 'Lost your tongue?'

'Everything's connected,' Ulrik whispered quickly.

'Everything's connected,' nodded the man. 'Remember that. Next time.'

'He'd get Mother Theresa to admit to triple murder,' Sigmund Berli said cynically, and tapped the report the policeman had written after questioning Ulrik Gjemselund. 'Or Nelson Mandela to admit to genocide. Or Jesus to . . .'

'I get the picture, Sigmund. Got it straight away, in fact.'

They were walking. Adam had insisted on going to Frogner Park first. Sigmund protested all the way. They didn't have much time. It was freezing cold. Sigmund was wearing unsuitable shoes and his wife was in a bad mood because of all the overtime. He couldn't understand why they should waste twenty minutes in a park full of ugly statues and aggressive dogs on the loose.

'I need some air,' Adam explained. 'I need to think, OK? And that's not easy with you chattering away like a five-year-old. So shut up. Enjoy the exercise. We need it, both of us.'

He thought: 'Johanne's wrong' and picked up pace. He felt an unfamiliar twinge under his ribcage. He'd never doubted her abilities before. He'd admired them. Needed them. He needed her and he was losing her. Her instincts were wrong. Her intellect weakened by sleepless nights and a greedy baby. 'The theory doesn't hold. If the murderer wanted to create an uproar, make a noise, get attention, he wouldn't have chosen Vegard Krogh. Vibeke Heinerback, yes. Everyone knows her. But Vegard Krogh? A sham of an artist, a quasi-intellectual fool? Who practically no one had heard of? Johanne's wrong and we're back to square one. We don't know what we're looking for. Where to look.'

'Why don't we just call the guy in?' Sigmund was surly. He had short legs and had to jog to keep up with his colleague. 'Why do we always have to visit people at home all the time? Bloody hell, Adam, we're wasting taxpayers' money by throwing away all this time.'

'People's tax money is used for far worse things than us trying to find a way out of the mess we're in,' Adam levelled. 'Give over. We're nearly there.'

'I don't believe that Gjemselund boy. Rudolf Fjord's not a poof, you know. He doesn't look like one. Why the hell would he pay that runt for sex? Huh? A tall, good-looking guy who the ladies love! My wife reads all those magazines, you know, with pictures from premieres and parties and all that, and he's definitely not a poof.'

Adam stopped. He took a deep breath. The air was so cold that it caught in his throat.

'Sigmund,' he said, calmly. 'Sometimes I get the impression

that you're just plain stupid. But as I know that you're not, I must ask you to . . .'

He warmed his ears with his hands. Took another deep breath and shouted, suddenly:

'*Shut up!*'

Then he set off again.

They passed through the heavily ornate gates onto Kirkeveien in silence. Two coaches were parked diagonally outside. Adam pulled his scarf tighter round his neck. A flock of traditionally dressed Africans in wide, colourful garments were boarding one of the coaches. It was hard to imagine why tourists came to Norway, Sigmund thought. And in February, when there was snow everywhere and you got slush all the way up your legs, it was incomprehensible.

'You've got to admit that those dresses are silly,' he muttered.

'You look pretty ridiculous too with leather patches on your arse, a red bolero and silver buckles on your shoes,' Adam retorted, 'but that doesn't seem to stop you wearing your national costume. It's probably some sort of official gubbins. What time is it?'

'Nearly six,' Sigmund complained. 'I'm cold as hell. And anyway, it's not a bol . . . bolero. It's a woollen jacket.'

Eleven minutes later Adam's finger ran up and down a list of names on a metal plate beside a grey door.

'Rudolf Fjord,' he murmured and pushed the bell.

No one answered. Sigmund banged his feet together to keep warm and muttered under his breath. A young woman walked up with a bag over her shoulder. She fished out a bunch of keys and smiled at Adam.

'Hi', she said, as if she knew him.

'Hi,' he replied.

'Going in?'

She held the door open and he caught it. The woman had red hair. She ran up the stairs, whistling like a girl, leaving behind a scent of fresh air and light perfume.

'Have a good evening,' she called. They heard a door open and close again.

'So here we are,' Sigmund said, and looked up the stairs.

'Third floor,' Adam said, and went over to an ancient lift with iron folding gates. 'I'm not sure this will hold both of us.'

'Max load 250 kilos,' Sigmund read on an enamel sign. 'We'll risk it, eh?'

It worked. Just. The lift whined and groaned and stopped a foot before the third floor. Adam struggled to get the door open. The gates were jammed against the floor.

'I'll think I'll take the stairs on the way down,' groaned Adam, and finally managed to get out.

It was an impressive building, even if the lift was ancient. The stairwell was wide and carpeted. The windows out to the back had diamonds of red and blue glass that threw a play of colours on the walls. There were two front doors on the third floor. Between them hung a glass-framed painting of a golden-brown landscape somewhere in southern Europe.

Adam hadn't even rung Rudolf Fjord's bell before the door opposite opened.

'Hallo,' said a woman in her seventies.

She was beautiful in a posh way, Sigmund noted. Slim and quite small. Groomed hair. Skirt and sweater and a pair of neat leather slippers. She was wringing her hands and seemed to be distressed.

'I'm terribly sorry to butt in, I know it's none of my business,' she said. Adam noticed now that despite her old-fashioned, almost subservient appearance, her eyes were sharp. The two men had been weighed up and measured at once.

'Are you friends of Mr Fjord? Or colleagues, perhaps?'

Her smile was sincere enough and the worried furrow in her brow was genuine.

'I have to admit that I've been listening in case anyone came,' she said before they had a chance to answer. 'For once I was grateful to hear the noise of that thing.'

272

A thin finger with a manicured nail pointed to the lift.

'You see, Rudolf is such a boon to us here. He looks after us. Sorts everything out. When I broke my leg just before Christmas . . .' She modestly lifted her left leg. It was beautiful, slim and whole. '. . . He popped by every day and did my shopping. We're good neighbours, Rudolf and I. But now I'm . . . oh, I do apologize.'

With practised hands, she undid the chain and came towards the two men.

'Halldis Helleland.'

She offered her hand. The two men mumbled their surnames.

'I am so worried,' said the woman. 'Rudolf came home about nine o'clock last night. I happened to come in at the same time. He had been to the theatre with a lady friend. Rudolf and I always have a natter when we bump into each other. Sometimes he even comes in for coffee. Or a glass of something. He is always so . . .'

'She's like a weasel,' Adam thought. 'An energetic, curious weasel, with playful hands and darting eyes that see everything.'

She patted her hair, coughed a little.

'. . . Nice,' she concluded.

'But not last night,' Adam suggested questioningly.

'No! He barely answered when I spoke to him. Looked pale. I asked if he was unwell, but he said he was fine. Be that as it may, when . . .' Halldis Helleland's smile took ten years off her. There was a flash of gold from her beautiful teeth and she had deep dimples. 'He's a man in his prime and I'm an old widow. I understand perfectly that he may not always have time for me. But . . .'

She hesitated.

'It was unusual behaviour,' Adam contributed. 'He behaved very differently from normal.'

'Exactly,' said a grateful Mrs Helleland. 'And since then, I'm ashamed to say that I've been keeping my ears open.'

She looked Adam straight in the eye.

'Not very nice, I admit, but sound *does* carry easily in this building and I feel that we should all . . . look out for one another.'

273

'I quite agree,' Adam assured her. 'And did you hear anything?'

'Nothing,' she said in obvious distress. 'That is the problem. I usually hear footsteps from the flat. Music. Sometimes the TV. The only . . .' The furrow reappeared on her brow. 'The telephone has rung,' she said decisively. 'Four times. Rung and rung.'

'Maybe he went out again,' Sigmund suggested.

Halldis Helleland gave him a reproachful look, as if he had insinuated that she was asleep at her post. She pointed to two newspapers on the doormat.

'The morning and evening edition,' she said, meaningfully. 'The man is a newspaper obsessive. Unless he sneaked out during the night when I was asleep, I say he's at home. And he hasn't even taken in the papers!'

'He may well have done just that,' Adam said. 'He may have gone out last night.'

'I'll ring the police,' the woman said with some force. 'If you won't believe that I know Rudolf Fjord well enough to know that something is wrong, I shall phone the authorities.'

She turned around and walked back towards her own door.

'Wait a moment,' Adam said in a calm voice. 'Mrs Helleland, we are from the police.'

She spun round.

'Excuse me?'

Her agile hands quickly brushed over her hair again before she smiled with relief and added:

'Of course. It's that awful business with Vibeke Heinerback. Terrible. It did so affect poor Rudolf. Of course, you're here to get more information. But then . . .'

She cocked her head to one side then the other – small, quick movements. Now she really did look like a weasel, with a pointed noise and small, darting eyes.

'Then we should go in,' she decided. 'But first I must ask to see your ID. Just a moment, I'll go and get the keys.'

Before the two policemen could say anything, she'd disappeared.

274

'I don't like the sound of that,' Adam said.

'Of what?' Sigmund asked. 'She's got the key! And you can say what you like, the woman talks a lot of sense.'

'I don't want to think about what we might find.'

Halldis Helleland reappeared. She glanced at the ID cards that the two men held up and nodded.

'Rudolf had his bathroom done up last autumn,' she explained, and put the key in the lock. 'It looks super now. But with the workmen coming in and out, it seemed best that I had a set of keys. You never know who you can trust. And I've just kept them. There!'

The door was open.

Adam went in.

It was dark in the hallway. All the doors to the rooms were shut.

'The drawing room is this way,' Mrs Helleland said, meeker now.

She slipped under Adam's arm and walked to the end of the hall. Then she stopped in front of a double door.

'Perhaps it's best . . .' she started and nodded to Adam.

He opened the door.

A chandelier lay on the table. The prisms were tangled. One lonely prism dangled over the edge of the table. Rudolf Fjord was hanging from a rope slung over a hook in the centre of an enormous ceiling rose, to which the chandelier had obviously until recently been attached. His tongue was blue and swollen. His eyes were open. The body hung absolutely still.

'I think you should go back to your own flat and wait there,' Adam said. Mrs Helleland had not dared to look into the drawing room yet.

Without asking, without even so much as glancing into the room, she obeyed. The front door was left open behind her. They heard her steps crossing the hall. Her door closing.

'Shit,' said Sigmund Berli, and walked over to the body.

He pulled up Rudolf Fjord's trouser leg and touched the white skin.

'Completely cold.'

'Can you see a letter?'

Adam didn't move. He just stood there, frozen, and watched the movement that Sigmund had set in motion. The body turned incredibly slowly round its own axis.

An upturned chair lay on the floor.

'Johanne was certainly right about one thing,' Adam thought. 'She was right about the price of this case. The cost is too high. We're stumbling around in the dark. Lifting up a corner of some-one's life here, pulling a thread there. Then it all goes to pieces. We can't find what we're looking for, but we carry on. Obviously Rudolf Fjord couldn't. Who told him? Was it Ulrik? Was it Ulrik who phoned to warn an old customer, to say that his secret was out? That there was no point in parading around with women any more, pretending to be a man of the world?'

'No letter, not here anyway.'

'Keep looking.'

'But I have . . .'

'Keep on looking. And call the duty officer. Straight away.'

Rudolf Fjord had not killed Vibeke Heinerback, Adam was sure of that. He couldn't bring himself to move. 'He had dinner with some party colleagues in Bærum on the night that she was murdered. His alibi was good. He was never a suspect. But we still couldn't let him be. We can never let anyone be,' he thought to himself.

'There's no letter here.' Sigmund Berli sounded irritated. 'He hanged himself because he was frightened of being caught with his trousers down. Not much to write home about, maybe.'

'And that,' Adam said, and finally managed to walk over to the body, which had stopped turning. '. . . the fact that Rudolf Fjord may have paid for sex with Trond Arnesen's lover, is something that we will keep to ourselves. There are limits to how much damage we can do to other people's lives and . . .' He looked up at Rudolf Fjord's face. The broad, masculine chin seemed bigger now and his eyes were bloodshot. He looked like a stranded deep-water fish. '. . . reputation,' Adam finished. 'We'll keep that to ourselves. OK?'

'OK,' Sigmund agreed. 'Fine by me. Oslo Police are on their way. Ten minutes, they said.'

They got there in eight.

When Kari Mundal answered the phone four hours later, annoyed that someone should ring at half past ten on a Friday night, it only took a minute before she sank down on the chair by the little mahogany shelf in the hall. She listened to what the party secretary had to say and barely managed to answer his questions adequately. When the conversation finally closed, she stayed sitting where she was. The chair was uncomfortable and it was dark and cold in the hall. But she couldn't get up.

She had rung Rudolf yesterday. There was nothing else she could do. She had tossed and turned on Wednesday night, weighing up the pros and cons of blowing the whistle, and by Thursday morning she had made up her mind.

And it had been fatal, she realized that now.

Without having decided how she would pursue the matter, she had phoned him. Without having thought about how the party, and thereby Kjell Mundal, would cope with such a scandal, she had told him what she knew.

'I was so angry,' she thought, hearing only her own breathing, shallow and fast. 'I was so disappointed and angry. Wasn't thinking straight. I just wanted him to know that he wasn't out of the woods yet. He needed to know that his secret hadn't gone to the grave with Vibeke. I was so angry. And so very disappointed.'

'What's the matter, dear?'

Kjell Mundal emerged from the sitting room. Light flooded through the double door and nearly blinded her. Her husband was a dark figure in the doorway with his pipe in one hand and a newspaper in the other.

'Rudolf is dead,' she said.

'Rudolf?'

'Yes.'

Her husband moved towards her. She could still hear only her own breathing, her own pulse. He turned on the light and it hurt her eyes. She was crying.

'What are you talking about?' he asked and took her hand.

'Rudolf has committed suicide,' she whispered. 'They're not quite sure when. Yesterday, possibly. They don't know. I don't know.'

'Committed suicide? *Taken his own life?*' Kjell Mundal bellowed. 'But why in the world would that idiot go and take his own life?'

The party secretary had told her that no letter had been found. Not in the flat, nor on his PC. They would, of course, carry on searching, but for the moment, nothing had been found.

'No one knows,' Kari Mundal said, and let go of his hand. 'No one knows anything yet.'

'I hope you didn't write a letter, Rudolf,' Kari Mundal thought. 'I hope that your mother, poor soul, never finds out why you were so frightened that you had to take your own life.'

'I need a drink,' Kjell Mundal said, and swore savagely. 'And so do you.'

She followed him, without saying any more.

It was a busy evening, with telephone calls and lots of visitors. No one noticed that the normally vivacious woman was completely silent, for the first time in her long life. Everyone talked at once. Some were desperate. Some cried. People came and went until far into the night. Kari Mundal made coffee and tea, mixed strong drinks and prepared sandwiches at midnight. But she said nothing.

As dawn approached, when Kjell had finally fallen asleep, she got up and went downstairs. In her handbag, in a compartment of her voluminous purse, was a copy of the telling invoice. She took it out and went over to the fireplace. There she lit a match. Only when the flames licked her fingers did she let go of the paper.

Two days later she made up a pretext to look at the old accounts again. She immediately found what she was looking for.

The original invoice was torn to shreds and flushed down the toilet on the second floor, an old-fashioned toilet with a high-level cistern and a porcelain handpull on a gold chain.

No suicide note was ever found. For a while, a couple of police-men in Oslo thought that they knew why Rudolf Fjord had hanged himself in his own drawing room, so soon after he'd been elected as the much-celebrated leader of one of the largest polit-ical parties in Norway. They never said anything. After some years, the episode faded and was forgotten.

An elderly lady at Snarøya, to the west of Oslo, was the only person who knew the reason why he had committed suicide.

And she never forgot.

Fifteen

'Leap year,' shouted Kristiane. 'Leap bound bang bang!'

'No pretend guns in the house,' Johanne reprimanded, and took the plastic spatula she was brandishing at her out of her hand.

'Honestly, you can't seriously call that a pretend gun,' Adam said, irritated.

'Bang, bang! What's a leap year?'

'It's a year that has a day like today,' Adam explained, and hunkered down beside her. 'The twenty-ninth of February. Days like this come only once every four years. Maybe they're shy.'

'Shy,' repeated Kristiane. 'Leap year. Peep here. Bang!'

She stopped and put her hair behind her ears, like her mother had just done.

'But what's the scientific explanation?' She was serious. 'I want to understand, not just be told something funny.'

The adults exchanged looks, Johanne's was anxious and Adam's was proud.

'Well, the Earth takes a bit longer than 365 days to . . .'

He stroked his head and looked over at Johanne for help.

'To go round its own axis?'

'That takes twenty-four hours, Adam.'

'To go round the sun?'

Johanne just smiled and wrung out a cloth.

'To go right round the sun,' he said with conviction to Kristiane. 'That's what we call a year, but it's a tiny bit longer . . . So, every now and then, we have to gather together all the extra bits that add up to make a full day. Every fourth year. And then there was something about Gregory and Julius, but I can't remember that.'

'You're clever,' Kristiane said. 'Julius is a chimpanzee in the

280

zoo, Adam. I'm going to play leap years with Leonard and today Daddy is coming to collect me. You're not my daddy.'

'No, but I love you very much.'

Then she shot off, with Jack at her heels. The small feet clattered down the stairs and the door slammed behind them. Adam snorted and got up, with pride.

'I wonder how many times we'll have to go through that whole rigmarole that I'm not her father,' he said. 'We'll have to get the access agreement sorted out soon. It's been chaotic this winter. Wasn't she supposed to stay at Isak's on Friday?'

'What's the matter with you?' Johanne asked, and stroked his hair. 'Is it just the Rudolf Fjord case, or is it . . .'

'Just? *Just?*' He pulled his head away, a bit too abruptly. 'It's bloody not "just" when your job forces people to suicide.'

'You haven't driven anyone to suicide, Adam. You know that.'

He sat down on the nearest bar stool. A half-eaten celery stick was lying on a dirty plate. He picked it up and took a bite.

'No, actually, I don't know that,' he said and took another bite.

'My love,' she said and he had to smile.

She kissed him on the ear, on the neck.

'You haven't killed anyone,' she whispered. 'You catch spiders and then let them out into the garden. Rudolf Fjord took his own life. He chose to die. By his own volition. Of course it's . . .'

She stood up and looked him in the eye.

'Of course it's not your fault. You know that.'

'I miss you,' he said, chewing on the celery.

'Miss me? I'm here, you fool.'

'Not quite,' he answered. 'None of us are all here. Not like before.'

'It will get better,' she thought. 'Soon. I've finally started to sleep now. Not a lot, but a lot more. Spring will soon be here. Ragnhild is growing. Getting stronger. Everything will get better. If only this case were over and you . . .'

'Have you considered taking some time off?' she asked lightly, and started to stack the dirty plates in the dishwasher.

'Time off?'

'Yes, take your paternity leave. Properly.'

'As if we can afford that . . .'

He chewed and chewed and stared at the green, half-eaten stick.

'I could start working again,' she said. 'Wouldn't it be good to have this case off your hands? To forget it? Let someone else take over, someone else take . . .'

'Nonsense.'

He scratched his groin.

'Isn't it strange,' he said, with his eyes narrowed. 'Isn't it strange to choose death rather than . . .'

'Don't change the subject. Have you actually considered it?'

'You're entitled to most leave, Johanne. Which is only fair and reasonable. You've just given birth, you're breastfeeding. It's good for Ragnhild. So it's good for us.'

He threw the remains of the celery at the rubbish bin in the cupboard under the sink, as if to underline that the conversation was closed. He missed.

'But isn't it peculiar,' he continued and opened out his hands, 'that a person should choose to take his life because he risks being outed as a homosexual? In 2004? For Christ's sake, they're everywhere! We've got hordes of lesbians at work and they don't seem to feel persecuted or bothered and we . . .'

'Actually, strictly speaking, you don't know much about that,' she said, and picked up the celery. 'You barely know them.'

'Come on, the *finance minister* of Norway is gay, for Christ's sake. And no one seems to be too bothered about that!'

Johanne smiled and it annoyed him.

'The finance minister is a . . . *soigné* gentleman from the west end,' she said. 'Discreet, professional and according to what little we know of him, an excellent cook. He's lived with the same man for centuries. That's a *bit* . . .' She held her finger and thumb together in an exaggerated gesture. '. . . Different,' she continued, 'from someone who buys sex from young boys while parading

282

around with blondes on his arm whenever there's a camera nearby.'

Adam said nothing. He put his head down on his arms.

'Why don't you have a little sleep?' she said quietly, and stroked his back. 'You were up all night.'

'I'm not tired,' he said into his sleeve.

'What are you then?'

'Depressed.'

'Can I do anything for you?'

'No.'

'Adam . . .'

'The worst thing is that Rudolf was cleared as a suspect so early on in the case,' he said angrily and sat up. 'His alibi was fine. There was nothing to indicate that he was behind it. Quite the opposite, according to his colleagues in the Storting, he was devastated. So why couldn't we just leave the man in peace? What the hell does it matter to us who he's fucking?'

'Adam,' she tried again, and held his neck between her hands.

'Listen to me,' he said and pushed her away.

'I'm listening. It's just a bit difficult to answer when what you're saying isn't . . . very sensible. You had every reason to investigate Rudolf Fjord in more detail. Especially after the argument you heard between him and Kari Mundal. At the memorial service out at . . .'

'I remember it well enough,' he cut her off, cross. 'But it can't be more than five days since you sat here and drew a profile of a killer that was *nothing* like Rudolf Fjord. Why did I then have to pursue . . .'

'You never believed in that profile,' she said curtly, and got out the washing-up powder. 'Not then and not now. And to be honest, I think you should stop moping.'

'Moping? *Moping?*'

'Yes, you're moping. Feeling sorry for yourself. You can just stop it now.'

She slammed the dishwasher shut, put the box of powder back

on the shelf in the cupboard and turned to face him, with her right hand on her hip. And grinned.

'Meany,' he mumbled, and smiled reluctantly back. 'Anyway, you said yourself that the profile had a number of weak points. Vegard Krogh didn't fit. He wasn't well known enough.'

Johanne picked up Sulamit the fire engine, which had been abandoned on the floor. The eyes on the radiator grille had lost their pupils and stared blindly at her. She fidgeted with the broken ladder.

'I've been doing some more thinking,' she said.

'And?'

Do you remember . . . do you remember when we were sitting here with Sigmund? Not last Tuesday, but a few weeks ago?'

'Of course.'

'He asked me what would be the worst imaginable murder.'

'Yes.'

'And I answered that it would have to be something like a killer without a motive.'

'Yes.'

'They don't exist.'

'Right. So what did you mean then?'

'I meant . . . I still think my reasoning stands, by the way. A killer who chooses his victims completely arbitrarily, without a motive for the individual murders, would be extremely difficult to catch. Assuming that a number of other factors are in place, of course. Such as the killer doing a good job, to put it simply.'

'Aha . . .'

He nodded and put his hand on his stomach.

She put Sulamit down with a thump.

'Surely you can't be hungry again. It's less than an hour since you ate. Now listen.'

'I'm all ears,' Adam said.

'The problem is that it's difficult to imagine a completely random series of victims,' Johanne said, and sat down on the stool beside him. 'People never function in a vacuum! We're never unbiased, we all have our likes and dislikes, we . . .'

She pressed her fingers together, so that her hands looked like a tent, and then she put her nose in the opening.

'Let's imagine,' she continued, in full concentration. Her voice sounded quite nasal when she sat like that. '. . . a murderer who decides to kill. For whatever reason. We'll come back to that. But he decides to kill, not because he wants to take someone's life, but because he . . .'

'It's difficult to imagine that anyone can be murdered in cold blood, unless the murderer actually wants them dead.'

'Try to imagine it all the same,' she said impatiently. She folded her hands and clasped them together until the knuckles turned white. 'The murderer would possibly choose the first victim fairly randomly. Like when we were children and spun the globe. Then, wherever your finger hit . . .'

'. . . You would go in twenty-five years' time,' he finished. 'I even read a children's book about something like that. *The Kept Promise.*'

'Do you remember what tended to happen the second time you tried?'

'I cheated,' he said, and smiled. 'Opened my eyes ever so slightly to make sure I got somewhere more exciting than my mate.'

'In the end I would stand there with open eyes and aim,' Johanne admitted. 'I wanted to go to Hawaii.'

'And your point is . . .'

'I've read in the papers,' she said, letting him stroke the back of her hand, 'that they're calling these cases the perfect crime. Not so strange really, considering how helpless the police seem to be. But I think perhaps we should shift the focus and instead say that we're in fact talking about *the perfect murderer*. But . . .'

She chewed her lip and reached out for a caper from one of the bowls.

'The point is that there is no such thing,' she said, studying the stalk. 'The perfect murderer is completely free of any context. The perfect murderer feels nothing – no fear, no horror, no hate and certainly no love. People have a tendency to think that mad murderers have no feelings and are completely incapable of relating to other human beings. They forget that even Marc Dutroux, the epitome of a paedophile monster, was married. Hitler inflicted terrible suffering on the Jews and sent six million to their death, but it's said that he was very fond of his dog. And presumably he was even kind to it.'

'Did he have a dog?'

She shrugged her shoulders.

'Think so. But you get my point, at least.'

'No.'

She got up slowly, still chewing on the stubborn caper. She looked around the room and then went over to Kristiane's toy box.

'I am a person who has decided to kill,' she said, and swallowed before stalling his objection: 'Just forget why, for the moment.'

She picked up a red ball and held it out in front of her in her right hand, in a dramatic pose, like Hamlet and the skull. Adam chuckled.

'Don't laugh,' she said, in a level voice. 'This is my world. I know a lot about crime. It's my subject. I know there's a connection between the motive and how a case is solved. I know that I'm more likely to get away with murder if no one can find a connection between me and the victim. So, I spin the globe . . .'

She closed her eyes and blindly pressed her finger into the red rubber.

'I have chosen a completely random victim,' she said. 'And I kill that person. Everything works out. No one suspects me. I get a taste for more.'

She looked up.

'But in some way, I've changed. All our actions, everything that happens, affects us. I feel . . . successful. I want to do it again. I feel . . . alive.'

She froze. Adam opened his mouth.

'Shh,' she said sharply. 'Shh!'

They could hear the children running from room to room

downstairs. Jack was barking angrily. Then they heard a muffled, cross, grown-up voice, through the floor.

'Maybe I should go down and get her,' Adam said. 'Sounds like . . .'

'Shh,' she said again. She had a distant look in her eyes and she had frozen in a theatrical comedy pose, with one leg tantalizingly in front of the other. The ball was still in her right hand.

'Alive,' she repeated, as if she was tasting the word.

Suddenly, she grabbed the ball with both hands and threw it to the floor. It bounced against the fireplace and knocked over a plant that was standing on the floor, without Johanne seeming to bother.

'Alive,' she said for the third time. 'These murders are a form of . . . extreme sport.'

'What?'

Adam stared at Johanne. He tried to see beyond the unfamiliar, frightened expression, beyond her unfamiliar behaviour; he tried to see inside her mind. She stood as if in a trance.

'Extreme sport,' she repeated, without paying him any attention, '. . . a way of feeling alive. That's how people describe it. The adrenalin kick. The rush. The feeling of defying death and succeeding, time and again. Nearly dying is the most intense way of feeling alive. Actually feeling life. Understanding it better. The rest of us just ask why? Why push yourself to get to the top of Mount Everest when the journey is, in every sense, paved with dead bodies? What would drive someone to throw themselves from a high cliff in Mexico when the slightest misjudgement could mean that the waves below hurled you straight back into the cliff face?'

'Johanne,' Adam tried, and put up his hand.

'They say it gives them the feeling of being alive.' She answered her own questions.

She still didn't look at him. Instead she got hold of Kristiane's rag doll from the windowsill. She pulled to it to her by the leg and then hugged it, long and hard.

'Johanne,' he tried again.

'I just don't understand it,' she whispered, 'but that's the explanation they give. That's what they say when it's all over and they're smiling at the camera, at their friends. Their stick their fingers up at life. And laugh. And then they go and do it all over again. And again. And again . . .'

This time he got up and went over to her. Pulled the doll from her hands and put his arms round her. He didn't know if she was crying, so he kept still.

'As if life isn't valuable enough in itself,' she mumbled into his chest. 'As if human triviality is not bad enough. As if loving someone, having children, getting old, isn't frightening enough.'

She pushed him away. He didn't want to let go, but she was determined and forced him to. But she did look him straight in the eye when she continued:

'We can see it everywhere, Adam. More and more, new variations all the time. Jackass stunts for young people. They set themselves alight, dive from a roof on a bike. People are bored. *People are bored to death!*'

She was nearly screaming and slapped him on the chest. Her voice trembled. 'Did you know that some people play a kind of Russian roulette with HIV? Others heighten their orgasm through strangulation? And sometimes they die before they come. Die!'

She was laughing now, hysterically. She went over to the island unit and managed to perch on a stool. She covered her face with her hands.

'Death is the only real news for people today,' she said. 'I can't remember who said that, but it's true. Death is extremely titillating, as it is the only thing we will never understand. It's the only thing we know nothing about.'

'So what you're saying,' Adam tried to bring her back to day to day reality, 'is that we're talking about a killer who's . . . bored?'

'Yes. His motive isn't to do with who he kills, but rather that they are killed.'

'Johanne . . .'

'It has to be,' she insisted. 'Killing someone is the most extreme of all extreme actions you can take. The murderer . . . It fits, Adam. It fits with the theory that he didn't kill Fiona Helle. He was just sitting there. Somewhere. Bored. Then Mats Bohus killed his mother, in a grotesque way, and Norway lost the plot. The murder had all the right ingredients: a famous victim, the characteristics of ritual, strong symbolism. The reaction was deafening. I can hardly imagine anything more stimulating, a more exciting trigger than that murder. Especially as it had so many similarities to the first murder in another series, in another story about . . .'

'Now listen to what you're saying,' Adam insisted. He had raised his voice now. 'If we summarize your profile, we've got the following. A: . . .'

With his right index finger, he pointed to his left thumb.

'The murderer knows everything that's worth knowing about crime. B: at some point or another, he has heard Warren's lecture about Proportional Retribution.'

'Or heard about it,' corrected Johanne.

'Which means that he may not necessarily be Norwegian,' Adam added, and pulled a face. 'Third: killing for this person is a kind of hobby, a way to relieve a boring, humdrum life. He chooses . . .'

'. . . His victims on an apparently random bases,' Johanne concluded. Her cheeks were flushed and her eyes were shiny. 'At least to begin with. He has only one criterion. The person has to be famous. He wants maximum effect. It's the thrill he's after. He's playing, Adam.'

'And then we're back to square one,' he said, and rubbed his cheek in resignation. 'Vegard Krogh was not famous.'

'He was famous enough,' she corrected him with great intensity. 'There was enough commotion about his death, for goodness' sake! Especially as he was number three in a series of celebrity murders. The murderer knew that. He knew that Vegard Krogh was sufficiently well known and that was why he decided to forgo . . . randomization!'

'What?'

'Only a computer can achieve a completely random selection, Adam. We humans, we let ourselves be swayed, consciously or unconsciously. Vegard Krogh was chosen because he . . .'

Once again the look in her eyes became distant and dark. She pulled at a tangle of hair and chewed it. The palaver downstairs had died down a while ago. The children had been sent out to play in the rain. Adam could hear them in the garden.

'The murderer wanted him dead,' she said slowly. 'The motive was first and foremost . . . the game. The challenge of killing someone and getting away with it. But the murderer gave in to temptation this time. By choosing someone he wanted to get even with.'

'Everyone wanted to get even with Vegard,' Adam groaned. 'And your profile doesn't match any of the people we've come across, spoken to or in any way suspected in connection with this case. And do you have any idea how many people that is? Do you know how many statements we've taken?'

'A lot, I should think.'

'Several hundred! Nearly a thousand statements. And not one of them, not a single witness, matches your description of . . . What shall we do? Where is he, what needs to be . . .'

'He won't stop. Not yet. I guess we just have to wait.'

'Wait for what?'

'For . . .'

'The world's best mummy,' shouted Kristiane.

She had her raincoat on and her boots were soaking. They squelched as she ran over the floor and threw herself into her mother's lap. Jack was in hot pursuit. He stopped in the middle of the floor, between the sitting room and open-plan kitchen, and shook himself. A shower of water sprayed around him. Sand and fine gravel pattered down on to the parquet.

'The best dog in the world,' Kristiane said. 'The best Kristiane. And Daddy. And Adam. And house. And . . .'

'Afternoon, all! The door was open so I just came up. Is her bag ready?'

Isak laughed and patted the eager, happy dog.

'I've been sailing,' he said, 'so I'm just as wet as Kristiane. Great weather for sailing though! Cold as hell. Good wind. But then it started to rain. Shame. Come on then, princess! We're going go-karting today! Won't that be fun!'

He trailed his dirty shoes over the floor. Picked up the fire engine, gave a big smile and put it in his pocket.

'Bye, Mummy! Bye, Adam!'

The girl danced after her father. Adam and Johanne sat in silence and listened to them rummaging around in her room. He put his hand on her thigh when she wanted to go in and help. Five minutes later they heard Isak's Audi TT accelerate powerfully down Haugesvei.

'I bet he forgot her pyjamas and toothbrush,' Johanne said, and tried to ignore Adam's exasperated sigh when he answered:

'He can buy a toothbrush at any petrol station, Johanne. And she can sleep in a T-shirt. Isak remembered Sulamit and that's what's most important. Don't make such . . .'

She got up suddenly and went out to the bathroom.

'I'm boring,' she thought to herself, and started to load the washing machine. 'I'm unexciting and unsophisticated. I know. I'm responsible and very rarely spontaneous. I'm boring. But I certainly never get bored.'

The man sitting in the chair with a target pinned to his breast pocket with a safety pin was an unpopular star. His long hair was tied back in a ponytail. He had a widow's peak that gave him a diabolic look. There was something primitive about the way his brows jutted out over his eyes; his eyebrows were joined, like a fat, hairy caterpillar crawling across his face. His nose was straight, narrow and sophisticated. His lips were full. An unbecoming goatee sprouted on his chin below his mouth. His tongue was just visible between his eye-teeth, which had been filed into points.

The corners of his mouth turned down in an unattractive grimace. Above his head, a zinc bucket was attached to the wall with a nail.

Håvard Stefansen was a professional biathlete. His greatest achievement as a senior to date was two individual silver medals in the world championships. He had won three world cup titles last season. And as he was only twenty-four, he was one of Norway's great hopes for the Winter Olympics in Turin in 2006.

As long as he could control himself, the national team coach had publicly warned him only six weeks ago.

During the course of his first two seasons in the senior national team, Håvard Stefansen had been sent home from meets and competitions four times. He was an arrogant winner and an appalling loser. He usually openly slandered his competitors when he lost a race. He accused them of taking drugs. They cheated. He treated foreigners and his own team mates with contempt. Håvard Stefansen was rude and egocentric and no one wanted to share a room with him. Which didn't seem to bother him.

The public didn't like him either, and he had never had personal sponsors. Boasting and menacing tattoos were not usual in his chosen sport. When he raced, he was often met with boos or silence, and in some weird way he seemed to get a kick out of that. His speed increased and his shooting improved every month, yet he did nothing to change his terrible reputation.

Now it was too late.

It was the night of the 2nd of March and the bullseye on the target over his heart had been hit. His eyes were glassy. When Adam Stubo leant over the body, he thought he saw slight bruising on the eyelids, as if someone had forced them open.

'He wasn't killed in here,' said an officer from the Oslo Police. His ginger hair was poking out from under the paper cap. 'That seems fairly clear. He was stabbed in the back with a knife. While he was asleep, we assume. No indications of a struggle, but the bed is full of blood. The tracks are obvious out here. It looks like his clothes were just thrown on. We think he was killed in his sleep and then dragged out here, dressed and arranged on the chair.'

'The bullet hole,' Adam muttered. He felt queasy.

'Lead pellet, sir,' the other replied. 'He was shot with an air rifle. This is some kind of indoor shooting range.' He pointed to the target covering the top of the bucket. 'For air guns only, of course. The pellets are caught in the bucket. Air rifles only make a "pff" sound, which explains why no one heard anything. If the guy was alive when he was shot, it would presumably have hurt like hell, but nothing more. That, on the other hand . . .'

The policeman, who had just introduced himself as Erik Henriksen, pointed to Håvard Stefansen's right hand. It was half open and resting on his groin. His index finger was missing. Only a ragged stump remained.

'His trigger finger,' Henriksen said. 'And if you look over here . . .'

He went to the other end of the corridor, his paper overalls rustling as he moved. An air rifle was attached to a sawhorse with tape and rope. The barrel of the gun was balanced on a slanting broom handle. Håvard Stefansen's finger was on the trigger of the gun, which was aimed at his heart. The finger was blue and the nail was slightly too long.

'I have to go out,' Adam said. 'I'm sorry, I just have to . . .'

'Even if this is our case,' Erik Henriksen said, 'I thought it would be best if you guys had a look. It's suspiciously like . . .'

'A sports celebrity,' Adam thought desperately. 'That's what we were waiting for. And I couldn't do anything. Couldn't guard every sports celebrity in the country. Couldn't raise the alarm. It would only have caused panic. And I couldn't know anything for certain. Johanne believed and thought and felt, but we couldn't be sure. What could I have done? What should I do?'

'How did the killer get in?' Adam forced himself to ask, determined to stick it out. 'Break in? Window?'

'We're on the fourth floor,' Henriksen pointed out, with a hint of irritation. This NCIS bloke was certainly not living up to his reputation. 'But take a look at this.'

Although the flat was in an old building, the front door looked new and had a solid, modern lock. Henriksen used his pen as a pointer.

'Old trick, really. A small piece of wood has been pushed into the keyhole and here . . .'

The pen moved over the spring bolt.

'It's stuck,' he said. 'Matches, presumably.'

'God,' Adam mumbled. 'A simple old con trick.'

'At the moment, we're assuming that the door was open when Håvard Stefansen was at home and awake. Somebody tampered with the lock. The flat is big enough for someone to get on with their business out here while he was eating, for example. And as this is the top floor, there's less risk of being seen.'

He put his pen back in the breast pocket of the white overalls.

'It's uncertain whether Håvard Stefansen even tried to lock the door before he went to bed. A tough guy like him, with all these weapons in the house, maybe he wasn't that bothered. But if he tried, it would have been difficult.'

'He's getting bolder,' Adam managed to think to himself through his thumping headache. He narrowed his eyes. 'He's more and more daring. Has to have more. Like climbers who always have to go higher, steeper, to live dangerously. He's getting there now. This victim must have been physically more powerful than him. But he knew that and took precautions. Killed Håvard Stefansen when he was asleep. A simple ambush. No symbolism, no sophisticated tricks. It didn't matter to him. It's us who are supposed to get the message. The outside world. Not the victim. He wants us to be shocked by this tableau: the marksman aiming at his own heart of steel. It's us he wants to provoke. Us. Me?'

'The guy slept with a ponytail?' Adam asked, just to have something to say.

'Looks cool, dunnit!'

Detective Sergeant Henriksen shrugged and added:

'Maybe the killer put his hair in a ponytail, to make him look . . . more like himself, kind of thing. Make the illusion stronger. And he succeeded, didn't he? Fu . . .'

He stopped swearing just in time. Perhaps out of respect to the dead. A colleague stuck his head round the door from the stairs.

'Hi,' he whispered. 'Erik, the woman's here. The one who called us. She found the body.'

Erik Henriksen nodded and raised his hand to signal that he would be there in a minute.

'Have you seen enough?' he asked.

'More than enough,' Adam nodded, and followed him out of the flat.

A woman was standing on the landing. She was solid, with dark hair that fell in big, untidy curls. Her skin looked healthy and weatherworn. It was difficult to determine her age. She was wearing jeans and a chunky green sweater. The stair lighting reflected in her small glasses, which made it hard to see her eyes. Adam thought there was something familiar about her.

'This is Wencke Bencke,' said the policeman who had just called them. 'She lives underneath. Was going up into the loft to put away some suitcases. The door was open, so she . . .'

'. . . I rang the bell,' she took over. 'When there was no answer, I took the liberty of going in. I guess you know already what I found. I rang the police immediately.'

'Wencke Bencke,' Erik Henriksen said, and took off his comical paper cap. 'Wencke Bencke, the crime writer?'

She gave an inscrutable smile and nodded.

Not to Henriksen, who had asked the question. Nor was the smile intended for the uniformed policeman, who looked as if he was about to pull out a piece of paper and ask for an autograph.

It was Adam she was looking at. It was him she turned to, held out her hand and said:

'Adam Stubo, isn't it? A pleasure to meet you, finally.'

Her handshake was firm, almost hard. Her hand was big and broad and the skin was unusually warm. He let go quickly, as if he had burnt himself.

Sixteen

The celebrity killer was a monster.

The press had calmed down when Fiona Helle's murderer turned out to be a patient in a psychiatric hospital, with a motive that most people could understand. For a while it seemed that the journalists had caught on to the idea that these might be copycat murders. That it perhaps wasn't the work of a serial murderer, but rather a frightening constellation of individual, gruesome murders. When Rudolf Fjord chose to take his own life, the press had been surprisingly subdued, giving the tragic death sober coverage.

When Håvard Stefansen was found dead, sitting on a chair as a target in his own improvised shooting range, people in Norway went mad.

Psychologists were pulled back into the picture. Along with private detectives and foreign police chiefs, researchers and crime analysts. Experts discussed and explained in column after column, and on all the channels. Within twenty-four hours, the serial murderer was back on everyone's tongue. He was a monster. A twisted psychopath. Over the course of a few days, the celebrity murderer took on mythical proportions, with features akin to those found only in dark Gothic tales.

The royal family went abroad and the palace couldn't say when they were likely to return. Rumour had it that security at the Storting had been reinforced, but the head of security, tense and serious, refused to comment. First nights at the theatre were cancelled. Planned concerts were shelved. A high-profile marriage between a well-known politician and a business tycoon was stopped three days before the wedding. Postponed until the autumn, explained the sombre bridegroom, and assured everyone that love was still blooming.

Even ordinary people, most of whom had never had their name in the papers or their photo printed in a colour magazine, threw away cinema tickets and decided not to go out that weekend after all. A mixture of shock and curiosity, fear and tension, malice and genuine despair made people stick to those they knew.

It was safest.

Johanne Vik and Adam Stubo were also at home. It was now Thursday the 4th of March and nearly half past eight in the evening. Ragnhild was asleep. The TV was on, with the sound turned down. Neither of them was watching.

They had barely spoken to each other for two days. Both of them carried a fear that was too great to share with the other. The murderer had chosen an athlete this time. Only one case remained from Warren Scifford's lecture on Proportional Retribution, and Johanne and Adam conversed with a stiff and false friendliness. Life in the semi-detached in Tåsen was hectic as everyday activities helped to disguise the fear.

For a while at last.

Adam was putting up the shelves in the bathroom. They had been stored in the cupboard for half a year now. Johanne expected to hear Ragnhild crying at any minute; his hammering would wake the dead. But she couldn't face talking to him. She sat on the sofa and turned the pages of a book. It was impossible to read.

'Tonight's evening news has been extended by an hour,' said a very faint voice on the TV.

Johanne found the remote control. The voice got louder. The opening music and graphics rolled.

The presenter was dressed in black, as if he was going to a funeral. He didn't smile as he usually did at the start of the programme. Johanne couldn't remember ever having seen the long-serving presenter wear a tie.

The chief of police was also dressed for the occasion. The already slim woman had lost a lot of weight over the past few weeks and her uniform hung off her. She sat straight and tense on her chair, as if on duty. For once she had problems giving a clear answer to the questions she was asked.

'Adam,' Johanne called. 'You should come and see this.'

Angry hammering from the bathroom.

'Adam!'

She went to get him. He was down on all fours, trying to separate two shelves.

'Bloody hell,' he said tersely. 'These bloody instructions are all wrong.'

'There's a special programme about your case,' Johanne told him.

'It's not *my* case. I don't own it.'

'Don't be silly. Come on. Come and watch it. The shelves won't run away.'

He put the hammer down.

'Look,' he said, ashamed, and pointed at the floor. 'I smashed one of the tiles. Sorry. I didn't think . . .'

'Come on,' she said curtly and went back into the sitting room.

'. . . we do of course have a number of leads in this case,' said the chief of police on the screen. 'Or cases, I should perhaps say. However, they are not explicit and it will take some time to sort this out. We're looking at a complex web of events.'

'Leads,' Adam muttered. He had followed Johanne into the sitting room and slumped down in the other sofa. 'Show me them, then. Show me your leads!'

He wiped his face with a corner of his shirt and grabbed a luke-warm can of beer from the table.

'Can you understand that people are worried?' asked the presenter as he leant forward and opened his arms in despair. 'Terrified! Following four horrific murders? And the investigation seems to have come to a *complete standstill*?'

'I must correct you there,' the chief of police said, and coughed into her hand. 'We're talking about three cases. The murder of Fiona Helle has been solved, according to the police and the authorities. Some investigation still needs to be carried out, but a charge will be made shortly . . .'

'Three cases,' the presenter interrupted. 'OK. And what leads do you have for those three cases?'

'I'm sure you understand that I can't give out any more details about an ongoing investigation. The only thing I can say this evening is that we are drawing on considerable resources . . .'

'Understand!' the presenter exclaimed. 'You ask for our understanding, when you seem to have no answers at all. People are barricading themselves in their homes, and . . .'

'He's frightened,' Adam said, and drank the dregs of the flat beer. 'He never gets angry. Isn't it more his style to wheedle and entice? To smile and let people make a fool of themselves?'

Johanne answered by turning up the volume even more.

'He's terrified,' Adam muttered. 'Him and a couple of thousand other Norwegians who live vicariously through that box.'

He pointed at the TV with the empty can.

'Shh.'

'Come over here.'

'What?'

'Can't you come over here and sit beside me?'

'I . . .'

'Please.'

The chief of police was finally allowed to go. While they swapped interviewees in the studio, they tried to run a report from the building where Håvard Stefansen had been found murdered two days earlier. The film got stuck. The panning shot from the entrance to a window on the fourth floor froze in mid-swing and became an unfocused still of a woman peering out from behind a curtain on the second floor, with a shocked expression. The sound was fuzzy. Something beeped. Suddenly the presenter was back on the screen.

'We apologize for the technical problems,' he coughed. 'But now I think we're . . .'

'We'll always be lovers,' murmured Adam, and smelt her hair;

she had curled up beside him and pulled a blanket over them both.

'Maybe,' she said, and stroked his arm. 'As long as you promise never to do any more DIY.'

'Welcome to the programme, Wencke Bencke.'

'What?' Adam sat up.

'Shh!'

'Thank you,' said Wencke Bencke, without a flicker of a smile.

'You are the author of no less than seventeen crime novels,' the presenter introduced her. 'All of which are about serial killers. You are deemed to be something of an expert in the field, and have gained widespread recognition for your thorough preparation and extensive research. Also within the police, as we found out today. Now, you were originally a lawyer, isn't that so?'

'Yes, that's right,' she replied, still serious. 'But there's not much of the lawyer left in me now. I've been writing novels since 1985.'

'We are particularly pleased to welcome you on the programme tonight, as it is actually twelve years since you gave an interview here in Norway. But it is, of course, the current tragic circumstances that have brought you here. All the same, I would like to start by asking a somewhat light-hearted question: how many people have *you* killed over the years?'

He leant forward in anticipation, as if he expected her to share a huge secret.

'I don't know any more,' she said, and smiled. Her teeth were unusually white and even for a woman who must be in her mid-forties. 'I've lost count. After all, quality is more important than quantity, even in my field. I concentrate on the details, not the numbers. I get my . . . pleasure from finding original twists, if you like.'

She pushed her fringe away from her forehead, but it just fell back immediately.

Johanne managed to free herself from Adam's arms. He was about to strangle her. He had just got hold of the *Dagbladet* paper

300

that was lying on the table. He looked at something and then dropped it on the floor. She turned round towards him and asked:

'What is it?'

. . . and you found the most recent victim, the TV droned, *. . . who was your closest neighbour. In your view, as an expert, what might lie behind . . .*

'What's wrong, darling?'

. . . the wish to be seen as something other than . . .

'Adam!'

His skin was sweaty. Grey.

'Adam,' she screamed and fell off the sofa. 'What's wrong with you?'

. . . more like cases from other countries. Not just the US, but also the UK and in Germany we know . . .

Johanne lifted her hand. Hit. The sound of her palm against his cheek made him look up at last.

'It's her,' he said.

. . . be cautious about jumping to conclusions about . . .

'It's her,' he repeated. 'That woman.'

'What's wrong, Adam?' Johanne screamed. 'I thought you were having a heart attack! I've told you a thousand times that you need to lose weight and cut out sugar and . . .'

. . . bearing in mind that I've been abroad for the past few months and only followed the case on the Internet and in the occasional newspaper, I would say that . . .

'Have you gone mad?' Johanne exclaimed. 'Have you gone stark raving mad? Why would . . .'

He was still pointing at the TV screen. The colour was returning to his face. His breathing had slowed. Johanne turned slowly back to the TV.

Wencke Bencke wore frameless glasses. The reflection of the sharp lights in the studio made it hard to see her eyes. Her suit was a touch too tight, as if she had bought it in the hope of losing some weight. There was a small brooch on the collar. A thin gold chain shone round her neck and she had a good colour for the time of year.

'I don't hold out much hope of that,' she answered to a question that Johanne had not heard. 'The police don't seem to have a clue, so I find it hard to imagine that the likelihood of the murders being solved is anything but slim.'

'Do you really believe that?' the presenter asked, with a gesture that invited a full reply.

'I don't understand,' Johanne said, and turned around again to try to get Adam's attention.

'Be quiet,' he said. 'Let me hear what she has to say!'

'Well, I'm afraid that's about all we have time for,' the presenter said. 'But in the light of the recent tragic events, I must ask in closing whether you ever get tired of it? Of thinking up murders and crimes for entertainment?'

Wencke Bencke straightened her glasses. Her nose seemed too small for her broad face and her glasses kept threatening to fall off.

'Yes,' she admitted. 'I do get tired of it. Sick and tired of it, sometimes. But writing crime is the only thing I can do. I'm getting older and . . .'

She waved a stubby finger and looked into the camera. Suddenly her eyes were visible. They were brown and sparkled with a smile that made her cheeks split into two deep dimples.

'. . . obviously the pay is fantastic, which helps.'

'Wencke Bencke, thank you very much . . .'

Click.

Johanne put down the remote control.

'What do you mean?' she whispered. 'You gave me such a fright, Adam. I thought you were about to die.'

'It's Wencke Bencke. She killed Vibeke Heinerback,' he said, squeezing the beer can with both hands. 'She killed Vegard Krogh. And she killed her neighbour, Håvard Stefansen. She's the celebrity killer. She has to be.'

Johanne sank down onto the coffee table. The house was quiet. Not a sound could be heard from outside. The neighbours downstairs were away. Johanne and Adam were alone and a light was turned off in the house over the road.

302

Suddenly crying could be heard from the children's room; the piercing, vulnerable cry of a six-week-old baby.

Wencke Bencke walked slowly through the swing doors at the reception of NRK TV. It was a chilly March evening with a cutting wind. When she looked up, she saw Venus twinkling against a patch of deep-blue sky between scudding dark clouds. She smiled at the journalists and let the photographers take yet more pictures before getting into the taxi and telling the driver her address.

Everything was different now. The difference was greater than she had ever hoped for. She'd noticed it at Gardemoen airport the previous Friday, when, with a broad smile, she thanked the air hostess for a pleasant trip. Whereas before she used to walk with a rounded back and heavy steps, she now stood up straight. She sauntered down the endless corridors with a tax-free bag swinging from her hand. She looked up and out. Noticed all the details of the beautiful building, the enormous limewood beams and the colour play of the artwork by the stairs down to the arrival hall. She waited patiently for her luggage and chatted with a red-haired child who poked her PC with curiosity. She smiled at the child's father and straightened the lapel of the new Armani coat she had bought in Galeries Lafayette in Nice, which made her look as new as she actually felt.

She was strong.

And supremely confident.

She had made a decision many years ago when she delivered her first manuscript and discovered that this was something she could do. She would become an expert in crime. A specialist in murder. Literary critics were an unreliable tribe. The reasoning of the media was predictable and petty: they would build you up, only to pull you down. Her editor had warned her about it, way back then. Looked at her with indescribably sad eyes, as if by making her debut as a crime writer Wencke Bencke had stepped into purgatory. And so she decided then and there:

She would never read a review.

And she would never, ever, make a mistake.

She would devise perfect plots. She would never misjudge the effect of a weapon. She would learn all there was to know about the human anatomy, about stab wounds and punches, bullet wounds and poison. Investigations and tactics. Chemistry, biology, psychology. She would build up an understanding of the business of crime, from the big powerful organizations down to the pathetic junkies who sat at the very bottom of the ladder, holding out a hand: *Can you spare any change?*

She hadn't managed to keep the first promise.

She read the reviews as soon as they came out.

But no one could say that Wencke Bencke didn't know what she was talking about.

And no one did.

She had studied and read constantly since 1985. Done field studies. Travelled. Observed and researched. And eventually she realized that theory could never surpass practice. She had to look to real life. The fictional universe wasn't concrete enough. Real life was full of details and unexpected turns. Just sitting at a desk, it was hard to imagine the multitude of seemingly insignificant, trivial events that could in fact be decisive in a murder case.

She started to catalogue real people.

Her archive dated back to 1995. She had needed a principal of a children's home and a policeman with a threadbare reputation for a book she was going to write. She was shocked at how easy it was to find them. Surveillance was boring, naturally, with hours of waiting and unimportant observations. Her notes were dry and dispassionate.

But it was easier to write.

The reviews were positive. Book number eight was received with considerable enthusiasm, as her first book had been. A couple of critics remarked that Wencke Bencke was fresher than she had been for a long time, almost revitalized.

They were wrong.

She was more bored than ever. She lived in a parallel world. She catalogued other people's lives without ever taking part. Her archive grew. She bought a steel cabinet, a fireproof device that was installed in the bedroom.

Sometimes she would sit in bed at night and read through a file. Often she got irritated. People led such similar lives. Work and children, infidelity and drink. There were renovation projects and divorces, financial problems and jumble sales for the football team. Whether they were politicians or dentists, rich or on the dole, men or women, the people she observed were all so bloody similar.

'I am unique,' she thought to herself, and settled back in the comfortable taxi seat. 'And now they can see me. Finally I'm being seen for what I am. An extraordinary expert. Not someone who publishes a book like handing in an exam every autumn, for bitchy comments. I can. I know. I do.

'He saw me. He was frightened. I could tell, the way he withdrew his hand and looked away. They see me now, but not like I see them. Not the way that I see her. Her file is fat. It's the biggest file I have. I have watched her for a long time and I know her.

'They see me now and there's nothing they can do.'

'Take a look at this.'

Adam held up page five of the day's edition of *Dagbladet* for her to see. He was still pale, but he didn't look fatally ill any more.

'Wencke Bencke,' said Johanne. She was walking around the room with Ragnhild over her shoulder. 'And?'

'Look at the pin. On her lapel.'

She carefully passed the baby over to him, took the newspaper and went a few steps closer to the lamp.

'It all fits,' he said, rocking Ragnhild. 'Too much of your profile fits. Wencke Bencke really does have crime as her profession. An internationally acclaimed crime writer! Superior to most when it comes to serial killers. Eccentric and difficult, if we're to believe the portraits that they've managed to put together, even though

305

she doesn't speak to Norwegian journalists. Until now, that is. Something must have changed. She's been a loner for a long time. Just like you said. Just how you put it in your profile.'

Ragnhild's eyes were heavy. He stroked her forehead and said: 'Look at her pin.'

The picture in *Dagbladet* was not particularly flattering. Wencke Bencke was just about to say something: her mouth was open and her eyes wide behind her glasses, which were perched on the end of her snub nose. But the outlines were sharp. The pin on the author's left lapel was clear.

'She knew who I was,' he said to no one in particular. 'It was me she was interested in.'

'This is worse than you think.'

'Worse . . .'

'Yes.'

'What d'you mean?'

She went into the bedroom without answering. He heard her rummaging around in the big chest of drawers. A cupboard door banged. The steps went further, into the closet, he guessed.

'Look.'

She had found what she was looking for. She took Ragnhild from him and put her down on her back under a baby gym on the floor. She gurgled and reached for the colourful figures. Johanne handed him the arch-lever file she had been looking for. It was white, with a big circular logo on the front.

'The FBI logo,' he said, and wrinkled his brow. 'Of course I recognize it. I've got a poster of it in my office. That's my point, that's why I . . .'

He pointed to the photograph in *Dagbladet*.

'Yes,' she said, 'but that's why it's worse than you think.'

She sat down beside him, on the edge of the sofa.

'Americans love their symbols,' she said, and straightened her glasses. 'The flag. The Pledge of Allegiance. Their monuments. Nothing is arbitrary. This blue . . .' She pointed to the emblem's background colour. '. . . Symbolizes justice, along with the scales in the top centre of the emblem. The circle contains thirteen stars to represent the thirteen original American states. The red and white stripes here are from the flag. Red stands for courage and strength. White for purity, light, truth and peace.'

'They obviously think that courage and strength are more important than truth and peace,' Adam observed, 'I think there are more red stripes than white.'

Johanne couldn't bring herself to smile.

'It's the same in the Stars and Stripes,' she said. 'One red stripe more than white. The toothed edge round the emblem symbolizes the challenges the FBI faces and the organization's strength.'

Ragnhild wriggled and kicked. The wooden figures banged against each other. Adam scratched his neck and mumbled:

'Impressive, but I don't see what you're driving at.'

'You see these two branches?'

She ran her finger along some branches on each side of the innermost, red and white shield.

'Laurels,' she told him. 'With a magnifying glass, you can count exactly forty-six leaves, the number of states in the USA in 1908, when the FBI was founded.'

'I'm still very impressed,' Adam said. 'But . . .'

'Now look at this.'

She held the newspaper photograph of Wencke Bencke up to the light.

'Her pin. The laurels. You see?'

'They're not laurels.'

He narrowed his eyes.

'No,' she confirmed.

'Are they feathers?' he asked.

'Yes.'

'Feathers instead of laurels. Why?'

'They're eagle feathers,' she told him.

'Eagle feathers?'

'Who used eagle feathers?'

'The native Indians.'

'Chieftains.'

'Chieftains,' he repeated lamely, confused.

Johanne walked over to Ragnhild. She gently lifted her up and put her across her shoulder. She breathed in the scent of soap and poo. A sludgy brown stain was spreading over the baby's romper leg. She held her tight.

'The Chief,' she said. 'Warren Scifford. A group of students got those pins made. A hundred or so. All hell broke loose when it was discovered. You don't muck about with the FBI heraldry. The pins became quite valuable after a while. People wore them on the inside of their jacket collars. A sort of membership badge, a sign that you were in the inner circle. One of Warren's disciples. He . . . he loved it, of course. Didn't want to know about it, but . . . loved it.'

'So that means that . . .'

'That means that Wencke Bencke knows Warren, in some way or another. She has either met him, heard him or spoken to someone who knows him.'

'Which in turn means . . .'

'That she wants us to see her,' Johanne said.

'What?'

'She's giving us an invitation. She's challenging us. She pops up on TV, after being silent for twelve years. She lets herself be photographed. She talks. She kills her neighbour and phones the police. She doesn't want to hide any more. She's been hiding for years and found it unbearable. She wants to be in the limelight, not out of it. And she's wearing that pin in the hope that she'll be recognized. By us. In the hope that we'll understand. She's playing with us.'

'Us? The two of us?'

Johanne didn't answer. She pulled a face at the increasingly pungent smell and disappeared into the bathroom. He followed.

'What do you mean?' he asked in a subdued voice.

She still didn't want to answer. She turned on the water and bent down to pick up a cloth, keeping one hand on Ragnhild's stomach where she lay on the changing table. Her poo was green and runny and Adam held his nose.

'Wasn't there a book that disappeared?' she asked.

'A book?'

'Don't hold your nose, Adam, it's your daughter.'

She let the water run over Ragnhild's bottom and continued:

'Yes, Trond Arnesen. He said a book was missing. And a watch. The watch was found, but was the book found? Pass me the cream.'

He rummaged around in the basket by the sink.

'There was a book,' he said slowly and stopped. He had a tube of zinc cream in one hand and a clean nappy in the other. 'That's right. I was quite preoccupied with the watch for a while. I'd forgotten the book. Completely. Especially once Trond found his damned watch. The book seemed pointless. It was a crime novel, I think, a book that Trond claimed had been lying on his bedside table, but . . .'

'Wencke Bencke,' she said. 'Wencke Bencke's latest novel.'

Her hands were unusually swift, almost impatient, as she slid the nappy in under the baby and then taped it on.

'It was her first murder,' she said, just as fast. 'She was careful. Vibeke Heinerback's house was isolated and she was on her own that night. Anyone who visited her website knew that. Not a dangerous murder. Almost risk free, if you knew what you were doing. Wencke Bencke knows what she's doing. So she took the book. It was a clever signature, but no one read it. No one understood what it meant. And the next time . . .'

The baby resisted. Johanne couldn't get her right arm into the sleeve and Ragnhild started to cry.

'Here, let me do it,' Adam murmured and took over.

Johanne sat down on the toilet seat with her elbows on her knees and her chin cupped in her hands.

'The next time she pushed it a bit more. Went further.'

Johanne seemed to be afraid of her own reasoning. Her voice

was low and was speaking more slowly. She sat up straight and chewed her thumb. Adam dressed Ragnhild in clean pyjamas. She made contented noises when he laid her on her stomach over his lower arm and held her to his body.

'The second time,' Johanne continued, without making any sign of getting up. 'The second time she chose Vegard Krogh. Who she hated. Presumably she was mad at him. He had mocked her for years. Ridiculed everything she stood for. Wencke Bencke knew that Vegard Krogh's . . .'

She hit her forehead with her hand.

'. . . *ridiculous* campaign,' she groaned, 'would give a tiny nudge in her direction. Not too obvious. Definitely not. He had lots of enemies. But still . . .'

Finally she got up. A fleeting smile crossed her face as she kissed the baby's head.

'Then she went the whole way. Killed her neighbour, rang the police. Was pulled into the investigation. She's in the spotlight, Adam. She is standing there, floodlit. In the centre of attention. And she's loving it. She's thumbing her nose at us and she knows she's won.'

'Won? She hasn't won yet! Now that we know what . . .'

She put her finger to her mouth and hushed him. Then she gently stroked Ragnhild's neck.

'She's asleep,' she whispered. 'Can you put her down?'

She went back into the sitting room. She took a bottle of wine out from the corner cupboard and opened it. Took the most beautiful glass she owned, a crystal glass from her grandparents' summer house. She'd had four of them originally, big glasses with fine chased-metal rings and thin gold leaf around the rims. Three had been broken. And this one was never used. She took it out a couple of times a month. Dusted it, looked at the pattern in the light from the lamp. It reminded her of long summers and salt water, of her grandfather on the terrace with a glass of white wine, his nose red from sun and happiness, with cake crumbs in his beard. He used to let her have a taste. She wet her tongue and pulled a face, then spat it out. He always laughed and gave her some Fanta instead, even if it wasn't Saturday.

She poured out the wine and watched it swirl around the glass.

'What do you mean, she's won?' Adam asked.

'Is she asleep?'

He nodded, and looked surprised when he saw which glass she had chosen. He went out into the kitchen to get another glass and helped himself.

'What d'you mean?' he repeated. 'Now we know it's her. Now we know where to look. In a way . . .'

'You won't manage it,' she said and took a drink.

'What d'you mean?'

His glass stood untouched on the dining table. Johanne turned to face the window. The garden looked sad, with some patches of snow left on the yellow, sodden lawn. The street lamps in Haugesvei had finally got new bulbs. A man in a yellow raincoat was out walking his dog. It wasn't on a leash and rushed from side to side of the road, sniffing the ground. It stopped by Johanne's old Golf and cocked its leg. It stood there for a long time, before following its master, tail wagging.

'She was in France,' she said, 'when Vibeke Heinerback was killed. And when Vegard Krogh was murdered in the woodland in Asker. You seem to have forgotten that.'

'Of course I haven't,' he said, a touch irritated. 'But both you and I know that she *can't* have been there. Unless she has an accomplice, a . . .'

'Wencke Bencke hasn't got an accomplice. She's a loner. She kills in order to feel alive, to prove her strength. To . . . grow. To show how clever . . . how *superior* she is.'

'Make up your mind,' he said. 'If she was in France, she can't have killed them. What do you actually mean?'

'Of course she wasn't there. Not all the time, at least. She must have travelled up and down in some way or another. We can speculate about how she succeeded. We can make up theories and

311

reconstructions. But the only thing that is certain is that we will never find out.'

'I don't know how you can say that,' he said, and put his arm round her. 'What makes you so sure? How can you . . .'

'Adam,' she interrupted, and looked up into his face.

His eyes were so clear. His eyebrows were growing long and looked like an old man's pointy optimistic brows. His skin was clear and smooth. His broad mouth was half open and she could feel his breath on hers; wine and a taint of garlic. She put her finger on the deep cleft in his chin.

'I've never said this before,' she whispered. 'And I hope I will never have reason to say it again. I am a profiler. Warren used to say that I was profiler by nature. That it was something I could never run away from.'

She laughed quietly and stroked her finger over his lips.

'For years I've tried to forget it. Do you remember how reluctant I was, that spring four years ago? When all those children were abducted and you wanted . . .'

She wasn't whispering any more. He bit her fingertip gently.

'I was working on my research. Digging deeper. I had more than enough with Kristiane and . . . then you came along. Our life here and Ragnhild. I don't want anything else. Why do you think that I've sat here night after night, working on a murder case that, strictly speaking, has nothing to do with me?'

'Because you're compelled to,' he said, his eyes not leaving hers.

'Because I'm compelled to,' she nodded. 'And I'm telling you this because I have to: Wencke Bencke has won. In all these weeks, you haven't found one, not *one* piece of evidence that is linked to her. Nothing. She doesn't want to be caught. She wants to be seen, but not caught.'

'But I still have to try,' Adam said. It sounded more like a question, as if he needed her blessing.

'Yes, you still have to try,' she confirmed. 'And the only hope you have is to find a way of proving that she was at the scene of the crime. Prove that she wasn't in France.'

'But you will never manage it,' she thought to herself again, but didn't repeat it out loud. Instead she drank the rest of her wine and said:

'The children can't stay here. Wencke Bencke still has one case left. We have to move the children.'

And with that, she went to phone her mother, even though it was nearly midnight.

'So what you're saying,' the head of the NCIS said, and scratched his ear with his pinkie, 'is that the whole investigation should be reorganized on the basis of a missing crime novel and a brooch? *A bloody brooch?*'

'A pin,' corrected Adam. 'It's a pin.'

The head of the NCIS was seriously overweight. His stomach bulged over his belt like a sack of potatoes. His shirt was stretched over his navel. He had stayed silent while Lars Kirkeland and Adam Stubo gave their reports. Even when the rest of the small gathering had discussed the case for more than half an hour, the boss had not said a word. Only his small, plump fingers had given him away, as they rapped impatiently on the table whenever anyone spoke for more than twenty seconds.

His double chins were quivering in anger. He got up with great difficulty. Went to the flipchart, where the name Wencke Bencke was written in red letters under a timeline with three dates. He stopped and snorted three times. Adam was unsure whether it was with scorn or whether he had breathing difficulties. He smoothed down his comb-over with his right hand, before tearing off the sheet and scrunching it up.

'Let me put it this way,' he said, and turned his small, beady eyes on Adam. 'You are one of my most valued colleagues. That is why I've sat here for more than an hour listening to this . . .' He pulled at his moustache, which curled cheerfully at the corners of his mouth and normally made him look like a fat, friendly uncle. '. . . rubbish,' he concluded. 'With all due respect.'

No one said anything. Adam looked at his colleagues. Six of the

313

most experienced investigators in Norway sat around the table and did not look up. Playing with a cup. Fiddling with their glasses. Lars Kirkeland appeared to be deeply engrossed in his doodles. Only Sigmund Berli looked up. His face was red and distressed and he looked as if he was about to stand up. Instead, he put up his hand, as if he was asking permission to speak.

'Is it not worth a try? I mean, we're in deadlock as it is! If you ask me, this is . . .'

'No one is asking you,' the boss said. 'Enough has been said. Lars has given a detailed report of the investigation so far. Everyone here knows that there is no . . . hocus-pocus in police work. Meticulousness, people. Patience. No one knows better than we do that hard work and the systematic processing of all new evidence is the only way to go. We are a modern organization, but not so modern that we would throw weeks of intensive, good police work out the window because some woman feels and thinks and believes that maybe she knows.'

'That's my wife you're talking about,' Adam said in a level voice. 'And I will not allow you to call her some woman.'

'Johanne is just some other woman,' the boss said, equally calm. 'In this context, that is what she is. I apologize if my choice of words offends you. I have the greatest respect for your wife and I am fully aware of how useful she was in that kidnapping case a few years ago. And that is one of the reasons why I have . . .'

He passed his hand over his scalp again. The thin strands of hair looked like they'd been drawn on his head.

'. . . been tolerant,' he said, 'of your somewhat dubious handling of case documents. But the case is very different now.'

'Different!' Sigmund spluttered. 'We know nothing. Not a bloody thing! What Lars just presented was actually an endless string of technical findings that lead absolutely nowhere and tactical analyses that basically mean only one thing: we have no idea where to look! Jesus, we . . .'

He stopped himself.

'Sorry,' he said feebly. 'But listen . . .'

The boss raised his hand.

'No,' he said. 'The last thing we need now is more criticism in the press. If we go after this Wencke Bencke . . .'

He peered into the wastepaper basket as if the crime writer was in there, together with her name written in red felt-tip.

'If we even *look* in her direction, all hell will break loose. She's becoming extremely popular, as far as I can see. I saw her on TV twice yesterday, and according to NRK's previews she's the main guest on *First and Last* tonight.'

He sucked in through his teeth. The sound was annoying. Then he smacked his tongue and twirled his moustache with his thumb and forefinger.

'And if, God forbid, there is any truth in this hypothesis of yours,' he added, and looked at Adam, 'in this absurd spaced-out theory based on old lectures and boredom, then the woman's a hard nut to crack.'

'Therefore it's better not to try,' Adam said, and looked straight at him.

'Spare me your sarcasm.'

'But you'd rather have three unsolved murders than a fuss in the press,' Adam said, and shrugged his shoulders. 'Fine by me.'

The head of NCIS stroked his immense belly. Stuck his thumb in under his tight belt. Sucked through his teeth again. Hoisted his trousers, which immediately slipped back down to the crevice below his gut.

'OK,' he said eventually. 'I'll give you two weeks. Three. For three weeks, you are absolved from doing anything other than finding out Wencke Bencke's movements around the times of the murders. And only that. D'you hear?'

Adam nodded.

'No other capers. No digging around in other parts of her life. I don't want any trouble. OK? Find out if her alibi does have any cracks. And my tip is, start with the last murder. With Håvard Stefansen. She was certainly close by when he was killed.'

Adam nodded again.

'If I hear *one* word that that woman is being investigated . . .'

His face was beetroot now and the sweat was shining on his forehead.

'. . . from anyone other than the people round this table, and who . . .'

His fat little hand slammed down onto the table.

'. . . *are damn well going to keep their traps shut about this* . . .'

He took a deep breath and let it out between clenched teeth.

'. . . I will be very angry,' he concluded at last. 'And you know what that means.'

They all nodded, like eager schoolboys.

'And you,' the boss pointed at Sigmund, 'if you absolutely must be Adam's squire, that's fine by me. Three weeks. And not a day more. Otherwise, the investigation continues as before, Lars. The meeting is closed.'

The chairs scraped on the floor. Someone opened a window. Someone else laughed. Sigmund grinned and gestured that he had to go to his office to make a phone call.

'Adam,' the boss said, and pulled him to one side as the room emptied.

'Yes?'

'I don't like that last case,' he said quietly.

'Håvard Stefansen?'

'No, the last case in that old lecture. The one that hasn't happened yet. The fire. The policeman's house getting burnt down.'

Adam didn't answer. He just blinked and looked out of the window, distracted.

'I've asked Oslo Police to do a few extra rounds,' the boss carried on. 'At night. To Haugesvei.'

'Thank you,' Adam said, and held out his hand. 'Thank you. We've moved the kids to their grandparents.'

'Good,' muttered the boss and made to leave.

But for a short second he hesitated, with Adam's hand in his.

'And that's not because I believe in this profile of yours,' he said. 'It's just a precaution. OK?'

'OK,' Adam said in earnest.

'And,' the boss continued and whipped the cigar case from Adam's breast pocket. 'I'll take this. Please stop smoking in your office. I get such a bollocking from health and safety.'

'OK,' Adam said again, but this time with a broad smile.

He had imagined that it would be more glamorous. Maybe not quite Hollywood, with the stars' names glittering on their doors, but an aura of something special. There was nothing special about the puce-coloured room at the top of a long staircase, with tepid coffee in a thermos and tea bags in a paper cup. There were two bench-like sofas along one wall, where five people sat, waiting for something. Adam had no idea what function they had. They weren't famous and they did nothing. Sat there in sloppy clothes drinking coffee while they looked at the clock, constantly. Just below the ceiling in the corner was a monitor, where he could see the studio. People with headsets wandered backwards and forwards as if they had all the time in the world.

'Hi,' he mumbled to two uniformed policemen who were standing by the stairs, looking out for whoever approached.

As security had been stepped up in connection with all NRK's activities, it had been easy to gain access to the studio. He only needed to show his ID to the young lad down in reception and he was pointed in the right direction. He nodded and smiled, but no one seemed to bother. Some of them were talking while the others ran in and out of the room. The chair opposite the monitor was empty. Adam sat down and grabbed a paper, so that he wouldn't look completely lost.

'Adam Stubo,' said a voice, and someone touched his shoulder.

He turned towards the voice and then got up.

'Wencke Bencke,' he said.

'I get the impression you're following me,' she said, and smiled.

'Not at all. Just tighter security measures.'

He waved his hand in the direction of the two policemen.

'Well, that certainly is tight security measures,' she said, and

317

straightened her glasses. 'Using an experienced and respected homicide investigator as security during the recording of a light entertainment programme is impressive. But perhaps not the best use of resources?'

She was still smiling. Her voice was friendly, almost teasing. But he caught a look behind her glasses that made him straighten up.

'We have to use what we've got, you know.'

He was sweating, so he took off his coat.

'These days,' he added.

He threw his coat over the back of the chair he had just got up from.

'These days,' she repeated. 'What sort of days are they?'

'A murderer on the loose,' he said.

'Or several,' she smiled. 'As far as I can tell, you aren't even sure if it's one and the same man.'

'I'm sure,' he answered. 'One man. Or woman for that matter. Not to be sexist. These days.'

Her cheeks split into dimples, from her eyes to her jaw.

'Better to be on the safe side,' she nodded.

She didn't want to go. The presenter came up the stairs, greeted everyone, had his nose powdered again by a sprightly young girl, then disappeared into the studio. Wencke Bencke didn't move. Her eyes were locked onto Adam's face.

'Nice pin you've got there,' he said with deliberation.

'This one?' She patted her lapel, without looking at it. 'Bought it in a second-hand shop in New York.'

'It's got a special history,' he said.

'Yes,' she nodded. 'That's why I bought it.'

'So you know . . . You know why the laurels have been replaced with . . .'

'Eagle feathers? The Chief, of course!'

Her laughter was soft and dark. The chatter in the room had died down, as if their conversation fascinated more than just the two of them.

318

'The Chief?' Adam asked. 'D'you know him?'

'Warren Scifford? No. That would be an exaggeration. I know of him, naturally. Have probably read everything he's written. I once had the pleasure of meeting him. At St Olaf's College. In Minnesota. I followed a series of lectures there. I'm sure he wouldn't remember me. But it's impossible to forget Warren Scifford.'

She looked down at the pin, at last. Stroked it with a stubby finger.

'Ask your wife,' she said lightly, without looking up. 'Warren is a man you never forget.'

Everything was spinning for Adam. His head felt light, he put his hand to his throat and tried to swallow.

'But . . . know?' he stuttered incoherently.

She looked at the ceiling, as if she was savouring her last words.

'No,' she replied.

Then she leant towards him. Her face was barely a hand's breadth from his.

'What are you doing here, Stubo? Truthfully, I mean?'

It was uncomfortably quiet. The make-up girls' chat from the adjoining room filled the stillness with a slight hum. Her eyes were darker now, almost black behind the clear spectacle lenses. He noticed that she had a fleck on her iris, a white patch that was eating into her left eye; he couldn't see anything but the yellow-ish-white defect in Wencke Bencke's staring eye.

'We have to go in now,' whispered a woman with big headphones on and a timetable under her arm. 'We're going on air.'

Wencke Bencke straightened up. Pushed her fringe away from her face; it fell down again.

'Are you coming?' asked the production assistant and pulled her by the arm.

'There are lots of Norwegians at St Olaf's,' said Wencke Bencke, without showing any sign of moving. 'And people of Norwegian descent. Maybe that's why . . .'

'I'm sorry, but we really must . . .'

319

The production assistant put her hand on her arm. Wencke took three slow steps backwards.

'Perhaps that's why Warren always ends his lectures by saying . . .'

'Come,' said the woman with the headphones, obviously annoyed now.

'. . . That Johanne Vik is the best profiler he's ever met. Or maybe it's just true.'

Then she disappeared into the studio. The heavy steel door swung slowly shut behind her.

'Is everything OK, sir?' the younger policeman asked. He seemed worried and offered Adam a glass of water. 'Detective Inspector? Is everything . . .'

But the detective inspector was glued to the monitor. The titles were rolling, a hare and a tortoise danced around in a psychedelic labyrinth and forced Adam to lean against a chair for support. The presenter appeared on the floor to enthusiastic applause from the carefully primed studio audience.

Wencke Bencke sat down.

Her suit was deep red.

The presenter laughed at something she said. Adam wasn't listening. He was staring at a small pin that was nearly invisible on the screen. Only every now and then the metal would flash in the studio lights, when the author moved, when she leant forward, as the presenter did. They exchanged confidences in front of a million viewers, and Adam heard nothing until the fair-haired man asked:

'And what did you do down there? On the Riviera, I mean, in the middle of winter.'

'I've been writing,' she said. 'I'm working on a novel about a crime writer who starts killing people because she's bored.'

Everyone laughed. They laughed in the studio, a vibration, a rumbling over the floor. They laughed in the small room where Adam was standing, laughed long and loud, and the presenter laughed longest and loudest.

'You can say what you like,' Wencke Bencke concluded when things quietened down. She put her hand on the man's thigh, soft and maternal. 'If there's anyone who knows what there is to know about murder, it's us. And what's more . . .'

She smiled and finished:

'We know how to get away with it.'

'Bloody hell, Adam. That's some story.'

In a house in Sagveien, just behind the old mills by the Aker River, a good fire was burning in the brick fireplace. It was late at night. Adam was leaning back in a deep wing chair. When he closed his eyes he could hear the waterfall at Mølla, where the river roared towards the fjord some kilometres further south, swollen by the spring thaw. Outside the windows it was dark and wet. Inside it was warm and sleepy.

Adam had told the story that he wasn't supposed to tell.

'Yes,' he said. 'It's quite a tale.'

The other man got up and came back with two glasses from the kitchen. Adam could hear the ice cubes clinking.

'Here,' said Bjørn Busk, and handed him a generous whisky before putting another log on the fire and sitting down in the other chair. 'Is Johanne at home alone?'

'No, she's staying with her parents. But only for one night. She has this idea that Wencke Bencke knows where we are, at any given time, so she doesn't want to stay in the same place as the kids. It's the two of us that the woman is after. Not the children. We'll stay at home. Kristiane will stay with Isak for a while and Johanne's mother will look after Ragnhild, at night that is. God knows how long we can stand it.'

Bjørn Busk put his feet on a pouffe and took a sip of whisky.

'You're absolutely convinced,' he said thoughtfully.

'That's she's out to get us? No. But I am one hundred per cent certain that she killed Vibeke Heinerback, Vegard Krogh and Håvard Stefansen. And I've never actually . . .' He stopped, and stared at the light playing in the amber drink. '. . . said that before,' he finished. 'That I'm certain that she's guilty. In a case that is chemically cleansed of evidence.'

'I'm glad you said that yourself,' Bjørn Busk smiled. 'Because as far as I can tell, there's nothing to give reasonable cause for suspicion.'

'Which is why I've come to you. In the middle of the night. Without calling.'

'No problem. After Sara moved out . . .'

'I'm so sorry, Bjørn. I should've got in touch when I heard. I should've . . .'

'Forget it. That's life. We all run around. Are busy. Have enough with our lives, without having to get involved in other people's problems. I'm fine, Adam. In a way . . . I've got over it. And I really appreciate you coming here tonight.'

Bjørn Busk smiled and put down his glass on the small table between them. He was a big man, the same age as Adam. They had been friends ever since they went into their first classroom together in 1962, with cropped hair and blue satchels slung over their narrow, suntanned shoulders.

'It could be said,' he mused, 'that our criminal justice system doesn't really take account of motiveless murders. If there is no real evidence, or it's weak, we tend to build on the motive. I've never quite seen it like that before, but . . .'

He took a drink. A deep furrow appeared in his brow.

'. . . As normal citizens have to be protected from arbitrary interference by the authorities, by setting standards for reasonable doubt before an actual investigation can be instigated . . .'

'Enough, that's all a bit legal, Bjørn. The point is that if we can't find a motive, we can't do a damn thing. Unless of course the murderer is caught with a knife dripping with blood, his trousers down, or by three witnesses with cameras.'

'Perhaps a bit extreme, the way you put it. But yes, that's roughly what I meant.'

They chuckled. Then it was quiet.

'You're asking me to do something that's actually illegal,' Bjørn said.

Adam opened his mouth to protest.

'Not illegal,' ran through his mind. 'I'm just asking you to stretch the limits a bit. To look through your fingers. Take a chance, that's all. In the name of justice.'

'Yes,' he said instead. 'I guess I am.'

'There are no grounds for compulsory disclosure. Absolutely none whatsoever. Or for disclosure at all, for that matter.'

'Without an order, I won't have a chance of checking her account,' Adam said. He could feel the heat from the whisky burning his cheeks. 'And without checking her account, I haven't got a hope in hell of finding out where she was when the murders took place.'

'Couldn't you just ask her?'

Bjørn peered at him over the top of his glasses.

'Ask her . . . hah!'

'If you can check her account, I mean. Not about where she was. From your description of her, it wouldn't surprise me if she said yes. Your story is about a woman who wants to be seen. Who wants you to get a glimpse of her, out of reach, but still . . . there. Present. Like a fairy in the woods. If you've seen one, you'll swear on your life that they exist. But you can never prove it.'

The wood crackled on the fire. Every now and then the flames flared up with blue tongues. The hint of burnt resin mingled with the smell of the malt whisky – tar and burnt bark. Bjørn reached for a wooden box on the shelf and opened the lid.

'Take one,' he said, and Adam felt his eyes go moist.

'Thank you,' he said. 'Thank you.'

They prepared their cigars in silence. Adam struck a match and had to hold back a sigh of sleepy pleasure.

'You should know that Wencke Bencke,' he said, and blew a smoke ring up towards the ceiling, 'has thought of everything. I don't know whether we could get anything from her account statements. Probably not. Judging by what she's managed so far, she will have thought about that. She's sharp and she knows her stuff. It would be unbelievable if she hadn't covered all her tracks, even the electronic ones. But if she hasn't . . .'

He put the cigar in his mouth. The dry, fine tobacco stuck to his lips. The smoke was mild and almost felt cool against his palate.

'If, contrary to expectation, she has overlooked such an important thing, it will only be because she *hasn't* overlooked it.'

He laughed and looked at the short, fat cigar.

'Then it would be part of the game. She is so sure, so utterly convinced that we will never find anything to nail her with, that she feels safe. She knows that we can't get access without her permission. Or get an order on the basis of reasonable doubt. We have neither. And she knows it.'

Bjørn pushed the ashtray over to him.

'I have to have that order,' Adam said and knocked his cigar on the edge of the ashtray. 'I know that it's a lot to ask. But you have to understand that . . .'

The wind had changed. It was a westerly now. The rain had been replaced by sleet. A flash of lightening illuminated the garden. The naked trees were visible for a moment, sharp with flat shadows, like an unsuccessful photograph. The thunder followed a few seconds later.

'Thunder and lightning at this time of year,' muttered Bjørn. 'A bit early, isn't it? And when it's so cold?'

'You're a judge,' Adam said and puffed on his cigar. 'You've been in the judicial system for . . . how long?'

'Eighteen years. Plus two as an associate lawyer. That's twenty years.'

'Twenty years. And have you ever, in all those years, come face to face with . . . evil? I don't mean situational madness, a kind of materially determined opportunism. I don't mean wretchedness, character disorders or egoism. I mean pure, genuine evil. Have you ever come across it?'

'Does it exist?'

'Yes.'

They drank in silence. The smoke lay like a comfortable, scented blanket under the ceiling.

'Do you have anyone who can submit a request?' Bjørn asked.

'What do we have young, easily manipulated lawyers for . . .'

They smiled, without looking at each other.

'Make sure it gets to the courts on Wednesday,' Bjørn Busk said. 'Not before and not after. Then there's a certain chance that it will end up on my desk. But I'm not promising anything.'

'Thank you,' Adam said, and made a move to get up.

'Can't you stay for a while?' Bjørn asked. 'Sit down. We've got whisky in our glasses and this box is full.'

He tapped the wooden lid with his fingers. Adam leant back in the chair. He put his feet on the pouffe in between them.

'If you insist,' he said, and shut his eyes. 'If you dare to have me here.'

'It's pouring with rain,' Bjørn Busk replied. 'The house won't burn down tonight.'

Seventeen

There was some satisfaction in the fact that they were frightened.

She had seen their fear, even though she no longer bothered to check that often. Every evening about seven, they carried the youngest child out into the car and drove a couple of kilometres to Johanne's childhood home. The strange one, who always carried a fire engine around with her that she should have grown out of years ago, was staying with her father. She often came to visit them in Haugesvei, but as far as Wencke Bencke could make out she never slept there.

Not that it really mattered.

Things had changed.

Everything.

It was Sunday the 21st of March and she was pottering about in the flat, tidying. She had been busy recently. Not only was she working hard on her manuscript, but the interviews and TV appearances took time. She had barely been home in the last couple of days, except to change clothes. And they were now strewn over chairs in the sitting room and the bedroom floor.

Old friends had suddenly reappeared. Not that they were any more interesting, but they had at least changed their attitude, which basically meant very little. She couldn't be bothered with everyone who came back to knock on her door, enthused by all the attention Wencke Bencke was now getting.

The most important thing was that she was being taken seriously at last. She was an expert. Not in fiction, but in fact. She was no longer the epitome of commercialism and an easy read, the trademark of culture in decline. Now she was in the opposition, a sceptic, someone who was critical of the authorities and an eloquent debater.

She was barely recognizable. Even to herself.

She stopped in the bathroom. Looked at herself in the mirror. She looked older. That must be the weight loss. She no longer just had crow's feet when she smiled; the wrinkles now followed her cheekbones as if the skin on her face was slightly too heavy.

It didn't matter. Age instilled her analyses with authority, gave substance to all the comments she was now asked to give and gave happily. No longer just about the serial killings, but also the disappearance in Vestlandet, a nasty rape case in Trondheim and a sensational bank robbery in Stavanger. Wencke Bencke was the expert that everyone wanted to hear.

And it was Fiona Helle's murder that had started it all.

Wencke Bencke opened the drawer of new make-up. She wasn't used to it. She tried to put mascara on her short lashes.

She missed.

The thought of Fiona Helle always made her hands shaky. She tried to breathe normally and turned on the tap. Cold water running over her wrists helped to clear her head.

She hadn't really felt any pleasure when she read about the murder, what now seemed like a lifetime ago. At the time, her feeling was closer to rage, a liberating rage, against the victim. She remembered the evening remarkably well. It was a Wednesday evening in January. The smell of asphalt hung in the air, as the road above the house had been repaired. She was restless, but couldn't do anything other than move from chair to chair in front of the panorama window with a view of the bay and Cap Ferrat.

The appalling Internet connection had nearly prevented her from surfing the day's papers in Norway. When she finally did log on, she stayed up all night.

Something happened.

Whereas previously she had been irritated, and on occasion provoked, this time she was overwhelmed by rage.

Fiona Helle sold other people's lives for her own fame and

fortune. The show was an affront to *her*, Wencke Bencke, with all its life lies and biology. It was *her* that Fiona Helle spat on every time she entertained the viewers with vulnerable people's dreams in her one-hour, lightweight programme; the dreams that were once *Wencke Bencke's dreams*, though she had never dared to admit it.

'I must learn how to do this,' Wencke Bencke thought as she pulled the mascara brush from the sticky black contents of the silver cylinder. 'I'm not old yet. I still have a lot to do and I'm changing. I'm no longer just an observer, I am being observed. I must learn to look good.'

Ten years ago, when her true history had come to light on an ageing document, she was already paralysed. She was on the verge of becoming invisible. She didn't belong anywhere. No one wanted to know her. She wrote books that everyone read, but no one admitted to it. Her father was a parasite, he wanted money, money, money. Her false mother barely spoke to her and couldn't understand what she called '*Wencke's horrible scribblings*'.

Her real mother, the woman who gave birth to her in pain and then died, would have been proud of her. She would have loved her, in spite of her heavy body, her unattractive face and increasingly closed nature.

Her mother would have kept all her novels in the bookshelves in the sitting room, and maybe had a scrapbook with clippings.

She couldn't face finding out more. Wencke Bencke knew nothing about the woman who had died twenty minutes after her daughter was born. Instead, she started to catalogue other people's lives. She became a better author.

And grew more and more invisible.

She didn't care about the world, just as the world obviously did not care about her.

But that was then. Not now.

It was a waste of time trying to put on make-up. Her hands felt too big; she wasn't used to the tiny brush in the eye-shadow compact. The lipstick was too brazen, too red.

It smelt of asphalt, she remembered, that evening in Villefranche. Wet, soft tar mixed with the brine of the sea and rain. She went to bed at dawn, but couldn't sleep. Somewhere in her head was a thought that kept evading her. It took a week before she grasped it. All these years, she had thought, all these years of futile work that had given her nothing but money and dissatisfaction. Then there it was, right in front of her, a shining new opportunity. All the preparations were made. She could just begin. Fiona Helle's tongue had been cut out and beautifully wrapped. Wencke Bencke smiled coldly when she read that; she laughed furiously and remembered another case, from another world, six years ago. She remembered a man with intense eyes, extreme energy and fascinating stories, remembered how she had moved closer and closer to the front with every lecture, with questions and observant comments. He gave her a fleeting smile and then bent down over an elegant brunette, quoting Longfellow, and winked. Wencke Bencke gave him a book with a respectful dedication in the front. He left it behind on the desk. In the evenings she followed him; he went to the pub where he was boisterous and told stories, surrounded by women who took it in turns to take him home.

She was already too old then. She was invisible and he bragged about Johanne Vik.

All this came back to her and she realized what she should do. She would no longer wait for something that would never happen. She would be the one who made it happen.

And she had succeeded.

And now she had to learn to put make-up on, to display her new self. She just had to stop thinking about the past so much, getting so emotional.

Forget Fiona Helle!

Wencke Bencke closed the drawer in the bathroom and went into the bedroom. She picked up clothes on the way. Her wardrobe was steadily expanding. She shopped regularly, nearly every week; she was no longer afraid of asking shop assistants for advice.

More than a hundred people's lives were stored in the filing cabinet by the wall. She stroked the ice-cold handle. Put her finger on the lock. Leant against the solid weight of steel.

People's good and bad habits, rhythms, desires and needs had been noted, analysed and catalogued. Wencke Bencke knew them better than they knew themselves; she was clinically neutral, the cold observer. She knew enough about over a hundred people to be able to disguise them lightly and then kill them with pen and paper. She knew their lives inside out. When she woke up that sunny January morning in Villefranche and decided to make fiction real, she had plenty to choose from.

She knew, both then and now, that she should select randomly. Arbitrary victims were the safest. But the temptation was too great. Vibeke Heinerback had always irritated her, though she never really knew why. The most important thing was that she could be taken for a racist. Everything had to fit. Johanne Vik had to have a chance of understanding. If not after the first murder, then later.

And Rudolf Fjord would tumble in any case.

He was pathetic.

Wencke Bencke opened the metal cabinet. Found a file. Read. She smiled at how good her memory was, how easy it was to recall all she had seen and written down.

Rudolf Fjord was despicable. He wouldn't survive if the police turned a searchlight on his life. If he didn't fall on one count, there were plenty of others that would nail him. His file was almost as extensive as Johanne Vik's. For a while she considered choosing him as her first victim. But then she decided against it. That would be too easy. Rudolf Fjord could sail his own sea.

She was right. He couldn't ride a storm.

Wencke Bencke closed the file. She pulled out another, much thinner, studied the name but didn't open it. A moment later she put it back and locked the cupboard.

Vegard Krogh deserved to die. She could hardly bear the thought of him. Now he was gone.

330

Wencke Bencke went out into the sitting room. It was tidier now. Some flowers had been standing for a few days too many and were giving off a potent smell; she had been given them by the committee of the Students' Association for taking part in a debate on chemical castration.

She opened the balcony door. The cold air caressed her face; it felt like it was wiping away all the wrinkles she had just been examining in the mirror.

For some reason, she couldn't quite come to terms with having sacrificed that whore in Stockholm. One prostitute more or less on Brunkebergstorg was, of course, neither here nor there. But there had been a kind of bond between them. Maybe it was the physical likeness. It hadn't taken long to find her; whores come in most colours and shapes. The woman was large, despite her obviously poor diet. Her hair was curly and dry. Even her glasses, which were so exclusive that they must have been stolen, were like hers.

And the woman fell for it.

She hadn't run away with the credit card. She could have spent as much as she liked before the card was blocked, then disappeared. But she had believed the promise that she would get lots of cash in return for doing what she was asked: to eat a good meal. Take a taxi. Buy something in a kiosk or two and be back at the hotel just before midnight. Be seen, but not say a word.

When they met again the next morning, the prostitute was almost happy. She was clean. She had eaten well. Had a good night's sleep in a warm bed, with no customers.

Of course she didn't get the money.

As expected she threatened to go to the police; she was smart enough to realize there was something suspicious about the offer she'd been made. As expected, she didn't do anything before injecting the heroin that Wencke Bencke had given her, a gesture of good will in return for her work well done.

As expected, she died of an overdose.

Now she was dead, cremated and no doubt laid to rest in an unmarked grave.

Wencke Bencke stood on the balcony and frowned at the thought of the dead whore. Then she lifted her face to the sky and decided never to give her another thought.

A light rain started to fall. It smelt of spring in Oslo, exhaust fumes and rotting rubbish.

Håvard Stefansen's death was simply a necessity. Johanne Vik had disappointed her; she didn't understand the pattern. She had to make it clearer, and Wencke Bencke finally stepped into the spotlight.

And she stayed there.

People recognized her on the street now. They smiled at her and some people asked for her autograph. One of the tabloids had run a three-page profile of the crime expert and international bestselling writer in its Saturday magazine: Wencke Bencke, photographed at her computer in her chaotic study, in front of a large, beautifully set dining table with a raised glass, on her balcony with a view over the town, smiling at the photographer. She'd had help from a stylist with the make-up.

She hadn't let them into the bedroom.

She went back into the sitting room. The smell of the flowers was nauseating. She took the vase out into the kitchen. Emptied out the water and put the flowers in a plastic bag.

The book would soon be finished.

At the bottom of her cupboard, where it wouldn't be found until she died, lay the most important file. On the cover, in big, regular capital letters, she had written:

ALIBIS.

For seventeen years, she had studied and researched. A good alibi was a prerequisite for a successful crime, the very foundations of a good thriller. She created and constructed, considered and discarded. The file grew slowly. Before she went to France, she had counted. Thirty-four documents. Thirty-four plausible alibis. She had already used some of them, others lay waiting for a new book, a more suitable story. None of them were perfect, because there was no such thing as a perfect alibi.

But her constructions were very, very good.

Three of them could never be used in a book.

They had been put to better use.

As they were not perfect, they kept her alive and on her toes. Every morning she felt that thrilling fear. When the doorbell rang, when the phone went, when a stranger stopped on the other side of the street, looked twice and then crossed the road towards her, she felt the fear; she was reminded of how valuable life had become.

On the way out to throw the flowers down the rubbish chute, she stopped and hesitated. The book she had taken from Vibeke Heinerback's bedroom was in the shoe cupboard in the hall. She had looked at it only last night. Felt the pages, felt the excitement of touching the paper that the young politician had taken to bed with her, read on the bus; maybe she had even sneaked a few pages during boring plenary sessions and the endless waiting around in the Storting.

It was Rudolf Fjord's copy.

She wanted to throw it away. She snatched it up and dropped it down the chute with the flowers. She stood there listening to the sound of the heavy book banging on metal, duller and duller until it ended in a muffled, nearly inaudible thump.

Someone might find it. Someone might wonder what a book belonging to Rudolf Fjord was doing in the rubbish room of the flats where Wencke Bencke lived and wrote. She hadn't destroyed it, hadn't torn out the page with the owner's name on it. She could have burnt the book or thrown it away somewhere else.

But there wouldn't be any excitement in that.

Wencke Bencke lived on a continuous high. She had thrown herself off the highest cliff.

'Three weeks,' Sigmund Berli said. 'Our three weeks are up.'

'Yes,' Adam Stubo replied. 'And we've got nothing. Nothing at all.'

On the desk in front of him there were two piles of printouts.

One contained statements for Wencke Bencke's three accounts from the period 1 January to 2 March, when Håvard Stefansen was murdered. The other was an itemized log from Telenor.

'When Vibeke Heinerback was killed,' Adam said, 'Wencke Bencke was in Stockholm. Just as she's said in several of these . . .' He kicked a pile of newspapers and magazines on the floor. '. . . Bloody interviews. About how shocked she was when she read about the murder, how . . . She's so damned cunning.'

For three weeks, Sigmund and Adam had worked alone. They had got their court order for compulsory disclosure, on the basis of a creatively modified and in part false petition. And since then, they had worked day and night, looked at Wencke Bencke's every move under a magnifying glass, only going home to change and get a few hours of unsettled sleep before returning to the painstaking work of reconstructing the woman's life by studying her money withdrawals, phone calls and where she had surfed the Internet.

Wencke Bencke was well off, but used surprisingly little money. She had renewed her wardrobe just before coming home, but even around Christmas her spending was absurdly low. She seldom rang anyone and was hardly ever contacted by anyone other than her various publishers in Europe. She hadn't spoken to her father since before Christmas.

She told the papers that she'd had a meeting with her publishers in Stockholm, a quick trip to plan the autumn's book launch and a tour. Sigmund rang and pretended to be a journalist; he fished for confirmation of the meeting. He was disturbingly unaffected by the growing number of lies that they had to tell. Adam, on the other hand, was deeply affected. Not only were they pushing the limits of what was permissible, they were doing the opposite of everything he had learnt and stood for in his years with the police.

Wencke Bencke had become an obsession.

They had used a week trying to work out the different ways in which she could have got from Stockholm to Oslo on the 6th of

February. They had juggled with possible times, studied maps and combed the passenger lists that Sigmund had managed to extract from the various carriers, using charm, threats and lies. At night they tramped around in the corridors, sticking yellow Post-it notes on the walls, with times on. Tried moving them closer together. Tried to find holes and weak points, a tiny opening in the solid wall of impossible times in Wencke Bencke's bank statements.

'Just can't get it to work,' Sigmund had concluded at around four o'clock every morning. 'I just can't get it to work.'

She had checked in at the hotel at three in the afternoon. Bought something in a kiosk at seventeen minutes past five. She took a taxi just before seven in the evening. At twenty-five to twelve, roughly the time that Vibeke Heinerback was murdered in her home in Lørenskog, Wencke Bencke had paid a substantial amount for a meal at a restaurant near the Dramaten theatre in the centre of Stockholm.

One morning, after working for sixteen hours with no results, Sigmund got on a plane to Stockholm, in a rage. He came back that afternoon defeated; the night porter was absolutely certain that he had seen Wencke Bencke returning to the hotel at around midnight on the night in question. He had nodded at the picture Sigmund showed him. No, they hadn't spoken, but he seemed to remember that the woman in room 237 had taken some ice from the machine in reception. It had something wrong with it, so he had to mop up the water on the floor after she'd gone. She had also dropped some clothes into the laundry that afternoon, and when he left them outside her door first thing next morning, he heard loud music coming from the room.

She had checked out at around ten o'clock.

The only thing that was odd about Wencke Bencke's trip to Stockholm was that she splashed out on herself, which was very unusual.

Otherwise, everything was just as it should be. Adam and Sigmund had given their all and got nothing in return. The deadline had passed.

'What do we do now?' Sigmund asked quietly.

'Yes, what do we . . .'

Adam played with the statements. When Vegard Krogh was killed, Wencke Bencke was apparently in France. Two days earlier, she'd withdrawn a substantial amount from her account and then didn't touch it for four days. The next transaction was in a fishmonger's in the old town in Nice.

Sigmund and Adam had been encouraged by this unaccounted-for period and used several days to investigate. Theoretically it was possible for her to have got to and from Norway using the cash. But her name did not appear on any of the passenger lists, nor was it registered with any of the car rental firms in Nice.

It was harder to get hold of the lists from Stockholm. She could easily have stolen a car. After three weeks' intensive work in the office, the only thing the two investigators knew was what they had been convinced of to begin with: Wencke Bencke had been in Oslo when the murders happened.

But they didn't know how she'd managed it.

They could carry on looking, investigating further.

That's what they should do. That's what they both wanted to do.

But to do that, it would have to be official.

Their deadline was already past and their colleagues had begun to make fun of them. They grinned when Adam and Sigmund came to lunch, pale and drawn. They sat by themselves and ate in silence.

When Håvard Stefansen was killed, Wencke Bencke had been sitting at her computer working, one floor below. She had given her witness statement and a very detailed statement at that. Hadn't seen or heard anything unusual, she was so engrossed in her work. She had been on the Internet for several hours, trying to find out more about South American spiders. It was only when she went to take her suitcases up into the loft, after her prolonged stay abroad, that she noticed the open door, stuck her head into the hallway and discovered the body. Then she rang the police. The story was consistent with the log from Telenor. It could hardly be called an alibi, but it didn't give them anything to go on either.

And Wencke Bencke blossomed. She was everywhere, and there was great anticipation about her new novel in the autumn.

Adam stood up abruptly. He gathered all the papers and stacked them together as one great document.

'We've lost,' he declared, and threw the pile into a box for shredding.

He stroked his hand over his head and added: 'Wencke Bencke has won. The only thing that we have after all these weeks of hard work is proof that . . .'

He laughed, quietly and reluctantly; he didn't want to finish the sentence.

'. . . That the woman is innocent,' Sigmund concluded slowly. 'We've worked day and night for three weeks without proving anything other than that . . . the woman's innocent. *We have proved Wencke Bencke's innocence!*'

'That is precisely what we have done,' Adam said, and gave a long yawn. 'And that's exactly what she intended. She knew this would happen. And you . . .'

He came round the desk. For a moment he stood looking hard at Sigmund, who had lost weight. His face was still round. His chin was still chubby, but his clothes were too loose. The lines around his nose were clearer and deeper than before. His eyes were bloodshot and he smelt of stale sweat when Adam gave him his hand, pulling him out of the chair.

'You are my best friend,' he said and gave him a hug. 'You are truly my Sancho Panza.'

Thursday 4 June 2004

Summer was just around the corner.

April and May had been and gone and the weather had been unusually warm and sunny. The leaves on the trees and flowers had sprung early this year, making spring hell on earth for people with allergies. The crown princes in Denmark and Spain had both married. Preparations were under way in Portugal for the European Cup and the Athenians were working against the clock to get ready for the Olympic Games in August. The world had been shocked by the abuse of prisoners in Abu Ghraib, but only enough for a few photographs to make the front pages of newspapers in Norway. The historical expansion of the European Union to the east didn't cause much of a stir either in the small rich country on the periphery of the Continent. People were more interested in the prolonged transport strike, which had resulted in empty shelves in shops and fights over toilet paper and nappies. Rosenborg won match after match in the football league and the revised national budget was passed without any political drama. If you looked carefully, you could still sometimes find the odd article about the unsolved murders of Vibeke Heinerback, Vegard Krogh and the biathlete Håvard Stefansen. But not often. Nothing had been written about the cases for a fortnight now.

A woman was sitting on a bench by the Aker River, reading the paper.

Johanne Vik had also used the spring to try to forget. She was well trained in the art. As the weeks and months passed and nothing more happened, it became impossible to keep the children in hiding. The house in Haugesvei had been under police observation, but that too seemed unnecessary after a while, certainly to those responsible for the Oslo Police's already strained budget. Patrol cars no longer included Haugesvei on their nightly rounds.

And no one had tried to set fire to the box-shaped, white semi-detached where the Vik–Stubo family lived with their children and a dog and friendly neighbours.

She had just started to sleep again too. She had found a daily rhythm. She went for walks.

The pram was standing beside her. The baby was asleep, covered by a light cotton blanket. Johanne glanced up at the sky every now and then; it looked as if the good weather might be coming to an end.

She enjoyed sitting like this. She came here every day. She bought the papers at the petrol station on Maridalsveien. Before she reached the bench under the willow tree, where the river took a swing between Sandaker and Bjølsen, the baby was asleep and she had an hour to herself.

Another woman walked towards her, down the path. She was probably in her mid-forties. Her hair was curling in the light breeze and she had sunglasses on.

'Johanne is so bloody predictable,' the woman thought to herself. 'Has she learnt nothing? She sits here every day, unless it's raining. She doesn't seem to be frightened any more. The children are at home again. It annoys me that I overestimated her.'

'Hallo,' the woman said as she walked up to Johanne. 'It is Johanne Vik, isn't it?'

Johanne stared at her. Wencke Bencke smiled when the other woman put her arm over the pram, her fingers splayed over the crocheted blanket.

'I've met your husband on a couple of occasions,' said the author. 'Is it OK if I sit down?'

Johanne didn't answer. She didn't move.

'Wencke Bencke, pleased to meet you. We've got mutual acquaintances, in fact. In addition to your husband, that is.'

339

She sat down. Her upper arm brushed Johanne's arm as she made herself comfortable, sitting confidently with her legs crossed. She bounced her upper foot.

'Terrible thing,' she said, and shook her head. 'All those celebrity murders. I was a witness in one of the cases. Perhaps you remember. It looks as if the poor victims are forgotten already, sadly.'

She nodded at the pile of papers between them.

'That's the way it goes. As long as there are no real suspects, the papers run out of things to write. And with those cases . . .'

She nodded at the papers again. Johanne sat poker-straight and paralysed, at the far end of the bench.

'. . . they seem to have come to a dead end. The police, I mean. Strange. Apparently there's no leads. They simply have nothing to go on.'

Johanne Vik had finally managed to pull herself together. She tried to get to her feet while clinging on to the pram and picking up a bag full of baby stuff.

'Wait,' Wencke Bencke said in a friendly voice, and gripped her arm. 'Can't you stay for a while? Just a few minutes. We have so much in common. There's so much I'd like to tell you.'

'Is it curiosity that keeps her sitting here,' she wondered. 'Or won't her legs carry her?'

Johanne sat still, with the bag on her lap and her arm protecting her daughter.

Wencke Bencke sat up straight on the bench and turned her head towards the younger woman.

'Have you ever suspected anyone other than me?' she asked, still friendly.

'She's not answering. She has no idea what to say. She's not curious any more. She's frightened. Why doesn't she shout? What would she shout?'

'I received this letter.'

Wencke Bencke pulled out a folded sheet from her back pocket. She unfolded it and flattened it over her knee.

'Notification of compulsory disclosure,' she explained. 'From the court. As prescribed by law, there's also information about how to proceed if I want to complain about your husband sticking his nose in my business.'

She held the letter up for a moment. Then she shook her head and put it back in her pocket.

'But I can't be bothered to. In fact, it suits me very well that I've already been cleared, in the event of any later accusations. The job's done, you might say.'

Her laughter was dark. She tried to tuck her hair behind her ear.

'The Stockholm trip must have puzzled you,' she said before getting the letter out of her pocket again.

She took it in her right hand and scrunched it up. Then she stood up and barred the way for the pram.

'Lovely little girl,' she said, and bent down over Ragnhild. 'She'll have a cleft in her chin.'

'Get away. *Get away!*'

Wencke Bencke took a step back.

'I'm not going to harm her,' she smiled. 'I'm not going to harm anyone!'

'I have to go,' Johanne Vik said, and struggled with the brakes on the pram. 'I don't want to talk to you.'

'Of course. I won't force you. I certainly didn't intend to distress you so. I just wanted to talk. About our shared interests and mutual . . .'

The brakes had got stuck. Johanne pulled the pram down the path. The rubber wheels screeched on the asphalt. Ragnhild woke up and started to howl. Wencke Bencke smiled and took off her sunglasses. Her eyes were lightly made up. They looked bigger and darker.

'She'll never go away,' thought Johanne. 'She'll never disappear. Not until she dies. Not until I manage to . . .'

'I've finished the book, by the way,' Wencke Bencke said, as she sauntered along behind the pram. 'It's good. I'll send you a copy when it's printed.'

Johanne stopped suddenly and opened her mouth to scream.

'Of course,' Wencke Bencke said, and lifted her hands, as if to stop her. 'You don't need to give me your address. I know perfectly well where you live.'

Then she gave a slight nod, turned her back and walked away down the path, in the opposite direction.

Postscript

This book opens with a quote by Walter Benjamin. The quote was used in Lars Fr. H. Svendsen's book, *Kjedsomhetens filosofi* (Universitetsforlaget 1999), which has been a great source of inspiration and help in writing *The Final Murder*.

On page 171, there is a quote from an unnamed source: 'And you're dying so slowly that you think you're alive'. I am obliged to say that this is taken from the title poem in a collection of poems by Bertrand Besigye (Gyldendal 1993).

I would like to thank Alexander Elgurén for his irrepressible enthusiasm and Randi Krogsveen for her invaluable help.

This book is for you, Tine, as all my books are.

Oslo, 18 June 2004
Anne Holt